'There were two men waiting. Feversham ran at the man who held the lantern. He was aware of the point of the spear, he ducked and beat it aside with his left arm, he leaped forward and struck with his right. The Arab fell at his feet. Feversham sprang across the white-robed body and ran eastwards towards the open desert.'

Captain Willoughby stopped.

'The strangest feature of those few fierce short minutes,' he said, 'was that Feversham felt no fear ...'

A. E. W. MASON

The Four Feathers

FONTANA/Collins

First published in 1902 by Smith, Elder & Co
Published in 1922 by John Murray Ltd
First issued in Fontana Books 1978

Made and printed in Great Britain by
William Collins Sons and Co Ltd Glasgow

THIS BOOK IS DEDICATED
TO
MISS ELSPETH ANGELA CAMPBELL

The character of Harry Feversham is developed from
a short story by the author, originally printed in the
Illustrated London News, and since republished.

CONTENTS

Chapter One

A CRIMEAN NIGHT

Lieutenant Sutch was the first of General Feversham's guests to reach Broad Place. He arrived about five o'clock on an afternoon of sunshine in mid June, and the old red-brick house, lodged on a southern slope of the Surrey hills, was glowing from a dark forest depth of pines with the warmth of a rare jewel. Lieutenant Sutch limped across the hall, where the portraits of the Fevershams rose one above the other to the ceiling, and went out on to the stone-flagged terrace at the back. There he found his host sitting erect like a boy, and gazing southwards towards the Sussex Downs.

'How's the leg?' asked General Feversham, as he rose briskly from his chair. He was a small wiry man, and, in spite of his white hairs, alert. But the alertness was of the body. A bony face, with a high narrow forehead and steel-blue inexpressive eyes, suggested a barrenness of mind.

'It gave me trouble during the winter,' replied Sutch. 'But that was to be expected.' General Feversham nodded, and for a little while both men were silent. From the terrace the ground fell steeply to a wide level plain of brown earth and emerald fields and dark clumps of trees. From this plain voices rose through the sunshine, small but very clear. Far away towards Horsham a coil of white smoke from a train snaked rapidly in and out amongst the trees; and on the horizon rose the Downs, patched with white chalk.

'I thought that I should find you here,' said Sutch.

'It was my wife's favourite corner,' answered Feversham, in a quite emotionless voice. 'She would sit here by the hour. She had a queer liking for wide and empty spaces.'

'Yes,' said Sutch. 'She had imagination. Her thoughts could people them.'

General Feversham glanced at his companion as though he

hardly understood. But he asked no questions. What he did not understand he habitually let slip from his mind as not worth comprehension. He spoke at once upon a different topic.

'There will be a leaf out of our table to-night.'

'Yes. Collins, Barberton, and Vaughan went this winter. Well, we are all permanently shelved upon the world's half-pay list as it is. The obituary column is just the last formality which gazettes us out of the Service altogether,' and Sutch stretched out and eased his crippled leg, which fourteen years ago that day had been crushed and twisted in the fall of a scaling-ladder.

'I am glad that you came before the others,' continued Feversham. 'I would like to take your opinion. This day is more to me than the anniversary of our attack upon the Redan. At the very moment when we were standing under arms in the dark — '

'To the west of the quarries, I remember,' interrupted Sutch, with a deep breath. 'How should one forget?'

'At that very moment Harry was born in this house. I thought, therefore, that if you did not object he might join us to-night. He happens to be at home. He will, of course, enter the service, and he might learn something, perhaps, which afterwards will be of use—one never knows.'

'By all means,' said Sutch, with alacrity. For since his visits to General Feversham were limited to the occasion of these anniversary dinners, he had never yet seen Harry Feversham.

Sutch had for many years been puzzled as to the qualities in General Feversham which had attracted Muriel Graham, a woman as remarkable for the refinement of her intellect as for the beauty of her person; and he could never find an explanation. He had to be content with his knowledge that for some mysterious reason she had married this man so much older than herself, and so unlike to her in character. Personal courage and an indomitable self-confidence were the chief, indeed the only qualities which sprang to light in General Feversham. Lieutenant Sutch went back in thought over twenty years as he sat on his garden-chair to a time before he had taken part, as an officer of the Naval Brigade, in that unsuccessful onslaught on the Redan. He remembered a season in London to which he had

8

come fresh from the China Station; and he was curious to see Harry Feversham. He did not admit that it was more than the natural curiosity of a man who, disabled in comparative youth, had made a hobby out of the study of human nature. He was interested to seé whether the lad took after his mother or his father – that was all.

So that night Harry Feversham took a place at the dinner-table and listened to the stories which his elders told, while Lieutenant Sutch watched him. The stories were all of that dark winter in the Crimea, and a fresh story was always in the telling before its predecessor was ended. They were stories of death, of hazardous exploits; of the pinch of famine and the chill of snow. But they were told in clipped words and with a matter-of-fact tone, as though the men who related them were only conscious of them as far-off things; and there was seldom a comment more pronounced that a mere 'that's curious,' or an exclamation more significant than a laugh.

But Harry Feversham sat listening as though the incidents thus carelessly narrated were happening actually at that moment and within the walls of that room. His dark eyes – the eyes of his mother – turned with each story from speaker to speaker, and waited wide-open and fixed until the last word was spoken. He listened fascinated and enthralled. And so vividly did the changes of expression shoot and quiver across his face, that it seemed to Sutch the lad must actually hear the drone of bullets in the air, actually resist the stunning shock of a charge, actually ride down in the thick of a squadron to where guns screeched out a tongue of flame from a fog. Once a major of artillery spoke of the suspense of the hours between the parading of the troops before a battle and the first command to advance; and Harry's shoulders worked under the intolerable strain of those lagging minutes.

But he did more than work his shoulders. He threw a single furtive, wavering glance backwards; and Lieutenant Sutch was startled, and indeed more than startled, he was pained. For this, after all, was Muriel Graham's boy.

The look was too familiar a one to Sutch. He had seen it on the faces of recruits during their first experience of a battle too often for him to misunderstand it. And one picture in particular rose before his mind. An advancing square at Inkermann, and a tall big soldier rushing forward from the line in the eagerness of his attack, and then stopping suddenly as though he suddenly understood that he was alone, and had to meet alone the charge of a mounted Cossack. Sutch remembered very clearly the fatal wavering glance which the big soldier had thrown backwards towards his companions – a glance accompanied by a queer sickly smile. He remembered, too, with equal vividness, its consequence. For though the soldier carried a loaded musket and a bayonet locked to the muzzle, he had without an effort of self-defence received the Cossack's lance-thrust in his throat.

Sutch glanced hurriedly about the table, afraid that General Feversham, or that some one of his guests, should have remarked the same look and the same smile upon Harry's face. But no one had eyes for the lad; each visitor was waiting too eagerly for an opportunity to tell a story of his own. Sutch drew a breath of relief and turned to Harry. But the boy was sitting with his elbows on the cloth and his head propped between his hands, lost to the glare of the room, and its glitter of silver, constructing again out of the swift succession of anecdotes a world of cries and wounds, and maddened riderless chargers and men writhing in a fog of cannon-smoke. The curtest, least graphic description of the biting days and nights in the trenches set the lad shivering. Even his face grew pinched, as though the iron frost of that winter was actually eating into his bones. Sutch touched him lightly on the elbow.

'You renew those days for me,' said he. 'Though the heat is dripping down the windows, I feel the chill of the Crimea.'

Harry roused himself from his absorption.

'The stories renew them,' said he.

'No. It is you listening to the stories.'

And before Harry could reply, General Feversham's voice broke sharply in from the head of the table –

'Harry, look at the clock!'

At once all eyes were turned upon the lad. The hands of the clock made the acutest of angles. It was close upon midnight, and from eight, without so much as a word or a question, he had sat at the dinner-table listening. Yet even now he rose with reluctance.

'Must I go, father?' he asked, and the General's guests intervened in a chorus. The conversation was clear gain to the lad, a first taste of powder which might stand him in good stead afterwards.

'Besides it's the boy's birthday,' added the major of artillery. 'He wants to stay, that's plain. You wouldn't find a youngster of fourteen sit all these hours without a kick of the foot against the table-leg unless the conversation entertained him. Let him stay, Feversham!'

For once General Feversham relaxed the iron discipline under which the boy lived.

'Very well,' said he. 'Harry shall have an hour's furlough from his bed. A single hour won't make much difference.'

Harry's eyes turned towards his father, and just for a moment rested upon his face with a curious steady gaze. It seemed to Sutch that they uttered a question, and, rightly or wrongly, he interpreted the question into words –

'Are you blind?'

But General Feversham was already talking to his neighbours, and Harry quietly sat down, and again propping his chin upon his hands, listened with all his soul. Yet he was not entertained; rather he was enthralled, he sat quiet under the compulsion of a spell. His face became unnaturally white, his eyes unnaturally large, while the flames of the candles shone ever redder and more blurred through a blue haze of tobacco-smoke, and the level of the wine grew steadily lower in the decanters.

Thus half of that one hour's furlough was passed; and then General Feversham, himself jogged by the unlucky mention of a name, suddenly blurted out in his jerky fashion –

'Lord Wilmington. One of the best names in England, if you please. Did you ever see his house in Warwickshire? Every inch of the ground you would think would have a voice to bid him play the man, if only in remembrance of his fathers . . . It seemed incredible and mere camp rumour, but the rumour grew. If it was whispered at the Alma, it was spoken aloud at Inkermann, it was shouted at Balaclava. Before Sebastopol the hideous thing was proved. Wilmington was acting as galloper to his General. I believe upon my soul the General chose him for the duty, so that the fellow might set himself right. There

11

were three hundred yards of bullet-swept flat ground, and a
message to be carried across them. Had Wilmington toppled
off his horse on the way, why, there were the whispers silenced
for ever. Had he ridden through alive he earned distinction
besides. But he didn't dare, he refused! Imagine it if you can!
He sat shaking on his horse, and declined. You should have
seen the General. His face turned the colour of that Burgundy.
'No doubt you have a previous engagement,' he said, in the
politest voice you ever heard – just that, not a word of abuse. A
previous engagement on the battle-field! For the life of me I
could hardly help laughing. But it was a tragic business for
Wilmington. He was broken, of course, and slunk back to
London. Every house was closed to him, he dropped out of his
circle like a lead bullet you let slip out of your hand into the
sea. The very women in Piccadilly spat if he spoke to them; and
he blew his brains out in a back bedroom off the Haymarket.
Curious that, eh? He hadn't the pluck to face the bullets when
his name was at stake, yet he could blow his own brains out
afterwards.'

Lieutenant Sutch chanced to look at the clock as the story
came to an end. It was now a quarter to one. Harry Feversham
had still a quarter of an hour's furlough, and that quarter of an
hour was occupied by a retired surgeon-general with a great
wagging beard, who sat nearly opposite to the boy.

'I can tell you an incident still more curious,' he said. 'The
man in this case had never been under fire before, but he was
of my own profession. Life and death were part of his business.
Nor was he really in any particular danger. The affair happened
during a hill campaign in India. We were encamped in a
valley, and a few Pathans used to lie out on the hillside at night
and take long shots into the camp. A bullet ripped through the
canvas of the hospital tent – that was all. The surgeon crept out
to his own quarters, and his orderly discovered him half an
hour afterwards lying in his blood stone dead.'

'Hit?' exclaimed the Major.

'Not a bit of it,' said the surgeon. 'He had quietly opened
his instrument-case in the dark, taken out a lancet, and severed
his femoral artery. Sheer panic, do you see, at the whistle of
a bullet.'

Even upon these men, case-hardened to horrors, the incident related in its bald simplicity wrought its effect. From some there broke a half-uttered exclamation of disbelief; others moved restlessly in their chairs with a sort of physical discomfort, because a man had sunk so far below humanity. Here an officer gulped his wine, there a second shook his shoulders as though to shake the knowledge off as a dog shakes water. There was only one in all that company who sat perfectly still in the silence which followed upon the story. That one was the boy Harry Feversham.

He sat with his hands now clenched upon his knees and leaning forward a little across the table towards the surgeon; his cheeks white as paper, his eyes burning and burning with ferocity. He had the look of a dangerous animal in the trap. His body was gathered, his muscles taut. Sutch had a fear that the lad meant to leap across the table and strike with all his strength in the savagery of despair. He had indeed reached out a restraining hand when General Feversham's matter-of-fact voice intervened, and the boy's attitude suddenly relaxed.

'Queer incomprehensible things happen. Here are two of them. You can only say they are the truth and pray God you may forget 'em. But you can't explain. For you can't understand.'

Sutch was moved to lay his hand upon Harry's shoulder.

'Can you?' he asked, and regretted the question almost before it was spoken. But it was spoken, and Harry's eyes turned swiftly towards Sutch, and rested upon his face, not, however, with any betrayal of guilt, but quietly, inscrutably. Nor did he answer the question, although it was answered in a fashion by General Feversham.

'Harry understand!' exclaimed the General with a snort of indignation. 'How should he? He's a Feversham.'

The question, which Harry's glance had mutely put before, Sutch in the same mute way repeated. 'Are you blind?' his eyes asked of General Feversham. Never had he heard an untruth so demonstrably untrue. A mere look at the father and the son proved it so. Harry Feversham wore his father's name, but he had his mother's dark and haunted eyes, his mother's breadth of forehead, his mother's delicacy of profile, his mother's imagination. It needed perhaps a stranger to recognise the truth. The father had been so long familiar with his son's aspect that it had no significance to his mind.

'Look at the clock, Harry.'

The hour's furlough had run out. Harry rose from his chair, and drew a breath.

'Good night, sir,' he said, and walked to the door.

The servants had long since gone to bed; and, as Harry opened the door, the hall gaped black like the mouth of night. For a second or two the boy hesitated upon the threshold, and seemed almost to shrink back into the lighted room as though in that dark void peril awaited him. And peril did – the peril of his thoughts.

He stepped out of the room and closed the door behind him. The decanter was sent again upon its rounds, there was a popping of soda-water bottles, the talk revolved again in its accustomed groove. Harry was in an instant forgotten by all but Sutch. The Lieutenant, although he prided himself upon his impartial and disinterested study of human nature, was the kindliest of men. He had more kindliness than observation by a great deal. Moreover, there were special reasons which caused him to take an interest in Harry Feversham. He sat for a little while with the air of a man profoundly disturbed. Then, acting upon an impulse, he went to the door, opened it noiselessly, as noiselessly passed out, and, without so much as a click of the latch, closed the door behind him.

And this is what he saw: Harry Feversham holding in the centre of the hall a lighted candle high above his head, and looking up towards the portraits of the Fevershams as they mounted the walls and were lost in the darkness of the roof. A muffled sound of voices came from the other side of the door-panels. But the hall itself was silent. Harry stood remarkably still, and the only thing which moved at all was the yellow flame of the candle as it flickered apparently in some faint draught. The light wavered across the portraits, glowing here upon a red coat, glittering there upon a corselet of steel. For there was not one man's portait upon the walls which did not glisten with the colours of a uniform, and there were the portraits of many men. Father and son, the Fevershams had been soldiers from the very birth of the family. Father and son, in lace collars and bucket boots, in Ramillies wigs and steel breast-plates, in velvet coats with powder on their hair, in shakos and swallow-tails, in high stocks and frogged coats, they looked down upon this last Feversham, summoning him to the like service. They were men of one stamp; no distinction of uniform could obscure their relationship – lean-faced men, hard as iron, rugged in feature, thin-lipped, with firm chins and straight level mouths, narrow foreheads, and the steel-blue inexpressive eyes; men of courage and resolution, no doubt, but without subtleties, or nerves, or that burdensome gift of imagination; sturdy men, a little wanting in delicacy, hardly conspicuous for intellect; to put it frankly men rather stupid – all of them, in a word, first-class fighting men, but not one of them a first-class soldier.

But Harry Feversham plainly saw none of their defects. To him they were one and all portentous and terrible. He stood before them in the attitude of a criminal before his judges, reading his condemnation in their cold unchanging eyes. Lieutenant Sutch understood more clearly why the flame of the candle flickered. There was no draught in the hall, but the boy's hand shook. And finally, as though he heard the mute voices of his judges delivering sentence and admitted its justice, he actually bowed to the portraits on the wall. As he raised his head, he saw Lieutenant Sutch in the embrasure of the doorway.

He did not start, he uttered no word; he let his eyes quietly rest upon Sutch and waited. Of the two it was the man who was embarrassed.

'Harry,' he said, and in spite of his embarrassment he had the tact to use the tone and the language of one addressing not a boy, but a comrade equal in years, 'we meet for the first time to-night. But I knew your mother a long time ago. I like to think that I have the right to call her by that much misused word – friend. Have you anything to tell me?'

'Nothing,' said Harry.

'The mere telling sometimes lightens a trouble.'

'It is kind of you. There is nothing.'

Lieutenant Sutch was rather at a loss. The lad's loneliness made a strong appeal to him. For lonely the boy could not but be, set apart as he was no less unmistakably in mind as in feature from his father and his father's fathers. Yet what more could he do? His tact again came to his aid. He took his card-case from his pocket.

'You will find my address upon this card. Perhaps some day you will give me a few days of your company. I can offer you on my side a day or two's hunting.'

A spasm of pain shook for a fleeting moment the boy's steady inscrutable face. It passed, however, swiftly as it had come.

'Thank you, sir,' Harry monotonously repeated. 'You are very kind.'

'And if ever you want to talk over a difficult question with an older man, I am at your service.'

He spoke purposely in a formal voice lest Harry with a boy's sensitiveness should think he laughed. Harry took the card and repeated his thanks. Then he went upstairs to bed.

Lieutenant Sutch waited uncomfortably in the hall until the light of the candle had diminished and disappeared. Something was amiss, he was very sure. There were words which he should have spoken to the boy, but he had not known how to set about the task. He returned to the dining-room, and with a feeling that he was almost repairing his omissions, he filled his glass and called for silence.

'Gentlemen,' he said, 'this is June 15th,' and there was great applause and much rapping on the table. 'It is the anniversary of our attack upon the Redan. It is also Harry Feversham's birthday. For us, our work is done. I ask you to drink the health of one of the youngsters who are ousting us. His work lies before him. The traditions of the Feversham family are very well known to us. May Harry Feversham carry on! May he add distinction to a distinguished name!'

At once all that company was on its feet.

'Harry Feversham!'

The name was shouted with so hearty a goodwill that the glasses on the table rang. 'Harry Feversham, Harry Feversham,' the cry was repeated and repeated, while old General Feversham sat in his chair, with a face aflush with pride. And a boy a minute afterwards in a room high up in the house heard the muffled words of a chorus –

> 'For he's a jolly good fellow,
> For he's a jolly good fellow,
> For he's a jolly good fellow,
> And so say all of us,'

and believed the guests upon this Crimean night were drinking his father's health. He turned over in his bed and lay shivering. He saw in his mind a broken officer slinking at night in the shadows of the London streets. He pushed back the flap of a tent and stooped over a man lying stone-dead in his blood, with an open lancet clenched in his right hand. And he saw that the face of the broken officer and the face of the dead surgeon were one; and that one face, the face of Harry Feversham.

Chapter Two

CAPTAIN TRENCH AND A
TELEGRAM

Thirteen years later, and in the same month of June, Harry Feversham's health was drunk again, but after a quieter fashion and in a smaller company. The company was gathered in a room high up in a shapeless block of buildings which frowns like a fortress above Westminster. A stranger crossing St James's Park southwards, over the suspension bridge, at night, who chanced to lift his eyes and see suddenly the tiers of lighted windows towering above him to so precipitous a height, might be brought to a stop with the fancy that here in the heart of London was a mountain and the gnomes at work. Upon the tenth floor of this building Harry had taken a flat during his year's furlough from his regiment in India; and it was in the dining-room of this flat that the simple ceremony took place. The room was furnished in a dark and restful

17

fashion, and since the chill of the weather belied the calendar, a comfortable fire blazed in the hearth. A bay window over which the blinds had not been lowered commanded London.

There were four men smoking about the dinner-table. Harry Feversham was unchanged except for a fair moustache which contrasted with his dark hair, and the natural consequences of growth. He was now a man of middle height, long-limbed and well-built like an athlete, but his features had not altered since that night when they had been so closely scrutinised by Lieutenant Sutch. Of his companions two were brother-officers on leave in England, like himself, whom he had that afternoon picked up at his club. Captain Trench, a small man, growing bald, with a small, sharp, resourceful face and black eyes of a remarkable activity, and Lieutenant Willoughby, an officer of quite a different stamp. A round forehead, a thick nose, and a pair of vacant and protruding eyes gave him an aspect of invincible stupidity. He spoke but seldom, and never to the point, but rather to some point long forgotten which he had since been laboriously revolving in his mind; and he continually twisted a moustache, of which the ends curled up towards his eyes with a ridiculous ferocity. A man whom one would dismiss from mind as of no consequence upon a first thought, and take again into one's consideration upon a second. For he was born stubborn as well as stupid; and the harm which his stupidity might do, his stubbornness would hinder him from admitting. He was not a man to be persuaded; having few ideas, he clung to them; it was no use to argue with him, for he did not hear the argument, but behind his vacant eyes all the while he turned over his crippled thoughts and was satisfied. The fourth at the table was Durrance, a lieutenant of the East Surrey Regiment, and Feversham's friend, who had come in answer to a telegram.

This was June of the year 1882, and the thoughts of civilians turned towards Egypt with anxiety, those of soldiers with an eager anticipation. Arabi Pasha, in spite of threats, was steadily strengthening the fortifications of Alexandria, and already a long way to the south, the other, the great danger, was swelling like a thunder-cloud. A year had passed since a young, slight, and tall Dongolawi, Mohammed Ahmed, had marched through the villages of the White Nile, preaching with the fire of a Wesley the coming of a Saviour. The passionate victims of the Turkish tax-gatherer had listened, had heard the promise repeated in the whispers of the wind in the withered grass, had found the holy names imprinted even upon the eggs they gathered up. In 1882 Mohammed had declared himself that Saviour, and had won his first battles against the Turks.

'There will be trouble,' said Trench, and the sentence was the text on which three of the four men talked. In a rare interval, however, the fourth, Harry Feversham, spoke upon a different subject.

'I am very glad you were all able to dine with me to-night. I telegraphed to Castleton as well, an officer of ours,' he explained to Durrance, 'but he was dining with a big man in the War Office, and leaves for Scotland afterwards, so that he could not come. I have news of a sort.'

The three men leaned forward, their minds still full of the dominant subject. But it was not about the prospect of war that Harry Feversham had news to speak.

'I only reached London this morning from Dublin,' he said, with a shade of embarrassment. 'I have been some weeks in Dublin.'

Durrance lifted his eyes from the tablecloth and looked quietly at his friend.

'Yes?' he asked steadily.

'I have come back engaged to be married.'

Durrance lifted his glass to his lips.

'Well, here's luck to you, Harry,' he said, and that was all. The wish, indeed, was almost curtly expressed, but there was nothing wanting in it to Feversham's ears. The friendship between these two men was not one in which affectionate phrases had any part. There was, in truth, no need of such. Both men were securely conscious of it; they estimated it at its true strong value; it was a helpful instrument which would not wear out, put into their hands for a hard, lifelong use; but it was not, and never had been, spoken of between them. Both men were grateful for it, as for a rare and undeserved gift; yet both knew that it might entail an obligation of sacrifice. But the sacrifices, were they needful, would be made, and they would not be mentioned. It may be, indeed, that the very knowledge of their friendship's strength constrained them to a particular reticence in their words to one another.

'Thank you, Jack!' said Feversham. 'I am glad of your good wishes. It was you who introduced me to Ethne. I cannot forget it.'

Durrance set his glass down without any haste. There followed a moment of silence, during which he sat with his eyes upon the table-cloth and his hands resting on the table-edge.

'Yes,' he said in a level voice. 'I did you a good turn then.'

He seemed on the point of saying more, and doubtful how to say it. But Captain Trench's sharp, quick, practical voice, a voice which fitted the man who spoke, saved him his pains.

'Will this make any difference?' asked Trench.

Feversham replaced his cigar between his lips.

'You mean, shall I leave the service?' he asked slowly. 'I don't know'; and Durrance seized the opportunity to rise from the table and cross to the window, where he stood with his back to his companions. Feversham took the abrupt movement for a reproach, and spoke to Durrance's back, not to Trench.

'I don't know,' he repeated. 'It will need thought. There is much to be said. On the one side, of course, there's my father, my career, such as it is. On the other hand, there is her father, Dermod Eustace.'

'He wishes you to chuck your commission?' asked Willoughby.

'He has no doubt the Irishman's objection to constituted authority,' said Trench, with a laugh. 'But need you subscribe to it, Feversham?'

'It is not merely that.' It was still to Durrance's back that he addressed his excuses. 'Dermod is old, his estates are going to ruin, and there are other things. You know, Jack?' The direct appeal he had to repeat, and even then Durrance answered it absently –

'Yes, I know'; and he added, like one quoting a catchword, ' "If you want any whisky, rap twice on the floor with your foot. The servants understand." '

'Precisely,' said Feversham. He continued, carefully weighing his words, and still intently looking across the shoulders of his companions to his friend.

'Besides, there is Ethne herself. Dermod for once did an appropriate thing when he gave her that name. For she is of her country and more, of her county. She has the love of it in her bones. I do not think that she could be quite happy in India, or indeed in any place which was not within reach of Donegal, the smell of its peat, its streams, and the brown friendliness of its hills. One has to consider that.'

He waited for an answer, and getting none went on again. Durrance, however, had no thought of reproach in his mind. He knew that Feversham was speaking – he wished very much that he would continue to speak for a little while – but he paid no heed to what was said. He stood looking steadfastly out of the windows. Over against him was the glare from Pall Mall striking upwards to the sky, and the chains of lights banked one above the other as the town rose northwards, and a rumble as of a million carriages was in his ears. At his feet, very far below, lay St James's Park, silent and black, a quiet pool of darkness in the midst of glitter and noise. Durrance had a great desire to escape out of this room into secrecy. But that he could not do without remark. Therefore he kept his back turned to his companion and leaned his forehead against the window, and hoped his friend would continue to talk. For he was face to face with one of the sacrifices which must not be mentioned, and which no sign must betray.

Feversham did continue, and if Durrance did not listen, on the other hand Captain Trench gave to him his closest attention. But it was evident that Harry Feversham was giving reasons seriously considered. He was not making excuses, and in the end Captain Trench was satisfied.

'Well, I drink to you, Feversham,' he said, 'with all the proper sentiments.'

'I too, old man,' said Willoughby, obediently following his senior's lead.

Thus they drank their comrade's health, and as their empty glasses rattled on the table, there came a knock upon the door.

The two officers looked up. Durrance turned about from the

window. Feversham said, 'Come in'; and his servant brought in to him a telegram.

Feversham tore open the envelope carelessly, as carelessly read the telegram, and then sat very still with his eyes upon the slip of pink paper, and his face grown at once extremely grave. Thus he sat for an appreciable time, not so much stunned as thoughtful. And in the room there was a complete silence. Feversham's three guests averted their eyes. Durrance turned again to his window; Willoughby twisted his moustache and gazed intently upwards at the ceiling; Captain Trench shifted his chair round and stared into the glowing fire, and each man's attitude expressed a certain suspense. It seemed that sharp upon the heels of Feversham's good news calamity had come knocking at the door.

'There is no answer,' said Harry, and fell to silence again. Once he raised his head and looked at Trench as though he had a mind to speak. But he thought the better of it, and so dropped again to the consideration of this message. And in a moment or two the silence was sharply interrupted, but not by any one of the expectant motionless three men within the room. The interruption came from without.

From the parade ground of Wellington Barracks the drums and fifes sounding the tattoo shrilled through the open window with a startling clearness like a sharp summons, and diminished as the band marched away across the gravel and again grew loud. Feversham did not change his attitude, but the look upon his face was now that of a man listening, and listening thoughtfully, just as he had read thoughtfully. In the years which followed that moment was to recur again and again to the recollection of each of Harry's three guests. The lighted room with the bright homely fire, the open window overlooking the myriad lamps of London, Harry Feversham seated with the telegram spread before him, the drums and fifes calling loudly, and then dwindling to a music very small and pretty – music which beckoned, where a moment ago it had commanded: all these details made up a picture of which the colours were not to fade by any lapse of time, although its significance was not apprehended now.

It was remembered that Feversham rose abruptly from his

chair, just before the tattoo ceased. He crumpled the telegram loosely in his hands, tossed it into the fire, and then, leaning his back against the chimney-piece and upon one side of the fire-place, said again –

'I don't know,' as though he had thrust that message, what-ever it might be, from his mind, and was summing up in this indefinite way the argument which had gone before. Thus that long silence was broken, and a spell was lifted. But the fire took hold upon the telegram and shook it, so that it moved like a thing alive and in pain. It twisted, and part of it unrolled, and for a second lay open and smooth of creases, lit up by the flame and as yet untouched; so that two or three words sprang, as it were, out of a yellow glare of fire and were legible. Then the flame seized upon that smooth part too, and in a moment shrivelled it into black tatters. But Captain Trench was all this while staring into the fire.

'You return to Dublin, I suppose?' said Durrance. He had moved back again into the room. Like his companions, he was conscious of an unexplained relief.

'To Dublin, no. I go to Donegal in three weeks' time. There is to be a dance. It is hoped you will come.'

'I am not sure that I can manage it. There is just a chance, I believe, should trouble come in the East, that I may go out on the Staff.' The talk thus came round again to the chances of peace and war, and held in that quarter till the boom of the Westminster clock told that the hour was eleven. Captain Trench rose from his seat on the last stroke; Willoughby and Durrance followed his example.

'I shall see you to-morrow,' said Durrance to Feversham.

'As usual,' replied Harry; and his three guests descended from his rooms and walked across the Park together. At the corner of Pall Mall, however, they parted company, Durrance mounting St James's Street, while Trench and Willoughby crossed the road into St James's Square. There Trench slipped his arm through Willoughby's, to Willoughby's surprise, for Trench was an undemonstrative man.

'You know Castleton's address?' he asked.

'Albemarle Street,' Willoughby answered, and added the number.

'He leaves Euston at twelve o'clock. It is now ten minutes past eleven. Are you curious, Willoughby? I confess to curiosity. I am an inquisitive methodical person, and when a man gets a telegram bidding him tell Trench something and he tells Trench nothing, I am curious as a philosopher to know what that something is! Castleton is the only other officer of our regiment in London. Castleton, too, was dining with a big man from the War Office. I think that if we take a hansom to Albemarle Street we shall just catch Castleton upon his doorstep.'

Mr Willoughby, who understood very little of Trench's meaning, nevertheless cordially agreed to the proposal.

'I think it would be prudent,' said he; and he hailed a passing cab. A moment later the two men were driving to Albemarle Street.

Chapter Three

THE LAST RIDE TOGETHER

Durrance, meanwhile, walked to his lodging alone, remembering a day, now two years since, when by a curious whim of old Dermod Eustace he had been fetched against his will to the house by the Lennon river in Donegal, and there, to his surprise, had been made acquainted with Dermod's daughter Ethne. For she surprised all who had first held speech with the father. Durrance had stayed for a night in the house, and through that evening she had played upon her violin, seated with her back towards her audience, as was her custom when she played, lest a look or a gesture should interrupt the concentration of her thoughts. the melodies which she had played rang in his ears now. For the girl possessed the gift of music, and the strings of her violin spoke to the questions of her bow. There was in particular an overture – the Melusine overture – which had the very sob of the waves. Durrance had listened wondering, for the violin had spoken to him of many things of which the girl

24

who played it could know nothing. It had spoken of long perilous journeys and the faces of strange countries; of the silver way across moonlit seas; of the beckoning voices from the under edges of the desert. It had taken a deeper, a more mysterious tone. It had told of great joys, quite unattainable, and of great griefs too, eternal, and with a sort of nobility by reason of their greatness; and of many unformulated longings beyond the reach of words; but with never a single note of mere complaint. So it had seemed to Durrance that night as he had sat listening while Ethne's face was turned away. So it seemed to him now when he knew that her face was still to be turned away for all his days. He had drawn a thought from her playing which he was at some pains to keep definite in his mind. The true music cannot complain.

Therefore it was that as he rode the next morning into the Row his blue eyes looked out upon the world from his bronzed face with not a jot less of his usual friendliness. He waited at half-past nine by the clump of lilacs and laburnums at the end of the sand, but Harry Feversham did not join him that morning, nor indeed for the next three weeks. Ever since the two men had graduated from Oxford it had been their custom to meet at this spot and hour, when both chanced to be in town, and Durrance was puzzled. It seemed to him that he had lost his friend as well.

Meanwhile, however, the rumours of war grew to a certainty, and when at last Feversham kept the tryst, Durrance had news.

'I told you luck might look my way. Well, she has. I go out to Egypt on General Graham's staff. There's talk we may run down the Red Sea to Suakin afterwards.'

The exhilaration of his voice brought an unmistakable envy into Feversham's eyes. It seemed strange to Durrance even at that moment of his good luck, that Harry Feversham should envy him – strange and rather pleasant. But he interpreted the envy in the light of his own ambitions.

'It is rough on you,' he said sympathetically, 'that your regiment has to stay behind.'

Feversham rode by his friend's side in silence. Then, as they came to the chairs beneath the trees, he said –

'That was expected. The day you dined with me I sent in my papers.'

'That night?' said Durrance, turning in his saddle. 'After we had gone?'

'Yes,' said Feversham, accepting the correction. He wondered whether it had been intended. But Durrance rode silently forward. Again Harry Feversham was conscious of a reproach in his friend's silence, and again he was wrong. For Durrance suddenly spoke heartily, and with a laugh.

'I remember. You gave us your reasons that night. But for the life of me I can't help wishing that we had been going out together. When do you leave for Ireland?'

'To-night.'

'So soon?'

They turned their horses and rode westwards again down the alley of trees. The morning was still fresh. The limes and chestnuts had lost nothing of their early green, and since the May was late that year, its blossoms still hung delicately white like snow upon the branches and shone red against the dark rhododendrons. The Park shimmered in a haze of sunlight, and the distant roar of the streets was as the tumbling of river water.

'It is a long time since we bathed in Sandford Lasher,' said Durrance.

'Or froze in the Easter vacations in the big snow-gully on Great End,' returned Feversham. Both men had the feeling that on this morning a volume in their book of life was ended, and since the volume had been a pleasant one to read, and they did not know whether its successors would sustain its promise, they were looking backwards through the leaves before they put it finally away.

'You must stay with us, Jack, when you come back,' said Feversham.

Durrance had schooled himself not to wince, and he did not even at that anticipatory 'us'. If his left hand tightened upon the thongs of his reins, the sign could not be detected by his friend.

'If I come back,' said Durrance. 'You know my creed. I

could never pity a man who died on active service. I would very much like to come by that end myself.'

It was a quite simple creed, consistent with the simplicity of the man who uttered it. It amounted to no more than this: that to die decently was worth a good many years of life. So that he uttered it without melancholy or any sign of foreboding. Even so, however, he had a fear that perhaps his friend might place another interpretation upon the words, and he looked quickly into his face. He only saw again, however, that puzzling look of envy in Feversham's eyes.

'You see there are worse things which can happen,' he continued. 'Disablement, for instance. Clever men could make a shift perhaps to put up with it. But what in the world should I do if I had to sit in a chair all my days? It makes me shiver to think of it,' and he shook his broad shoulders to unsaddle that fear. 'Well, this is the last ride. Let us gallop,' and he let out his horse.

Feversham followed his example, and side by side they went racing down the sand. At the bottom of the Row they stopped, shook hands, and with the curtest of nods parted. Feversham rode out of the Park, Durrance turned back and walked his horse up towards the seats beneath the trees.

Even as a boy in his home at Southpool in Devonshire upon a wooded creek of the Salcombe estuary, he had always been conscious of a certain restlessness, a desire to sail down that creek and out over the levels of the sea, a dream of queer outlandish countries and peoples beyond the dark familiar woods. And the restlessness had grown upon him, so that 'Guessens', even when he had inherited it with its farms and lands, had remained always in his thoughts as a place to come home to rather than an estate to occupy a life. He purposely exaggerated that restlessness now, and purposely set against it words which Feversham had spoken and which he knew to be true. Ethne Eustace would hardly be happy outside her county of Donegal. Therefore, even had things fallen out differently, as he phrased it, there might have been a clash. Perhaps it was as well that Harry Feversham was to marry Ethne – and not another than Feversham.

Thus at all events he argued as he rode, until the riders

27

vanished from before his eyes, and the ladies in their coloured frocks beneath the cool of the trees. The trees themselves dwindled to ragged mimosas, the brown sand at his feet spread out in a widening circumference and took the bright colour of honey; and upon the empty sand black stones began to heap themselves shapelessly like coal, and to flash in the sun like mirrors. He was deep in his anticipations of the Soudan, when he heard his name called out softly in a woman's voice, and, looking up, found himself close by the rails.

'How do you do, Mrs Adair?' said he, and he stopped his horse. Mrs Adair gave him her hand across the rails. She was Durrance's neighbour at Southpool, and by a year or two his elder – a tall woman remarkable for the many shades of her thick brown hair and the peculiar pallor on her face. But at this moment the face had brightened, there was a hint of colour in the cheeks.

'I have news for you,' said Durrance. 'Two special items. One, Harry Feversham is to be married.'

'To whom?' asked the lady, eagerly.

'You should know. It was in your house in Hill Street that Harry first met her. And I introduced him. He has been improving the acquaintance in Dublin.'

But Mrs Adair already understood; and it was plain that the news was welcome.

'Ethne Eustace,' she cried. 'They will be married soon?'

'There is nothing to prevent it.'

'I am glad,' and the lady sighed as though with relief. 'What is your second item?'

'As good as the first. I go out on General Graham's Staff.'

Mrs Adair was silent. There came a look of anxiety into her eyes, and the colour died out of her face.

'You are very glad, I suppose,' she said slowly.

Durrance's voice left her in no doubt.

'I should think I was. I go soon, too, and the sooner the better. I will come and dine some night, if I may, before I go.'

'My husband will be pleased to see you,' said Mrs Adair, rather coldly. Durrance did not notice the coldness, however. He had his own reasons for making the most of the opportunity which had come his way; and he urged his enthusiasm, and laid it bare in words more for his own benefit than with any thought of Mrs Adair. Indeed, he had always rather a vague impression of the lady. She was handsome in a queer, foreign way, not so uncommon along the coasts of Devonshire and Cornwall, and she had good hair, and was always well dressed. Moreover, she was friendly. And at that point, Durrance's knowledge of her came to an end. Perhaps her chief merit in his eyes was that she had made friends with Ethne Eustace. But he was to become better acquainted with Mrs Adair. He rode away from the Park with the old regret in his mind that the fortunes of himself and his friend were this morning finally severed. As a fact he had that morning set the strands of a new rope a-weaving which was to bring them together again in a strange and terrible relationship. Mrs Adair followed him out of the Park, and walked home very thoughtfully.

Durrance had just one week wherein to provide his equipment, and arrange his estate in Devonshire. It passed in a continuous hurry of preparation, so that his newspaper lay each day unfolded in his rooms. The General was to travel overland to Brindisi, and so on an evening of wind and rain towards the end of July Durrance stepped from the Dover Pier into the mail-boat for Calais. In spite of the rain and the gloomy night, a small crowd had gathered to give the General a send-off. As the ropes were cast off a feeble cheer was raised, and before the cheer had ended, Durrance found himself beset by a strange illusion. He was leaning upon the bulwarks idly wondering whether this was his last view of England, and with a wish that some one of his friends had come down to see him go, when it seemed to him suddenly that his wish was answered. For he caught a glimpse of a man standing beneath a gas-lamp, and that man was of the stature and wore the likeness of Harry Feversham. Durrance rubbed his eyes and looked again. But the wind made the tongue of light flicker uncertainly within the glass, the rain, too, blurred the quay. He could only be certain that a man was standing there, he could only vaguely distinguish beneath the lamp the whiteness of a face. It was an illusion, he said to himself. Harry Feversham was at that moment most likely listening to Ethne Eustace playing the violin under a clear sky in a high garden of Donegal. But even as he was turning from the bulwarks, there came a lull of the wind, the lights burned bright and steady on the pier, and the face leaped from the shadows distinct in feature and expression. Durrance leaned out over the side of the boat.

'Harry!' he shouted at the top of a wondering voice.

But the figure beneath the lamp never stirred. The wind blew the lights again this way and that, the paddles churning the water, the mail-boat passed beyond the pier. It was an illusion, he repeated, it was a coincidence. It was the face of a stranger very like to Harry Feversham. It could not be Feversham's, because the face which Durrance had seen so distinctly for a moment was a haggard, wistful face, a face stamped with an extraordinary misery, the face of a man cast out from among his fellows.

Durrance had been very busy all that week. He had clean forgotten the arrival of that telegram and the suspense which the long perusal of it had caused. Moreover, his newspaper had lain unopened in his rooms. But his friend Harry Feversham had come to see him off.

Chapter Four

THE BALL AT LENNON HOUSE

Yet Feversham had travelled to Dublin by the night mail after his ride with Durrance in the Row. He had crossed Lough Swilly on the following forenoon by a little cargo steamer, which once a week steamed up the Lennon river as far as Ramelton. On the quayside Ethne was waiting for him in her dog-cart; she gave him the hand and the smile of a comrade.

'You are surprised to see me,' said she, noting the look upon his face.

'I always am,' he replied. 'For always you exceed my thoughts of you'; and the smile changed upon her face – it became something more than the smile of a comrade.

'I shall drive slowly,' she said, as soon as his traps had been packed into the cart; 'I brought no groom on purpose. There will be guests coming to-morrow. We have only to-day.'

She drove along the wide causeway by the river-side, and turned up the steep, narrow street. Feversham sat silently by her side. It was his first visit to Ramelton, and he gazed about him, noting the dark thicket of tall trees which climbed on the far side of the river, the old grey bridge, the noise of the water above it as it sang over shallows, and the drowsy quiet of the town, with a great curiosity and almost a pride of ownership, since it was here that Ethne lived, and all these things were part and parcel of her life.

She was at that time a girl of twenty-one, tall, strong, and supple of limb, and with a squareness of shoulder proportionate to her height. She had none of that exaggerated slope which our grandmothers esteemed, yet she lacked no grace of womanhood on that account, and in her walk she was light-footed as a deer. Her hair was dark brown, and she wore it coiled upon the nape of her neck; a bright colour burned in her cheeks, and her eyes, of a very clear grey, met the eyes of those to whom she talked with a most engaging frankness. And in character she was the counterpart of her looks. She was honest, she had a certain simplicity, the straightforward simplicity of strength which comprises much gentleness and excludes violence. Of her courage there is a story still told in Ramelton, which Feversham could never remember without a thrill of wonder. She had stopped at a door on that steep hill leading down to the river, and the horse which she was driving took fright at the mere clatter of a pail and bolted. The reins were lying loose at the moment; they fell on the ground before Ethne could seize them. She was thus seated helpless in the dog-cart, and the horse was tearing down to where the road curves sharply over the bridge. The thing which she did, she did quite coolly. She climbed over the front of the dog-cart as it pitched and raced down the hill, and balancing herself along the shafts, reached the reins at the horse's neck, and brought the horse to a stop ten yards from the curve. But she had, too, the defects of her qualities, although Feversham was not yet aware of them.

Ethne, during the first part of this drive, was almost as silent as her companion, and when she spoke it was with an absent air, as though she had something of more importance in her thoughts. It was not until she had left the town and was out upon the straight undulating road to Letterkenny that she turned quickly to Feversham and uttered it.

'I saw this morning that your regiment was ordered from India to Egypt. You could have gone with it had I not come in your way. There would have been chances of distinction. I have hindered you, and I am very sorry. Of course, you could not know that there was any possibility of your regiment going, but I can understand it is very hard for you to be left behind. I blame myself.'

Feversham sat staring in front of him for a moment. Then he said, in a voice suddenly grown hoarse –

'You need not.'

'How can I help it? I blame myself the more,' she continued, 'because I do not see things quite like other women. For instance, supposing that you had gone to Egypt, and that the worst had happened, I should have felt very lonely, of course, all my days, but I should have known quite surely that when those days were over, you and I would see much of one another.'

She spoke without any impressive lowering of the voice, but in the steady level tone of one stating the simplest imaginable fact. Feversham caught his breath like a man in pain. But the girl's eyes were upon his face, and he sat still, staring in front of him without so much as a contraction of the forehead. But it seemed that he could not trust himself to answer. He kept his lips closed, and Ethne continued –

'You see, I can put up with the absence of the people I care about a little better perhaps than most people. I do not feel that I have lost them at all;' and she cast about for a while as if her thought was difficult to express. 'You know how things happen,' she resumed. 'One goes along in a dull sort of way, and then suddenly a face springs out from the crowd of one's acquaintances, and you know it at once and certainly for the face of a friend, or rather you recognise it, though you have never seen it before. It is almost as though you had come upon someone long looked for and now gladly recovered. Well, such friends – they are few, no doubt, but after all only the few really count – such friends one does not lose, whether they are absent, or even – dead.'

'Unless,' said Feversham, slowly, 'one has made a mistake. Suppose the face in the crowd is a mask, what then? One may make mistakes.'

Ethne shook her head decidedly.

'Of that kind, no. One may seem to have made mistakes, and perhaps for a long while. But in the end one would be proved not to have made them.'

And the girl's implicit faith took hold upon the man and tortured him, so that he could no longer keep silence.

'Ethne,' he cried, 'you don't know — ' But at that moment Ethne reined in her horse, laughed, and pointed with her whip.

They had come to the top of a hill a couple of miles from Ramelton. The road ran between stone walls enclosing open fields upon the left, and a wood of oaks and beeches on the right. A scarlet letter-box was built into the left-hand wall, and at that Ethne's whip was pointed.

'I wanted to show you that,' she interrupted. 'It was there I used to post my letters to you during the anxious times.' And so Feversham let slip his opportunity of speech.

'The house is behind the trees to the right,' she continued.

'The letter-box is very convenient,' said Feversham.

'Yes,' said Ethne, and she drove on and stopped again where the park wall had crumbled.

'That's where I used to climb over to post the letters. There's a tree on the other side of the wall as convenient as the letter-box. I used to run down the half-mile of avenue at night.'

'There might have been thieves,' exclaimed Feversham.

'There were thorns,' said Ethne; and turning through the gates, she drove up to the porch of the long, irregular grey house. 'Well, we have still a day before the dance.'

'I suppose the whole country-side is coming?' said Feversham.

'It daren't do anything else,' said Ethne, with a laugh. 'My father would send the police to fetch them if they stayed away, just as he fetched your friend Mr Durrance here. By the way, Mr Durrance has sent me a present – a Guarnerius violin.'

The door opened, and a thin, lank old man with a fierce peaked face like a bird of prey came out upon the steps. His face softened, however, into friendliness when he saw Feversham, and a smile played upon his lips. A stranger might have thought that he winked. But his left eyelid continually dropped over the eye.

'How do you do?' he said. 'Glad to see you. Must make yourself at home. If you want any whisky, stamp twice on the floor with your foot. The servants understand;' and with that he went straightway back into the house.

The biographer of Dermod Eustace would need to bring a wary mind to his work. For though the old master of Lennon House has not lain twenty years in his grave, he is already swollen into a legendary character. Anecdotes have grown upon his memory like barnacles, and any man in those parts with a knack of invention has only to foist his stories upon Dermod to ensure a ready credence. They are, however, definite facts. He practised an ancient and tyrannous hospitality, keeping open house upon the road to Letterkenny, and forcing bed and board even upon strangers, as Durrance had once discovered. He was a man of another century, who looked out with an angry eye upon a topsy-turvy world and would not be reconciled to it except after much alcohol. He was a sort of intoxicated Coriolanus, believing that the people should be shepherded with a stick, yet always mindful of his manners even to the lowliest of women. It was always said of him with pride by the townsfolk of Ramelton that, even at his worst, when he came galloping down the steep cobbled streets, mounted on a big white mare of seventeen hands, with his inseparable collie-dog for his companion – a gaunt, grey-faced, grey-haired man with a drooping eye, swaying with drink, yet by a miracle keeping his saddle – he had never ridden down anyone except a man. There are two points to be added. He was rather afraid of his daughter, who wisely kept him doubtful whether she was displeased with him or not, and he had conceived a great liking for Harry Feversham.

Harry saw little of him that day, however. Dermod retired

into the room which he was pleased to call his office, while Feversham and Ethne spent the afternoon fishing for salmon in the Lennon river. It was an afternoon restful as a Sabbath, and the very birds were still. From the house the lawns fell steeply, shaded by trees and dappled by the sunlight, to a valley, at the bottom of which flowed the river swift and black under overarching boughs. There was a fall, where the water slid over rocks with a smoothness so unbroken that it looked solid except just at one point. There a spur stood sharply up, and the river broke back upon itself in an amber wave through which the sun shone. Opposite this spur they sat for a long while, talking at times, but for the most part listening to the roar of the water, and watching its perpetual flow. And at last the sunset came, and the long shadows. They stood up, looked at each other with a smile, and so walked slowly back to the house. It was an afternoon which Feversham was long to remember. For the next night was the night of the dance, and as the band struck up the opening bars of the fourth waltz, Ethne left her position at the drawing-room door, and, taking Feversham's arm, passed out into the hall.

The hall was empty, and the front door stood open to the cool of the summer night. From the ballroom came the swaying lilt of the music and the beat of the dancers' feet. Ethne drew a breath of relief at her reprieve from her duties, and then, dropping her partner's arm, crossed to a side table.

'The post is in,' she said. 'There are letters, one, two, three for you, and a little box.'

She held the box out to him as she spoke, a little white jeweller's cardboard box, and was at once struck by its absence of weight.

'It must be empty,' she said.

Yet it was most carefully sealed and tied. Feversham broke the seals and unfastened the string. He looked at the address. The box had been forwarded from his lodgings, and he was not familiar with the hand-writing.

'There is some mistake,' he said as he shook the lid open; and then he stopped abruptly. Three white feathers fluttered out of the box, swayed and rocked for a moment in the air, and then, one after another, settled gently down upon the floor.

They lay like flakes of snow upon the dark polished boards. But they were not whiter than Harry Feversham's cheeks. He stood and stared at the feathers until he felt a light touch upon his arm. He looked and saw Ethne's gloved hand upon his sleeve.

'What does it mean?' she asked. There was some perplexity in her voice, but nothing more than perplexity. The smile upon her face and the loyal confidence of her eyes showed she had never a doubt that his first word would lift it from her. 'What does it mean?'

'That there are things which cannot be hid, I suppose,' said Feversham.

For a little while Ethne did not speak. The langurous music floated into the hall, and the trees whispered from the garden through the open door. Then she shook his arm gently, uttered a breathless little laugh, and spoke as though she were pleading with a child.

'I don't think you understand, Harry. Here are three white feathers. They were sent to you in jest? Oh, of course in jest. But it is a cruel kind of jest — '

'They were sent in deadly earnest.'

He spoke now, looking her straight in the eyes. Ethne dropped her hand from his sleeve.

'Who sent them?' she asked.

Feversham had not given a thought to that matter. The message was all in all, the men who had sent it so unimportant. But Ethne reached out her hand and took the box from him. There were three visiting-cards lying at the bottom, and she took them out and read them aloud.

'Captain Trench, Mr Castleton, Mr Willoughby. Do you know these men?'

'All three are officers of my old regiment.'

The girl was dazed. She knelt down upon the floor and gathered the feathers into her hand with a vague thought that merely to touch them would help her to comprehension. They lay upon the palm of her white glove, and she blew gently upon them and they swam up into the air and hung fluttering and rocking. As they floated downwards she caught them again, and so she slowly felt her way to another question.

'Were they justly sent?' she asked.

'Yes,' said Harry Feversham.

He had no thought of denial or evasion. He was only aware that the dreadful thing for so many years dreadfully anticipated had at last befallen him. He was known for a coward. The word which had long blazed upon the wall of his thoughts in letters of fire was now written large in the public places. He stood as he had once stood before the portraits of his fathers, mutely accepting condemnation. It was the girl who denied, as she still kneeled upon the floor.

'I do not believe that is true,' she said. 'You could not look me in the face so steadily were it true. Your eyes would seek the floor, not mine.'

'Yet it is true.'

'Three little white feathers,' she said slowly; and then, with a sob in her throat. 'This afternoon we were under the elms down by the Lennon river – do you remember, Harry? – just you and I. And then come three little white feathers; and the world's at an end.'

'Oh don't!' cried Harry, and his voice broke upon the word. Up till now he had spoken with a steadiness matching the steadiness of his eyes. But these last words of hers, the picture which they evoked in his memories, the pathetic simplicity of her utterance caught him by the heart. But Ethne seemed not to hear the appeal. She was listening with her face turned towards the ballroom. The chatter and laughter of the voices there grew louder and nearer. She understood that the music had ceased. She rose quickly to her feet, clenching the feathers in her hand, and opened a door. It was the door of her sitting-room.

'Come,' she said.

Harry followed her into the room, and she closed the door, shutting out the noise.

'Now,' she said, 'will you tell me, if you please, why the feathers have been sent.'

She stood quietly before him; her face was pale, but Feversham could not gather from her expression any feeling which she might have beyond a desire and a determination to get at

37

the truth. She spoke, too, with the same quietude. He answered, as he had answered before, directly, and to the point, without any attempt at mitigation.

'A telegram came. It was sent by Castleton. It reached me when Trench and Willoughby were dining with me. It told me that my regiment would be ordered on active service in Egypt. Castleton was dining with a man likely to know, and I did not question the accuracy of his message. He told me to tell Trench. I did not, I thought the matter over with the telegram in front of me. Castleton was leaving that night for Scotland, and he would go straight from Scotland to rejoin the regiment. He would not, therefore, see Trench for some weeks at the earliest, and by that time the telegram would very likely be forgotten, or its date confused. I did not tell Trench. I threw the telegram into the fire, and that night sent in my papers. But Trench found out somehow. Durrance was at dinner, too – good God, Durrance!' he suddenly broke out. 'Most likely he knows like the rest.'

It came upon him as something shocking and strangely new that his friend Durrance, who, as he knew very well, had been wont rather to look up to him, in all likelihood counted him a thing of scorn. But he heard Ethne speaking. After all, what did it matter whether Durrance knew, whether every man knew from the South Pole to the North, since she, Ethne, knew.

'And is this all?' she asked.

'Surely it is enough,' said he.

'I think not,' she answered, and she lowered her voice a little as she went on. 'We agreed, didn't we, that no foolish misunderstandings should ever come between us. We were to be frank, and to take frankness each from the other without offence. So be frank with me! Please!' and she pleaded. 'I could, I think, claim it as a right. At all events I ask for it as I shall never ask for anything else in all my life.'

There was a sort of explanation of his act, Harry Feversham remembered. But it was so futile when compared with the overwhelming consequence. Ethne had unclenched her hands, the three feathers lay before his eyes upon the table. They could not be explained away; he wore 'coward' like a blind man's label; besides, he could never make her understand. However, she wished for the explanation, and had a right to it; she had been generous in asking for it, with a generosity not very common amongst women. So Feversham gathered his wits, and explained –

'All my life I have been afraid that some day I should play the coward, and from the very first I knew that I was destined for the army. I kept my fear to myself. There was no one to whom I could tell it. My mother was dead, and my father — ' he stopped for a moment with a deep intake of the breath. He could see his father, that lonely iron man, sitting at this very moment in his mother's favourite seat upon the terrace, and looking over the moonlit fields towards the Sussex Downs; he could imagine him dreaming of honours and distinctions worthy of the Fevershams to be gained immediately by his son in the Egyptian campaign. Surely that old man's stern heart would break beneath this blow! The magnitude of the bad thing which he had done, the misery which it would spread, were becoming very clear to Harry Feversham. He dropped his head between his hands and groaned aloud.

'My father,' he resumed, 'would, nay, could never have understood. I know him. When danger came his way it found him ready, but he did not foresee. That was my trouble always. I foresaw. Any peril to be encountered, any risk to be run – I foresaw them. I foresaw something else besides. My father would talk in his matter-of-fact way of the hours of waiting before the actual commencement of a battle, after the troops had been paraded. The mere anticipation of this suspense and the strain of those hours was a torture to me. I foresaw the possibility of cowardice. Then one evening, when my father had his old friends about him on one of his Crimean nights, two dreadful stories were told – one of an officer, the other of a surgeon, who had both shirked. I took those stories up to bed with me. They never left my memory; they became a part of me. I saw myself behaving now as one, now as the other of those two men had behaved, perhaps in the crisis of a battle bringing ruin upon my country, certainly dishonouring my father and all the dead men whose portraits hung ranged in the hall. I tried to get the best of my fears. I hunted, but with a map of the country-side in my mind. I foresaw every hedge, every pit, every treacherous bank.'

'Yet you rode straight,' interrupted Ethne. 'Mr Durrance told me so.'

'Did I?' said Feversham vaguely, 'Well, perhaps I did, once the hounds were off. Durrance never knew what the moments of waiting before the coverts were drawn meant to me! So when this telegram came I took the chance it seemed to offer, and resigned.'

He ended his explanation. He had spoken warily, having something to conceal. However, earnestly she might ask for frankness, he must at all costs, for her sake, hide something from her. But at once she suspected it.

'Were you afraid too of disgracing me? Was I in any way the cause that you resigned?'

Feversham looked her in the eyes and lied:

'No.'

'If you had not been engaged to me you would still have sent in your papers?'

'Yes.'

Ethne slowly stripped a glove off her hand. Feversham turned away.

'I think that I am rather like your father,' she said. 'I don't understand;' and in the silence which followed upon her words Feversham heard something whirr and rattle upon the table. He looked and saw that she had slipped her engagement ring off her finger. It lay upon the table, the stones winking at him.

'And all this – all that you have told to me,' she exclaimed suddenly, with her face very stern, 'you would have hidden from me. You would have married me and hidden it had not these three feathers come?'

The words had been on her lips from the beginning, but she had not uttered them lest by a miracle he should after all have some unimagined explanation which would re-establish him in her thoughts. She had given him every chance. Now, however, she struck and laid bare the worst of his disloyalty. Feversham flinched, and he did not answer, but allowed his silence to consent. Ethne, however, was just; she was in a way curious too: she wished to know the very bottom of the matter before she thrust it into the back of her mind.

'But yesterday,' she said, 'you were going to tell me something. I stopped you to point out the letter-box;' and she laughed in a queer empty way. 'Was it about the feathers?'

'Yes,' answered Feversham, wearily. What did these persistent questions matter, since the feathers had come, since her ring lay flickering and winking on the table. 'Yes, I think what you were saying rather compelled me.'

'I remember,' said Ethne, interrupting him rather hastily, 'about seeing much of one another – afterwards. We will not speak of such things again,' and Feversham swayed up on his feet as though he would fall. 'I remember, too, you said one could make mistakes. You were right, I was wrong. One can do more than seem to make them. Will you, if you please, take back your ring?'

Feversham picked up the ring and held it in the palm of his hand, standing very still. He had never cared for her so much, he had never recognised her value so thoroughly as at this moment when he lost her. She gleamed in the quiet room, wonderful, most wonderful, from the bright flowers in her hair to the white slipper on her foot. It was incredible to him that he should ever have won her. Yet he had, and disloyally had lost her. Then her voice broke in again upon his reflections.

'These, too, are yours. Will you take them please?'

She was pointing with her fan to the feathers upon the table. Feversham obediently reached out his hand, and then drew it back in surprise.

'There are four,' he said.

Ethne did not reply, and looking at her fan Feversham understood. It was a fan of ivory and white feathers. She had broken off one of those feathers and added it on her own account to the three.

The thing which she had done was cruel, no doubt. But she wished to make an end – a complete, irrevocable end; though her voice was steady, and her face, despite its pallor calm, she was really tortured with humiliation and pain. All the details of Harry Feversham's courtship, the interchange of looks, the

41

letters she had written and received, the words which had been spoken, tingled and smarted unbearably in her recollections. Their lips had touched – she recalled it with horror. She desired never to see Harry Feversham after this night. Therefore she added her fourth feather to the three.

Harry Feversham took the feathers as she bade him, without a word of remonstrance, and indeed with a sort of dignity which even at that moment surprised her. All the time, too, he had kept his eyes steadily upon hers, he had answered her questions simply, there had been nothing abject in his manner; so that Ethne already began to regret this last thing which she had done. However, it *was* done. Feversham had taken the four feathers.

He held them in his fingers as though he was about to tear them across. But he checked the action. He looked suddenly towards her, and kept his eyes upon her face for some little while. Then very carefully he put the feathers into his breast pocket. Ethne at this time did not consider why. She only thought that here was the irrevocable end.

'We should be going back, I think,' she said. 'We have been some time away. Will you give me your arm?' In the hall she looked at the clock. 'Only eleven o'clock,' she said wearily. 'When we dance here, we dance till daylight. We must show brave faces until daylight.'

And, with her hand resting upon his arm, they passed into the ball-room.

Chapter Five

THE PARIAH

Habit assisted them; the irresponsible chatter of the ball-room sprang automatically to their lips; the appearance of enjoyment never failed from off their faces; so that no one at Lennon House that night suspected that any swift cause of severance had come between them. Harry Feversham watched

Ethne laugh and talk as though she had never a care, and was perpetually surprised, taking no thought that he wore the like mask of gaiety himself. When she swung past him the light rhythm of her feet almost persuaded him that her heart was in the dance. It seemed that she could even command the colour upon her cheeks. Thus they both wore brave faces as she had bidden. They even danced together. But all the while Ethne was conscious that she was holding up a great load of pain and humiliation which would presently crush her, and Feversham felt those four feathers burning at his breast. It was wonderful to him that the whole company did not know of them. He never approached a partner without the notion that she would turn upon him with the contemptuous name which was his upon her tongue. Yet he felt no fear on that account. He would not indeed have cared had it happened, had the word been spoken. He had lost Ethne. He watched her and looked in vain amongst her guests, as indeed he surely knew he would, for a fit comparison. There were women, pretty, graceful, even beautiful, but Ethne stood apart by the particular character of her beauty. The broad forehead, the perfect curve of the eyebrows; the great, steady, clear grey eyes, the full red lips which could dimple into tenderness and shut level with resolution, and the royal grace of her carriage, marked her out to Feversham's thinking, and would do so in any company. He watched her in a despairing amazement that he had ever had a chance of owning her.

Only once did her endurance fail, and then only for a second. She was dancing with Feversham, and as she looked towards the windows she saw that the daylight was beginning to show very pale and cold upon the other side of the blinds.

'Look!' she said, and Feversham suddenly felt all her weight upon his arms. Her face lost its colour, and grew tired and very grey. Her eyes shut tightly and then opened again. He thought that she would faint. 'The morning at last!' she exclaimed; and then, in a voice as weary as her face, 'I wonder whether it is right that one should suffer so much pain.'

'Hush!' whispered Feversham. 'Courage! A few minutes more – only a very few!' He stopped and stood in front of her until her strength returned.

'Thank you!' she said gratefully; and the bright wheel of the dance caught them in its spokes again.

It was strange that he should be exhorting her to courage, she thanking him for help, but the irony of this queer momentary reversal of their position occurred to neither of them. Ethne was too tired by the strain of those last hours, and Feversham had learned from that one failure of her endurance, from the drawn aspect of her face and the depths of pain in her eyes, how deeply he had wounded her. He no longer said, 'I have lost her,' he no longer thought of his loss at all. He heard her words: 'I wonder whether it is right that one should suffer so much pain.' He felt that they would go ringing down the world with him, persistent in his ears, spoken upon the very accent of her voice. He was sure that he would hear them at the end above the voices of any who should stand about him when he died, and hear in them his condemnation. For it was not right.

The ball finished shortly afterwards. The last carriage drove away, and those who were staying in the house sought the smoking-room or went upstairs to bed, according to their sex. Feversham, however, lingered in the hall with Ethne. She understood why.

'There is no need,' she said, standing with her back to him as she lighted a candle. 'I have told my father. I told him everything.'

Feversham bowed his head in acquiescence.

'Still, I must wait and see him,' he said.

Ethne did not object, but she turned and looked at him quickly with her brows drawn in a frown of perplexity. To wait for her father under such circumstances seemed to argue a certain courage. Indeed, she herself felt some apprehension as she heard the door of the study open and Dermod's footsteps on the floor. Dermod walked straight up to Harry Feversham, looking for once in a way what he was, a very old man, and stood there staring into Feversham's face with a muddled and bewildered expression. Twice he opened his mouth to speak, but no words came. In the end he turned to the table and lit his candle and Harry Feversham's. Then he turned back towards Feversham, and rather quickly, so that Ethne took a step forward as if to get between them. But he did nothing more than stare at Feversham again and for a long time. Finally, he took up his candle.

'Well — ' he said, and stopped. He snuffed the wick with the scissors, and began again. 'Well — ' he said, and stopped again. Apparently his candle had not helped him to any suitable expressions. He stared into the flame now instead of into Feversham's face, and for an equal length of time. He could think of nothing whatever to say, and yet he was conscious that something must be said. In the end he said lamely –

'If you want any whisky stamp twice on the floor with your foot. The servants understand.'

Thereupon he walked heavily up the stairs. The old man's forbearance was perhaps not the least part of Harry Feversham's punishment.

It was broad daylight when Ethne was at last alone within her room. She drew up the blinds and opened the windows wide. The cool fresh air of the morning was as a draught of spring water to her. She looked out upon a world as yet unillumined by colours, and found therein an image of her days to come. The dark, tall trees looked black; the winding paths a singular dead white; the very lawns were dull and grey, though the dew lay upon them like a network of frost. It was a noisy world, however, for all its aspect of quiet. For the blackbirds were calling from the branches and the grass, and down beneath the overhanging trees the Lennon flowed in music between its banks. Ethne drew back from the window. She had much to do that morning before she slept. For she designed with her natural thoroughness to make an end at once of all her associations with Harry Feversham. She wished that from the moment when next she waked she might never come across a single thing which could recall him to her memory. And with a sort of stubborn persistence she went about the work.

But she changed her mind. In the very process of collecting together the gifts which he had made to her, she changed her mind. For each gift that she looked upon had its history, and the days before this miserable night had darkened on her happiness came one by one slowly back to her as she looked. She determined to keep one thing which had belonged to

Harry Feversham, a small thing, a thing of no value. At first she chose a penknife, which he had once lent to her and she had forgotten to return. But the next moment she dropped it, and rather hurriedly. For she was, after all, an Irish girl, and though she did not believe in superstitions, where superstitions were concerned she preferred to be on the safe side. She selected his photograph in the end, and locked it away in a drawer.

She gathered the rest of his presents together, packed them carefully in a box, fastened the box, addressed it and carried it down to the hall, that the servants might despatch it in the morning. Then coming back to her room she took his letters, made a little pile of them on the hearth and set them alight. They took some while to consume, but she waited, sitting upright in her armchair while the flame crept from sheet to sheet, discolouring the paper, blackening the writing like a stream of ink, and leaving in the end only flakes of ashes like feathers, and white flakes like white feathers. The last sparks were barely extinguished when she heard a cautious step on the gravel beneath her window.

It was broad daylight, but her candle was still burning on the table at her side, and with a quick instinctive movement she reached out her arm and put the light out. Then she sat very still and rigid, listening. For awhile she heard only the blackbirds calling from the trees in the garden and the throbbing music of the river. Afterwards she heard the footsteps again, cautiously retreating; and in spite of her will, in spite of her formal disposal of the letters and the presents, she was mastered all at once, not by pain or humiliation, but by an overpowering sense of loneliness. She seemed to be seated high on an empty world of ruins. She rose quickly from her chair, and her eyes fell upon a violin-case. With a sigh of relief she opened it, and a little while after one or two of the guests who were sleeping in the house chanced to wake up, and heard floating down the corridors the music of a violin played very lovingly and low. Ethne was not aware that the violin which she held was the Guarnerius violin which Durrance had sent to her. She only understood that she had a companion to share her loneliness.

Chapter Six

HARRY FEVERSHAM'S PLAN

It was the night of August 30th. A month had passed since the ball at Lennon House, but the uneventful country-side of Donegal was still busy with the stimulating topic of Harry Feversham's disappearance. The townsmen in the climbing street and the gentry at their dinner-tables gossiped to their hearts' contentment. It was asserted that Harry Feversham had been seen on the very morning after the dance and at five minutes to six – though according to Mrs Brien O'Brien it was ten minutes past the hour – still in his dress-clothes, and with a white, suicide's face, hurrying along the causeway by the Lennon Bridge. It was suggested that a drag-net would be the only way to solve the mystery. Mr Dennis Rafferty, who lived on the road to Rathmullen, indeed, went so far as to refuse salmon on the plea that he was not a cannibal, and the saying had a general vogue. Their conjectures as to the cause of the disappearance were no nearer to the truth. For there were only two who knew, and those two went steadily about the business of living as though no catastrophe had befallen them. They held their heads a trifle more proudly perhaps. Ethne might have become a little more gentle, Dermod a little more irascible, but these were the only changes. So gossip had the field to itself.

But Harry Feversham was in London, as Lieutenant Sutch discovered, on the night of the 30th. All that day the town had been perturbed by rumours of a great battle fought at Kassassin the desert east of Ismailia. Messengers had raced ceaselessly through the streets, shouting tidings of victory and tidings of disaster. There had been a charge by moonlight of General Drury-Lowe's Cavalry Brigade, which had rolled up Arabi's left flank and captured his guns. It was rumoured that an English general had been killed, that the York and Lancaster

Regiment had been cut up. London was uneasy, and at eleven o'clock at night a great crowd of people had gathered beneath the gas-lamps in Pall Mall, watching with pale upturned faces the lighted blinds of the War Office. The crowd was silent and impressively still. Only if a figure moved for an instant across the blinds a thrill of expectation passed from man to man, and the crowd swayed in a continuous movement from edge to edge. Lieutenant Sutch, careful of his wounded leg, was standing on the outskirts with his back to the parapet of the Junior Carlton Club, when he felt himself touched upon the arm. He saw Harry Feversham at his side. Feversham's face was working and extraordinarily white, his eyes were bright like the eyes of a man in a fever, and Sutch at the first was not sure that he knew or cared who it was to whom he talked.

'I might have been out there in Egypt to-night,' said Harry, in a quick, troubled voice. 'Think of it! I might have been out there, sitting by a camp-fire in the desert, talking over the battle with Jack Durrance; or dead perhaps. What would it have mattered? I might have been in Egypt to-night!'

Feversham's unexpected appearance, no less than his wandering tongue, told Sutch that somehow his fortunes had gone seriously wrong. He had many questions in his mind, but he did not ask a single one of them. He took Feversham's arm and led him straight out of the throng.

'I saw you in the crowd,' continued Feversham. 'I thought that I would speak to you, because – do you remember, a long time ago you gave me your card? I have always kept it because I have always feared that I would have reason to use it. You said that if one was in trouble, the telling might help.'

Sutch stopped his companion.

'We will go in here. We can find a quiet corner in the upper smoking-room;' and Harry looking up, saw that he was standing by the steps of the Army and Navy Club.

'Good God, not there!' he cried in a sharp low voice, and moved quickly into the roadway, where no light fell directly on his face. Sutch limped after him. 'Not to-night. It is late. To-morrow if you will, in some quiet place, and after nightfall. I do not go out in the daylight.'

Again Lieutenant Sutch asked no questions.

'I know a quiet restaurant,' he said. 'If we dine there at nine we shall meet no one whom we know. I will meet you just before nine to-morrow night at the corner of Swallow Street.'

They dined together accordingly on the following evening at a table in the corner of the Criterion grill-room. Feversham looked quickly about him as he entered the room.

'I dine here often when I am in town,' said Sutch. 'Listen!' The throbbing of the engines working the electric light could be distinctly heard, their vibrations could be felt.

'It reminds me of a ship,' said Sutch, with a smile. 'I can almost fancy myself in the gunroom again. We will have dinner. Then you shall tell me your story.'

'You have heard nothing of it?' asked Feversham, suspiciously.

'Not a word;' and Feversham drew a breath of relief. It had seemed to him that everyone must know. He imagined contempt on every face which passed him in the street.

Lieutenant Sutch was even more concerned this evening than he had been the night before. He saw Harry Feversham clearly now in a full light. Harry's face was thin and haggard with lack of sleep, there were black hollows beneath his eyes; he drew his breath and made his movements in a restless, feverish fashion, his nerves seemed strung to breaking point. Once or twice between the courses he began his story, but Sutch would not listen until the cloth was cleared.

'Now,' said he, holding out his cigar-case. 'Take your time, Harry.'

Thereupon Feversham told him the whole truth, without exaggeration or omission, forcing himself to a slow, careful, matter-of-fact speech, so that in the end Sutch almost fell into the illusion that it was just the story of a stranger which Feversham was recounting merely to pass the time. He began with the Crimean night at Broad Place, and ended with the ball at Lennon House.

'I came back across Lough Swilly early that morning,' he said in conclusion, 'and travelled at once to London. Since then I have stayed in my rooms all day, listening to the bugles calling in the barrack-yard beneath my windows. At night I

49

prowl about the streets or lie in bed waiting for the Westminster clock to sound each new quarter of an hour. On foggy nights, too, I can hear steam-sirens on the river. Do you know when the ducks start quacking in St James's Park?' he asked with a laugh. 'At two o'clock to the minute.'

Sutch listened to the story without an interruption. But halfway through the narrative he changed his attitude, and in a significant way. Up to the moment when Harry told of his concealment of the telegram, Sutch had sat with his arms upon the table in front of him, and his eyes upon his companion. Thereafter he raised a hand to his forehead, and so remained with his face screened while the rest was told. Feversham had no doubt of the reason. Lieutenant Sutch wished to conceal the scorn he felt, and could not trust the muscles of his face. Feversham, however, mitigated nothing, but continued steadily and truthfully to the end. But even after the end was reached Sutch did not remove his hand, nor for some little while did he speak. When he did speak, his words came upon Feversham's ears with a shock of surprise. There was no contempt in them, and though his voice shook, it shook with a great contrition.

'I am much to blame,' he said. 'I should have spoken that night at Broad Place, and I held my tongue. I shall hardly forgive myself.' The knowledge that it was Muriel Graham's son who had thus brought ruin and disgrace upon himself was uppermost in the lieutenant's mind. He felt that he had failed in the discharge of an obligation, self-imposed, no doubt, but a very real obligation none the less. 'You see, I understood,' he continued remorsefully. 'Your father, I am afraid, never would.'

'He never will,' interrupted Harry.

'No,' Sutch agreed. 'Your mother, of course, had she lived would have seen clearly, but few women, I think, except your mother. Brute courage? Women make a god of it. That girl for instance — ' and again Harry Feversham interrupted.

'You must not blame her. I was defrauding her into marriage.'

Sutch took his hand suddenly from his forehead.

'Suppose that you had never met her, would you still have sent in your papers?'

'I think not,' said Harry slowly. 'I want to be fair. Disgracing my name and those dead men in the hall I think I would have risked. I could not risk disgracing her.'

And Lieutenant Sutch thumped his fist despairingly upon the table. 'If only I had spoken at Broad Place. Harry, why didn't you let me speak? I might have saved you many unnecessary years of torture. Good heavens! What a childhood you must have spent with that fear all alone with you. It makes me shiver to think of it. I might even have saved you from this last catastrophe. For I understood. I understood.'

Lieutenant Sutch saw more clearly into the dark places of Harry Feversham's mind than Harry Feversham did himself; and because he saw so clearly he could feel no contempt. The long years of childhood, and boyhood, and youth, lived apart in Broad Place in the presence of the uncomprehending father and the relentless dead men on the walls had done the harm. There had been no one in whom the boy could confide. The fear of cowardice had sapped incessantly at his heart. He had walked about with it; he had taken it with him to his bed. It had haunted his dreams. It had been his perpetual menacing companion. It had kept him from intimacy with his friends, lest an impulsive word should betray him. Lieutenant Sutch did not wonder that in the end it had brought about this irretrievable mistake. For Lieutenant Sutch understood.

'Did you ever read "Hamlet"?' he asked.

'Of course,' said Harry, in reply.

'Ah, but did you consider it? The same disability is clear in that character. The thing which he foresaw, which he thought over, which he imagined in the act and in the consequence – that he shrank from, upbraiding himself even as you have done. Yet when the moment of action comes, sharp and immediate, does he fail! No, he excels, and just by reason of that foresight. I have seen men in the Crimea, tortured by their imaginations before the fight – once the fight had begun you must search amongst the Oriental fanatics for their match. "Am I a coward?" Do you remember the lines?

"Am I a coward?
Who calls me villain? Breaks my pate across?
Plucks off my beard, and blows it in my face?"

There's the case in a nutshell. If only I had spoken on that night!'

One or two people passed the table on the way out. Sutch stopped and looked round the room. It was nearly empty. He glanced at his watch and saw that the hour was eleven. Some plan of action must be decided upon that night. It was not enough to hear Harry Feversham's story. There still remained the question, what was Harry Feversham, disgraced and ruined, now to do? How was he to recreate his life? How was the secret of his disgrace to be most easily concealed?

'You cannot stay in London, hiding by day, slinking about by night,' he said with a shiver. 'That's too like — ' and he checked himself. Feversham, however, completed the sentence.

'That's too like Wilmington,' said he, quietly, recalling the story which his father had told so many years ago, and which he had never forgotten even for a single day. 'But Wilmington's end will not be mine. Of that I can assure you. I shall not stay in London.'

He spoke with an air of decision. He had indeed mapped out already the plan of action concerning which Lieutenant Sutch was so disturbed. Sutch, however, was occupied with his own thoughts.

'Who knows of the feathers? How many people?' he asked. 'Give me their names.'

'Trench, Castleton, Willoughby,' began Feversham.

'All three in Egypt. Besides, for the credit of their regiment they are likely to hold their tongues when they return. Who else?'

'Dermod Eustace and – and – Ethne.'

'They will not speak.'

'You, Durrance perhaps, and my father.'

Sutch leaned back in his chair and stared.

'Your father! You wrote to him?'

'No. I went into Surrey and told him.'

Again remorse for that occasion, recognised and not used, seized upon Lieutenant Sutch.

'Why didn't I speak that night?' he said impotently. 'A coward, and you go quietly down to Surrey and confront your father with that story to tell to him! You do not even write!

You stand up and tell it to him face to face. Harry, I reckon myself as good as another when it comes to bravery, but for the life of me I could not have done that.'

'It was not – pleasant,' said Feversham, simply: and this was the only description of the interview between father and son which was vouchsafed to anyone. But Lieutenant Sutch knew the father and knew the son. He could guess at all which that one adjective implied. Harry Feversham told the results of his journey into Surrey.

'My father continues my allowance. I shall need it, every penny of it – otherwise, I should have taken nothing. But I am not to go home again. I did not mean to go home for a long while in any case, if at all.'

He drew his pocket-book from his breast, and took from it the four white feathers. These he laid before him on the table.

'You have kept them?' exclaimed Sutch.

'Indeed, I treasure them,' said Harry, quietly. 'That seems strange to you. To you they are the symbols of my disgrace. To me they are much more. They are my opportunities for retrieving it.' He looked about the room, separated three of the feathers, pushed them forward a little on the table-cloth, and then leaned across towards Sutch.

'What if I could compel Trench, Castleton, and Willoughby to take back from me, each in his turn, the feather he sent? I do not say that it is likely. I do not say even that it is possible. But there is a chance that it may be possible, and I must wait upon that chance. There will be few men leading active lives as these three do who do not at some moment stand in great peril and great need. To be in readiness for that moment is from now my career. All three are in Egypt. I leave for Egypt to-morrow.'

Upon the face of Lieutenant Sutch there came a look of great and unexpected happiness. Here was an issue of which he had never thought, and it was the only issue, as he knew for certain, once he was aware of it. This student of human nature disregarded without a scruple the prudence and the calculation proper to the character which he assumed. The obstacles in Harry Feversham's way, the possibility that at the last moment he might shrink again, the improbability that three such opportunities would occur – these matters he over-looked. His eyes already shone with pride, the three feathers for him were already taken back. The prudence was on Harry Feversham's side.

'There are endless difficulties,' he said. 'Just to cite one. I am a civilian, these three are soldiers, surrounded by soldiers; so much the less opportunity therefore for a civilian.'

'But it is not necessary that the three men should be them-selves in peril,' objected Sutch, 'for you to convince them that the fault is retrieved.'

'Oh no. There may be other ways,' agreed Feversham. 'The plan came suddenly into my mind, indeed at the moment when Ethne bade me take up the feathers and added the fourth. I was on the point of tearing them across when this way out of it sprang clearly up in my mind. But I have thought it over since during these last weeks while I sat listening to the bugles in the barrack yard. And I am sure there is no other way. But it is well worth trying. You see, if the three take back their feathers' – he drew a deep breath, and in a very low voice, with his eyes upon the table so that his face was hidden from Sutch, he added – 'why, then she perhaps might take hers back too.'

'Will she wait, do you think?' asked Sutch; and Harry raised his head quickly.

'Oh no,' he exclaimed, 'I had no thought of that. She has not even a suspicion of what I intend to do. Nor do I wish her to have one until the intention is fulfilled. My thought was different' – and he began to speak with hesitation for the first time in the course of that evening. 'I find it difficult to tell you – Ethne said something to me the day before the feathers came – something rather sacred. I think that I will tell you, because what she said is just what sends me out upon this errand. But for her words, I would very likely never have thought of it. I find in them my motive and a great hope. They may seem strange to you, Mr Sutch. But I ask you to believe that they are very real to me. She said – it was when she knew no more than that my regiment was ordered to Egypt; she was blaming herself because I had resigned my commission, for which there was no need, because – had I fallen, although she would have felt lonely all her life, she would none the less have surely known that she and I would see much of one another – afterwards.'

Feversham had spoken his words with difficulty, not looking at his companion, and he continued with his eyes still averted:

'Do you understand? I have a hope that if – this fault can be repaired' – and he pointed to the feathers – 'we might still, perhaps, see something of one another – afterwards.'

It was a strange proposition, no doubt, to be debated across the soiled table-cloth of a public restaurant, but neither of them felt it strange or even fanciful. They were dealing with the simple serious issues, and they had reached a point where they could not be affected by any incongruity in their surroundings. Lieutenant Sutch did not speak for some while after Harry Feversham had done, and in the end Harry looked up at his companion, prepared for almost a word of ridicule. But he saw Sutch's right hand outstretched towards him.

'When I come back,' said Feversham, and he rose from his chair. He gathered the feathers together and replaced them in his pocket-book.

'I have told you everything,' he said. 'You see, I wait upon chance opportunities; the three may not come in Egypt. They may never come at all, and in that case I shall not come back at all. Or they may come only at the very end, and after many years. Therefore I thought that I would like just one person to know the truth thoroughly in case I do not come back. If you hear definitely that I never can come back, I would be glad if you would tell my father.'

'I understand,' said Sutch.

'But don't tell him everything – I mean not the last part – not what I have just said about Ethne and my chief motive. For I do not think he would understand. Otherwise you will keep silence altogether. Promise!'

Lieutenant Sutch promised, but with an absent face, and Feversham consequently insisted.

'You will breathe no word of this, to man or woman, however hard you may be pressed, except to my father under the circumstances which I have explained,' said Feversham.

Lieutenant Sutch promised a second time and without an

instant's hesitation. It was quite natural that Harry should lay some stress upon the pledge, since any disclosure of his purpose might very well wear the appearance of a foolish boast, and Sutch himself saw no reason why he should refuse it. So he gave the promise and fettered his hands. His thoughts, indeed, were occupied with the limit Harry had set upon the knowledge which was to be imparted to General Feversham. Even if he died with his mission unfulfilled, Sutch was to hide from the father that which was best in the son, at the son's request. And the saddest part of it, to Sutch's thinking, was that the son was right in so requesting. For what he had said was true: the father could not understand. Lieutenant Sutch was brought back to the causes of the whole miserable business: the premature death of the mother, who could have understood; the want of comprehension in the father, who was left; and his own silence on the Crimean night at Broad Place.

'If only I had spoken,' he said sadly. He dropped the end of his cigar into his coffee-cup, and, standing up, reached for his hat. 'Many things are irrevocable, Harry,' he said. 'But one never knows whether they are irrevocable or not until one has found out. It is always worth while finding out.'

The next evening Feversham crossed to Calais. It was a night as wild as that on which Durrance had left England; and, like Durrance, Feversham had a friend to see him off. For the last thing which his eyes beheld as the packet swung away from the pier was the face of Lieutenant Sutch beneath a gas-lamp. The lieutenant maintained his position after the boat had passed into the darkness and until the throb of its paddles could no longer be heard. Then he limped through the rain to his hotel, aware, and regretfully aware, that he was growing old. It was long since he had felt regret on that account, and the feeling was very strange to him. Ever since the Crimea he had been upon the world's half-pay list, as he had once said to General Feversham, and what with that and the recollection of a certain magical season before the Crimea, he had looked forward to old age as an approaching friend. To-night, however, he prayed that he might live just long enough to welcome back Muriel Graham's son with his honour redeemed and his great fault atoned.

Chapter Seven

THE LAST RECONNAISSANCE

'No one,' said Durrance, and he strapped his field-glasses into the leather case at his side.

'No one, sir,' Captain Mather agreed.

'We will move forward.'

The scouts went on ahead, the troops resumed their formation, the two seven-pounder mountain guns closed up behind, and Durrance's detachment of the Camel Corps moved down from the gloomy ridge of Khor Gwob, thirty-five miles south-west of Suakin, into the plateau of Sinkat. It was the last reconnaissance in strength before the evacuation of the Eastern Soudan.

All through that morning the camels had jolted slowly up the gulley of shale between red precipitous rocks, and when the rocks fell back, between red mountain-heaps all crumbled into a desolation of stones. Hardly a patch of grass or the ragged branches of a mimosa had broken the monotony of ruin. And after that arid journey the green bushes of Sinkat in the valley below comforted the eye with the pleasing aspect of a park. The troopers sat their saddles with a greater alertness.

They moved in a diagonal line across the plateau towards the mountains of Erkoweet, a silent company on a plain still more silent. It was eleven o'clock. The sun rose towards the centre of a colourless, cloudless sky, the shadows of the camels shortened upon the sand, and the sand itself glistened white as a beach of the Scilly Islands. There was no draught of air that morning to whisper amongst the rich foliage, and the shadows of the branches lay so distinct and motionless upon the ground that they might themselves have been branches strewn there on some past day by a storm. The only sounds that were audible were the sharp clank of weapons, the soft ceaseless padding of

57

the camels' feet, and at times the whirr of a flight of pigeons disturbed by the approaching cavalcade. Yet there was life on the plateau, though of a noiseless kind. For as the leaders rode along the curves of sand, trim and smooth between the shrubs like carriage drives, they would see from time to time, far ahead of them, a herd of gazelle start up from the ground and race silently, a flash of dappled brown and white, to the enclosing hills. It seemed that here was a country during this last hour created.

'Yet this way the caravans passed southwards to Erkoweet and the Khor Baraka. Here the Suakis built their summer-houses,' said Durrance, answering the thought in his mind.

'And there Tewfik fought, and died with his four hundred men,' said Mather, pointing forwards.

. For three hours the troops marched across the plateau. It was the month of May, and the sun blazed upon them with an intolerable heat. They had long since lost their alertness. They rode rocking drowsily in their saddles and prayed for the evening and the silver shine of stars. For three hours the camels went mincing on with their queer smirking motions of the head, and then quite suddenly a hundred yards ahead Durrance saw a broken wall with window-spaces which let the sky through.

'The fort,' said he.

Three years had passed since Osman Digna had captured and destroyed it, but during these three years its roofless ruins had sustained another siege, and one no less persistent. The quick-growing trees had so closely girt and encroached upon it to the rear and to the right and to the left, that the traveller came upon it unexpectedly, as Childe Roland upon the Dark Tower in the plain. In the front, however, the sand still stretched open to the walls, where three great Gemeiza trees of dark and spreading foliage spaced like sentinels.

In the shadow to the right front of the fort, where the bushes fringed the open sand with the level regularity of a river bank, the soldiers unsaddled their camels and prepared their food. Durrance and Captain Mather walked round the fort, and as they came to the southern corner, Durrance stopped.

'Hallo,' said he.

'Some Arab has camped here,' said Mather, stopping in his turn. The grey ashes of a wood fire lay in a little heap upon a blackened stone.

'And lately,' said Durrance.

Mather walked on, mounted a few rough steps to the crumbled archway of the entrance, and passed into the unroofed corridors and rooms. Durrance turned the ashes over with his boot. The stump of a charred and whitened twig glowed red. Durrance set his foot upon it, and a tiny thread of smoke spurted into the air.

'Very lately,' he said to himself, and he followed Mather into the fort. In the corners of the mud walls, in any fissure, in the very floor, young trees were sprouting. Rearwards a steep glacis and a deep fosse defended the works. Durrance sat himself down upon the parapet of the wall above the glacis, while the pigeons wheeled and circled overhead, thinking of the long months during which Tewfik must daily have strained his eyes from this very spot towards the pass over the hills from Suakin, looking as that other general far to the south had done, for the sunlight flashing on the weapons of the help which did not come. Mather sat by his side and reflected in quite another spirit.

'Already the Guards are steaming out through the coral reefs towards Suez. A week and our turn comes,' he said. 'What a God-forsaken country!'

'I come back to it,' said Durrance.

'Why?'

'I like it. I like the people.'

Mather thought the taste unaccountable, but he knew nevertheless that, however unaccountable in itself, it accounted for his companion's rapid promotion and success. Sympathy had stood Durrance in the stead of much ability. Sympathy had given him patience and the power to understand, so that during these three years of campaign he had left far quicker and far abler men behind him, in his knowledge of the sorely harassed tribes of the eastern Soudan. He liked them; he could enter into their hatred of the old Turkish rule, he could understand their fanaticism, and their pretence of fanaticism under the compulsion of Osman Digna's hordes.

'Yes, I shall come back,' he said, 'and in three months' time. For one thing, we know – every Englishman in Egypt too knows – that this can't be the end. I want to be here when the work's taken in hand again. I hate unfinished things.'

The sun beat relentlessly upon the plateau; the men, stretched in the shade, slept; the afternoon was as noiseless as the morning; Durrance and Mather sat for some while compelled to silence by the silence surrounding them. But Durrance's eyes turned at last from the amphitheatre of hills, they lost their abstraction, they became intently fixed upon the shrubbery beyond the glacis. He was no longer recollecting Tewfik Bey and his heroic defence, or speculating upon the work to be done in the years ahead. Without turning his head, he saw that Mather was gazing in the same direction as himself.

'What are you thinking about?' he asked suddenly of Mather. Mather laughed, and answered thoughtfully –

'I was drawing up the menu of the first dinner I will have when I reach London. I will eat it alone, I think, quite alone, and at Epitaux. It will begin with a watermelon. And you?'

'I was wondering why, now that the pigeons have got used to our presence, they should be wheeling in and out of one particular tree. Don't point to it, please! I mean the tree beyond the ditch, and to the right of two small bushes.'

All about them they could see the pigeons quietly perched upon the branches, spotting the foliage like a purple fruit. Only above the one tree they circled and timorously called.

'We will draw that covert,' said Durrance. 'Take a dozen men and surround it quietly.'

He himself remained on the glacis watching the tree and the thick undergrowth. He saw six soldiers creep round the shrubbery from the left, six more from the right. But before they could meet, and ring the tree in, he saw the branches violently shaken, and an Arab with a roll of yellowish dammar wound about his waist, and armed with a flat-headed spear and a shield of hide, dashed from the shelter and raced out between the soldiers into the open plain. He ran for a few yards only. For Mather gave a sharp order to his men, and the Arab, as though he understood that order, came to a sudden stop before a rifle could be lifted to a shoulder. He walked quietly back to

Mather. He was brought up on to the glacis, where he stood before Durrance without insolence or servility.

He explained in Arabic that he was a man of the Kababish tribe named Abou Fatma, and friendly to the English. He was on his way to Suakin.

'Why did you hide?' asked Durrance.

'It was safer. I knew you for my friends. But, my gentleman, did you know me for yours?'

Then Durrance said quickly, 'You speak English,' and Durrance spoke in English.

The answer came without hesitation.

'I know a few words.'

'Where did you learn them?'

'In Khartum.'

Thereafter he was left alone with Durrance on the glacis, and the two men talked together for the best part of an hour. At the end of that time the Arab was seen to descend the glacis, cross the trench, and proceed towards the hills. Durrance gave the order for the resumption of the march.

The water-tanks were filled, the men replenished their zam-shyehs, knowing that of all thirsts in this world the afternoon thirst is the very worst, saddled their camels, and mounted to the usual groaning and snarling. The detachment moved north-westwards from Sinkat, at an acute angle to its morning's march. It skirted the hills opposite to the pass from which it had descended in the morning. The bushes grew sparse. It came into a black country of stones scantily relieved by yellow tasselled mimosas.

Durrance called Mather to his side.

'That Arab had a strange story to tell me. He was Gordon's servant in Khartum. At the beginning of 1884, eighteen months ago, in fact, Gordon gave him a letter which he was to take to Berber, whence the contents were to be telegraphed to Cairo. But Berber had just fallen when the messenger arrived there. He was seized upon and imprisoned the day after his arrival. But during the one day which he had free he hid the letter in the wall of a house, and so far as he knows it has not been discovered.'

'He would have been questioned if it had been,' said Mather.

'Precisely, and he was not questioned. He escaped from Berber at night, three weeks ago. The story is curious, eh?'

'And the letter still remains in the wall? It is curious. Perhaps the man was telling lies.'

'He had the chain mark on his ankles,' said Durrance.

The cavalcade turned to the left into the hills on the northern side of the plateau, and climbed again over shale.

'A letter from Gordon,' said Durrance in a musing voice, 'scribbled perhaps upon the rooftop of his palace, by the side of his great telescope – a sentence written in haste, and his eye again to the lens, searching over the palm trees for the smoke of the steamers – and it comes down the Nile to be buried in a mud wall in Berber. Yes, it's curious,' and he turned his face to the west and the sinking sun. Even as he looked, the sun dipped behind the hills. The sky above his head darkened rapidly to violet; in the west it flamed a glory of colours rich and iridescent. The colours lost their violence and blended delicately into one rose hue, the rose lingered for a little, and, fading in its turn, left a sky of the purest emerald green transfused with light from beneath the rim of the world.

'If only they had let us go last year westward to the Nile,' he said with a sort of passion. 'Before Khartum had fallen, before Berber had surrendered. But they would not.'

The magic of the sunset was not at all in Durrance's thoughts. The story of the letter had struck upon a chord of reverence within him. He was occupied with the history of that honest, great, impracticable soldier, who, despised by officials and thwarted by intrigues, a man of few ties and much loneliness, had gone unflaggingly about his work, knowing the while that the moment his back was turned the work was in an instant all undone.

Darkness came upon the troops, the camels quickened their pace, the cicadas shrilled from every tuft of grass. The detachment moved down towards the well of Disibil. Durrance lay long awake that night on his camp bedstead spread out beneath the stars. He forgot the letter in the mud wall. Southwards the Southern Cross hung slanting in the sky, above him glittered the curve of the Great Bear. In a week he would sail for England; he lay awake, counting up the years since the packet had cast off from Dover pier, and he found that the tale of them was good. Kassassin, Tel-el-Kebir, the rush down the Red Sea, Tokar, Tamai, Tamanieb – the crowded moments came vividly to his mind. He thrilled even now at the recollection of the Hadendowas leaping and stabbing through the breach of McNeil's zareeba six miles from Suakin; he recalled the obdurate defence of the Berkshires, the steadiness of the Marines, the rallying of the broken troops. The years had been good years, years of plenty, years which had advanced him to the brevet-rank of lieutenant-colonel.

'A week more – only a week,' murmured Mather, drowsily.

'I shall come back,' said Durrance, with a laugh.

'Have you no friends?'

And there was a pause.

'Yes, I have friends. I shall have three months wherein to see them.'

Durrance had written no word to Harry Feversham during these years. Not to write letters was indeed a part of the man. Correspondence was a difficulty to him. He was thinking now that he would surprise his friends by a visit to Donegal, or he might find them perhaps in London. He would ride once again in the Row. But in the end he would come back. For his friend was married, and to Ethne Eustace, and as for himself his life's work lay here in the Soudan. He would certainly come back. And so, turning on his side, he slept dreamlessly while the hosts of the stars trampled across the heavens above his head.

Now, at this moment Abou Fatma of the Kababish tribe was sleeping under a boulder on the Khor Gwob. He rose early and continued along the broad plains to the white city of Suakin. There he repeated the story which he had told to Durrance to one Captain Willoughby, who was acting for the time as deputy-governor. After he had come from the Palace he told his story again, but this time in the native bazaar. He told it in Arabic, and it happened that a Greek seated outside a café close at hand overheard something of what was said. The Greek took Abou Fatma aside, and with a promise of much merissa, wherewith to intoxicate himself, induced him to tell it a fourth time and very slowly.

'Could you find the house again?' asked the Greek.

Abou Fatma had no doubts upon that score. He proceeded to draw diagrams in the dust, not knowing that during his imprisonment the town of Berber had been steadily pulled down by the Mahdists and rebuilt to the north.

'It will be wise to speak of this to no one except me,' said the Greek, jingling some significant dollars, and for a long while the two men talked secretly together. The Greek happened to be Harry Feversham, whom Durrance was proposing to visit in Donegal. Captain Willoughby was Deputy-Governor of Suakin, and after three years of waiting one of Harry Feversham's opportunities had come.

Chapter Eight

LIEUTENANT SUTCH IS TEMPTED TO LIE

Durrance reached London one morning in June, and on that afternoon took the first walk of the exile, into Hyde Park, where he sat beneath the trees marvelling at the grace of his country-women and the delicacy of their apparel, a solitary figure, sun-burnt and stamped already with that indefinable expression of the eyes and face which marks the men set apart in the distant corners of the world. Amongst the people who strolled past him, one, however, smiled, and, as he rose from his chair, Mrs Adair came to his side. She looked him over from head to foot with a quick and almost furtive glance which might have told even Durrance something of the place which he held in her thoughts. She was comparing him with the picture which she had of him, now three years old. She was looking for the small marks of change which those three years might have brought about, and with eyes of apprehension. But Durrance only noticed that she was dressed in black. She understood the question in his mind and answered it.

'My husband died eighteen months ago,' she explained in a

quiet voice. 'He was thrown from his horse during a run with the Pytchley. He was killed at once.'

'I had not heard,' Durrance answered awkwardly. 'I am very sorry.'

Mrs Adair took a chair beside him and did not reply. She was a woman of perplexing silences; and her pale and placid face with its cold correct outline gave no clue to the thoughts with which she occupied them. She sat without stirring. Durrance was embarrassed. He remembered Mr Adair as a good-humoured man, whose one chief quality was his evident affection for his wife, but with what eyes the wife had looked upon him he had never up till now considered. Mr Adair indeed had been at the best a shadowy figure in that small household, and Durrance found it difficult even to draw upon his recollections for any full expression of regret. He gave up the attempt and asked –

'Are Harry Feversham and his wife in town?'

Mrs Adair was slow to reply.

'Not yet,' she said, after a pause, but immediately she corrected herself, and said a little hurriedly, 'I mean – the marriage never took place.'

Durrance was not a man easily startled, and even when he was his surprise was not expressed in exclamations.

'I don't think I understand. Why did it never take place?' he asked.

Mrs Adair looked sharply at him as though inquiring for the reason of his deliberate tones.

'I don't know why,' she said. 'Ethne can keep a secret if she wishes;' and Durrance nodded his assent. 'The marriage was broken off on the night of a dance at Lennon House.'

Durrance turned at once to her.

'Just before I left England three years ago?'

'Yes. Then you knew?'

'No. Only you have explained to me something which occurred on the very night that I left Dover. What has become of Harry?'

Mrs Adair shrugged her shoulders.

'I do not know. I have met no one who does know. I do

not think that I have met anyone who has even seen him since that time. He must have left England.'

Durrance pondered on this mysterious disappearance. It was Harry Feversham then whom he had seen upon the pier as the Channel boat cast off. The man with the troubled and despairing face was after all his friend.

'And Miss Eustace?' he asked after a pause, with a queer timidity. 'She has married since?'

Again Mrs Adair took her time to reply.

'No,' said she.

'Then she is still at Ramelton?'

Mrs Adair shook her head.

'There was a fire at Lennon House a year ago. Did you ever hear of a constable called Bastable?'

'Indeed, I did. He was the means of introducing me to Miss Eustace and her father. I was travelling from Londonderry to Letterkenny. I received a letter from Mr Eustace, whom I did not know, but who knew from my friends at Letterkenny that I was coming past his house. He asked me to stay the night with him. Naturally enough, I declined, with the result that Bastable arrested me on a magistrate's warrant as soon as I landed from the ferry.'

'That is the man,' said Mrs Adair, and she told Durrance the history of the fire. It appeared that Bastable's claim to Dermod's friendship rested upon his skill in preparing a particular brew of toddy, which needed a single oyster simmering in the saucepan to give it its perfection of flavour. About two o'clock of a June morning the spirit-lamp on which the saucepan stewed had been overset; neither of the two confederates in drink had their wits about them at the moment, and the house was half burnt and the rest of it ruined by water before the fire could be got under.

'There were consequences still more distressing than the destruction of the house,' she continued. 'The fire was a beacon warning to Dermod's creditors for one thing, and Dermod, already overpowered with debts, fell in a day upon complete ruin. He was drenched by the water-hoses besides, and took a chill which nearly killed him, from the effects of which he has never recovered. You will find him a broken man. The estates are let, and Ethne is now living with her father in a little mountain village in Donegal.'

Mrs Adair had not looked at Durrance while she spoke. She kept her eyes fixed steadily in front of her, and indeed she spoke without feeling on one side or the other, but rather like a person constraining herself to speech because speech was a necessity. Nor did she turn to look at Durrance when she had done.

'So she has lost everything,' said Durrance.

'She still has a home in Donegal,' returned Mrs. Adair.

'And that means a great deal to her?' said Durrance, slowly. 'Yes, I think you are right.'

'It means,' said Mrs Adair, 'that Ethne with all her ill-luck has reason to be envied by many other women.'

Durrance did not answer that suggestion directly. He watched the carriages drive past, he listened to the chatter and the laughter of the people about him, his eyes were refreshed by the women in their light-coloured frocks; and all the time his slow mind was working towards the lame expression of his philosophy. Mrs Adair turned to him with a slight impatience in the end.

'Of what are you thinking?' she asked.

'That women suffer much more than men when the world goes wrong with them,' he answered, and the answer was rather a question than a definite assertion. 'I know very little, of course. I can only guess. But I think women gather up into themselves what they have been through much more than we do. To them, what is past becomes a real part of them, as much a part of them as a limb; to us it's always something external, at the best the rung of a ladder, at the worst a weight on the heel. Don't you think so too? I phrase the thought badly. But put it this way: Women look backwards, we look ahead, so misfortune hits them harder, eh?'

Mrs Adair answered in her own way. She did not expressly agree. But a certain humility became audible in her voice.

'The mountain village at which Ethne is living,' she said in a low voice, 'is called Glenalla. A track strikes up towards it from the road half-way between Rathmullen and Ramelton.'

She rose as she finished the sentence and held out her hand. 'Shall I see you?'

'You are still in Hill Street?' said Durrance. 'I shall be for a time in London.'

Mrs Adair raised her eyebrows. She looked always by nature for the intricate and concealed motive, so that conduct which sprang from a reason, obvious and simple, was likely to baffle her. She was baffled now by Durrance's resolve to remain in town. Why did he not travel at once to Donegal, she asked herself, since thither his thoughts undoubtedly preceded him. She heard of his continual presence at his Service Club, and could not understand. She did not even have a suspicion of his motive when he himself informed her that he had travelled into Surrey and had spent a day with General Feversham.

It had been an ineffectual day for Durrance. The General kept him steadily to the history of the campaign from which he had just returned. Only once was he able to approach the topic of Harry Feversham's disappearance, and at the mere mention of his son's name the old General's face set like plaster. It became void of expression and inattentive as a mask.

'We will talk of something else, if you please,' said he; and Durrance returned to London, not an inch nearer to Donegal.

Thereafter he sat under the great tree in the inner courtyard of his club, talking to this man and to that, and still unsatisfied with the conversation. All through that June the afternoons and evenings found him at his post. Never a friend of Feversham's passed by the tree but Durrance had a word for him, and the word led always to a question. But the question elicited no answer except a shrug of the shoulders, and a 'Hanged if I know!'

Harry Feversham's place knew him no more; he had dropped even out of the speculations of his friends.

Towards the end of June, however, an old retired naval officer limped into the courtyard, saw Durrance, hesitated, and began with a remarkable alacrity to move away.

Durrance sprang up from his seat.

'Mr Sutch,' said he. 'You have forgotten me?'

'Colonel Durrance, to be sure,' said the embarrassed lieutenant. 'It is some while since we met, but I remember you very well now. I think we met – let me see – where was it? An old man's memory Colonel Durrance, is like a leaky ship. It comes to harbour with its cargo of recollections swamped.'

Neither the lieutenant's present embarrassment nor his previous hesitation escaped Durrance's notice.

'We met at Broad Place,' said he. 'I wish you to give me news of my friend Feversham. Why was his engagement to Miss Eustace broken off? Where is he now?'

The lieutenant's eyes gleamed for a moment with satisfaction. He had always been doubtful whether Durrance was aware of Harry's fall into disgrace. Durrance plainly did not know.

'There is only one person in the world, I believe,' said Sutch, 'who can answer both your questions.'

Durrance was in no way disconcerted.

'Yes. I have waited here a month for you,' he replied.

Lieutenant Sutch pushed his fingers through his beard, and stared down at his companion.

'Well, it is true,' he admitted. 'I can answer your questions, but I will not.'

'Harry Feversham is my friend.'

'General Feversham is his father, yet he knows only half the truth. Miss Eustace was betrothed to him, and she knows no more. I pledged my word to Harry that I would keep silence.'

'It is not curiosity which makes me ask.'

'I am sure that, on the contrary, it is friendship,' said the lieutenant, cordially.

'Not that entirely. There is another aspect of the matter. I will not ask you to answer my questions, but I will put a third one to you. It is one harder for me to ask than for you to answer. Would a friend of Harry Feversham be at all disloyal to that friendship, if' – and Durrance flushed beneath his sunburn – 'if he tried his luck with Miss Eustace?'

The question startled Lieutenant Sutch.

'You?' he exclaimed; and he stood considering Durrance, remembering the rapidity of his promotion, speculating upon his likelihood to take a woman's fancy. Here was an aspect of the case, indeed, to which he had not given a thought, and he was no less troubled than startled. For there had grown up within him a jealousy on behalf of Harry Feversham as strong as a mother's for a favourite second son. He had nursed with a most pleasurable anticipation a hope that, in the end, Harry would come back to all that he once had owned, like a re-throned king. He stared at Durrance and saw the hope stricken. Durrance looked the man of courage which his record proved him to be, and Lieutenant Sutch had his theory of women. 'Brute courage – they make a god of it.'

'Well?' asked Durrance.

Lieutenant Sutch was aware that he must answer. He was sorely tempted to lie. For he knew enough of the man who questioned him to be certain that the lie would have its effect. Durrance would go back to the Soudan, and leave his suit unpressed.

'Well?'

Sutch looked up at the sky and down upon the flags. Harry had foreseen that this complication was likely to occur; he had not wished that Ethne should wait. Sutch imagined him at this very moment, lost somewhere under the burning sun, and compared that picture with the one before his eyes – the successful soldier taking his ease at his club. He felt inclined to break his promise, to tell the whole truth, to answer both the questions which Durrance had first asked. And again the pitiless monosyllable demanded his reply.

'Well?'

'No,' said Sutch, regretfully. 'There would be no disloyalty.'

And on that evening Durrance took the train for Holyhead.

Chapter Nine

AT GLENALLA

The farm-house stood a mile above the village in a wild moorland country. The heather encroached upon its garden, and the bridle-path ended at its door. On three sides an amphitheatre of hills, which changed so instantly to the season that it seemed one could distinguish from day to day a new gradation in their colours, harboured it like a ship. No trees grew upon those hills, the granite cropped out amidst the moss and heather; but they had a friendly sheltering look, and Durrance came almost to believe that they put on their different draperies of emerald green, and purple, and russet brown consciously to delight the eyes of the girl they sheltered. The house faced the long slope of country to the inlet of the Lough. From the windows the eye reached down over the sparse thickets, the few tilled fields, the white-washed cottages, to the tall woods upon the bank, and caught a glimpse of bright water and the gulls poising and dipping above it. Durrance rode up the track upon an afternoon and knew the house at once. For as he approached, the music of a violin floated towards him from the windows like a welcome. His hand was checked upon the reins, and a particular strong hope, about which he had allowed his fancies to play, rose up within him and suspended his breath.

He tied up his horse and entered in at the gate. A formless barrack without, the house within was a place of comfort. The room into which he was shown, with its brasses and its gleaming oak and its wide prospect, was bright as the afternoon itself. Durrance imagined it, too, with the blinds drawn upon a winter's night, and the fire red on the hearth, and the wind skirling about the hills and rapping on the panes.

Ethne greeted him without the least mark of surprise.

'I thought that you would come,' she said, and a smile shone upon her face.

Durrance laughed suddenly as they shook hands, and Ethne wondered why. She followed the direction of his eyes towards the violin which lay upon a table at her side. It was pale in colour, there was a mark, too, close to the bridge, where a morsel of worm-eaten wood had been replaced.

'It is yours,' she said. 'You were in Egypt. I could not well send it back to you there.'

'I have hoped lately, since I knew,' returned Durrance, 'that, nevertheless, you would accept it.'

'You see I have,' said Ethne; and looking straight into his eyes she added, 'I accepted it some while ago. There was a time when I needed to be assured that I had sure friends. And a thing tangible helped. I was very glad to have it.'

Durrance took the instrument from the table, handling it delicately like a sacred vessel.

'You have played upon it? The Melusine overture perhaps,' said he.

'Do you remember that?' she returned with a laugh. 'Yes, I have played upon it, but only recently. For a long time I put my violin away. It talked to me too intimately of many things which I wished to forget;' and these words, like the rest, she spoke without hesitation or any down-dropping of the eyes.

Durrance fetched up his luggage from Rathmullen the next day, and stayed at the farm for a week. But up to the last hour of his visit no further reference was made to Harry Feversham by either Ethne or Durrance, although they were thrown much into each other's company. For Dermod was even more broken than Mrs Adair's description had led Durrance to expect. His speech was all dwindled to monosyllables; his frame was shrunken, and his clothes bagged upon his limbs; his very stature seemed lessened; even the anger was clouded from his eye; he had become a stay-at-home, dozing for the most part of the day by a fire, even in that July weather; his longest walk was to the little grey church which stood naked upon a mound some quarter of a mile away and within view of the windows, and even that walk taxed his strength. He was an old man fallen upon decrepitude, and almost out of recognition, so that his gestures and the rare tones of his voice struck upon Durrance as something painful, like the mimicry of a dead man. His collie dog seemed to age in company, and, to see them side by side, one might have said, in sympathy.

Durrance and Ethne were thus thrown much together. By day in the wet weather or the fine, they tramped the hills, while she, with the colour glowing in her face, and her eyes most jealous and eager, showed him her country and exacted his admiration. In the evenings she would take her violin, and sitting as of old with an averted face, she would bid the strings speak of the heights and depths. Durrance sat watching the sweep of her arm, the absorption of her face, and counting up his chances. He had not brought with him to Glenalla Lieutenant Sutch's anticipations that he would succeed. The shadow of Harry Feversham might well separate them. For another thing, he knew very well that poverty would fall more lightly upon her than upon most women. He had indeed had proofs of that. Though the Lennon House was ruined altogether, and its lands gone from her, Ethne was still amongst her own people. They still looked eagerly for her visits; she was still the princess of that country-side. On the other hand, she took a frank pleasure in his company, and she led him to speak of his three years' service in the East. No detail was too insignificant for her inquiries, and while he spoke her eyes continually sounded him, and the smile upon her lips continually approved. Durrance did not understand what she was after. Possibly no one could have understood unless he was aware of what had passed between Harry Feversham and Ethne. Durrance wore the likeness of a man, and she was anxious to make sure that the spirit of a man informed it. He was a dark lantern to her. There might be a flame burning within, or there might be mere vacancy and darkness. She was pushing back the slide so that she might be sure.

She led him thus to speak of Egypt upon the last day of his visit. They were seated upon the hillside, on the edge of a stream which leaped from ledge to ledge down a miniature gorge of rock, and flowed over deep pools between the ledges very swiftly, a torrent of clear black water.

'I travelled once for four days amongst the mirages,' he said. 'Lagoons, still as a mirror and fringed with misty trees. You could almost walk your camel up to the knees in them, before the lagoon receded and the sand glared at you. And one cannot imagine that glare. Every stone within view dances and shakes like a heliograph; you can see – yes, actually see – the heat flow breast-high across the desert as swift as this stream here, only pellucid. So till the sun sets ahead of you level with your eyes! Imagine the nights which follow – nights of infinite silence, with a cool friendly wind blowing from horizon to horizon – and your bed spread for you under the great dome of stars. Oh!' he cried, drawing a deep breath. 'But that country grows on you. It's like the Southern Cross – four over-rated stars when first you see them, but in a week you begin to look

73

for them, and you miss them when you travel north again.' He raised himself upon his elbow and turned suddenly towards her. 'Do you know – I can speak for myself but I never feel alone in those empty spaces. On the contrary, I always feel very close to the things I care about and to the few people I care about too.'

Her eyes shone very brightly upon him, her lips parted in a smile. He moved nearer to her upon the grass, and sat with his feet gathered under him upon one side, and leaning upon his arm.

'I used to imagine you out there,' he said. 'You would have loved it – from the start before daybreak, in the dark, to the camp-fire at night. You would have been at home. I used to think so as I lay awake wondering how the world went with my friends.'

'And you go back there?' she said.

Durrance did not immediately answer. The roar of the torrent throbbed about them. When he did speak, all the enthusiasm had gone from his voice. He spoke gazing into the stream.

'To Wadi Halfa. For two years. I suppose so.'

Ethne kneeled up on the grass at his side.

'I shall miss you,' she said.

She was kneeling just behind him as he sat on the ground, and again there fell a silence between them.

'Of what are you thinking?' she asked.

'That you need not miss me,' he said, and he was aware that she drew back and sank down upon her heels. 'My appointment at Halfa – I might shorten its term. I might perhaps avoid it altogether. I have still half my furlough.'

She did not answer, nor did she change her attitude. She remained very still, and Durrance was alarmed, and all his hopes sank. For a stillness of attitude he knew to be with her as definite an expression of distress as a cry of pain with another woman. He turned about towards her. Her head was bent, but she raised it as he turned, and though her lips smiled, there was a look of great trouble in her eyes. Durrance was a man like another. His first thought was whether there was some obstacle which would hinder her from compliance, even though she herself were willing.

'There is your father,' he said.

'Yes,' she answered, 'there is my father too. I could not leave him.'

'Nor need you,' said he, quickly. 'That difficulty can be surmounted. To tell the truth, I was not thinking of your father at the moment.'

'Nor was I,' said she.

Durrance turned away and sat for a little while staring down the rocks into a wrinkled pool of water just beneath. It was, after all, the shadow of Feversham which stretched between himself and her.

'I know, of course,' he said, 'that you would never feel trouble, as so many do, with half your heart. You would neither easily care nor lightly forget.'

'I remember enough,' she returned in a low voice, 'to make your words rather a pain to me. Some day perhaps I may bring myself to tell everything which happened at that ball three years ago, and then you will be better again to understand why I am a little distressed. All that I can tell you now is this: I have a great fear that I was to some degree the cause of another man's ruin. I do not mean that I was to blame for it. But if I had not been known to him his career might perhaps never have come to so abrupt an end. I am not sure, but I am afraid. I asked whether it was so, and I was told "no", but I think very likely that generosity dictated that answer. And the fear stays. I am much distressed by it. I lie awake with it at night. And then you come whom I greatly value, and you say quietly, "Will you please spoil my career too?" ' And she struck one hand sharply into the other and cried, 'But that I will not do.'

And again he answered –

'There is no need that you should. Wadi Halfa is not the only place where a soldier can find work to his hand.'

His voice had taken a new hopefulness. For he had listened intently to the words which she had spoken, and he had construed them by the dictionary of his desires. She had not said that friendship bounded all her thoughts of him. Therefore he need not believe it. Women were given to a hinting modesty of speech, at all events the best of them. A man might read a little more emphasis into their tones, and underline their words and still be short of their meaning, as he argued. A subtle delicacy graced them in nature. Durrance was near to Benedick's mood. 'One whom I value;' 'I shall miss you;' there might be a double meaning in the phrases. When she said that she needed to be assured that she had sure friends, did she not mean that she needed their companionship? But the argument, had he been acute enough to see it, proved how deep he was sunk in error. For what this girl spoke, she habitually meant, and she habitually meant no more. Moreover, upon this occasion she had particularly weighed her words.

'No doubt,' she said, '*a* soldier can. But can this soldier find work so suitable? Listen, please, till I have done. I was so very glad to hear all that you have told me about your work and your journeys. I was still more glad because of the satisfaction with which you told it. For it seemed to me, as I listened and as I watched, that you had found the one true straight channel along which your life could run swift and smoothly and un-harassed. And so few do that – so very few!' And she wrung her hands and cried, 'And now you spoil it all.'

Durrance suddenly faced her. He ceased from argument; he cried in a voice of passion –

'I am for you, Ethne! There's the true straight channel, and upon my word I believe you are for me. I thought – I admit it – at one time I would spend my life out there in the East, and the thought contented me. But I had schooled myself into con-tentment, for I believed you married.' Ethne ever so slightly flinched, and he himself recognised that he had spoken in a voice overloud, so that it had something almost of brutality.

'Do I hurt you?' he continued. 'I am sorry. But let me speak the whole truth out, I cannot afford reticence, I want you to know the first and last of it. I say now that I love you. Yes; but I could have said it with equal truth five years ago. It is five years since your father arrested me at the ferry down there on Lough Swilly, because I wished to press on to Letter-kenny, and not delay a night by stopping with a stranger. Five years since I first saw you, first heard the language of your violin. I remember how you sat with your back towards me. The light shone on your hair, I could just see your eyelashes and the colour of your cheeks. I remember the sweep of your arm . . . My dear, you are for me; I am for you.'

But she drew back from his outstretched hands.

'No,' she said very gently, but with a decision he could not mistake. She saw more clearly into his mind than he did himself. The restlessness of the born traveller, the craving for the large and lonely spaces in the outlandish corners of the world, the incurable intermittent fever to be moving, ever moving amongst strange people and under strange skies – these were deep-rooted qualities of the man. Passion might obscure them for awhile, but they would make their appeal in the end, and the appeal would torture. The home would become a prison. Desires would so clash within him, there could be no happiness. That was the man. For herself, she looked down the slope of the hill across the brown country. Away on the right waved the woods about Ramelton, at her feet flashed a strip of the Lough; and this was her country; she was its child and the sister of its people.

'No,' she repeated, as she rose to her feet.

Durrance rose with her. He was still not so much disheartened as conscious of a blunder. He had put his case badly, he should never have given her the opportunity to think that marriage would be an interruption of his career.

'We will say good-bye here,' she said, 'in the open. We shall be none the less good friends because three thousand miles hinder us from shaking hands.'

They shook hands as she spoke.

'I shall be in England again in a year's time,' said Durrance. 'May I come back?'

Ethne's eyes and her smile consented.

'I should be sorry to lose you altogether,' she said, 'although even if I did not see you I should know that I had not lost your friendship.' She added, 'I should also be glad to hear news of you and what you are doing, if ever you have the time to spare.'

'I may write?' he exclaimed eagerly.

'Yes,' she answered, and his eagerness made her linger a little doubtfully upon the word. 'That is, if you think it fair. I mean, it might be best for you, perhaps, to get rid of me entirely from your thoughts,' and Durrance laughed and without any bitterness; so that in a moment Ethne found herself laughing too, though at what she laughed she would have discovered it difficult to explain. 'Very well, write to me then.' And she added drily, 'But it will be about – other things.'

And again Durrance read into her words the interpretation he desired; and again she meant just what she said, and not a word more.

She stood where he left her, a tall, strong-limbed figure of womanhood, until he was gone out of sight. Then she climbed down to the house, and going into her room took one of her violins from its case. But it was the violin which Durrance had given to her, and before she had touched the strings with her bow she recognised it and put it suddenly away from her in its case. She snapped the case to. For a few moments she sat motionless in her chair, then she quickly crossed the room, and, taking her keys, unlocked a drawer. At the bottom of the drawer there lay hidden a photograph, and at this she looked for a long while, and very wistfully.

Durrance meanwhile walked down to the trap which was waiting for him at the gates of the house and saw that Dermod Eustace stood in the road with his hat upon his head.

'I will walk a few yards with you, Colonel Durrance,' said Dermod. 'I have a word for your ear.'

Durrance suited his stride to the old man's faltering steps, and they walked behind the dogcart, and in silence. It was not the mere personal disappointment which weighed upon Durrance's spirit. But he could not see with Ethne's eyes, and as his gaze took in that quiet corner of Donegal, he was filled with a great sadness lest all her life should be passed in this seclusion, her grave dug in the end under the wall of the tiny church, and her memory linger only in a few white cottages scattered over the moorland, and for a very little while. He was recalled by the pressure of Dermod's hand upon his elbow. There was a gleam of inquiry in the old man's faded eyes, but it seemed that speech itself was a difficulty.

'You have news for me?' he asked, after some hesitation. 'News of Harry Feversham? I thought that I would ask you before you went away.'

'None,' said Durrance.

'I am sorry,' replied Dermod, wistfully, 'though I have no reason for sorrow. He struck us a cruel blow, Colonel Durrance. I should have nothing but curses for him in my mouth and my heart. A black-throated coward my reason calls him, and yet I would be very glad to hear how the world goes with him. You were his friend. But you do not know?'

It was actually of Harry Feversham that Dermod Eustace was speaking; and Durrance, as he remarked the old man's wistfulness of voice and face, was seized with a certain remorse that he had allowed Ethne so to thrust his friend out of his thoughts. He speculated upon the mystery of Harry Feversham's disappearance at times as he sat in the evening upon his verandah above the Nile at Wadi Halfa, piecing together the few hints which he had gathered. 'A black-throated coward,' Dermod had called Harry Feversham, and Ethne had said enough to assure him that something graver than any dispute, something which had destroyed all her faith in the man, had put an end to their betrothal. But he could not conjecture at the particular cause, and the only consequence of his perplexed imaginings was the growth of a very real anger within him against the man who had been his friend. So the winter passed, and summer came to the Soudan, and the month of May.

Chapter Ten

THE WELLS OF OBAK

In the month of May Durrance lifted his eyes from Wadi Halfa and began eagerly to look homewards. But in the contrary direction, five hundred miles to the south of his frontier town, on the other side of the great Nubian desert and the Belly of Stones, the events of real importance to him were occurring without his knowledge. On the deserted track between Berber and Suakin the wells of Obak are sunk deep amongst mounds of shifting sand. Eastwards a belt of trees divides the dunes from a hard stony plain built upon with granite hills; westwards the desert stretches for fifty-eight waterless miles to Mahobey and Berber on the Nile, a desert so flat that the merest tuft of grass knee-high seems at the distance of a mile a tree promising shade for a noonday halt, and a pile of stones no bigger than one might see by the side of any roadway in repair achieves the stature of a considerable hill. In this particular May there could be no spot more desolate than the wells of Obak. The sun blazed upon it from six in the morning with an intolerable heat, and all night the wind blew across it piercingly cold, and played with the sand as it would, building pyramids house-high and levelling them, tunnelling valleys, silting up long slopes, so that the face of the country was continually changed. The vultures and the sand-grouse held it undisturbed in a perpetual tenancy. And to make the spot yet more desolate there remained scattered here and there the bleached bones and skeletons of camels to bear evidence that about these wells once the caravans had crossed and halted; and the remnants of a house built of branches bent in hoops showed that once Arabs had herded their goats and made their habitation there. Now the sun rose and set and the hot sky pressed upon an empty round of honey-coloured earth. Silence brooded there like night upon the waters; and the absolute stillness made it a place of mystery and expectation.

Yet in this month of May one man sojourned by the wells, and sojourned secretly. Every morning at sunrise he drove two camels, swift riding mares of the pure Bisharin breed, from the belt of trees, watered them, and sat by the well-mouth for the space of three hours. Then he drove them back again into the shelter of the trees, and fed them delicately with dhoura upon a cloth; and for the rest of the day he appeared no more. For five mornings he thus came from his hiding-place and sat looking towards the sand-dunes and Berber, and no one approached him. But on the sixth, and as he was on the point of returning to his shelter, he saw the figures of a man and a donkey suddenly outlined against the sky upon a crest of the sand. The Arab seated by the well looked first at the donkey, and, remarking its grey colour, half rose to his feet. But as he rose he looked at the man who drove it, and saw that while his jellab was drawn forward over his face to protect it from the sun, his bare legs showed of an ebony blackness against the sand. The donkey driver was a negro. The Arab sat down again and waited with an air of the most complete indifference for the stranger to descend to him. He did not even move or turn when he heard the negro's feet treading the sand close behind him.

'Salam aleikum,' said the negro as he stopped. He carried a long spear and a short one, and a shield of hide. These he laid upon the ground and sat by the Arab's side.

The Arab bowed his head and returned the salutation.

'Aleikum es salam,' said he, and he waited.

'It is Abou Fatma?' asked the negro.

The Arab nodded an assent.

'Two days ago,' the other continued, 'a man of the Bisharin, Moussa Fedil, stopped me in the market-place of Berber, and, seeing that I was hungry, gave me food. And when I had eaten, he charged me to drive this donkey to Abou Fatma at the wells of Obak.'

Abou Fatma looked carelessly at the donkey as though now for the first time he had remarked it.

'Tayeeb,' he said, no less carelessly. 'The donkey is mine,' and he sat inattentive and motionless as though the negro's business were done, and he might go.

The negro, however, held his ground.

'I am to meet Moussa Fedil again on the third morning from now, in the market-place of Berber. Give me a token which I may carry back, so that he may know I have fulfilled the charge, and reward me.'

Abou Fatma took his knife from the small of his back, and picking up a stick from the ground, notched it three at each end.

'This shall be a sign to Moussa Fedil;' and he handed the stick to his companion. The negro tied it securely into a corner of his wrap, loosed his water-skin from the donkey's back, filled it at the well and slung it about his shoulders. Then he picked up his spears and his shield. Abou Fatma watched him labour up the slope of loose sand and disappear again on the further incline of the crest. Then in his turn he rose, and hastily. When Harry Feversham had set out from Obak six days before to traverse the fifty-eight miles of barren desert to the Nile, this grey donkey had carried his water-skins and food.

Abou Fatma drove the donkey down amongst the trees, and fastening it to a stem examined its shoulders. In the left shoulder a tiny incision had been made and the skin neatly stitched up again with fine thread. He cut the stitches, and pressing open the two edges of the wound, forced out a tiny package little bigger than a postage stamp. The package was a goat's bladder, and enclosed within the bladder was a note written in Arabic and folded very small. Abou Fatma had not been Gordon's body servant for nothing; he had been taught during his service to read. He unfolded the note, and this is what was written –

'The houses which were once Berber are destroyed and a new town of wide streets is building. There is no longer any sign by which I may know the ruins of Yusef's house from the ruins of a hundred houses; nor does Yusef any longer sell rock-salt in the bazaar. Yet wait for me another week.'

The Arab of the Bisharin who wrote the letter was Harry Feversham. Wearing the patched jubbeh of the Dervishes over his stained skin, his hair frizzed on the crown of his head and falling upon the nape of his neck in locks matted and gummed into the semblance of seaweed, he went about his search for Yusef through the wide streets of New Berber with its gaping pits. To the south, and separated by a mile or so of desert, lay the old town where Abou Fatma had slept one night and hidden the letters, a warren of ruined houses facing upon narrow alleys and winding streets. The front walls had all been pulled down, the roofs carried away, only the bare inner walls were left standing, so that Feversham when he wandered amongst them vainly at night seemed to have come into long lanes of fives courts, crumbling into decay. And each court was only distinguishable from its neighbour by a degree of ruin. Already the foxes made their burrows beneath the walls.

He had calculated that one night would have been the term of his stay in Berber. He was to have crept through the gate in the dusk of the evening, and before the grey light had quenched the stars his face should be set towards Obak. Now he must go steadily forward amongst the crowds like a man that has business of moment, dreading conversation lest his tongue should betray him, listening ever for the name of Yusef to strike upon his ears. Despair kept him company at times, and fear always. But from the sharp pangs of these emotions a sort of madness was begotten in him, a frenzy of obstinacy, a belief fanatical as the dark religion of those amongst whom he moved, that he could not now fail and the world go on, that there could be no injustice in the whole scheme of the universe great enough to lay this heavy burden upon the one man least fitted to bear it and then callously to destroy him because he tried.

Fear had him in its grip on that morning three days after he had left Abou Fatma at the wells, when coming over a slope he first saw the sand stretched like a lagoon up to the dark brown walls of the town, and the overshadowing foliage of the big date palms rising on the Nile bank beyond. Within those walls were the crowded Dervishes. It was surely the merest madness for a man to imagine that he could escape detection there, even for an hour. Was it right, he began to ask, that a man should even try? The longer he stood the more insistent did this question grow. The low mud walls grew strangely sinister; the welcome green of the waving palms, after so many arid days of sun and sand and stones, became an ironical invitation to death. He began to wonder whether he had not already done enough for honour in venturing so near.

The sun beat upon him; his strength ebbed from him as though his veins were opened. If he were caught, he thought, as surely he would be – oh, very surely! He saw the fanatical faces crowding fiercely about him . . . were not mutilations practised? . . . He looked about him, shivering even in that strong heat, and the great loneliness of the place smote upon him, so that his knees shook. He faced about and commenced to run, leaping in a panic alone and unpursued across the naked desert under the sun, while from his throat feeble cries broke inarticulately.

He ran, however, only for a few yards, and it was the very violence of his flight which stopped him. These four years of anticipation were as nothing then? He had schooled himself in the tongue, he had lived in the bazaars to no end? He was still the craven who had sent in his papers. The quiet confidence with which he had revealed his plan to Lieutenant Sutch over the table in the Criterion Grill Room was the mere vainglory of a man who continually deceived himself. And Ethne? . . .

He dropped upon the ground, and drawing his coat over his head lay, a brown spot indistinguishable from the sand about him, an irregularity in the great waste surface of earth. He shut the prospect from his eyes, and over the thousands of miles of continent and sea he drew Ethne's face towards him. A little while and he was back again in Donegal. The summer night whispered through the open doorway in the hall; in a room near by people danced to music. He saw the three feathers fluttering to the floor; he read the growing trouble in Ethne's face. If he could do this thing, and the still harder thing which now he knew to lie beyond, he might perhaps some day see that face cleared of its trouble. There were significant words too in his ears: 'I should have no doubt that you and I would see much of one another afterwards.' Towards the setting of the sun he rose from the ground, and walking down towards Berber, passed between the gates.

Chapter Eleven

DURRANCE HEARS NEWS OF
FEVERSHAM

A month later Durrance arrived in London and discovered a letter from Ethne awaiting him at his club. It told him simply that she was staying with Mrs Adair, and would be glad if he would find time to call, but there was a black border to the paper and the envelope. Durrance called at Hill Street the next afternoon and found Ethne alone.

'I did not write to Wadi Halfa,' she explained at once, 'for I thought that you would be on your way home before my letter could arrive. My father died towards the end of May.'

'I was afraid when I got your letter that you would have this to tell me,' he replied. 'I am very sorry. You will miss him.'

'More than I can say,' said she, with a quiet depth of feeling. 'He died one morning early – I think I will tell you if you would care to hear,' and she related to him the manner of Dermod's death, of which a chill was the occasion rather than the cause; for he died of a gradual dissolution rather than a definite disease.

It was a curious story which Ethne had to tell, for it seemed that just before his death Dermod recaptured something of his old masterful spirit. 'We knew that he was dying,' said Ethne. 'He knew it too, and at seven o'clock of the afternoon after — ' She hesitated for a moment and resumed – 'after he had spoken for a little while to me, he called his dog by name. The dog sprang at once on to the bed, though his voice had not risen above a whisper, and crouching quite close, pushed its muzzle with a whine under my father's hand. Then he told me to leave him and the dog altogether alone. I was to shut the door upon him. The dog would tell me when to open it again. I obeyed him and waited outside the door until one o'clock. Then a loud sudden howl moaned through the house.' She stopped for a while. This pause was the only sign of distress which she gave, and in a few minutes she went on speaking quite simply without any of the affectations of grief. 'It was trying to wait outside that door while the afternoon faded and the night came. It was night, of course, long before the end. He would have no lamp left in his room. One imagined him just the other side of that thin door-panel, lying very still and silent in the great four-poster bed with his face towards the hills, and the light failing. One imagined the room slipping away into darkness, and the windows continually looming into a greater importance, and the dog by his side and no one else right to the very end. He would have it that way, but it was rather hard for me.'

Durrance said nothing in reply, but gave her in full measure what she most needed, the sympathy of his silence. He imagined those hours in the passage, six hours of twilight and darkness; he could picture her standing close by the door, with her ear perhaps to the panel, and her hand upon her heart to check its loud beating. There was something rather cruel, he thought, in Dermod's resolve to die alone. It was Ethne who broke the silence.

'I said that my father spoke to me just before he told me to leave him. Of whom do you think he spoke?'

She was looking directly at Durrance as she put the question. From neither her eyes nor the level tone of her voice could he gather anything of the answer, but a sudden throb of hope caught away his breath.

'Tell me!' he said in a sort of suspense as he leaned forward in his chair.

'Of Mr Feversham,' she answered, and he drew back again, and rather suddenly. It was evident that this was not the name which he had expected. He took his eyes from hers and stared downwards at the carpet, so that she might not see his face.

'My father was always very fond of him,' she continued gently, 'and I think that I would like to know if you have any knowledge of what he is doing or where he is.'

Durrance did not answer nor did he raise his face. He reflected upon the strange strong hold which Harry Feversham kept upon the affections of those who had once known him well; so that even the man whom he had wronged, and upon whose daughter he had brought much suffering, must remember him with kindliness upon his death-bed. The reflection was not without its bitterness to Durrance at this moment, and this bitterness he was afraid that his face and voice might both betray. But he was compelled to speak, for Ethne insisted.

'You have never come across him, I suppose?' she asked.

Durrance rose from his seat and walked to the window before he answered. He spoke looking out into the street, but though he thus concealed the expression of his face, a thrill of deep anger sounded through his words, in spite of his efforts to subdue his tones.

'No,' he said, 'I never have,' and suddenly his anger had its way with him; it chose as well as informed his words. 'And I never wish to,' he cried. 'He was my friend, I know. But I cannot remember that friendship now. I can only think that if he had been the true man we took him for, you would not have waited alone in that dark passage during those six hours.' He turned again to the centre of the room and asked abruptly:

'You are going back to Glenalla?'

'Yes.'

'You will live there alone?'

'Yes.'

For a little while there was silence between them. Then Durrance walked round to the back of her chair.

'You once said that you would perhaps tell me why your engagement was broken off.'

'But you know,' she said. 'What you said at the window showed that you knew.'

'No, I do not. One or two words your father let drop. He asked me for news of Feversham the last time that I spoke with him. But I know nothing definite. I should like you to tell me.'

Ethne shook her head and leaned forward with her elbows on her knees. 'Not now,' she said, and silence again followed her words. Durrance broke it again.

'I have only one more year at Halfa. It would be wise to leave Egypt then, I think. I do not expect much will be done in the Soudan for some little while. I do not think that I will stay there – in any case. I mean even if you should decide to remain alone at Glenalla.'

Ethne made no pretence to ignore the suggestion of his words. 'We are neither of us children,' she said; 'you have all your life to think of. We should be prudent.'

'Yes,' said Durrance, with a sudden exasperation, 'but the right kind of prudence. The prudence which knows that it's worth while to dare a good deal.'

Ethne did not move. She was leaning forward with her back towards him, so that he could see nothing of her face, and for a long while she remained in this attitude, quite silent and very still. She asked a question at the last, and in a very low and gentle voice.

'Do you want me so very much?' And before he could answer she turned quickly towards him. 'Try not to,' she exclaimed earnestly. 'For this one year try not to. You have much to occupy your thoughts. Try to forget me altogether;' and there was just sufficient regret in her tone, the regret at the prospect of losing a valued friend, to take all the sting from her words, to confirm Durrance in his delusion that but for her fear that she would spoil his career, she would answer him in very different words. Mrs Adair came into the room

87

before he could reply, and thus he carried away with him his delusion.

He dined that evening at his club, and sat afterwards smoking his cigar under the big tree where he had sat so persistently a year before in his vain quest for news of Harry Feversham. It was much the same sort of clear night as that on which he had seen Lieutenant Sutch limp into the courtyard and hesitate at the sight of him. The strip of sky was cloudless and starry overhead; the air had the pleasant languor of a summer night in June; the lights flashing from the windows and doorways gave to the leaves of the trees the fresh green look of spring; and outside in the roadway the carriages rolled with a thunderous hum like the sound of the sea. And on this night, too, there came a man into the courtyard who knew Durrance. But he did not hesitate. He came straight up to Durrance and sat down upon the seat at his side. Durrance dropped the paper at which he was glancing and held out his hand.

'How do you do?' said he. This friend was Captain Mather.

'I was wondering whether I should meet you when I read the evening paper. I knew that it was about the time one might expect to find you in London. You have seen, I suppose?'

'What?' asked Durrance.

'Then you haven't,' replied Mather. He picked up the newspaper which Durrance had dropped and turned over the sheets, searching for the piece of news which he required. 'You remember that last reconnaissance we made from Suakin?'

'Very well.'

'We halted by the Sinkat fort at midday. There was an Arab hiding in the trees at the back of the glacis.'

'Yes.'

'Have you forgotten the yarn he told you?'

'About Gordon's letters and the wall of a house in Berber. No, I have not forgotten.'

'Then here's something which will interest you,' and Captain Mather, having folded the paper to his satisfaction, handed it to Durrance and pointed to a paragraph. It was a short paragraph; it gave no details; it was the merest summary, and Durrance read it through between the puffs of his cigar.

'The fellow must have gone back to Berber, after all,' said

he. 'A risky business. Abou Fatma – that was the man's name.'

The paragraph made no mention of Abou Fatma, or indeed of any man except Captain Willoughby, the Deputy-Governor of Suakin. It merely announced that certain letters which the Mahdi had sent to Gordon summoning him to surrender Khartum, and inviting him to become a convert to the Mahdist religion, together with copies of Gordon's curt replies, had been recovered from a wall in Berber and brought safely to Captain Willoughby at Suakin.

'They were hardly worth risking a life for,' said Mather.

'Perhaps not,' replied Durrance, a little doubtfully. 'But, after all, one is glad they have been recovered. Perhaps the copies are in Gordon's own hand. They are, at all events, of an historic interest.'

'In a way, no doubt,' said Mather. 'But even so, their recovery throws no light upon the history of the siege. It can make no real difference to anyone, not even to the historian.'

'That is true,' Durrance agreed, and there was nothing more untrue. In the same spot where he had sought for news of Feversham news had now come to him – only he did not know. He was in the dark; he could not appreciate that here was news which, however little it might trouble the historian, touched his life at the springs. He dismissed the paragraph from his mind, and sat thinking over the conversation which had passed that afternoon between Ethne and himself, and without discouragement. Ethne had mentioned Harry Feversham, it was true – had asked for news of him. But she might have been – nay, she probably had been – moved to ask because her father's last words had referred to him. She had spoken his name in a perfectly steady voice, he remembered; and, indeed, the mere fact that she had spoken it at all might be taken as a sign that it had no longer any power with her. There was something hopeful to his mind in her very request that he should try during this one year to omit her from his thoughts. For it seemed almost to imply that if he could not, she might at the end of it, perhaps, give to him the answer for which he longed. He allowed a few days to pass, and then called again at Mrs Adair's house. But he found only Mrs Adair. Ethne had left London and returned to Donegal. She had left rather suddenly, Mrs Adair told him, and Mrs Adair had no sure knowledge of the reason of her going.

Durrance, however, had no doubt as to the reason. Ethne was putting into practice the policy which she had commended to his thoughts. He was to try to forget her, and she would help him to success so far as she could by her absence from his sight. And in attributing this reason to her Durrance was right. But one thing Ethne had forgotten. She had not asked him to cease to write to her, and accordingly in the autumn of that year the letters began again to come from the Soudan. She was frankly glad to receive them, but at the same time she was troubled. For in spite of their careful reticence, every now and then a phrase leaped out – it might be merely the repetition of some trivial sentence which she had spoken long ago and long ago forgotten – and she could not but see that in spite of her prayer she lived perpetually in his thoughts. There was a strain of hopefulness too as though he moved in a world painted with new colours and suddenly grown musical. Ethne had never freed herself from the haunting fear that one man's life had been spoilt because of her; she had never faltered from her determination that this should not happen with a second. Only with Durrance's letters before her she could not evade a new and perplexing question. By what means was that possibility to be avoided? There were two ways. By choosing which of them could she fulfil her determination? She was no longer so sure as she had been the year before, that his career was all in all. The question recurred to her again and again. She took it out with her on the hill-side with the letters, and pondered and puzzled over it and got never an inch nearer to a solution. Even her violin failed her in this strait.

Chapter Twelve

DURRANCE SHARPENS HIS WITS

It was a night of May, and outside the mess-room at Wadi Halfa three officers were smoking on a grass knoll above the Nile. The moon was at its full and the strong light had robbed even the planets of their lustre. The smaller stars were not visible at all, and the sky, washed of its dark colour, curved overhead, pearly-hued and luminous. The three officers sat in their lounge chairs and smoked silently, while the bull-frogs croaked from an island in mid-river. At the bottom of the small steep cliff on which they sat, the Nile, so sluggish was its flow, shone like a burnished mirror, and from the opposite bank the desert stretched away to infinite distances, a vast plain with scattered hummocks, a plain white as a hoar frost on the surface of which the stones sparkled like jewels. Behind the three officers of the garrison the roof of the mess-room verandah threw a shadow on the ground; it seemed a solid piece of blackness.

One of the three officers struck a match and held it to the end of his cigar. The flame lit up a troubled and anxious face.

'I hope that no harm has come to him,' he said, as he threw the match away. 'I wish that I could say I believed it.'

The speaker was a man of middle age and the colonel of a Soudanese battalion. He was answered by a man whose hair had gone grey, it is true. But grey hair is frequent in the Soudan, and his unlined face still showed that he was young. He was Lieutenant Calder of the Engineers. Youth, however, in this instance had no optimism wherewith to challenge Colonel Dawson.

'He left Halfa eight weeks ago, eh?' he said gloomily.

'Eight weeks to-day,' replied the Colonel.

It was the third officer, a tall, spare, long-necked major of the Army Service Corps, who alone hazarded a cheerful prophecy.

'It's early days to conclude Durrance has got scuppered,' said he. 'One knows Durrance. Give him a camp-fire in the desert, and a couple of sheiks to sit round it with him, and he'll buck to them for a month and never feel bored at the end. While here there are letters, and there's an office, and there's a desk in the office and everything he loathes and can't do with. You'll see Durrance will turn up right enough, though he won't hurry about it.'

'He is three weeks overdue,' objected the Colonel, 'and he's methodical after a fashion. I am afraid.'

Major Walters pointed out his arm to the white empty desert across the river.

'If he had travelled that way, westwards, I might agree,' he said. 'But Durrance went east through the mountain country towards Berenice and the Red Sea. The tribes he went to visit were quiet even in the worst times when Osman Digna lay before Suakin.'

The Colonel, however, took no comfort from Walters' confidence. He tugged at his moustache and repeated, 'He is three weeks overdue.'

Lieutenant Calder knocked the ashes from his pipe and re-filled it. He leaned forward in his chair as he pressed the tobacco down with his thumb, and he said slowly –

'I wonder. It is just possible that some sort of trap was laid for Durrance. I am not sure. I never mentioned before what I knew, because until lately I did not suspect that it could have anything to do with his delay. But now I begin to wonder. You remember the night before he started?'

'Yes,' said Dawson, and he hitched his chair a little nearer. Calder was the one man in Wadi Halfa who could claim something like intimacy with Durrance. Despite their difference in rank there was no great disparity in age between the two men, and from the first, when Calder had come inexperienced and fresh from England, but with a great ardour to acquire a comprehensive experience, Durrance in his reticent way had been at pains to show the new-comer considerable friendship. Calder therefore might be likely to know.

'I, too, remember that night,' said Walters. 'Durrance dined at the mess, and went away early to prepare for his journey.'

'His preparations were made already,' said Calder. 'He went away early, as you say. But he did not go to his quarters. He walked along the river bank to Tewfikieh.'

Wadi Halfa was the military station, Tewfikieh a little frontier town to the north separated from Halfa by a mile of river-bank. A few Greeks kept stores there, a few bare and dirty cafés faced the street between native cook-shops and tobacconists; a noisy little town where the negro from the Dinka country jostled the fellah from the Delta and the air was torn with many dialects; a thronged little town which yet lacked to European ears one distinctive element of a throng. There was no ring of footsteps. The crowd walked on sand, and for the most part with naked feet, so that if for a rare moment the sharp high cries and the perpetual voices ceased, the figures of men and women flitted by noiseless as ghosts. And even at night, when the streets were most crowded and the uproar loudest, it seemed that underneath the noise and almost appreciable to the ear, there lay a deep and brooding silence, the silence of deserts and the East.

'Durrance went down to Tewfikieh at ten o'clock that night,' said Calder. 'I went to his quarters at eleven. He had not returned. He was starting eastwards at four in the morning, and there was some detail of business on which I wished to speak to him before he went. So I waited for his return. He came in about a quarter of an hour afterwards and told me at once that I must be quick since he was expecting a visitor. He spoke quickly and rather restlessly. He seemed to be labouring under some excitement. He barely listened to what I had to say, and he answered me at random. It was quite evident that he was moved, and rather deeply moved, by some unusual feeling, though at the nature of the feeling I could not guess. For at one moment it seemed certainly to be anger, and the next moment he relaxed into a laugh, as though in spite of himself he was glad. However, he bundled me out, and as I went I heard him telling his servant to go to bed, because, though he expected a visitor, he would admit the visitor himself.'

'Well!' said Dawson, 'and who was the visitor?'

'I do not know,' answered Calder. 'The one thing I do know is that when Durrance's servant went to call him at four o'clock for his journey, he found Durrance still sitting on the verandah outside his quarters, as though he still expected his visitor. The visitor had not come.'

'And Durrance left no message?'

'No. I was up myself before he started. I thought that he was puzzled and worried. I thought, too, that he meant to tell me what was the matter. I still think that he had that in his mind, but that he could not decide. For even after he had taken his seat upon his saddle and his camel had risen from the ground, he turned and looked down towards me. But he thought better of it, or worse, as the case may be. At all events, he did not speak. He struck the camel on the flank with his stick, and rode slowly past the post-office and out into the desert, with his head sunk upon his breast. I wonder whether he rode into a trap. Who could this visitor have been whom he meets in the street of Tewfikieh, and who must come so secretly to Wadi Halfa? What can have been his business with Durrance? Important business, troublesome business – so much is evident. And he did not come to transact it. Was the whole thing a lure to which we have not the clue? Like Colonel Dawson, I am afraid.'

There was a silence after he had finished, which Major Walters was the first to break. He offered no argument – he simply expressed again his unalterable cheerfulness.

'I don't think Durrance has got scuppered,' said he, as he rose from his chair.

'I know what I shall do,' said the Colonel. 'I shall send out a strong search party in the morning.'

And the next morning, as they sat at breakfast on the verandah he at once proceeded to describe the force which he meant to dispatch. Major Walters, too, it seemed, in spite of his hopeful prophecies, had pondered during the night over Calder's story, and he leaned across the table to Calder.

'Did you inquire whom Durrance talked with at Tewfikieh on that night?' he asked.

'I did, and there's a point that puzzles me,' said Calder. He was sitting with his back to the Nile and his face towards the glass doors of the mess-room, and he spoke to Walters, who was directly opposite. 'I could not find that he talked to more than one person, and that one person could not by any likelihood have been the visitor he expected. Durrance stopped in front of a café where some strolling musicians, who had somehow wandered up to Tewfikieh, were playing and singing for their night's lodging. One of them, a Greek, I was told, came outside into the street and took his hat round. Durrance threw a sovereign into the hat, the man turned to thank him, and they talked for a little time together' – and as he came to this point he raised his head. A look of recognition came into his face. He laid his hands upon the table-edge, and leaned forward with his feet drawn back beneath his chair as though he was on the point of springing up. But he did not spring up. His look of recognition became one of bewilderment. He glanced round the table and saw that Colonel Dawson was helping himself to cocoa, while Major Walters' eyes were on his plate. There were other officers of the garrison present, but not one had remarked his movement and its sudden arrest. Calder leaned back, and staring curiously in front of him and over the Major's shoulder, continued his story. 'But I could never hear that Durrance spoke to anyone else. He seemed, except that one knows to the contrary, merely to have strolled through the village and back again to Wadi Halfa.'

'That doesn't help us much,' said the Major.

'And it's all you know?' asked the Colonel.

'No, not quite all,' returned Calder, slowly; 'I know for instance, that the man we are talking about is staring me straight in the face.'

At once everybody at the table turned towards the mess-room.

'Durrance!' cried the Colonel, springing up.

'When did you get back?' said the Major.

Durrance, with the dust of his journey still powdered upon his clothes, and a face burnt to the colour of red brick, was standing in the doorway, and listening with a remarkable intentness to the voices of his fellow-officers. It was perhaps noticeable that Calder, who was Durrance's friend, neither rose from his chair nor offered any greeting. He still sat

95

watching Durrance; he still remained curious and perplexed; but as Durrance descended the three steps into the verandah there came a quick and troubled look of comprehension into his face.

'We expected you three weeks ago,' said Dawson, as he pulled a chair away from an empty place at the table.

'The delay could not be helped,' replied Durrance. He took the chair and drew it up.

'Does my story account for it?' asked Calder.

'Not a bit. It was the Greek musician I expected that night,' he explained with a laugh. 'I was curious to know what stroke of ill-luck had cast him out to play the zither for a night's lodging in a café at Tewfikieh. That was all,' and he added slowly in a softer voice, 'Yes, that was all.'

'Meanwhile you are forgetting your breakfast,' said Dawson, as he rose. 'What will you have?'

Calder leaned ever so slightly forward with his eyes quietly resting on Durrance. Durrance looked round the table, and then called the mess-waiter. 'Moussa, get me something cold,' said he, and the waiter went back into the mess-room. Calder nodded his head with a faint smile, as though he understood that here was a difficulty rather cleverly surmounted.

'There's tea, cocoa, and coffee,' he said. 'Help yourself, Durrance.'

'Thanks,' said Durrance. 'I see, but I will get Moussa to bring me a brandy-and-soda, I think;' and again Calder nodded his head.

Durrance ate his breakfast and drank his brandy-and-soda, and talked the while of his journey. He had travelled further eastwards than he had intended. He had found the Ababdeh Arabs quiet amongst their mountains. If they were not disposed to acknowledge allegiance to Egypt, on the other hand, they paid no tribute to Mahommed Ahmet. The weather had been good, ibex and antelope plentiful. Durrance on the whole had reason to be content with his journey. And Calder sat and watched him, and disbelieved every word that he said. The other officers went about their duties; Calder remained behind, and waited until Durrance should finish. But it seemed that Durrance never would finish. He loitered over his breakfast,

96

and when that was done he pushed his plate away and sat talking. There was no end to his questions as to what had passed at Wadi Halfa during the last eight weeks, no limit to his enthusiasm over the journey from which he had just returned. Finally, however, he stopped with a remarkable abruptness, and said with some suspicion to his companion –

'You are taking life easily this morning.'

'I have not eight weeks' arrears of letters to clear off, as you have, Colonel,' Calder returned with a laugh; and he saw Durrance's face cloud and his forehead contract.

'True,' he said, after a pause. 'I had forgotten my letters.' And he rose from his seat at the table, mounted the steps, and passed into the mess-room.

Calder immediately sprang up, and with his eyes followed Durrance's movements. Durrance went to a nail which was fixed in the wall close to the glass doors and on a level with his head. From that nail he took down the key of his office, crosséd the room, and went out through the further door. That door he left open, and Calder could see him walk down the path between the bushes through the tiny garden in front of the mess, unlatch the gate, and cross the open space of sand towards his office. As soon as Durrance had disappeared Calder sat down again, and, resting his elbows on the table, propped his face between his hands. Calder was troubled. He was a friend of Durrance; he was the one man in Wadi Halfa who possessed something of Durrance's confidence; he knew that there were certain letters in a woman's handwriting waiting for him in his office. He was very deeply troubled. Durrance had aged during these eight weeks. There were furrows about his mouth where only faint lines had been visible when he had started out from Halfa; and it was not merely desert dust which had discoloured his hair. His hilarity, too, had an artificial air. He had sat at the table constraining himself to the semblance of high spirits. Calder lit his pipe, and sat for a long while by the empty table.

Then he took his helmet and crossed the sand to Durrance's office. He lifted the latch noiselessly; as noiselessly he opened the door, and he looked in. Durrance was sitting at his desk with his head bowed upon his arms and all his letters unopened

97

at his side. Calder stepped into the room and closed the door loudly behind him. At once Durrance turned his face to the door.

'Well?' said he.

'I have a paper, Colonel, which requires your signature,' said Calder. 'It's the authority for the alterations in C barracks. You remember?'

'Very well. I will look through it and return it to you, signed, at lunch-time. Will you give it to me, please?'

He held out his hand towards Calder. Calder took his pipe from his mouth, and, standing thus in full view of Durrance, slowly and deliberately placed it into Durrance's outstretched palm. It was not until the hot bowl burnt his hand that Durrance snatched his arm away. The pipe fell and broke upon the floor. Neither of the two men spoke for a few moments, and then Calder put his arm round Durrance's shoulders, and asked in a voice gentle as a woman's –

'How did it happen?'

Durrance buried his face in his hands. The great control which he had exercised till now he was no longer able to sustain. He did not answer, nor did he utter any sound, but he sat shivering from head to foot.

'How did it happen?' Calder asked again, and in a whisper.

Durrance put another question –

'How did you find out?'

'You stood in the mess-room doorway listening to discover whose voice spoke from where. When I raised my head and saw you, though your eyes rested on my face there was no recognition in them. I suspected then. When you came down the steps into the verandah I became almost certain. When you would not help yourself to food, when you reached out your arm over your shoulder so that Moussa had to put the brandy-and-soda safely into your palm, I was sure.'

'I was a fool to try and hide it,' said Durrance. 'Of course I knew all the time that I couldn't for more than a few hours. But even those few hours somehow seemed a gain.'

'How did it happen?'

'There was a high wind,' Durrance explained. 'It took my helmet off. It was eight o'clock in the morning. I did not mean to move my camp that day, and I was standing outside my tent in my shirt-sleeves. So you see that I had not even the collar of a coat to protect the nape of my neck. I was fool enough to run after my helmet; and – you must have seen the same thing happen a hundred times – each time that I stooped to pick it up it skipped away; each time that I ran after it, it stopped and waited for me to catch it up. And before one was aware what one was doing one had run a quarter of a mile. I went down, I was told, like a log just when I had the helmet in my hand. How long ago it happened I don't quite know, for I was ill for a time, and afterwards it was difficult to keep count, since one couldn't tell the difference between day and night.'

Durrance, in a word, had gone blind. He told the rest of his story. He had bidden his followers carry him back to Wadi Halfa, and then influenced by the natural wish to hide his calamity as long as he could, he had enjoined upon them silence. Calder heard the story through to the end, and then rose at once to his feet.

'There's a doctor. He is clever, and, for a Syrian, knows a good deal. I will fetch him here privately, and we will hear what he says. Your blindness may be merely temporary.'

The Syrian doctor, however, pursed up his lips and shook his head. He advised an immediate departure to Cairo. It was a case for a specialist. He himself would hesitate to pronounce an opinion, though, to be sure, there was always hope of a cure.

'Have you ever suffered an injury in the head!' he asked. 'Were you ever thrown from your horse? Were you wounded?'

'No,' said Durrance.

The Syrian did not disguise his conviction that the case was grave; and after he had departed both men were silent for some time. Calder had a feeling that any attempt at consolation would be futile in itself, and might, moreover, in betraying his own fear that the hurt was irreparable, only discourage his companion. He turned to the pile of letters and looked them through.

'There are two letters here, Durrance,' he said gently, 'which you might perhaps care to hear. They are written in a woman's hand, there is an Irish postmark. Shall I open them?'

'No!' exclaimed Durrance, suddenly; and his hand dropped quickly upon Calder's arm. 'By no means.'

Calder, however, did not put down the letters. He was anxious, for private reasons of his own, to learn something more of Ethne Eustace than the outside of her letters could reveal. A few rare references made in unusual moments of confidence by Durrance had only informed Calder of her name, and assured him that his friend would be very glad to change it if he could. He looked at Durrance – a man so trained to vigour and activity that his very sunburn seemed an essential quality rather than an accident of the country in which he lived; a man, too, who came to the wild, uncited places of the world with the joy of one who comes into an inheritance; a man to whom these desolate tracts were home, and the fireside and the hedged fields and made roads merely the other places; and he understood the magnitude of the calamity which had befallen him. Therefore he was most anxious to know more of this girl who wrote to Durrance from Donegal, and to gather from her letters, as from a mirror in which her image was reflected, some speculation as to her character. For if she failed, what had this friend of his any longer left?

'You would like to hear them, I expect,' he insisted. 'You have been away eight weeks.' And he was interrupted by a harsh laugh.

'Do you know what I was thinking when I stopped you?' said Durrance. 'Why, that I would read the letters after you had gone. It takes time to get used to being blind after your eyes have served you pretty well all your life.' And his voice shook ever so little. 'You will have to help me to answer them, Calder. So read them. Please read them.'

Calder tore open the envelopes and read the letters through and was satisfied. They gave a record of the simple doings of her mountain village in Donegal, and in the simplest terms. But the girl's nature shone out in the telling. Her love of the country-side and of the people who dwelt there was manifest. She could see the humour and the tragedy of the small village troubles. There was a warm friendliness for Durrance more-over expressed, not so much in a sentence as in the whole spirit of the letters. It was evident that she was most keenly interested in all that he did, that, in a way, she looked upon his career as a thing in which she had a share, even if it was only a friend's share. And when Calder had ended he looked again at Durrance, but now with a face of relief. It seemed, too, that Durrance was relieved.

'After all, one has something to be thankful for,' he cried. 'Think! Suppose that I had been engaged to her? She would never have allowed me to break it off, once I had gone blind. What an escape!'

'An escape,' exclaimed Calder.

'You don't understand. But I knew a man who went blind, a good fellow, too, before – mind that, before! But a year after! You couldn't have recognised him. He had narrowed down into the most selfish, exacting, egotistical creature it is possible to imagine. I don't wonder, I hardly see how he could help it, I don't blame him. But it wouldn't make life easier for a wife, would it? A helpless husband who can't cross a road without his wife at his elbow is bad enough. But make him a selfish beast into the bargain, full of questions, jealous of her power to go where she will, curious as to every person with whom she speaks – and what then? My God, I am glad that girl refused me. For that I am most grateful.'

'She refused you?' asked Calder, and the relief passed from his face and voice.

'Twice,' said Durrance. 'What an escape! You see, Calder, I shall be more trouble even than the man I told you of. I am not clever. I can't sit in a chair and amuse myself by thinking, not having any intellect to buck about. I have lived out of doors and hard, and that's the only sort of life that suits me. I tell you, Calder, you won't be very anxious for much of my society in a year's time,' and he laughed again and with the same harshness.

'Oh, stop that,' said Calder; 'I will read the rest of your letters to you.'

He read them, however, without much attention to their contents. His mind was occupied with the two letters from Ethne Eustace, and he was wondering whether there was any deeper emotion than mere friendship hidden beneath the words. Girls refused men for all sorts of queer reasons which had no sense in them, and very often they were sick and sorry about it afterwards; and very often they meant to accept the men all the time.

'I must answer the letters from Ireland,' said Durrance, when he had finished. 'The rest can wait.'

Calder held a sheet of paper upon the desk and told Durrance when he was writing on a slant and when he was writing on the blotting-pad; and in this way Durrance wrote to tell Ethne that a sunstroke had deprived him of his sight. Calder took that letter away. But he took it to the hospital and asked for the Syrian doctor. The doctor came out to him, and they walked together under the trees in front of the building.

'Tell me the truth,' said Calder.

The doctor blinked behind his spectacles.

'The optic nerve is, I think, destroyed,' he replied.

'Then there is no hope?'

'None, if my diagnosis is correct.'

Calder turned the letter over and over, as though he could not make up his mind what in the world to do with it.

'Can a sunstroke destroy the optic nerve?' he asked at length.

'A mere sunstroke? No,' replied the doctor. 'But it may be the occasion. For the cause one must look deeper.'

Calder came to a stop, and there was a look of horror in his eyes. 'You mean – one must look to the brain?'

'Yes.'

They walked on for a few paces. A further question was in Calder's mind, but he had some difficulty in speaking it, and when he had spoken he waited for the answer in suspense.

'Then this calamity is not all. There will be more to follow – death or — ' but that other alternative he could not bring himself to utter. Here, however, the doctor was able to reassure him.

'No. That does not follow.'

Calder went back to the mess-room and called for a brandy-and-soda. He was more disturbed by the blow which had fallen upon Durrance that he would have cared to own; and he put the letter upon the table and thought of the message of renunciation which it contained, and he could hardly restrain his fingers from tearing it across. It must be sent, he knew, its destruction would be of no more than a temporary avail. Yet he could hardly bring himself to post it. With the passage of every minute he realised more clearly what blindness meant to Durrance. A man not very clever, as he himself was ever the first to acknowledge, and always the inheritor of the other places – how much more it meant to him than to the ordinary run of men! Would the girl, he wondered, understand as clearly? It was very silent that morning on the verandah at Wadi Halfa; the sunlight blazed upon desert and river; not a breath of wind stirred the foliage of any bush. Calder drank his brandy-and-soda and slowly that question forced itself more and more into the front of his mind. Would the woman over in Ireland understand? He rose from his chair as he heard Colonel Dawson's voice in the mess-room, and taking up his letter walked away to the post-office. Durrance's letter was despatched, but somewhere in the Mediterranean it crossed a letter from Ethne, which Durrance received a fortnight later at Cairo. It was read out to him by Calder, who had obtained leave to come down from Wadi Halfa with his friend. Ethne wrote that she had, during the last months, considered all that he had said when at Glenalla and in London; she had read, too, his letters and understood that in his thoughts of her there had been no change, and that there would be none; she therefore went back upon her old argument that she would by marriage be doing him an injury, and she would marry him upon his return to England.

'That's rough luck, isn't it?' said Durrance, when Calder had read the letter through. 'For here's the one thing I have always wished for, and it comes when I can no longer take it.'

'I think you will find it very difficult to refuse to take it,' said Calder. 'I do not know Miss Eustace, but I can hazard a guess from the letters of hers which I have read to you. I do not think that she is a woman who will say "yes" one day, and then because bad times come to you, say "no" the next, or allow you to say "no" for her either. I have a sort of notion that since she cares for you and you for her, you are doing little less than insulting her if you imagine that she cannot marry you and still be happy.'

Durrance thought over that aspect of the question, and began to wonder. Calder might be right. Marriage with a blind man! It might, perhaps, be possible, if upon both sides there was love, and the letter from Ethne proved – did it not? – that on both sides there *was* love. Besides there were some trivial compensations which might help to make her sacrifice less burdensome. She could still live in her own country and move in her own home. For the Lennon house could be rebuilt and the estates cleared of their debt.

'Besides,' said Calder, 'there is always a possibility of a cure.'

'There is no such possibility,' said Durrance with a decision which quite startled his companion. 'You know that as well as I do,' and he added with a laugh, 'you needn't start so guiltily. I haven't overheard a word of any of your conversation about me.'

'Then what in the world makes you think that there's no chance?'

'The voice of every doctor who has encouraged me to hope. Their words – yes – their words tell me to visit specialists in Europe, and not lose heart, but their voices give the lie to their words. If one cannot see, one can at all events hear.'

Calder looked thoughtfully at his friend. This was not the only occasion on which of late Durrance had surprised his friends by an unusual acuteness. Calder glanced uncomfortably at the letter which he was still holding in his hand.

'When was that letter written?' said Durrance suddenly, and immediately upon the question he asked another. 'What makes you jump?'

Calder laughed and explained hastily. 'Why, I was looking at the letter at the moment when you asked, and your question came so pat that I could hardly believe you did not see what I was doing. It was written on the fifteenth of May.'

'Ah,' said Durrance, 'the day I returned to Wadi Halfa blind.'

Calder sat in his chair without a movement. He gazed anxiously at his companion, it seemed almost as though he was afraid; his attitude was one of suspense.

'That's a queer coincidence,' said Durrance with a careless laugh; and Calder had an intuition that he was listening with the utmost intentness for some movement on his own part perhaps, a relaxation of his attitude perhaps, perhaps a breath of relief. Calder did not move, however; and he drew no breath of relief.

Chapter Thirteen

DURRANCE BEGINS TO SEE

Ethne stood at the drawing-room window of the house in Hill Street. Mrs Adair sat in front of her tea-table. Both women were waiting, and they were both listening for some particular sound to rise up from the street and penetrate into the room. The window stood open that they might hear it the more quickly. It was half-past five in the afternoon. June had come round again with the exhilaration of its sunlight, and London had sparkled into a city of pleasure and green trees. In the houses opposite the windows were gay with flowers, and in the street below the carriages rolled easily towards the Park. A jingle of bells rose upwards suddenly and grew loud. Mrs Adair raised her head quickly.

'That's a cab,' she said.

'Yes.'

Ethne leaned forward and looked down. 'But it's not stopping here;' and the jingle grew fainter and died away.

Mrs Adair looked at the clock.

'Colonel Durrance is late,' she said, and she turned curiously towards Ethne. It seemed to her that Ethne had spoken her 'yes' with much more of suspense than eagerness; her attitude as she leaned forward at the window had been almost one of apprehension; and though Mrs Adair was not quite sure, she fancied that she detected relief when the cab passed by the house and did not stop. 'I wonder why you didn't go to the station and meet Colonel Durrance?' she asked slowly.

The answer came promptly enough.

'He might have thought that I had come because I looked

upon him as rather helpless, and I don't wish him to think that. He has his servant with him.' Ethne looked again out of the window, and once or twice she made a movement as if she was about to speak, and then thought silence the better part. Finally, however, she made up her mind.

'You remember the telegram I showed to you?'

'From Lieutenant Calder, saying that Colonel Durrance had gone blind?'

'Yes. I want you to promise never to mention it. I don't want him to know that I ever received it.'

Mrs Adair was puzzled, and she hated to be puzzled. She had been shown the telegram, but she had not been told that Ethne had written to Durrance, pledging herself to him immediately upon its receipt. Ethne, when she showed the telegram, had merely said, 'I am engaged to him.' Mrs Adair at once believed that the engagement had been of some standing, and she had been allowed to continue in that belief.

'You will promise?' Ethne insisted.

'Certainly, my dear, if you like,' returned Mrs Adair, with an ungracious shrug of the shoulders. 'But there is a reason, I suppose. I don't understand why you exact the promise.'

'Two lives must not be spoilt because of me.'

There was some ground for Mrs Adair's suspicion that Ethne expected the blind man, to whom she was betrothed, with apprehension. It is true that she was a little afraid. Just twelve months had passed since, in this very room, on just such a sunlit afternoon, Ethne had bidden Durrance try to forget her, and each letter which she had since received had shown that, whether he tried or not, he had not forgotten. Even that last one received three weeks ago, the note scrawled in the handwriting of a child, from Wadi Halfa, with the large unsteady words straggling unevenly across the page, and the letters running into one another, wherein he had told his calamity and renounced his suit – even that proved, and perhaps more surely than its hopeful forerunners – that he had not forgotten. As she waited at the window she understood very clearly that it was she herself who must buckle to the hard work of forgetting. Or if that was impossible, she must be careful always that by no word let slip in a forgetful moment she betrayed that she had not forgotten.

'No,' she said, 'Two lives shall not be spoilt because of me,' and she turned towards Mrs Adair.

'Are you quite sure, Ethne,' said Mrs Adair, 'that the two lives will not be more surely spoilt by this way of yours – the way of marriage? Don't you think that you will come to feel Colonel Durrance, in spite of your will, something of a hindrance and a drag? Isn't it possible that he may come to feel that too? I wonder. I very much wonder.'

'No,' said Ethne decisively. 'I shall not feel it, and he must not.'

The two lives, according to Mrs Adair, were not the lives of Durrance and Harry Feversham, but of Durrance and Ethne herself. There she was wrong; but Ethne did not dispute the point, she was indeed rather glad that her friend was wrong; and she allowed her to continue in her wrong belief.

Ethne resumed her watch at the window, foreseeing her life, planning it out so that never might she be caught off her guard. The task would be difficult, no doubt, and it was no wonder that in these minutes while she waited fear grew upon her lest she should fail. But the end was well worth the effort, and she set her eyes upon that. Durrance had lost everything which made life to him worth living the moment he went blind – everything, except one thing. 'What should I do if I were crippled?' he had said to Harry Feversham on the morning when for the last time they had ridden together in the Row. 'A clever man might put up with it. But what should I do if I had to sit in a chair all my days?' Ethne had not heard the words, but she understood the man well enough without them. He was by birth the inheritor of the other places, and he had lost his heritage. The things which delighted him, the long journeys, the faces of strange countries, the camp-fire a mere spark of red light amidst black and empty silence, the hours of sleep in the open under bright stars, the cool night wind of the desert, and the work of government – all these things he had lost. Only one thing remained to him – herself, and only, as she knew very well, herself so long as he could believe she wanted him. And while she was still occupied with her resolve the cab for which she waited stopped unnoticed at the door. It was not until Durrance's servant had actually rung the bell that her attention was again attracted to the street.

'He has come!' she said, with a start.

Durrance, it was true, was not particularly acute; he had never been inquisitive; he took his friends as he found them; he put them under no microscope. It would have been easy at any time, Ethne reflected, to quiet his suspicions, should he have ever come to entertain any. But *now* it would be easier than ever. There was no reason for apprehension. Thus she argued, but in spite of the argument she rather nerved herself to an encounter, then went forward to welcome her betrothed.

Mrs Adair slipped out of the room so that Ethne was alone when Durrance entered at the door. She did not move immediately, she retained her attitude and position, expecting that the change in him would for the first moment shock her. But she was surprised; for the particular changes which she had expected were noticeable only through their absence. His face was worn, no doubt, his hair had gone grey, but there was no air of helplessness or uncertainty, and it was that which for his own sake she most dreaded. He walked forward into the room as though his eyes saw; his memory seemed to tell him exactly where each piece of furniture stood. The most that he did was once or twice to put out a hand where he expected a chair.

Ethne drew silently back into the window rather at a loss with what words to greet him, and immediately he smiled and came straight towards her.

'Ethne,' he said.

'It isn't true then,' she exclaimed. 'You have recovered.' The words were forced from her by the readiness of his movement.

'It is quite true, and I have not recovered,' he answered. 'But you moved at the window and so I knew that you were there.'

'How did you know? I made no noise.'

'No, but the window's open. The noise in the street became suddenly louder, so I knew that someone in front of the window had moved aside. I guessed that it was you.'

Their words were thus not perhaps the most customary

greeting between a couple meeting on the first occasion after they have become engaged, but they served to hinder embarrassment. Ethne shrank from any perfunctory expression of regret, knowing that there was no need for it, and Durrance had no wish to hear it. For there were many things which these two understood each other well enough to take as said. They did no more than shake hands when they had spoken, and Ethne moved back into the room.

'I will give you some tea,' she said, 'then we can talk.'

'Yes, we must have a talk, mustn't we?' Durrance answered seriously. He threw off his serious air, however, and chatted with good humour about the details of his journey home. He even found a subject of amusement in his sense of helplessness during the first days of his blindness; and Ethne's apprehensions rapidly diminished. They had indeed almost vanished from her mind when something in his attitude suddenly brought them back.

'I wrote to you from Wadi Halfa,' he said. 'I don't know whether you could read the letter.'

'Quite well,' said Ethne.

'I got a friend of mine to hold the paper and tell me when I was writing on it or merely on the blotting-pad,' he continued with a laugh. 'Calder – of the Sappers – but you don't know him.'

He shot the name out rather quickly, and it came upon Ethne with a shock that he had set a trap to catch her. The curious stillness of his face seemed to tell her that he was listening with an extreme intentness for some start, perhaps even a checked exclamation which would betray that she knew something of Calder of the Sappers. Did he suspect, she asked herself? Did he know of the telegram? Did he guess that her letter was sent out of pity? She looked into Durrance's face, and it told her nothing except that it was very alert. In the old days, a year ago, the expression of his eyes would have answered her quite certainly, however close he held his tongue.

'I could read the letter without difficulty,' she answered gently. 'It was the letter you would have written. But I had written to you before, and of course your bad news could make no difference. I take back no word of what I wrote.'

Durrance sat with his hands upon his knees, leaning forward a little. Again Ethne was at a loss. She could not tell from his manner or his face whether he accepted or questioned her answer; and again she realised that a year ago while he had his sight she would have been in no doubt.

'Yes, I know you. You would take nothing back,' he said at length. 'But there is my point of view.'

Ethne looked at him with apprehension.

'Yes?' she replied, and she strove to speak with unconcern. 'Will you tell me it?'

Durrance assented, and began in the deliberate voice of a man who has thought out his subject, knows it by heart, and has decided, moreover, the order of words by which it will be most lucidly developed.

'I know what blindness means to all men – a growing, narrowing egotism unless one is perpetually on one's guard. And will one be perpetually on one's guard? Blindness means that to all men,' he repeated emphatically. 'But it must mean more to me, who am deprived of every occupation. If I were a writer I could still dictate. If I were a business man I could conduct my business. But I am a soldier, and not a clever soldier. Jealousy, a continual and irritable curiosity – there is no Paul Pry like your blind man – a querulous claim upon your attention – these are my special dangers.' And Ethne laughed gently in contradiction of his argument.

'Well, perhaps one may hold them off,' he acknowledged, 'but they are to be considered. I have considered them. I am not speaking to you without thought. I have pondered and puzzled over the whole matter night after night since I got your letter, wondering what I should do. You know how gladly, with what gratitude, I would have answered you "Yes, let the marriage go on," if I dared. If I dared! But I think – don't you? – that a great trouble rather clears one's wits. I used to lie awake at Cairo and think; and the unimportant trivial considerations gradually dropped away; and a few straight and simple truths stood out rather vividly. One felt that one had to cling to them and with all one's might, because nothing else was left.'

'Yes, that I do understand,' Ethne replied in a low voice.

She had gone through just such an experience herself. It might have been herself, and not Durrance, who was speaking. She looked up at him, and for the first time began to understand that after all she and he might have much in common. She repeated over to herself with an even firmer determination: 'Two lives shall not be spoilt because of me.'

'Well?' she asked.

'Well, here's one of the very straight and simple truths. Marriage between a man crippled like myself, whose life is done, and a woman like you, active and young, whose life is in its flower, would be quite wrong unless each brought to it much more than friendship. It would be quite wrong if it implied a sacrifice for you.'

'It implies no sacrifice,' she answered firmly.

Durrance nodded. It was evident that the answer contented him, and Ethne felt that it was the intonation to which he listened rather than the words. His very attitude of concentration showed her that. She began to wonder whether it would be so easy after all to quiet his suspicions now that he was blind; she began to realise that it might possibly on that very account be all the more difficult.

'Then do you bring more than friendship?' he asked suddenly. 'You will be very honest, I know. Tell me.'

Ethne was in a quandary. She knew that she must answer, and at once and without ambiguity. In addition, she must answer honestly.

'There is nothing,' she replied, and as firmly as before, 'nothing in the world which I wish for so earnestly as that you and I should marry.'

It was an honest wish, and it was honestly spoken. She knew nothing of the conversation which had passed between Harry Feversham and Lieutenant Sutch in the grill-room of the Criterion Restaurant; she knew nothing of Harry's plans; she had not heard of the Gordon letters recovered from the mud-wall of a ruined house in the city of the Dervishes on the Nile bank. Harry Feversham had, so far as she knew and meant, gone for ever completely out of her life. Therefore her wish was an honest one. But it was not an exact answer to Durrance's question, and she hoped that again he would listen to

111

the intonation rather than to the words. However, he seemed content with it.

'Thank you, Ethne,' he said, and he took her hand and shook it. His face smiled at her. He asked no other questions. There was not a doubt, she thought; his suspicions were quieted; he was quite content. And upon that Mrs Adair came with discretion into the room.

She had the tact to greet Durrance as one who suffered under no disadvantage, and she spoke as though she had seen him only the week before.

'I suppose Ethne has told you of our plan,' she said as she took her tea from her friend's hand.

'No, not yet,' Ethne answered.

'What plan?' asked Durrance.

'It is all arranged,' said Mrs Adair. 'You will want to go home to Guessens in Devonshire. I am your neighbour – a couple of fields separate us, that's all. So Ethne will stay with me during the interval before you are married.'

'That's very kind of you, Mrs Adair,' Durrance exclaimed. 'Because, of course, there will be an interval.'

'A short one, no doubt,' said Mrs Adair.

'Well, it's this way. If there's a chance that I may recover my sight, it would be better that I should seize it at once. Time means a good deal in these cases.'

'Then there is a chance?' cried Ethne.

'I am going to see a specialist here to-morrow,' Durrance answered. 'And, of course, there's the oculist at Wiesbaden. But it may not be necessary to go so far. I expect that I shall be able to stay at Guessens and come up to London when it is necessary. Thank you very much, Mrs Adair. It is a good plan.' And he added slowly, 'From my point of view there could be no better.'

Ethne watched Durrance drive away with his servant to his old rooms in St James's Street, and stood by the window after he had gone, in much the same attitude and absorption as that which had characterised her before he had come. Outside in the street the carriages were now coming back from the Park, and there was just one other change. Ethne's apprehensions had taken a more definite shape.

She believed that suspicion was quieted in Durrance for to-day, at all events. She had not heard his conversation with Calder in Cairo. She did not know that he believed there was no cure which could restore him to sight. She had no remotest notion that the possibility of a remedy might be a mere excuse. But none the less she was uneasy. Durrance had grown more acute. Not only his senses had been sharpened – that, indeed, was to be expected – but trouble and thought had sharpened his mind as well. It had become more penetrating. She felt that she was entering upon an encounter of wits, and she had a fear lest she should be worsted. 'Two lives shall not be spoilt because of me,' she repeated, but it was a prayer now, rather than a resolve. For one thing she recognised quite surely: Durrance saw ever so much more clearly now that he was blind.

Chapter Fourteen

CAPTAIN WILLOUGHBY
REAPPEARS

During the months of July and August Ethne's apprehensions grew, and once at all events they found expression on her lips.

'I am afraid,' she said one morning as she stood in the sunlight at an open window of Mrs Adair's house upon a creek of the Salcombe estuary. In the room behind her Mrs Adair smiled quietly.

'Of what? That some accident happened to Colonel Durrance yesterday in London?'

'No,' Ethne answered slowly, 'not of that. For he is at this moment crossing the lawn towards us.'

Again Mrs Adair smiled, but she did not raise her head from the book which she was reading, so that it might have been some passage in the book which so amused and pleased her.

'I thought so,' she said, but in so low a voice that the

words barely reached Ethne's ears. They did not penetrate to her mind, for as she looked across the stone-flagged terrace and down the broad shallow flight of steps to the lawn, she asked abruptly –

'Do you think he has any hope whatever that he will recover his sight?'

The question had not occurred to Mrs Adair before, and she gave it now no importance in her thoughts.

'Would he travel up to town so often to see his oculist if he had none?' she asked in reply. 'Of course he hopes.'

'I am afraid,' said Ethne, and she turned with a sudden movement towards her friend. 'Haven't you noticed how quick he has grown and is growing. Quick to interpret your silences, to infer what you do not say from what you do, to fill out your sentences, to make your movements the commentary of your words. Laura, haven't you noticed? At times I think the very corners of my mind are revealed to him. He reads me like a child's lesson-book.'

'Yes,' said Mrs Adair, 'you are at a disadvantage. You no longer have your face to screen your thoughts.'

'And his eyes no longer tell me anything at all,' Ethne added.

There was truth in both remarks. So long as Durrance had had Ethne's face with its bright colour and her steady, frank, grey eyes visible before him, he could hardly weigh her intervals of silence and her movements against her spoken words with the detachment which was now possible to him. On the other hand, whereas before she had never been troubled by doubt as to what he meant or wished or intended, now she was often in the dark. Durrance's blindness, in a word, had produced an effect entirely opposite to that in which might have been expected. It had reversed their positions.

Mrs Adair, however, was more interested in Ethne's unusual burst of confidence. There was no doubt of it, she reflected. The girl, once remarkable for a quiet frankness of word and look, was declining into a creature of shifts and agitation.

'There is something then to be concealed from him?' she asked quietly.

'Yes.'

'Something rather important?'

'Something which at all costs I must conceal,' Ethne exclaimed, and was not sure even while she spoke that Durrance had not already found it out. She stepped over the threshold of the window on to the terrace. In front of her the lawn stretched to a hedge; on the far side of that hedge a couple of grass fields lifted and fell in gentle undulations; and beyond the fields she could see amongst a cluster of trees the smoke from the chimneys of Colonel Durrance's house. She stood for a little while hesitating upon the terrace. On the left the lawn ran down to a line of tall beeches and oaks which fringed the creek. But a broad space had been cleared to make a gap upon the bank, so that Ethne could see the sunlight on the water and the wooded slope on the further side, and a sailing-boat some way down the creek tacking slowly against the light wind. Ethne looked about her, as though she was summoning her resources, and even composing her sentences ready for delivery to the man who was walking steadily towards her across the lawn. If there was hesitation upon her part, there was none at all, she noticed, on the part of the blind man. It seemed that Durrance's eyes took in the path which his feet trod, and with the stick which he carried in his hand he switched at the blades of grass like one that carries it from habit rather than for any use. Ethne descended the steps and advanced to meet him. She walked slowly as if to a difficult encounter.

But there was another who only waited an opportunity to engage in it with eagerness. For as Ethne descended the steps Mrs Adair suddenly dropped the book which she had pretended to resume and ran towards the window. Hidden by the drapery of the curtain, she looked out and watched. The smile was still upon her lips, but a fierce light had brightened in her eyes, and her face had the drawn look of hunger.

'Something which at all costs she must conceal,' she said to herself, and she said it in a voice of exultation. There was contempt too in her tone, contempt for Ethne Eustace, the woman of the open air, who was afraid, who shrank from marriage with a blind man, and dreaded the restraint upon her freedom. It was that shrinking which Ethne had to conceal – Mrs Adair had no doubt of it. 'For my part I am glad,' she said, and she was – fiercely glad that blindness had disabled Durrance. For if her opportunity ever came, as it seemed to her now more and more likely to come, blindness reserved him to her, as no man was ever reserved to any woman. So jealous was she of his every word and look that his dependence upon her would be the extreme of pleasure. She watched Ethne and Durrance meet on the lawn at the foot of the terrace steps. She saw them turn and walk side by side across the grass towards the creek. She noticed that Ethne seemed to plead, and in her heart she longed to overhear.

And Ethne was pleading.

'You saw your oculist yesterday?' she said quickly, as soon as they met. 'Well, what did he say?'

Durrance shrugged his shoulders.

'That one must wait. Only time can show whether a cure is possible or not,' he answered, and Ethne bent forward a little and scrutinised his face as though she doubted that he spoke the truth.

'But must you and I wait?' she asked.

'Surely,' he returned. 'It would be wiser on all counts.' And thereupon he asked her suddenly a question of which she did not see the drift. 'It was Mrs Adair, I imagine, who proposed this plan that I should come home to Guessens and that you should stay with her here across the fields?'

Ethne was puzzled by the question, but she answered it directly and truthfully. 'I was in great distress when I heard of your accident. I was so distressed that at the first I could not think what to do. I came to London and told Laura, since she is my friend, and this was her plan. Of course I welcomed it with all my heart;' and the note of pleading rang in her voice. She was asking Durrance to confirm her words, and he understood that. He turned towards her with a smile.

'I know that very well, Ethne,' he said gently.

Ethne drew a breath of relief, and the anxiety passed for a while from her face.

'It was kind of Mrs Adair,' he resumed; 'but it is rather hard on you, who would like to be back in your own country. I remember very well a sentence which Harry Feversham — ' He spoke the name quite carelessly, but paused just for a moment after he had spoken it. No expression upon his face

showed that he had any intention in so pausing, but Ethne
suspected one. He was listening, she suspected, for some movement of uneasiness, perhaps of pain, into which she might
possibly be betrayed. But she made no movement. 'A sentence
which Harry Feversham spoke a long while since,' he continued, 'in London just before I left London for Egypt. He
was speaking of you, and he said, "She is of her country and
more of her county. I do not think she could be happy in any
place which was not within reach of Donegal." And when I
remember that it seems rather selfish that I should claim to
keep you here at so much cost to you.'

'I was not thinking of that,' Ethne exclaimed, 'when I asked
why we must wait. That makes me out most selfish. I was
merely wondering why you preferred to wait, why you insist
upon it. For of course, although one hopes and prays with all
one's soul that you will get your sight back, the fact of a cure
can make no difference.'

She spoke slowly, and her voice again had a ring of pleading.
This time Durrance did not confirm her words, and she repeated them with a greater emphasis.

'It can make no difference.'

Durrance started like a man roused from an abstraction.

'I beg your pardon, Ethne,' he said. 'I was thinking at the
moment of Harry Feversham. There is something which I
want you to tell me. You said a long time ago at Glenalla that
you might one day bring yourself to tell it me, and I should
rather like to know now. You see Harry Feversham was my
friend. I want you to tell me what happened that night at
Lennon House to break off your engagement, to send him
away an outcast.'

Ethne was silent for a while, and then she said gently, 'I
would rather not. It is all over and done with. I don't want you
to ask me ever.'

Durrance did not press for an answer in the slightest degree.

'Very well,' he said cheerily, 'I won't ask you. It might hurt
you to answer, and I don't want, of course, to cause you
pain.'

'It's not on that account that I wish to say nothing,' Ethne
explained earnestly. She paused and chose her words. 'It isn't

117

that I am afraid of any pain. But what took place, took place such a long while ago – I look upon Mr Feversham as a man whom one has known well and who is now dead.'

They were walking towards the wide gap in the line of trees upon the bank of the creek, and as Ethne spoke she raised her eyes from the ground. She saw that the little boat which she had noticed tacking up the creek while she hesitated upon the terrace had run its nose into the shore. The sail had been lowered, the little pole mast stuck up above the grass bank of the garden, and upon the bank itself a man was standing and staring vaguely towards the house as though not very sure of his ground.

'A stranger has landed from the creek,' she said. 'He looks as if he has lost his way. I will go on and put him right.'

She ran forward as she spoke, seizing upon that stranger's presence as a means of relief, even if the relief was only to last for a minute. Such relief might be felt, she imagined, by a witness in a court when the judge rises for his half-hour at luncheon time. For the close of an interview with Durrance left her continually with the sense that she had just stepped down from a witness-box where she had been subjected to a cross-examination so deft that she could not quite clearly perceive its tendency, although from the beginning she suspected it.

The stranger at the same time advanced to her. He was a man of the middle size with a short snub nose, a pair of vacuous protruding eyes, and a moustache of some ferocity. He lifted his hat from his head and disclosed a round forehead which was going bald.

'I have sailed down from Kingsbridge,' he said, 'but I have never been in this part of the world before. Can you tell me if this house is called The Pool?'

'Yes, you will find Mrs Adair if you go up the steps on to the terrace,' said Ethne.

'I came to see Miss Eustace.'

Ethne turned back to him with surprise.

'I am Miss Eustace.'

The stranger contemplated her in silence.

'So I thought.'

He twirled first one moustache and then the other before he spoke again.

'I have had some trouble to find you, Miss Eustace. I went all the way to Glenalla – for nothing. Rather hard on a man whose leave is short!'

'I am very sorry,' said Ethne, with a smile; 'but why have you been put to this trouble?'

Again the stranger curled a moustache. Again his eyes dwelt vacantly upon her before he spoke.

'You have forgotten my name, no doubt, by this time.'

'I do not think that I have ever heard it,' she answered.

'Oh yes, you have, believe me. You heard it five years ago. I am Captain Willoughby.'

Ethne drew sharply back; the bright colour paled in her cheeks; her lips set in a firm line, and her eyes grew very hard. She glowered at him silently.

Captain Willoughby was not in the least degree discomposed. He took his time to speak, and when he did it was rather with the air of a man forgiving a breach of manners than of one making his excuses.

'I can quite understand that you do not welcome me, Miss Eustace, but none of us could foresee that you would be present when the three white feathers came into Feversham's hands.'

Ethne swept the explanation aside.

'How do you know that I was present?' she asked.

'Feversham told me.'

'You have seen him?'

The cry leaped loudly from her lips. It was just a throb of the heart made vocal. It startled Ethne as much as it surprised Captain Willoughby. She had schooled herself to omit Harry Feversham from her thoughts, and to obliterate him from her affections, and the cry showed to her how incompletely she had succeeded. Only a few minutes since she had spoken of him as one whom she looked upon as dead, and she had believed that she spoke the truth.

'You have actually seen him,' she repeated in a wondering voice. She gazed at her stolid companion with envy. 'You have spoken to him? And he to you? When?'

119

'A year ago, at Suakin. Else why should I be here?'

The question came as a shock to Ethne. She did not guess the correct answer; she was not, indeed, sufficiently mistress of herself to speculate upon any answer, but she dreaded it, whatever it might be.

'Yes,' she said slowly, and almost reluctantly. 'After all, why are you here?'

Willoughby took a letter-case from his breast, opened it with deliberation, and shook out from one of its pockets into the palm of his hand, a tiny, soiled white feather. He held it out to Ethne.

'I have come to give you this.'

Ethne did not take it. In fact, she positively shrank from it.

'Why?' she asked unsteadily.

'Three white feathers, three separate accusations of cowardice, were sent to Feversham by three separate men. This is actually one of those feathers which were forwarded from his lodgings to Ramelton five years ago. I am one of the three men who sent them. I have come to tell you that I withdraw my accusation. I take my feather back.'

'And you bring it to me?'

'He asked me to.'

Ethne took the feather in her palm, a thing in itself so light and fragile, and yet so momentous as a symbol, and the trees and the garden began to whirl suddenly about her. She was aware that Captain Willoughby was speaking, but his voice had grown extraordinarily distant and thin; so that she was annoyed, since she wished very much to hear all that he had to say. She felt very cold, even upon that August day of sunlight. But the presence of Captain Willoughby, one of the three men whom she never would forgive, helped her to command herself. She would give no exhibition of weakness before any one of the detested three, and with an effort she recovered herself when she was on the very point of swooning.

'Come,' she said, 'I will hear your story. Your news was rather a shock to me. Even now I do not quite understand.'

She led the way from that open space to a little plot of grass above the creek. On three sides thick hedges enclosed it, at the back rose the tall elms and poplars, in front the water flashed and broke in ripples, and beyond the water the trees rose again and were overtopped by sloping meadows. A gap in the hedge made an entrance into this enclosure, and a garden seat stood in the centre of the grass.

'Now,' said Ethne, and she motioned to Captain Willoughby to take a seat at her side. 'You will take your time perhaps. You will forget nothing. Even his words if you remember them! I shall thank you for his words. She held the white feather clenched in her hand. Somehow Harry Feversham had redeemed his honour, somehow she had been unjust to him; and she was to learn how. She was in no hurry. She did not even feel one pang of remorse that she had been unjust. Remorse, no doubt, would come afterwards. At present the mere knowledge that she had been unjust was too great a happiness to admit of abatement. She opened her hand and looked at the feather. And as she looked, memories sternly repressed for so long, regrets which she had thought stifled quite out of life, longings which had grown strange, filled all her thoughts. The Devonshire meadows were about her, the salt of the sea was in the air, but she was back again in the midst of that one season at Dublin during a spring five years ago, before the feathers came to Ramelton.

Willoughby began to tell his story, and almost at once even the memory of that season vanished.

Ethne was in the most English of counties, the county of Plymouth and Dartmouth and Brixham and the Start, where the red cliffs of its coastline speak perpetually of dead centuries, so that one cannot put into any harbour without some thought of the Spanish Main and of the little barques and pinnaces which adventured manfully out on their long voyages with the tide. Up this very creek the clink of the shipbuilders' hammers had rung, and the soil upon its banks was vigorous with the memories of British sailors. But Ethne had no thought for these associations. The country-side was a shifting mist before her eyes, which now and then let through a glimpse of that strange wide country in the East, of which Durrance had so often told her. The only trees which she saw were the stunted mimosas of the desert; the only sea the great stretches of yellow sand; the only cliffs the sharp-peaked pyramidal black rocks rising abruptly from its surface. It was part of the irony of her position that she was able so much more completely to appreciate the trials which one lover of hers had undergone through the confidences which had been made to her by the other.

Chapter Fifteen

THE STORY OF THE
FIRST FEATHER

'I will not interrupt you,' said Ethne, as Willoughby took his seat beside her, and he had barely spoken a score of words before she broke that promise.

'I am Deputy-Governor of Suakin,' he began. 'My Chief was on leave in May. You are fortunate enough not to know Suakin, Miss Eustace, particularly in May. No white woman can live in that town. It has a sodden intolerable heat peculiar to itself. The air is heavy with brine, you can't sleep at night for its oppression. Well, I was sitting in the verandah on the first floor of the palace about ten o'clock at night, looking out over the harbour and the distillation works, and wondering whether it was worth while to go to bed at all, when a servant told me that a man, who refused to give his name, wished particularly to see me. The man was Feversham. There was only a lamp burning in the verandah, and the night was dark, so that I did not recognise him until he was close to me.'

And at once Ethne interrupted.

'How did he look?'

Willoughby wrinkled his forehead and opened his eyes wide.

'Really I do not know,' he said doubtfully. 'Much like other men, I suppose, who have been a year or two in the Soudan, a trifle overtrained and that sort of thing.'

'Never mind,' said Ethne, with a sigh of disappointment. For five years she had heard no word of Harry Feversham. She fairly hungered for news of him, for the sound of his habitual phrases, for the description of his familiar gestures. She had the woman's anxiety for his bodily health, she wished to know whether he had changed in face or figure, and, if so, how and in what measure. But she glanced at the obtuse, unobservant countenance of Captain Willoughby, and she understood that however much she craved for these particulars, she must go without.

'I beg your pardon,' she said. 'Will you go on?'

'I asked him what he wanted,' Willoughby resumed, 'and why he had not sent in his name. "You would not have seen me if I had," he replied, and he drew a packet of letters out of his pocket. Now, those letters, Miss Eustace, had been written a long while ago by General Gordon in Khartum. They had been carried down the Nile as far as Berber. But the day after they reached Berber, that town surrendered to the Mahdists. Abou Fatma, the messenger who carried them, hid them in the wall of the house of an Arab called Yusef, who sold rock-salt in the market-place. Abou was then thrown into prison on suspicion, and escaped to Suakin. The letters remained hidden in that wall until Feversham recovered them. I looked over them and saw that they were of no value, and I asked Feversham bluntly why he, who had not dared to accompany his regiment on active service, had risked death and torture to get them back.'

Standing upon that verandah, with the quiet pool of water in front of him, Feversham had told his story quietly and without exaggeration. He had related how he had fallen in with Abou Fatma at Suakin, how he had planned the recovery of the letters, how the two men had travelled together as far as Obak, and since Abou Fatma dared not go further, how he himself, driving his grey donkey, had gone on alone to Berber. He had not even concealed that access of panic which had loosened his joints when first he saw the low brown walls of the town and the towering date palms behind on the bank of the Nile; which had sent him running and leaping across the empty desert in the sunlight, a marrowless thing of fear. He made, however, one omission. He said nothing of the hours which he had spent crouching upon the hot sand, with his coat drawn over his head, while he drew a woman's face towards him

123

across the continents and seas and nerved himself to endure by the look of sorrow which it wore.

'He went down into Berber at the setting of the sun,' said Captain Willoughby, and it was all that he had to say. It was enough, however, for Ethne Eustace. She drew a deep breath of relief, her face softened, there came a light into her grey eyes, and a smile upon her lips.

'He went down into Berber,' she repeated softly.

'And found that the old town had been destroyed by the orders of the Emir, and that a new one was building upon its southern confines,' continued Willoughby. 'All the landmarks, by which Feversham was to know the house in which the letters were hidden, had gone. The roofs had been torn off, the houses dismantled, the front walls carried away. Narrow alleys of crumbling fives-courts – that was how Feversham described the place – crossing this way and that and gaping to the stars. Here and there perhaps a broken tower rose up, the remnant of a rich man's house. But of any sign which could tell a man where the hut of Yusef, who had once sold rock-salt in the market-place, had stood, there was no hope in those acres of crumbling mud. The foxes had already made their burrows there.'

The smile faded from Ethne's face, but she looked again at the white feather lying in her palm, and she laughed with a great contentment. It was yellow with the desert dust. It was a proof that in this story there was to be no word of failure.

'Go on,' she said.

Willoughby related the despatch of the negro with the donkey to Abou Fatma at the wells of Obak.

'Feversham stayed for a fortnight in Berber,' Willoughby continued. 'A week during which he came every morning to the well and waited for the return of his negro from Obak, and a week during which that negro searched for Yusef, who had once sold rock-salt in the market-place. I doubt, Miss Eustace, if you can realise, however hard you try, what that fortnight must have meant to Feversham – the anxiety, the danger, the continued expectation that a voice would bid him halt and a hand fall upon his shoulder, the urgent knowledge that if the hand fell, death would be the least part of his penalty. I imagine the town – a town of low houses and broad streets of sand, dug here and there into pits for mud wherewith to build the houses, and overhead the blistering sun and a hot shadow-less sky. In no corner was there any darkness or concealment. And all day a crowd jostled and shouted up and down these streets – for that is the Mahdist policy to crowd the towns so that all may be watched and every other man may be his neighbour's spy. Feversham dared not seek the shelter of a roof at night, for he dared not trust his tongue. He could buy his food each day at the booths, but he was afraid of any conversation. He slept at night in some corner of the old deserted town, in the acres of the ruined fives-courts. For the same reason he must not slink in the byways by day lest any should question him about his business; nor listen on the chance of hearing Yusef's name in the public places lest other loiterers should joke with him and draw him into their talk. Nor dare he in the daylight prowl about those crumbled ruins. From sunrise to sunset he must go quickly up and down the streets of the town like a man bent upon urgent business which permits no delay. And that continued for a fortnight, Miss Eustace! A weary, trying life, don't you think? I wish I could tell you of it as vividly as he told me that night upon the balcony of the Palace at Suakin.'

Ethne wished it too with all her heart. Harry Feversham had made his story very real that night to Captain Willoughby; so that even after the lapse of fifteen months this unimaginative creature was sensible of a contrast and a deficiency in his manner of narration.

'In front of us was the quiet harbour and the Red Sea, above us the African stars. Feversham spoke in the quietest manner possible, but with a peculiar deliberation and with his eyes fixed upon my face, as though he was forcing me to feel with him and to understand. Even when he lighted his cigar he did not avert his eyes. For by this time I had given him a cigar and offered him a chair, I had really, I assure you, Miss Eustace. It was the first time in four years that he had sat with one of his equals, or indeed with any of his countrymen on a footing of equality. He told me so. I wish I could remember all that he told me.' Willoughby stopped and cudgelled his brains help-lessly. He gave up the effort in the end.

'Well,' he resumed, 'after Feversham had skulked for a fortnight in Berber, the negro discovered Yusef, no longer selling salt, but tending a small plantation of dhurra on the river's edge. From Yusef, Feversham obtained particulars enough to guide him to the house where the letters were concealed in the inner wall. But Yusef was no longer to be trusted. Possibly Feversham's accent betrayed him. The more likely conjecture is that Yusef took Feversham for a spy, and thought it wise to be beforehand and to confess to Mohammed-el-Kheir, the Emir, his own share in the concealment of the letters. That, however, is a mere conjecture. The important fact is this. On the same night Feversham went alone to old Berber.'

'Alone!' said Ethne. 'Yes?'

'He found the house fronting a narrow alley, and the sixth of the row. The front wall was destroyed, but the two side walls and the back wall still stood. Three feet from the floor and two feet from the right-hand corner the letters were hidden in that inner wall. Feversham dug into the mud bricks with his knife; he made a hole wherein he could slip his hand. The wall was thick, he dug deep, stopping now and again to feel for the packet. At last his fingers clasped and drew it out; as he hid it in a fold of his jibbeh, the light of a lantern shone upon him from behind.'

Ethne started as though she had been trapped herself. Those acres of roofless fives-courts, with here and there a tower showing up against the sky, the lonely alleys, the dead silence here beneath the stars, the cries and the beatings of drums and the glare of lights from the new town, Harry Feversham alone with the letters, with, in a word, some portion of his honour redeemed, and finally, the lantern light flashing upon him in the solitary place – the scene itself and the progress of the incidents were so visible to Ethne at that moment, that even with the feather in her open palm she could hardly bring herself to believe that Harry Feversham had escaped.

'Well, well?' she asked.

'He was standing with his face to the wall, the light came from the alley behind him. He did not turn, but out of the corner of his eye he could see a fold of a white robe hanging motionless. He carefully secured the package, with a care indeed and a composure which astonished him even at that moment. The shock had strung him to a concentration and lucidity of thought unknown to him till then. His fingers were trembling, he remarked, as he tied the knots, but it was with excitement, and an excitement which did not flurry. His mind worked rapidly but quite coolly, quite deliberately. He came to a perfectly definite conclusion as to what he must do. Every faculty which he possessed was extraordinarily clear, and at the same time extraordinarily still. He had his knife in his hand, he faced about suddenly and ran. There were two men waiting. Feversham ran at the man who held the lantern. He was aware of the point of a spear, he ducked and beat it aside with his left arm, he leaped forward and struck with his right. The Arab fell at his feet, the lantern was extinguished. Feversham sprang across the white-robed body and ran eastwards towards the open desert. But in no panic; he had never been so collected. He was followed by the second soldier. He had foreseen that he would be followed. If he was to escape it was indeed necessary that he should be. He turned a corner, crouched behind a wall, and as the Arab came running by he leaped out upon his shoulders. And again as he leaped he struck.'

Captain Willoughby stopped at this point of his story and turned towards Ethne. He had something to say which perplexed and at the same time impressed him, and he spoke with a desire for an explanation.

'The strangest feature of those few fierce short minutes,' he said, 'was that Feversham felt no fear. I don't understand that, do you? From the first moment when the lantern shone upon him from behind to the last when he turned his feet eastwards, and ran through the ruined alleys and broken walls towards the desert and the Wells of Obak, he felt no fear.'

This was the most mysterious part of Harry Feversham's story to Captain Willoughby. Here was a man who so shrank from the possibilities of battle, that he must actually send in his papers rather than confront them; yet when he stood in dire and immediate peril he felt no fear. Captain Willoughby might well turn to Ethne for an explanation.

There had been no mystery in it to Harry Feversham, but a great bitterness of spirit. He had sat on the verandah at Suakin whittling away at the edge of Captain Willoughby's table with the very knife which he had used in Berber to dig out the letters, and which had proved so handy a weapon when the lantern shone out behind him – the one glimmering point of light in that vast acreage of ruin. Harry Feversham had kept it carefully uncleansed of blood; he had treasured it all through his flight across the two hundred and forty odd miles of desert into Suakin; it was, next to the white feathers, the thing which he held most precious of his possessions, and not merely because it would serve as a corroboration of his story to Captain Willoughby, but because the weapon enabled him to believe and realise it himself. A brown clotted rust dulled the whole length of the blade, and often during the first two days and nights of his flight, when he travelled alone, hiding and running and hiding again, with the dread of pursuit always at his heels, he had taken the knife from his breast, and stared at it with incredulous eyes, and clutched it close to him like a thing of comfort. He had lost his way amongst the sand-hills of Obak on the evening of the second day, and had wandered vainly, with his small store of dates and water exhausted, until he had stumbled and lay prone, parched and famished and enfeebled, with the bitter knowledge that Abou Fatma and the Wells were somewhere within a mile of the spot on which he lay. But even at that moment of exhaustion the knife had been a talisman and a help. He grasped the rough wooden handle, all too small for a Western hand, and he ran his fingers over the rough rust upon the blade, and the weapon spoke to him and bade him take heart, since once he had been put to the test and had not failed. But long before he saw the white houses of Suakin that feeling of elation vanished, and the knife became an emblem of the vain tortures of his boyhood and the miserable folly which culminated in his resignation of his commission. He understood now the words which Lieutenant Sutch had spoken in the grill-room of the Criterion Restaurant, when citing Hamlet as his example, 'The thing which he saw, which he thought over, which he imagined in the act and in the consequence – that he shrank from. Yet when the moment of action comes sharp and immediate, does he fail?' And remembering the words, Harry Feversham sat one May night four years afterwards in Captain Willoughby's verandah, whittling away at the table with his knife, and saying over and over again in a bitter, savage voice, 'It was an illusion, but an illusion which has caused a great deal of suffering to a woman I would have shielded from suffering. But I am well paid for it, for it has wrecked my life besides.'

Captain Willoughby could not understand, any more than General Feversham could have understood, or than Ethne had. But Willoughby could at all events remember and repeat, and Ethne had grown by five years of unhappiness since the night when Harry Feversham, in the little room off the hall at Lennon House, had told her of his upbringing, of the loss of his mother, of the impassable gulf between his father and himself, and of the fear of disgrace which had haunted his nights and disfigured the world for him by day.

'Yes, it was an illusion,' she cried. 'I understand. I might have understood a long while since, but I would not. When those feathers came he told me why they were sent, quite simply, with his eyes on mine. When my father knew of them, he waited quite steadily and faced my father.'

There was other evidence of the like kind not within Ethne's knowledge. Harry Feversham had journeyed down to Broad Place in Surrey, and made his confession no less unflinchingly to the old General. But Ethne knew enough. 'It was the possibility of cowardice from which he shrank, not the possibility of hurt,' she exclaimed. 'If only one had been a little older, a little less sure about things, a little less narrow! I should have listened. I should have understood. At all events, I should not, I think, have been cruel.'

Not for the first time did remorse for that fourth feather which she had added to the three seize upon her. She sat now crushed by it into silence. Captain Willoughby, however, was a stubborn man, unwilling upon any occasion to admit an error. He saw that Ethne's remorse by implication condemned himself, and that he was not prepared to suffer.

'Yes; but these fine distinctions are a little too elusive for practical purposes,' he said. 'You can't run the world on fine

129

distinctions; so I cannot bring myself to believe that we three men were at all to blame, and if we were not, you of all people can have no reason for self-reproach.'

Ethne did not consider what he precisely meant by the last reference to herself. For as he leaned complacently back in his seat anger against him flamed suddenly hot in her. Occupied by his story, she had ceased to take stock of the story-teller. Now that he had ended she looked him over from head to foot. An obstinate stupidity was the mark of the man to her eye. How dare he sit in judgment upon the meanest of his fellows, let alone Harry Feversham? she asked, and in the same moment recollected that she herself had endorsed his judgment. Shame tingled through her blood; she sat with her lips set, keeping Willoughby under watch from the corners of her eyes, and waiting to pounce savagely the moment he opened his lips. There had been noticeable throughout his narrative a manner of condescension towards Feversham. 'Let him use it again!' thought Ethne. But Captain Willoughby said nothing at all, and Ethne herself broke the silence. 'Who of you three first thought of sending the feathers?' she asked aggressively. 'Not you?'

'No, I think it was Trench,' he replied.

'Ah, Trench!' Ethne exclaimed. She struck one clenched hand, the hand which held the feather, viciously into the palm of the other. 'I will remember that name.'

'But I share his responsibility,' Willoughby assured her. 'I do not shrink from it at all. I regret very much that we caused you pain and annoyance, but I do not acknowledge to any mistake in this matter. I take my feather back now, and I annul my accusation. But that is your doing.'

'Mine?' asked Ethne. 'What do you mean?'

Captain Willoughby turned with surprise to his companion.

'A man may live in the Soudan and yet not be wholly ignorant of women and their great quality of forgiveness. You gave the feathers back to Feversham in order that he might redeem his honour. That is evident.'

Ethne sprang to her feet before Captain Willoughby had come to the end of his sentence, and stood a little in front of him, with her face averted, and in an attitude remarkably still.

Willoughby in his ignorance, like many another stupid man before him, had struck with a shrewdness and a vigour which he could never have compassed by the use of his wits. He had pointed abruptly and suddenly to Ethne a way which she might have taken and had not, and her remorse warned her very clearly that it was the way which she ought to have taken. But she could rise to the heights. She did not seek to justify herself in her own eyes, nor would she allow Willoughby to continue in his misconception. She recognised that here she had failed in charity and justice, and she was glad that she had failed, since her failure had been the opportunity of greatness to Harry Feversham.

'Will you repeat what you said?' she asked in a low voice; 'and ever so slowly, please.'

'You gave the feathers back into Feversham's hand —'

'He told you that himself?'

'Yes,' and Willoughby resumed: 'In order that he might by his subsequent bravery compel the men who sent them to take them back, and so redeem his honour.'

'He did not tell you that?'

'No. I guessed it. You see, Feversham's disgrace was, on the face of it, impossible to retrieve. The opportunity might never have occurred – it was not likely to occur. As things happened, Feversham still waited for three years in the bazaar at Suakin before it did. No, Miss Eustace, it needed a woman's faith to conceive that plan – a woman's encouragement to keep the man who undertook it to his work.'

Ethne laughed and turned back to him. Her face was tender with pride, and more than tender. Pride seemed in some strange way to hallow her, to give an unimagined benignance to her eyes, an unearthly brightness to the smile upon her lips and the colour upon her cheeks. So that Willoughby, looking at her, was carried out of himself.

'Yes,' he cried, 'you were the woman to plan this redemption.'

Ethne laughed again and very happily.

'Did he tell you of a fourth white feather?' she asked.

'No.'

'I shall tell you the truth,' she said, as she resumed her seat. 'The plan was of his devising from first to last. Nor did I

131

encourage him to its execution. For until to-day I never heard a word of it. Since the night of that dance in Donegal I have had no message from Mr Feversham, and no news of him. I told him to take up those three feathers because they were his, and I wished to show him that I agreed with the accusations of which they were the symbols. That seems cruel? But I did more. I snapped a fourth white feather from my fan and gave him that to carry away, too. It is only fair that you should know. I wanted to make an end for ever and ever, not only of my acquaintanceship with him, but of every kindly thought he might keep of me, of every kindly thought I might keep of him. I wanted to be sure myself, and I wanted him to be sure, that we should always be strangers now and – and afterwards,' and the last words she spoke in a whisper. Captain Willoughby did not understand what she meant by them. It is possible that only Lieutenant Sutch and Harry Feversham himself would have understood.

'I was sad and sorry enough when I had done it,' she resumed. 'Indeed, indeed, I think I have always been sorry since. I think that I have never at any minute during these five years quite forgotten that fourth white feather and the quiet air of dignity with which he took it. But to-day I am glad.' And her voice, though low, rang rich with the fullness of her pride. 'Oh, very glad! For this was his thought, his deed. They are both all his, as I would have them be. I had no share, and of that I am very proud. He needed no woman's faith, no woman's encouragement.'

'Yet he sent this back to you,' said Willoughby, pointing in some perplexity to the feather which Ethne held.

'Yes,' she said, 'yes. He knew that I should be glad to know.' And suddenly she held it close to her breast. Thus she sat for a while with her eyes shining, until Willoughby rose to his feet and pointed to the gap in the hedge by which they had entered the enclosure.

'By Jove! Jack Durrance,' he exclaimed.

Durrance was standing in the gap, which was the only means or entering or going out.

Chapter Sixteen

CAPTAIN WILLOUGHBY RETIRES

Ethne had entirely forgotten even Colonel Durrance's existence. From the moment when Captain Willoughby had put that little soiled feather which had once been white, and was now yellow, into her hand, she had had no thought for anyone but Harry Feversham. She had carried Willoughby into that enclosure, and his story had absorbed her and kept her memory on the rack, as she filled out with this or that recollected detail of Harry's gestures, or voice, or looks, the deficiencies in her companion's narrative. She had been swept away from that August garden of sunlight and coloured flowers, and those five most weary years, during which she had held her head high and greeted the world with a smile of courage, were blotted from her experience. How weary they had been perhaps she never knew until she raised her head and saw Durrance at the entrance in the hedge.

'Hush!' she said to Willoughby; and her face paled and her eyes shut tight for a moment with a spasm of pain. But she had no time to spare for any indulgence of her feelings. Her few minutes' talk with Captain Willoughby had been a holiday, but the holiday was over. She must take up again the responsibilities with which those five years had charged her, and at once. If she could not accomplish that hard task of forgetting – and she now knew very well that she never would accomplish it – she must do the next best thing, and give no sign that she had not forgotten. Durrance must continue to believe that she brought more than friendship into the marriage account.

He stood at the very entrance to the enclosure, he advanced into it. He was so quick to guess, it was not wise that he should meet Captain Willoughby or even know of his coming. Ethne looked about her for an escape, knowing very well that she would look in vain. The creek was in front of them, and three

133

walls of high thick hedge girt them in behind and at the sides. There was but one entrance to this enclosure, and Durrance himself barred the path to it.

'Keep still,' she said in a whisper. 'You know him?'

'Of course. We were together for three years at Suakin. I heard that he had gone blind. I am glad to know that it is not true.' This he said, noticing the freedom of Durrance's gait.

'Speak lower,' returned Ethne. 'It is true. He *is* blind.'

'One would never have thought it. Consolations seem so futile. What can I say to him?'

'Say nothing!'

Durrance was still standing just within the enclosure, and, as it seemed, looking straight towards the two people seated on the bench.

'Ethne,' he said, rather than called; and the quiet unquestioning voice made the illusion that he saw extraordinarily complete.

'It's impossible that he is blind,' said Willoughby. 'He sees us.'

'He sees nothing.'

Again Durrance called 'Ethne,' but now in a louder voice and a voice of doubt.

'Do you hear? He is not sure,' whispered Ethne. 'Keep very still.'

'Why?'

'He must not know you are here;' and lest Willoughby should move she caught his arm tight in her hand. Willoughby did not pursue his inquiries. Ethne's manner constrained him to silence. She sat very still, still as she wished him to sit, and in a queer huddled attitude; she was even holding her breath; she was staring at Durrance with a great fear in her eyes; her face was strained forward, and not a muscle of it moved, so that Willoughby, as he looked at her, was conscious of a certain excitement, which grew on him for no reason but her remarkable apprehension. He began unaccountably himself to fear lest he and she should be discovered.

'He is coming towards us,' he whispered.

'Not a word – not a movement.'

'Ethne,' Durrance cried again. He advanced further into the

enclosure and towards the seat. Ethne and Captain Willoughby sat rigid, watching him with their eyes. He passed in front of the bench and stopped actually facing them. Surely, thought Willoughby, he sees. His eyes were upon them; he stood easily, as though he were about to speak. Even Ethne, though she very well knew that he did not see, began to doubt her knowledge.

'Ethne!' he said again, and this time in the quiet voice which he had first used. But since again no answer came, he shrugged his shoulders and turned towards the creek. His back was towards them now, but Ethne's experience had taught her to appreciate almost indefinable signs in his bearing, since nowadays his face showed her so little. Something in his attitude, in the poise of his head, even in the carelessness with which he swung his stick, told her that he was listening, and listening with all his might. Her grasp tightened on Willoughby's arm. Thus they remained for the space of a minute, and then Durrance turned suddenly and took a quick step towards the seat. Ethne, however, by this time knew the man and his ingenuities; she was prepared for some such unexpected movement. She did not stir, there was not audible the merest rustle of her skirt, and her grip still constrained Willoughby.

'I wonder where in the world she can be,' said Durrance to himself aloud, and he walked back and out of the enclosure. Ethne did not free Captain Willoughby's arm until Durrance had disappeared from sight.

'That was a close shave,' Willoughby said when at last he was allowed to speak. 'Suppose Durrance had sat down on the top of us?'

'Why suppose, since he did not?' Ethne asked calmly. 'You have told me everything?'

'So far as I remember.'

'And all that you have told me happened in the spring?'

'The spring of last year,' said Willoughby.

'Yes. I want to ask you a question. Why did you not bring this feather to me last summer?'

'Last year my leave was short. I spent it in the hills north of Suakin after ibex.'

'I see,' said Ethne, quietly; 'I hope you had good sport.'

'It wasn't bad.'

135

Last summer Ethne had been free. If Willoughby had come home with his good news instead of shooting ibex on Jebel Araft, it would have made all the difference in her life, and the cry was loud at her heart: 'Why didn't you come?' But outwardly she gave no sign of the irreparable harm which Willoughby's delay had brought about. She had the self-command of a woman who has been sorely tried, and she spoke so unconcernedly that Willoughby believed her questions prompted by the merest curiosity.

'You might have written,' she suggested.

'Feversham did not suggest that there was any hurry. It would have been a long and difficult matter to explain in a letter. He asked me to go to you when I had an opportunity, and I had no opportunity before. To tell the truth, I thought it very likely that I might find Feversham had come back before me.'

'Oh no,' returned Ethne, 'there could be no possibility of that. The other two feathers still remain to be redeemed before he will ask me to take back mine.'

Willoughby shook his head. 'Feversham can never persuade Castleton and Trench to cancel their accusations as he persuaded me.'

'Why not?'

'Major Castleton was killed when the square was broken at Tamai.'

'Killed?' cried Ethne; and she laughed in a short and satisfied way. Willoughby turned and stared at her, disbelieving the evidence of his ears. But her face showed him quite clearly that she was thoroughly pleased. Ethne was a Celt, and she had the Celtic feeling that death was not a very important matter. She could hate, too, and she could be hard as iron to the men she hated. And these three men she hated exceedingly. It was true that she had agreed with them, that she had given a feather, the fourth feather, to Harry Feversham just to show that she agreed, but she did not trouble her head about that. She was very glad to hear that Major Castleton was out of the world and done with.

'And Colonel Trench too?' she said.

'No,' Willoughby answered. 'You are disappointed? But he

is even worse off than that. He was captured when engaged on a reconnaissance. He is now a prisoner in Omdurman.'

'Ah!' said Ethne.

'I don't think you can have any idea,' said Willoughby, severely, 'of what captivity in Omdurman implies. If you had, however much you disliked the captive, you would feel some pity.'

'Not I,' said Ethne, stubbornly.

'I will tell you something of what it does imply.'

'No. I don't wish to hear of Colonel Trench. Besides, you must go. I want you to tell me one thing first,' said she as she rose from her seat. 'What became of Mr Feversham after he had given you that feather?'

'I told him that he had done everything which could be reasonably expected; and he accepted my advice. For he went on board the first steamer which touched at Suakin on its way to Suez, and so left the Soudan.'

'I must find out where he is. He must come back. Did he need money?'

'No. He still drew his allowance from his father. He told me that he had more than enough.'

'I am glad of that,' said Ethne; and she bade Willoughby wait within the enclosure until she returned, and went out by herself to see that the way was clear. The garden was quite empty. Durrance had disappeared from it, and the great stone terrace of the house and the house itself, with its striped sunblinds, looked a place of sleep. It was getting towards one o'clock, and the very birds were quiet amongst the trees. Indeed the quietude of the garden struck upon Ethne's senses as somewhat almost strange. Only the bees hummed drowsily about the flowerbeds, and the voice of a lad was heard calling from the slopes of meadow on the far side of the creek. She returned to Captain Willoughby.

'You can go now,' she said. 'I cannot pretend friendship for you, Captain Willoughby, but it was kind of you to find me out and tell me your story. You are going back at once to Kingsbridge? I hope so. For I do not wish Colonel Durrance to know of your visit or anything of what you have told me.'

'Durrance was a friend of Feversham's – his great friend,' Willoughby objected.

'He is quite unaware that any feathers were sent to Mr Feversham, so there is no need he should be informed that one of them has been taken back,' Ethne answered. 'He does not know why my engagement to Mr Feversham was broken off. I do not wish him to know. Your story would enlighten him, and he must not be enlightened.'

'Why?' asked Willoughby. He was obstinate by nature, and he meant to have the reason for silence before he promised to keep it. Ethne gave it to him at once very simply.

'I am engaged to Colonel Durrance,' she said. It was her fear that Durrance already suspected that no stronger feeling than friendship attached her to him. If once he heard that the fault which broke her engagement to Harry Feversham had been most bravely atoned, there could be no doubt as to the course which he would insist upon pursuing. He would strip himself of her, the one thing left to him, and that she was stubbornly determined he should not do. She was bound to him in honour, and it would be a poor way of manifesting her joy that Harry Feversham had redeemed his honour if she straightway sacrificed her own.

Captain Willoughby pursed up his lips and whistled.

'Engaged to Jack Durrance!' he exclaimed. 'Then I seem to have wasted my time in bringing you that feather;' and he pointed towards it. She was holding it in her open hand, and she drew her hand sharply away, as though she feared for a moment that he meant to rob her of it.

'I am most grateful for it,' she returned.

'It's a bit of a muddle, isn't it?' Willoughby remarked. 'It seems a little rough on Feversham perhaps, what? It's a little rough on Jack Durrance, too, when you come to think of it.' Then he looked at Ethne. He noticed her careful handling of the feather; he remembered something of the glowing look with which she had listened to his story, something of the eager tones in which she had put her questions; and he added: 'I shouldn't wonder if it was rather rough on you, too, Miss Eustace.'

Ethne did not answer him, and they walked together out of

the enclosure towards the spot where Willoughby had moored his boat. She hurried him down the bank to the water's edge, intent that he should sail away unperceived.

But Ethne had counted without Mrs Adair, who all that morning had seen much in Ethne's movements to interest her. From the drawing-room window she had watched Ethne and Durrance meet at the foot of the terrace-steps, she had seen them walk together towards the estuary, she had noticed Willoughby's boat as it ran aground in the wide gap between the trees, she had seen a man disembark, and Ethne go forward to meet him. Mrs Adair was not the woman to leave her post of observation at such a moment, and from the cover of the curtains she continued to watch with all the curiosity of a woman in a village who draws down the blind, that unobserved she may get a better peep at the stranger passing down the street. Ethne and the man from the boat turned away and disappeared amongst the trees, leaving Durrance forgotten and alone. Mrs Adair thought at once of that enclosure at the water's edge. The conversation lasted for some while, and since the couple did not promptly reappear, a question flashed into her mind. 'Could the stranger be Harry Feversham?' Ethne had no friends in this part of the world. The question pressed upon Mrs Adair. She longed for an answer, and of course for that particular answer which would convict Ethne Eustace of duplicity. Her interest grew into an excitement when she saw Durrance, tired of waiting, follow upon Ethne's steps. But what came after was to interest her still more.

Durrance reappeared, to her surprise alone, and came straight to the house, up the terrace, into the drawing-room.

'Have you seen Ethne?' he asked.

'Is she not in the little garden by the water?' Mrs Adair asked.

'No. I went into it and called to her. It was empty.'

'Indeed,' said Mrs Adair. 'Then I don't know where she is. Are you going?'

'Yes, home.'

Mrs Adair made no effort to detain him at that moment.

'Perhaps you will come in and dine to-night. Eight o'clock.'

'Thanks, very much. I shall be pleased,' said Durrance, but

he did not immediately go. He stood by the window idly swinging to and fro the tassel of the blind.

'I did not know until to-day that it was your plan that I should come home, and Ethne stay with you until I found out whether a cure was likely or possible. It was very kind of you, Mrs Adair, and I am grateful.'

'It was a natural plan to propose as soon as I heard of your ill-luck.'

'And when was that?' he asked unconcernedly. 'The day after Calder's telegram reached her from Wadi Halfa, I suppose.'

Mrs Adair was not deceived by his attitude of carelessness. She realised that his expression of gratitude had deliberately led up to this question.

'Oh, so you knew of that telegram,' she said. 'I thought you did not.' For Ethne had asked her not to mention it on the very day when Durrance returned to England.

'Of course I knew of it,' he returned; and without waiting any longer for an answer he went out on to the terrace.

Mrs Adair dismissed for the moment the mystery of the telegram. She was occupied by her conjecture that in the little garden by the water's edge Durrance had stood and called aloud for Ethne, while within twelve yards of him, perhaps actually within his reach, she and someone else had kept very still and given no answer. Her conjecture was proved true. She saw Ethne and her companion come out again on to the open lawn. Was it Feversham? She must have an answer to that question. She saw them descend the bank towards the boat, and, stepping from her window, ran.

Thus it happened that as Willoughby rose from loosening the painter, he saw Mrs Adair's disappointed eyes gazing into his. Mrs Adair called to Ethne, who stood by Captain Willoughby, and came down the bank to them.

'I noticed you cross the lawn from the drawing-room window,' she said.

'Yes?' answered Ethne, and she said no more. Mrs Adair, however, did not move away, and an awkward pause followed. Ethne was forced to give in.

'I was talking to Captain Willoughby;' and she turned to him. 'You do not know Mrs Adair, I think?'

'No,' he replied, as he raised his hat. 'But I know Mrs Adair very well by name. I know friends of yours, Mrs Adair – Durrance, for instance; and of course I knew — '

A glance from Ethne brought him abruptly to a stop. He began vigorously to push the nose of his boat from the sand.

'Of course what?' asked Mrs Adair, with a smile.

'Of course I knew of you, Mrs Adair.'

Mrs Adair was quite clear that this was not what Willoughby had been on the point of saying when Ethne turned her eyes quietly upon him and cut him short. He was on the point of adding another name. 'Captain Willoughby,' she repeated to herself. Then she said:

'You belong to Colonel Durrance's regiment, perhaps?'

'No, I belong to the North Surrey,' he answered.

'Ah! Mr Feversham's old regiment,' said Mrs Adair pleasantly. Captain Willoughby had fallen into her little trap with a guilelessness which provoked in her a desire for a closer acquaintanceship. Whatever Willoughby knew it would be easy to extract. Ethne, however, had disconcerting ways which at times left Mrs Adair at a loss. She looked now straight into Mrs Adair's eyes and said calmly:

'Captain Willoughby and I have been talking of Mr Feversham.' At the same time she held out her hand to the Captain. 'Good-bye,' she said.

Mrs Adair hastily interrupted.

'Colonel Durrance has gone home, but he dines with us to-night. I came out to tell you that, but I am glad that I came, for it gives me the opportunity to ask your friend to lunch with us if he will.'

Captain Willoughby, who already had one leg over the bows of his boat, withdrew it with alacrity.

'It's awfully good of you, Mrs Adair,' he began.

'It is very kind indeed,' Ethne continued, 'but Captain Willoughby has reminded me that his leave is very short, and we have no right to detain him. Good-bye.'

Captain Willoughby gazed with a vain appeal upon Miss Eustace. He had travelled all night from London, he had made the scantiest breakfast at Kingsbridge, and the notion of lunch appealed to him particularly at that moment. But her eyes rested on his with a quiet and inexorable command. He bowed, got ruefully into his boat, and pushed off from the shore.

'It's a little bit rough on me too, perhaps, Miss Eustace,' he said. Ethne laughed and returned to the terrace with Mrs Adair. Once or twice she opened the palm of her hand and disclosed to her companion's view a small white feather, at which she laughed again, and with a clear and rather low laugh. But she gave no explanation of Captain Willoughby's errand. Had she been in Mrs Adair's place she would not have expected one. It was her business and only hers.

Chapter Seventeen

THE MELUSINE OVERTURE

Mrs Adair, on her side, asked for no explanations. She was naturally behind her pale and placid countenance a woman of a tortuous and intriguing mind. She preferred to look through a keyhole even when she could walk straight in at the door; and knowledge which could be gained by a little manœuvring was always more desirable and precious in her eyes than any information which a simple question would elicit. She avoided, indeed, the direct question on a perverted sort of principle, and she thought a day very well spent if at the close of it she had outwitted a companion into telling her spontaneously some trivial and unimportant piece of news which a straightforward request would have at once secured for her at breakfast-time.

Therefore, though she was mystified by the little white feather upon which Ethne seemed to set so much store, and wondered at the good news of Harry Feversham which Captain Willoughby had brought, and vainly puzzled her brains in conjecture as to what in the world could have happened on that night at Ramelton so many years ago, she betrayed nothing whatever of her perplexity all through lunch; on the contrary, she plied her guest with conversation upon indifferent topics. Mrs Adair could be good company when she chose, and she chose now. But it was not to any purpose.

'I don't believe that you hear a single word I am saying,' she exclaimed.

Ethne laughed and pleaded guilty. She betook herself to her room as soon as lunch was finished, and allowed herself an afternoon of solitude. Sitting at her window she repeated slowly the story which Willoughby had told to her that morning, and her heart thrilled to it as to music divinely played. The regret that he had not come home and told it a year ago, when she was free, was a small thing in comparison with the story itself. It could not outweigh the great gladness which that brought to her – it had, indeed, completely vanished from her thoughts. Her pride, which had never recovered from the blow which Harry Feversham had dealt to her in the hall at Lennon House, was now quite restored, and by the man who had dealt the blow. She was aglow with it, and most grateful to Harry Feversham for that he had, at so much peril to himself, restored it. She was conscious of a new exhilaration in the sunlight, of a quicker pulsation in her blood. Her youth was given back to her upon that August afternoon.

Ethne unlocked a drawer in her dressing-case, and took from it the portrait alone of all Harry Feversham's presents she had kept. She rejoiced that she had kept it. It was the portrait of someone who was dead to her – that she knew very well, for there was no thought of disloyalty towards Durrance in her breast – but the someone was a friend. She looked at it with a great happiness and contentment, because Harry Feversham had needed no expression of faith from her to inspire him and no encouragement from her to keep him through the years on the level of his high inspiration. When she put it back again, she laid the white feather in the drawer with it and locked the two things up together.

She came back to her window. Out upon the lawn a light breeze made the shadows from the high trees dance, the sunlight mellowed and reddened. But Ethne was of her county, as Harry Feversham had long ago discovered, and her heart

143

yearned for it at this moment. It was the month of August. The first of the heather would be out upon the hillsides of Donegal, and she wished that the good news had been brought to her there. The regret that it had not was her crumpled rose-leaf. Here she was in a strange land; there the brown mountains, with their outcroppings of granite and the voices of the streams, would have shared, she almost thought, in her new happiness. Great sorrows or great joys had this in common for Ethne Eustace – they both drew her homewards, since there endurance was more easy and gladness more complete.

She had, however, one living tie with Donegal at her side, for Dermod's old collie dog had become her inseparable companion. To him she made her confidence, and if at times her voice broke in tears, why, the dog would not tell. She came to understand much which Willoughby had omitted, and which Feversham had never told. Those three years of concealment in the small and crowded city of Suakin, for instance, with the troops marching out to battle, and returning dust-strewn and bleeding and laurelled with victory. Harry Feversham had to slink away at their approach, lest some old friend of his – Durrance, perhaps, or Willoughby, or Trench – should notice him and penetrate his disguise. The panic which had beset him when first he saw the dark brown walls of Berber, the night in the ruined acres, the stumbling search for the well amongst the shifting sandhills of Obak – Ethne had vivid pictures of these incidents, and as she thought of each she asked herself, 'Where was I then? What was I doing?'

She sat in a golden mist until the lights began to change upon the still water of the creek, and the rocks wheeled noisily out from the tree tops to sort themselves for the night, and warned her of evening.

She brought to the dinner-table that night a buoyancy of spirit which surprised her companions. Mrs Adair had to admit that seldom had her eyes shone so starrily, or the colour so freshly graced her cheeks. She was more than ever certain that Captain Willoughby had brought stirring news; she was more than ever tortured by her vain efforts to guess its nature. But Mrs Adair, in spite of her perplexities, took her share in the talk, and that dinner passed with a freedom from embarrassment unknown since Durrance had come home to Guessens. For he, too, threw off a burden of restraint; his spirits rose to match Ethne's; he answered laugh with laugh, and from his face that habitual look of tension, the look of a man listening with all his might that his ears might make good the loss of his eyes, passed altogether away.

'You will play on your violin to-night, I think,' he said with a smile as they rose from the table.

'Yes,' she answered, 'I will – with all my heart.'

Durrance laughed and held open the door. The violin had remained locked in its case during these last two months. Durrance had come to look upon that violin as a gauge and test. If the world was going well with Ethne, the case was unlocked, the instrument was allowed to speak; if the world went ill, it was kept silent lest it should say too much, and open old wounds and lay them bare to other eyes. Ethne herself knew it for an indiscreet friend. But it was to be brought out to-night.

Mrs Adair lingered until Ethne was out of earshot.

'You have noticed the change in her to-night?' she said.

'Yes. Have I not?' answered Durrance. 'One has waited for it, hoped for it, despaired of it.'

'Are you so glad of the change?'

Durrance threw back his head. 'Do you wonder that I am glad? Kind, friendly, unselfish – these things she has always been. But there is more than friendliness evident to-night, and for the first time evident.'

There came a look of pity upon Mrs Adair's face, and she passed out of the room without another word. Durrance took all of that great change in Ethne to himself. Mrs Adair drew up the blinds of the drawing-room, opened the window and let the moonlight in; and then, as she saw Ethne unlocking the case of her violin, she went out on to the terrace. She felt that she could not sit patiently in her company. So that when Durrance entered the drawing-room he found Ethne alone there. She was seated in the window and already tightening the strings of her violin. Durrance took a chair behind her in the shadows.

'What shall I play to you?' she asked.

'The Melusine Overture,' he answered. 'You played it on

the first evening when I came to Ramelton. I remember so well how you played it then. Play it again to-night. I want to compare.'

'I have played it since.'

'Never to me.'

They were alone in the room; the windows stood open; it was a night of moonlight. Ethne suddenly crossed to the lamp and put it out. She resumed her seat, while Durrance remained in the shadow, leaning forward with his hands upon his knees, listening – but with an intentness of which he had given no sign that evening. He was applying, as he thought, a final test upon which his life and hers should be decided. Ethne's violin would tell him assuredly whether he was right or no. Would friendship speak from it or the something more than friendship?

Ethne played the overture, and as she played she forgot that Durrance was in the room behind her. In the garden the air was still and summer-warm and fragrant; on the creek the moonlight lay like a solid floor of silver; the trees stood dreaming to the stars; and as the music floated out across the silent lawn, Ethne had a sudden fancy that it might perhaps travel down the creek and over Salcombe Bar and across the moonlit seas, and strike small yet wonderfully clear like fairy music upon the ears of a man sleeping somewhere far away beneath the brightness of the southern stars with the cool wind of the desert blowing upon his face.

'If he could only hear!' she thought. 'If he could only wake and know that what he heard was a message of friendship!'

And with this fancy in her mind she played with such skill as she had never used before; she made of her violin a voice of sympathy. The fancy grew and changed as she played. The music became a bridge swung in mid-air across the world, upon which just for these few minutes she and Harry Feversham might meet and shake hands. They would separate, of course, forthwith, and each one go upon the allotted way. But these few minutes would be a help to both along the separate ways. The chords rang upon silence. It seemed to Ethne that they declaimed the pride which had come to her that day. Her fancy grew into a belief. It was no longer 'If he should hear!' but 'He *must* hear!' And so carried away was she from the discretion of thought that a strange hope suddenly sprung up and enthralled her.

'If he could answer!'

She lingered upon the last bars, waiting for the answer; and when the music had died down to silence she sat with her violin upon her knees, looking eagerly out across the moonlit garden.

And an answer did come, but it was not carried up the creek and across the lawn. It came from the dark shadows of the room behind her, and it was spoken through the voice of Durrance.

'Ethne, where do you think I heard that overture last played?'

Ethne was roused with a start to the consciousness that Durrance was in the room, and she answered like one shaken suddenly out of sleep.

'Why, you told me. At Ramelton, when you first came to Lennon House.'

'I have heard it since, though it was not played by you. It was not really played at all. But a melody of it, and not even that really, but a suggestion of a melody I heard stumbled out upon a zither, with many false notes, by a Greek in a bare little whitewashed café lit by one glaring lamp at Wadi Halfa.'

'This overture?' she said. 'How strange!'

'Not so strange after all. For the Greek was Harry Feversham.'

So the answer had come. Ethne had no doubt that it was an answer. She sat very still in the moonlight; only had anyone bent over her with eyes to see, he would have discovered that her eyelids were closed. There followed a long silence. She did not consider why Durrance, having kept this knowledge secret so long, should speak of it now. She did not ask what Harry Feversham was doing that he must play the zither in a mean café at Wadi Halfa. But it seemed to her that he had spoken to her as she to him. The music had, after all, been a bridge. It was not even strange that he had used Durrance's voice wherewith to speak to her.

'When was this?' she asked at length.

'In February of this year. I will tell you about it.'

'Yes, please, tell me.'

And Durrance spoke out of the shadows of the room.

Chapter Eighteen

THE ANSWER TO THE OVERTURE

Ethne did not turn towards Durrance or move at all from her attitude. She sat with her violin upon her knees, looking across the moonlit garden to the band of silver in the gap of the trees; and she kept her position deliberately. For it helped her to believe that Harry Feversham himself was speaking to her, she was able to forget that he was speaking through the voice of Durrance. She almost forgot that Durrance was even in the room. She listened with Durrance's own intentness, and anxious that the voice should speak very slowly, so that the message might take a long time in the telling, and she gather it all jealously to her heart.

'It was on the night before I started eastwards into desert – for the last time,' said Durrance, and the deep longing and regret with which he dwelt upon that 'last time' for once left Ethne quite untouched.

'Yes,' she said. 'That was in February. The middle of the month, wasn't it? Do you remember the day? I should like to know the exact day, if you can tell me.'

'The fifteenth,' said Durrance; and Ethne repeated the date meditatively.

'I was at Glenalla all February,' she said. 'What was I doing on the fifteenth? It does not matter.'

She had felt a queer sort of surprise all the time while Willoughby was telling his story that morning that she had not known, by some instinct, of these incidents at the actual moment of their occurrence. The surprise returned to her now. It was strange that she should have had to wait for this August night and this summer garden of moonlight and closed flowers before she learned of the meeting between Feversham and Durrance on February 15 and heard the message. And remorse came to her because of that delay. 'It was my own fault,' she said to herself. 'If I had kept my faith in him I should have known at once. I am well punished.' It did not at all occur to her that the message could convey any but the best of news. It would carry on the good tidings which she had already heard. It would enlarge and complete, so that this day might be rounded to perfection. Of this she was quite sure.

'Well?' she said. 'Go on!'

'I had been busy all that day in my office finishing up my work. I turned the key in the door at ten o'clock, thinking with relief that for six weeks I should not open it, and I strolled northwards out of Wadi Halfa along the Nile bank into the little town of Tewfikieh. As I entered the main street I saw a small crowd – Arabs, negroes, a Greek or two, and some Egyptian soldiers, standing outside the café, and lit up by a glare of light from within. As I came nearer I heard the sound of a violin and a zither, both most vilely played, jingling out a waltz. I stood at the back of the crowd, and looked over the shoulders of the men in front of me into the room. It was a place of four bare whitewashed walls, a bar stood in one corner, a wooden bench or two were ranged against the walls, and a single unshaded paraffin lamp swung and glared from the ceiling. A troupe of itinerant musicians were playing to that crowd of negroes and Arabs and Egyptians for a night's lodging and the price of a meal. There were four of them, and, so far as I could see, all four were Greeks. Two were evidently man and wife. They were both old, both slatternly and almost in rags; the man a thin, sallow-faced fellow with grey hair and a black moustache; the woman fat, coarse of face, unwieldy of body. Of the other two, one it seemed must be their daughter, a girl of seventeen, not good-looking really, but dressed and turned out with a scrupulous care, which in those sordid and mean surroundings lent her good looks. The care, indeed, with which she was dressed assured me she was their daughter, and, to tell the truth, I was rather touched by the thought that the father and mother would go in rags so that she at all costs might be trim. A clean ribbon bound back her hair, an untorn

149

frock of some white stuff clothed her tidily; even her shoes were neat. The fourth was a young man; he was seated in the window, with his back towards me, bending over his zither. But I could see that he wore a beard. When I came up the old man was playing the violin, though playing is not indeed the word. The noise he made was more like the squeaking of a pencil on a slate; it set one's teeth on edge; the violin itself seemed to squeal with pain. And while he fiddled, and the young man hammered at his zither, the old woman and the girl slowly revolved in a waltz. It may sound comic to hear about, but if you could have seen! . . . It fairly plucked at one's heart. I do not think that I have ever in my life witnessed anything quite so sad. The little crowd outside, negroes, mind you, laughing at the troupe, passing from one to the other any sort of low jest at their expense, and inside the four white people – the old woman, clumsy, heavy-footed, shining with heat, lumbering round slowly, panting with her exertions; the girl, lissom and young; the two men with their discordant, torturing music; and just above you the great planets and stars of an African sky, and just about you the great silent and spacious dignity of the moonlit desert. Imagine it! The very ineptness of the entertainment actually hurt one.'

He paused for a moment, while Ethne pictured to herself the scene which he had described. She saw Harry Feversham bending over the zither, and at once she asked herself, 'What was he doing with that troupe?' It was intelligible enough that he would not care to return to England. It was certain that he would not come back to her, unless she sent for him. And she knew from what Captain Willoughby had said that he expected no message from her. He had not left with Willoughby the name of any place where a letter could reach him. But what was he doing at Wadi Halfa, masquerading with this itinerant troupe? He had money; so much Willoughby had told her.

'You spoke to him?' she asked suddenly.

'To whom? Oh, to Harry?' returned Durrance. 'Yes, afterwards, when I found out it was he who was playing the zither.'

'Yes, how did you find out?' Ethne asked.

'The waltz came to an end. The old woman sank exhausted upon the bench against the whitewashed wall; the young man raised his head from his zither; the old man scraped a new chord upon his violin, and the girl stood forward to sing. Her voice had youth and freshness, but no other quality of music. Her singing was as inept as the rest of the entertainment. Yet the old man smiled, the mother beat time with her heavy foot, and nodded at her husband with pride in their daughter's accomplishment. And again in the throng the ill-conditioned talk, the untranslatable jests of the Arabs and the negroes went their round. It was horrible, don't you think?'

'Yes,' answered Ethne, but slowly in an absent voice. As she had felt no sympathy for Durrance when he began to speak, so she had none to spare for these three outcasts of fortune. She was too absorbed in the mystery of Harry Feversham's presence at Wadi Halfa. She was listening too closely for the message which he sent to her. Through the open window the moon threw a broad panel of silver light upon the floor of the room close to her feet. She sat gazing into it as she listened, as though it was itself a window through which, if she looked but hard enough, she might see, very small and far away, that lighted café blazing upon the street of the little town of Tewfikieh on the frontier of the Soudan.

'Well?' she asked. 'And after the song was ended?'

'The young man with his back towards me,' Durrance resumed, 'began to fumble out a solo upon the zither. He struck so many false notes, no tune was to be apprehended at the first. The laughter and noise grew amongst the crowd, and I was just turning away, rather sick at heart, when some notes, a succession of notes played correctly by chance, suddenly arrested me. I listened again, and a sort of haunting melody began to emerge – a weak thin thing with no soul in it, a ghost of a melody, and yet familiar. I stood listening in the street of sand, between the hovels fringed by a row of stunted trees, and I was carried away out of the East to Ramelton and to a summer night beneath a melting sky of Donegal, when you sat by the open window as you sit now and played the Melusine Overture, which you have played again to-night.'

'It was a melody from this overture?' she exclaimed.

'Yes, and it was Harry Feversham who played the melody. I did not guess it at once. I was not very quick in those days.'

'But you are now,' said Ethne.

'Quicker, at all events. I should have guessed it now. Then, however, I was only curious. I wondered how it was that an itinerant Greek came to pick up the tune. At all events, I determined to reward him for his diligence. I thought that you would like me to.'

'Yes,' said Ethne in a whisper.

'So, when he came out from the café, and with his hat in his hand passed through the jeering crowd. I threw a sovereign into the hat. He turned to me with a start of surprise. In spite of his beard I knew him. Besides, before he could check himself, he cried out "Jack!"'

'You can have made no mistake, then,' said Ethne in a wondering voice. 'No, the man who strummed upon the zither was — ' – the Christian name was upon her lips, but she had the wit to catch it back unuttered – 'was Mr Feversham. But he knew no music. I remember very well.' She laughed with a momentary recollection of Feversham's utter inability to appreciate any music except that which she herself evoked from her violin. 'He had no ear. You couldn't invent a discord harsh enough even to attract his attention. He could never have remembered any melody from the Melusine Overture.'

'Yet it was Harry Feversham,' he answered. 'Somehow he had remembered. I can understand it. He would have so little he cared to remember, and that little he would have striven with all his might to bring clearly back to mind. Somehow, too, by much practice, I suppose, he had managed to elicit from his zither some sort of resemblance to what he remembered. Can't you imagine him working the scrap of music out in his brain, humming it over, whistling it uncounted times with perpetual errors and confusions, until some fine day he got it safe and sure and fixed it in his thoughts? I can. Can't you imagine him then picking it out sedulously and laboriously on the strings? I can. Indeed, I can.'

Thus Ethne got her answer, and Durrance interpreted it to her understanding. She sat silent and very deeply moved by the story he had told to her. It was fitting that this overture, her favourite piece of music, should convey the message that he had not forgotten her, that in spite of the fourth white feather he thought of her with friendship. Harry Feversham had not striven so laboriously to learn that melody in vain. Ethne was stirred as she had thought nothing would ever again have the power to stir her. She wondered whether Harry, as he sat in the little bare white-washed café, and strummed out his music to the negroes and Greeks and Arabs gathered about the window, had dreamed, as she had done to-night, that somehow, thin and feeble as it was, some echo of the melody might reach across the world. She knew now for very certain that, however much she might in the future pretend to forget Harry Feversham, it would never be more than a pretence. The vision of the lighted café in the desert town would never be very far from her thoughts, but she had no intention of relaxing on that account from her determination to pretend to forget. The mere knowledge that she had at one time been unjustly harsh to Harry made her yet more resolved that Durrance should not suffer for any fault of hers.

'I told you last year, Ethne, at Hill Street,' Durrance resumed, 'that I never wished to see Feversham again. I was wrong. The reluctance was all on his side, and not at all on mine. For the moment that he realised he had called out my name he tried to edge backwards from me into the crowd, he began to gabble Greek, but I caught him by the arm, and I would not let him go. He had done you some great wrong. That I know; that I knew. But I could not remember it then. I only remembered that years before Harry Feversham had been my friend, my one great friend; that we had rowed in the same college boat at Oxford, he at stroke, I at seven; that the stripes on his jersey during three successive eights had made my eyes dizzy during those last hundred yards of spurt past the barges. We had bathed together in Sandford Lasher on summer afternoons. We had supper on Kennington Island; we had cut lectures and paddled up the Cher to Islip. And here he was at Wadi Halfa, herding with that troupe, an outcast, sunk to such a depth of ill-fortune that he must come to that squalid little town and play the zither vilely before a crowd of natives and a few Greek clerks for his night's lodging and the price of a meal.'

'No,' Ethne interrupted suddenly. 'It was not for that reason that he went to Wadi Halfa.'

'Why, then?' asked Durrance.

'I cannot think. But he was not in any need of money. His father had continued his allowance, and he had accepted it.'

'You are sure?'

'Quite sure. I heard it only to-day,' said Ethne.

It was a slip, but Ethne for once was off her guard that night. She did not even notice that she had made a slip. She was too engrossed in Durrance's story. Durrance himself, however, was not less preoccupied, and so the statement passed for the moment unobserved by either.

'So you never knew what brought Mr Feversham to Halfa?' she asked. 'Did you not ask him? Why didn't you? Why?'

She was disappointed, and the bitterness of her disappointment gave passion to her cry. Here was the last news of Harry Feversham, and it was brought to her incomplete, like the half-sheet of a letter. The omission might never be repaired.

'I was a fool,' said Durrance. There was almost as much regret in his voice now as there had been in hers; and because of that regret he did not remark the passion with which she had spoken. 'I shall not easily forgive myself. He was my friend, you see. I had him by the arm, and I let him go. I was a fool.' And he knocked upon his forehead with his fist.

'He tried Arabic,' Durrance resumed, 'pleading that he and his companions were just poor peaceable people, that if I had given him too much money, I should take it back, and all the while he dragged away from me. But I held him fast. I said, "Harry Feversham, that won't do," and upon that he gave in and spoke in English, whispering it. "Let me go, Jack, let me go." There was the crowd about us. It was evident that Harry had some reason for secrecy; it might have been shame, for all I knew, shame at his downfall. I said, "Come up to my quarters in Halfa as soon as you are free," and I let him go. All that night I waited for him on the verandah, but he did not come. In the morning I had to start across the desert. I almost spoke of him to a friend who came to see me start, to Calder, in fact – you know of him – the man who sent you the telegram,' said Durrance, with a laugh.

'Yes, I remember,' Ethne answered.

It was the second slip she made that night. The receipt of Calder's telegram was just one of the things which Durrance was not to know. But again she was unaware that she had made a slip at all. She did not even consider how Durrance had come to know or guess that the telegram had ever been despatched.

'At the very last moment,' Durrance resumed, 'when my camel had risen from the ground, I stooped down to speak to him, to tell him to see to Feversham. But I did not. You see, I knew nothing about his allowance. I merely thought that he had fallen rather low. It did not seem fair to him that another should know of it. So I rode on and kept silence.'

Ethne nodded her head. She could not but approve, however poignant her regret for the lost news.

'So you never saw Mr Feversham again?'

'I was away nine weeks. I came back blind,' he answered simply, and the very simplicity of his words went to Ethne's heart. He was apologising for his blindness, which had hindered him from inquiring. She began to wake to the comprehension that it was really Durrance who was speaking to her, but he continued to speak, and what he said drove her quite out of all caution.

'I went at once to Cairo, and Calder came with me. There I told him of Harry Feversham, and how I had seen him at Tewfikieh. I asked Calder when he got back to Halfa to make inquiries, to find and help Harry Feversham if he could. I asked him, too, to let me know the result. I received a letter from Calder a week ago, and I am troubled by it, very much troubled.'

'What did he say?' Ethne asked apprehensively, and she turned in her chair away from the moonlight towards the shadows of the room and Durrance. She bent forward to see his face, but the darkness hid it. A sudden fear struck through her and chilled her blood, but out of the darkness Durrance spoke.

'That the two women and the old Greek had gone back north-wards on a steamer to Assouan.'

'Mr Feversham remained at Wadi Halfa, then? That is so, isn't it?' she said eagerly.

'No,' Durrance replied. 'Harry Feversham did not remain. He slipped past Halfa the day after I started towards the east.

He went out in the morning, and to the south.'

'Into the desert?'

'Yes, but the desert to the south, the enemy's country. He went just as I saw him, carrying his zither. He was seen. There can be no doubt.'

Ethne was quite silent for a little while. Then she asked –

'You have that letter with you?'

'Yes.'

'I should like to read it.'

She rose from her chair and walked across to Durrance. He took the letter from his pocket and gave it to her, and she carried it over to the window. The moonlight was strong. Ethne stood close by the window, with a hand pressed upon her heart, and read it through once and again. The letter was explicit; the Greek who owned the café at which the troupe had performed admitted that Joseppi, under which name he knew Feversham, had wandered south carrying a water-skin and a store of dates, though why, he either did not know or would not tell. Ethne had a question to ask, but it was some time before she could trust her lips to utter it distinctly and without faltering.

'What will happen to him?'

'At the best, capture; at the worst death. Death by starvation, or thirst, or at the hands of the Dervishes. But there is just a hope it might be only capture and imprisonment. You see he was white. If caught, his captors might think him a spy; they would be sure he had knowledge of our plans and our strength. I think that they would most likely send him to Omdurman. I have written to Calder. Spies go out and in from Wadi Halfa. We often hear of things which happen in Omdurman. If Feversham is taken there, sooner or later I shall know. But he must have gone mad. It is the only explanation.'

Ethne had another, and she knew hers to be the right one. She was off her guard, and she spoke it aloud to Durrance.

'Colonel Trench,' said she, 'is a prisoner at Omdurman.'

'Oh yes,' answered Durrance. 'Feversham will not be quite alone. There is some comfort in that, and perhaps something may be done. When I hear from Calder I will tell you. Perhaps something may be done.'

It was evident that Durrance had misconstrued her remark.

He at all events was still in the dark as to the motive which had taken Feversham southwards beyond the Egyptian patrols. And he must remain in the dark. For Ethne did not even now slacken in her determination still to pretend to have forgotten. She stood at the window with the letter clenched in her hand. She must utter no cry, she must not swoon; she must keep very still and quiet, and speak when needed with a quiet voice, even though she knew that Harry Feversham had gone southwards to join Colonel Trench at Omdurman. But so much was beyond her strength. For as Colonel Durrance began to speak again, the desire to escape, to be alone with this terrible news, became irresistible. The cool quietude of the garden, the dark shadows of the trees, called to her.

'Perhaps you will wonder,' said Durrance, 'why I have told you to-night what I have up till now kept to myself. I did not dare to tell it you before. I want to explain why.'

Ethne did not notice the exultation in his voice, she did not consider what his explanation might be, she only felt that she could not now endure to listen to it. The mere sound of a human voice had become an unendurable thing. She hardly knew, indeed, that Durrance was speaking; she was only aware that a voice spoke, and that the voice must stop. She was close by the window, a single silent step, and she was across the sill and free. Durrance continued to speak out of the darkness, engrossed in what he said, and Ethne did not listen to a word. She gathered her skirts carefully, so that they should not rustle, and stepped from the window. This was the third slip which she made upon that eventful night.

Chapter Nineteen

MRS ADAIR INTERVENES

Ethne had thought to escape quite unobserved. But Mrs Adair was sitting upon the terrace in the shadow of the house, and not very far from the open window of the drawing-room. She saw

Ethne lightly cross the terrace and run down the steps into the garden, and she wondered at the precipitancy of her movements. Ethne seemed to be taking flight, and in a sort of desperation. The incident was singular to Mrs Adair. She had seen Ethne turn out the lamp, and the swift change of the room from light to dark, with its suggestion of secrecy and of the private talk of lovers, had been a torture to her. But she had not fled from the torture. She had sat listening, and the music as it floated out upon the garden, with its thrill of happiness, its accent of yearning, and the low, hushed conversation which followed upon its cessation in that darkened room, had struck upon a chord of imagination in her and had kindled her jealousy into a scorching flame. Then suddenly Ethne had taken flight. The possibility of a quarrel Mrs Adair dismissed from her thoughts, for she knew very well that Ethne was not of the kind which quarrels.

But something still more singular occurred. Durrance continued to speak in that room from which Ethne had escaped. The sound of his voice reached Mrs Adair's ears, though she could not distinguish the words. It was clear to her that he believed Ethne to be still with him. Mrs Adair rose from her seat, and, walking silently upon the tips of her toes, came close to the open window. She heard Durrance laugh light-heartedly, and she listened to the words he spoke. She could hear them plainly now, though she could not see the man who spoke them. He sat in the shadows.

'I began to find out,' he was saying, 'even on that first afternoon at Hill Street two months ago, that there was only friendship on your side. My blindness helped me. With your face and your eyes in view I should have believed without question just what you wished me to believe. But you had no longer those defences. I, on my side, had grown quicker. I began, in a word, to see. For the first time in my life I began to see.'

Mrs Adair did not move. Durrance, upon his side, appeared to expect no answer or acknowledgment. He spoke with the voice of enjoyment which a man uses recounting difficulties which have ceased to hamper him, perplexities which have been long since unravelled. He was completely absorbed in saying clearly what was in his mind.

'I should have definitely broken off our engagement, I suppose, at once; for I still believed, and as firmly as ever, that
there must be more than friendship on both sides. But I had
grown selfish. I warned you, Ethne, selfishness was the blind
man's particular fault. I waited and deferred the time of
marriage. I made excuses. I led you to believe that there was a
chance of recovery when I knew there was none. For I hoped,
as a man will, that with time your friendship might grow into
more than friendship. So long as there was a chance of that I –
Ethne, I could not let you go. So I listened for some new softness in your voice, some new buoyancy in your laughter, some
new deep thrill of the heart in the music which you played,
longing for it – how much! Well, to-night I have burnt my
boats. I have admitted to you that I knew friendship limited
your thoughts of me. I have owned to you that there is no
hope my sight will be restored. I have even dared to-night to
tell you what I have kept secret for so long – my meeting with
Harry Feversham and the peril he has run. And why? Because
for the first time I have heard to-night just those signs for which
I waited. The new softness, the new pride in your voice, the
buoyancy in your laughter, they have been audible to me all
this evening. The restraint and the tension were gone from your
manner. And when you played it was as though someone with
just your skill and knowledge played, but someone who let her
heart speak resonantly through the music as until to-night you
have never done. Ethne! Ethne!'

But at that moment Ethne was in the little enclosed garden
whither she had led Captain Willoughby that morning. Here
she was private; Dermod's collie dog had followed her; she
had reached the solitude and the silence which had become
necessities to her. A few more words from Durrance, and her
prudence would have broken beneath the strain. All that pretence of affection which during these last months she had so
sedulously built up about him like a wall, and which he was
never to look over, would have been struck down and levelled
to the ground. Durrance, indeed, had already looked over the
wall – was looking over it with amazed eyes at this instant; but
that Ethne did not know. The moonlight slept in silver upon
the creek, the tall trees stood dreaming to the stars; the lapping

of the tide against the bank was no louder than the music of a river. She sat down upon the bench and strove to gather some of the quietude of that summer night into her heart, and to learn from the growing things of nature about her something of their patience and their extraordinary perseverance.

But the occurrences of the day had overtaxed her, and she could not. Only this morning, and in this very garden, the good news had come, and she had regained Harry Feversham. For in that way she thought of Willoughby's message. This morning she had regained him, and this evening the bad news had come and she had lost him – and most likely right to the very end of mortal life. Harry Feversham meant to pay for his fault to the uttermost scruple, and Ethne cried out against his thoroughness, which he had learned from no other than herself. 'Surely,' she thought, 'he might have been content. In redeeming his honour in the eyes of one of the three he has done enough – he has redeemed it in the eyes of all.'

But he had gone south to join Colonel Trench in Omdurman. Of that squalid and shadowless town, of its hideous barbarities, of the horrors of its prison-house, Ethne knew nothing at all. But Captain Willoughby had hinted enough to fill her imagination with terrors. He had offered to explain to her what captivity in Omdurman implied, and she wrung her hands as she remembered that she had refused to listen. What cruelties might not be practised? Even now, at that very hour perhaps, on this night of summer — But she dared not let her thoughts wander that way . . .

The lapping of the tide against the banks was like the music of a river. It brought to Ethne's mind one particular river which had sung and babbled in her ears when, five years ago, she had watched out another summer night till dawn. Never had she so hungered for her own country and the companionship of its brown hills and streams. No, not even this afternoon, when she had sat at her window and watched the lights change upon the creek. Donegal had a sanctity for her; it seemed when she dwelled in it to set her, in a way, apart from and above earthly taints; and as her heart went out in a great longing towards it now, a sudden, fierce loathing for the concealments, the shifts, and manœuvres which she had practised, and still must practise, sprang up within her. A great weariness came upon her too. But she did not change from her fixed resolve. Two lives were not to be spoilt because she lived in the world. To-morrow she would gather up her strength and begin again. For Durrance must never know that there was another whom she placed before him in her thoughts.

Meanwhile, however, Durrance within the drawing-room brought his confession to an end.

'So, you see,' he said, 'I could not speak of Harry Feversham until to-night; for I was afraid that what I had to tell you would hurt you very much. I was afraid that you still remembered him, in spite of those five years. I knew, of course, that you were my friend. But I doubted whether in your heart you were not more than that to him. To-night, however, I could tell you without fear.'

Now, at all events, he expected an answer. Mrs Adair, still standing by the window, heard him move in the shadows.

'Ethne!' he said, with some surprise in his voice. And since again no answer came, he rose and walked towards the chair in which Ethne had sat. Mrs Adair could see him now. His hands felt for and grasped the back of the chair. He bent over it, as though he thought Ethne was leaning forward with her hands upon her knees.

'Ethne!' he said again; and there was in this iteration of her name more trouble and doubt than surprise. It seemed to Mrs Adair that he dreaded to find her silently weeping. He was beginning to speculate whether, after all, he had been right in his inference from Ethne's recapture of her youth to-night – whether the shadow of Feversham did not, after all, fall between them. He leaned further forward, feeling with his hand, and suddenly a string of Ethne's violin twanged loud. She had left it lying on the chair, and his fingers had touched it.

Durrance drew himself up straight and stood quite motionless and silent, like a man who has suffered a shock and is bewildered. He passed his hand across his forehead once or twice, and then, without calling upon Ethne again, he advanced to the open window.

Mrs Adair did not move, and she held her breath. There was just the width of the sill between them. The moonlight

161

struck full upon Durrance, and she saw a comprehension gradually dawn in his face that someone was standing close to him.

'Ethne,' he said a third time. He stretched out a hand timidly and touched her dress.

'It is not Ethne,' he cried with a start.

'No, it is not Ethne,' answered Mrs Adair quietly. Durrance drew back a step from the window, and for a little while was silent.

'Where has she gone?' he asked at length.

'Into the garden. She ran across the terrace and down the steps very quickly and silently. I saw her from my chair. Then I heard you speaking alone.'

'Can you see her now in the garden?'

'No. She went across the lawn towards the trees and their great shadows. There is only the moonlight in the garden now.'

Durrance stepped across the window-sill and stood by the side of Mrs Adair. The last slip which Ethne had made betrayed her inevitably to the man who had grown quick. There could be only one reason for her sudden, unexplained, and secret flight. He had told her that Feversham had wandered south from Wadi Halfa into the savage country, he had spoken his fears as to Feversham's fate without reserve, thinking that she had forgotten him, and indeed rather inclined to blame her for the callous indifference with which she received the news. The callousness was a mere mask, and she had fled because she no longer had the strength to hold it up before her face. His first suspicions had been right. Feversham still stood between Ethne and himself, and held them at arm's length.

'She ran as though she was in great trouble and hardly knew what she was doing,' Mrs Adair continued. 'Did you cause that trouble?'

'Yes.'

'I thought so, from what I heard you say.'

Mrs Adair wanted to hurt, and, in spite of Durrance's impenetrable face, she felt that she had succeeded. It was a small sort of compensation for the weeks of mortification which she had endured. There is something which might be said for Mrs Adair, extenuations might be pleaded even if no defence was

made. For she, like Ethne, was overtaxed that night. That calm
pale face of hers hid the quick passions of the south, and she
had been racked by them to the limits of endurance. There had
been something grotesque, something rather horrible in that
outbreak and confession by Durrance after Ethne had fled from
the room. He was speaking out his heart to an empty chair. She
herself had stood outside the window with a bitter longing that
he had spoken so to her and a bitter knowledge that he never
would. She was sunk deep in humiliation. The irony of the
position tortured her; it was like a jest of grim selfish gods
played off upon mortals to their hurt. And at the bottom of all
her thoughts rankled that memory of the extinguished lamp
and the low hushed voices speaking one to the other in darkness. Therefore she spoke to give pain, and was glad that
she gave it, even though it was to the man whom she
coveted.

'There's one thing which I don't understand,' said Durrance.
'I mean the change which we both noticed in Ethne to-night. I
mistook the cause of it. I was a fool. But there must have been
a cause. The gift of laughter had been restored to her. She
became just what she was five years ago.'

'Exactly,' Mrs Adair answered. 'Just what she was before
Mr Feversham disappeared from Ramelton. You are so quick,
Colonel Durrance. Ethne had good news of Mr Feversham
this morning.'

Durrance turned quickly towards her, and Mrs Adair felt a
keen pleasure at his abrupt movement. She had provoked the
display of some emotion, and the display of any emotion was
preferable to his composure.

'Are you quite sure?' he asked.

'As sure as that you gave her bad news to-night,' she replied.

But Durrance did not need the answer. Ethne had made another slip that evening, and, though unnoticed at the time, it
came back to Durrance's memory now. She had declared that
Feversham still drew an allowance from his father. 'I heard
it only to-day,' she had said.

'Yes, Ethne heard news of Feversham to-day,' he said slowly.
'Did she make a mistake five years ago? There was some wrong
thing Harry Feversham was supposed to have done. But was

163

there really more misunderstanding than wrong? Did she mis-judge him? Has she to-day learnt that she misjudged him?'

'I will tell you what I know. It is not very much. But I think it is fair that you should know it.'

'Wait a moment, please, Mrs Adair,' said Durrance sharply. He had put his questions rather to himself than to his com-panion, and he was not sure that he wished her to answer them. He walked abruptly away from her and leaned upon the balus-trade with his face towards the garden.

It seemed to him rather treacherous to allow Mrs Adair to disclose what Ethne herself evidently intended to conceal. But he knew why Ethne wished to conceal it. She wished him never to suspect that she retained any love for Harry Feversham. On the other hand, however, he did not falter from his own belief. Marriage between a man crippled like himself and a woman active and vigorous like Ethne could never be right unless both brought more than friendship. Here disloyalty seemed the truest loyalty of all. He turned back to Mrs Adair.

'Tell me what you know, Mrs Adair. Something might be done perhaps for Feversham. From Assouan or Suakin some-thing might be done. This news – this good news came, I sup-pose, this afternoon when I was at home.'

'No, this morning, when you were here. It was brought by a Captain Willoughby, who was once an officer in Mr Fever-sham's regiment.'

'He is now Deputy-Governor of Suakin,' said Durrance. 'I know the man. For three years we were together in that town. And he brought the news of Feversham? Well?'

'He sailed down from Kingsbridge. You and Ethne were walking across the lawn when he landed from the creek. Ethne left you and went forward to meet him. I saw them meet, be-cause I happened to be looking out of this window at the moment.'

'Yes, Ethne went forward. There was a stranger whom she did not know. I remember.'

'They spoke for a few moments, and then Ethne led him to-wards the trees at once, without looking back. They went to-gether into the little enclosed garden on the bank;' and Dur-rance started as she spoke. 'Yes, you followed them,' continued Mrs Adair curiously. She had been puzzled as to how Durrance had failed to find them there.

'They were there then,' he said slowly, 'on that seat, in the enclosure, all the while.'

Mrs Adair waited for a more definite explanation of the mystery, but she got none.

'Well?' he asked.

'They stayed there for a long while. You had gone home across the fields before they came outside into the open. I was in the garden, and indeed happened to be actually upon the bank.'

'So you saw Captain Willoughby? Perhaps you spoke to him?'

'Yes. Ethne introduced him; but she would not let him stay. She hurried him into his boat and back to Kingsbridge at once.'

'Then how do you know Captain Willoughby brought good news of Harry Feversham?'

'Ethne told me that they had been talking of him. His manner and her laugh showed me no less clearly that the news was good.'

'Yes,' said Durrance; and he nodded his head in assent. Captain Willoughby's tidings had given to Ethne that new pride and buoyancy which he had so readily taken to himself. Signs of the necessary something more than friendship – so he had accounted them; and he was right so far. But it was not he who had inspired them. His very penetration and insight had led him astray. He was silent for a few minutes, and Mrs Adair searched his face in the moonlight for some evidence that he resented Ethne's secrecy. But she searched in vain.

'And that is all?' said Durrance.

'Not quite. Captain Willoughby brought a token from Mr Feversham. Ethne carried it back to the house in her hand. Her eyes were upon it all the way; her lips smiled at it. I do not think there is anything so precious to her in all the world.'

'A token?'

'A little white feather,' said Mrs Adair, 'all soiled and speckled with dust. Can you read the riddle of that feather?'

'Not yet,' Durrance replied. He walked once or twice along the terrace and back, lost in thought. Then he went into the house and fetched his cap from the hall. He came back to Mrs Adair.

'It was kind of you to have told me this,' he said. 'I want you to add to your kindness. When I was in the drawing-room alone, and you came to the window, how much did you hear? What were the first words?'

Mrs Adair's answer relieved him of a fear. Ethne had heard nothing whatever of his confession.

'Yes,' he said, 'she moved to the window to read a letter by the moonlight. She must have escaped from the room the moment she had read it. Consequently she did not hear that I had no longer any hope of recovering my sight, and that I merely used the pretence of a hope in order to delay our marriage. I am glad of that – very glad.' He shook hands with Mrs Adair, and said good night. 'You see,' he added absently, 'if I hear that Harry Feversham is in Omdurman something might perhaps be done – from Suakin or Assouan something might be done. Which way did Ethne go?'

'Over to the water.'

'She had her dog with her, I hope?'

'The dog followed her,' said Mrs Adair.

'I am glad,' said Durrance. He knew quite well what comfort the dog would be to Ethne in this bad hour; and perhaps he rather envied the dog. Mrs Adair wondered that at a moment of such distress to him he could still spare a thought for so small an alleviation of Ethne's trouble. She watched him cross the garden to the stile in the hedge. He walked steadily forward upon the path like a man who sees. There was nothing in his gait or bearing to reveal that the one thing left to him had that evening been taken away.

Chapter Twenty

EAST AND WEST

Durrance found his body-servant waiting up for him when he had come across the fields to his own house of Guessens.

'You can turn the lights out and go to bed,' said Durrance; and he walked through the hall into his study. The name hardly described the room, for it had always been more of a gun-room than a study.

He sat for some while in his chair, and then began to walk gently about the room in the dark. There were many cups and goblets scattered about the room which Durrance had won in his past days. He knew them each one by their shape and position, and he drew a kind of comfort from the feel of them. He took them up one by one and touched them and fondled them, wondering whether, now that he was blind, they were kept as clean and bright as they used to be. This one, a thin-stemmed goblet, he had won in a regimental steeplechase at Colchester; he could remember the day, with its clouds and grey sky, and the dull look of the ploughed fields between the hedges. That pewter which stood upon his writing table, and which had formed a convenient holder for his pens, he had acquired very long ago in his college 'fours' when he was a freshman at Oxford. The hoof of a favourite horse mounted in silver stood as an ornament upon the mantelpiece. His trophies made the room a gigantic diary. He fingered his records of good days gone by, and came at last to his guns and rifles.

He took them down from their racks. They were to him much what Ethne's violin was to her, and had stories for his ear alone. He sat with a Remington across his knees and lived over again one long hot day in the hills to the west of Berenice, during which he had stalked a lion across stony open country and killed him at three hundred yards just before sunset. Another talked to him, too, of his first ibex, shot in the Khor Baraka, and of antelope stalked among the mountains northwards of Suakin. There was a little Greener gun which he had used upon mid-winter nights in a boat upon this very creek of the Salcombe estuary. He had brought down his first mallard with that; and he lifted it and slid his left hand along the under side of the barrel, and felt the butt settle comfortably into the hollow of his shoulder. But his weapons began to talk over-loudly in his ears, even as Ethne's violin, in the earlier days after Harry Feversham was gone and she was left alone, had spoken with too penetrating a note to her. As he handled the locks and was aware that he could no longer see the sights, the sum of his losses was presented to him in a very definite and incontestable way.

He put his guns away, and was seized suddenly with a desire to disregard his blindness – to pretend that it was no hindrance, and to pretend so hard that it should prove not to be one. The desire grew and shook him like a passion, and carried him winged out of the countries of dim stars straight to the East. The smell of the East and its noises, and the domes of its mosques, the hot sun, the rabble in its streets, and the steel-blue sky overhead caught at him till he was plucked from his chair and set pacing restlessly about his room.

He dreamed himself to Port Said, and was marshalled in the long procession of steamers down the waterway of the Canal. The song of the Arabs coaling the ship was in his ears, and so loud that he could see them as they went at night-time up and down the planks between the barges and the ship's deck – an endless chain of naked figures monotonously chanting, and lurid in the red glare of the braziers. He travelled out of the Canal, past the red headlands of the Sinaitic peninsula, into the chills of the Gulf of Suez. He zigzagged down the Red Sea, while the Great Bear swung northwards low down in the sky above the rail of the quarterdeck, and the Southern Cross began to blaze in the south. He touched at Tor and at Yambo; he saw the tall white houses of Yeddah lift themselves out of the sea, and admired the dark, brine-withered woodwork of their carved casements; he walked through the dusk of its roofed bazaars with the joy of the homesick after long years come home; and from Yeddah he crossed between the narrowing coral reefs into the land-locked harbour of Suakin.

Westward from Suakin stretched the desert, with all that it meant to this man whom it had smitten and cast out – the quiet padding of camels' feet in sand, the great rock-cones rising sheer and abrupt as from a rippleless ocean, towards which you march all day and get no nearer; the gorgeous momentary blaze of sunset colours in the west, the rustle of the wind through the short twilight when the west is a pure pale green and the east the darkest blue, and the downward swoop of the planets out of nothing to the earth. The inheritor of the other places dreamed himself back into his inheritance as he tramped to and fro, forgetful of his blindness and parched with desire as with a fever, until unexpectedly he heard the blackbirds and the swallows bustling and piping in the garden, and knew that outside his windows the world was white with dawn.

He waked from his dream at the homely sound. There were to be no more journeys for him; affliction had caged him and soldered a chain about his leg. He felt his way by the balustrade up the stairs to his bed. He fell asleep as the sun rose.

But at Dongola, on the great curve of the Nile southwards of Wadi Halfa, the sun was already blazing, and its inhabitants were awake. There was sport prepared for them this morning under the few palm trees before the house of the Emir Wad El Nejoumi. A white prisoner, captured a week before close to the wells of El Agia on the great Arbain road by a party of Arabs, had been brought in during the night, and now awaited his fate at the Emir's hands. The news spread quick as a spark through the town; already a crowd of men and women and children flocked to this rare and pleasant spectacle. In front of the palm trees an open space stretched to the gateway of the Emir's house; behind them a slope of sand descended flat and bare to the river.

Harry Feversham was standing under the trees, guarded by four of the Ansar soldiery. His clothes had been stripped from him; he wore only a torn and ragged jibbeh upon his body and a twist of cotton on his head to shield him from the sun; his bare shoulders and arms were scorched and blistered. His ankles were fettered; his wrists were bound with a rope of palm fibre; an iron collar was locked about his neck, to which a chain was attached; and this chain one of the soldiers held. He stood and smiled at the mocking crowd about him, and seemed well pleased, like a lunatic.

That was the character which he had assumed. If he could sustain it, if he could baffle his captors so that they were at a loss whether he was a man really daft or an agent with promises of help and arms to the disaffected tribes of Kordofan, then there was a chance that they might fear to dispose of him themselves and send him forward to Omdurman. But it was hard work. Inside the house the Emir and his counsellors were debating his destiny; on the river bank, and within his view, a high gallows stood out black and most sinister against the yellow sand. Harry Feversham was very glad of the chain about his neck and the fetters on his legs. They helped him to betray no panic, by assuring him of its futility.

These hours of waiting, while the sun rose higher and higher, and no one came from the gateway, were the worst he had ever as yet endured. All through that fortnight in Berber a hope of escape had sustained him, and when the lantern shone upon him from behind in the ruined acres, what had to be done must be done quickly there was no time for fear or thought. Here there was time and too much of it.

He had time to anticipate and foresee. He felt his heart sinking till he was faint, just as in those distant days when he had heard the hounds scuffling and whimpering in a covert and he himself had sat shaking upon his horse. He glanced furtively towards the gallows, and foresaw the vultures perched upon his shoulders, fluttering about his eyes. But the man had grown during his years of probation. The fear of physical suffering was not uppermost in his mind, nor even the fear that he would walk unmanfully to the high gallows, but a greater dread – that if he died now, here, at Dongola, Ethne would never take back that fourth feather, and his strong hope of the 'afterwards' would never come to its fulfilment. He was very glad of the collar about his neck and the fetters on his legs. He summoned his wits together, and, standing there alone, without a companion to share his miseries, laughed and scraped and grimaced at his tormentors.

An old hag danced and gesticulated before him, singing the while a monotonous song. The gestures were pantomimic, and menaced him with abominable mutilations. The words described in simple and unexpurgated language the grievous death-agonies which immediately awaited him and the eternity of torture in hell which he would subsequently suffer. Feversham understood, and inwardly shuddered; but he only imitated her gestures, and nodded and mowed at her as though she was singing to him of Paradise. Others, taking their war trumpets, placed the mouths against the prisoner's ears and blew with all their might.

'Do you hear, Kaffir?' cried a child, dancing with delight before him. 'Do you hear our ombeyehs? Blow louder! Blow louder!'

But the prisoner only clapped his hands and cried out that the music was good.

Finally there came to to the group a tall warrior with a long heavy spear. A cry was raised at his approach and a space was cleared. He stood before the captive and poised his spear, swinging it backwards and forwards, to make his arm supple before he thrust, like a bowler before he delivers a ball at a cricket match. Feversham glanced wildly about him, and seeing no escape, suddenly flung out his breast to meet the blow. But the spear never reached him. For as the warrior lunged from the shoulder, one of the four guards jerked the neck chain violently from behind, and the prisoner was flung half throttled upon his back. Three times, and each time to a roar of delight, this pastime was repeated, and then a solder appeared in the gateway of Nejoumi's house.

'Bring the Kaffir in!' he cried, and, followed by the curses and threats of the crowd, the prisoner was dragged under the arch across a courtyard into a dark room.

For a few moments Feversham could see nothing. Then his eyes began to adapt themselves to the gloom, and he distinguished a tall bearded man, who sat upon an angareb (the native bedstead of the Soudan), and two others, who squatted beside him on the ground. The man on the angareb was the Emir.

'You are a spy of the Government from Wadi Halfa,' he said.

'No, I am a musician,' returned the prisoner, and he laughed happily like a man that has made a jest.

Nejoumi made a sign, and an instrument with many broken strings was handed to the captive. Feversham seated himself upon the ground, and with slow fumbling fingers, breathing hard as he bent over the zither, he began to elicit a wavering melody. It was the melody to which Durrance had listened in the street of Tewfikieh on the eve of his last journey into the desert; and which Ethne Eustace had played only the night before in the quiet drawing-room at Southpool. It was the only melody which Feversham knew. When he had done Nejoumi began again.

'You are a spy.'

'I have told you the truth,' answered Feversham stubbornly, and Nejoumi took a different tone. He called for food, and the raw liver of a camel covered with salt and red pepper was placed before Feversham. Seldom has a man had smaller inclination to eat, but Feversham ate none the less even of that unattractive dish, knowing well that reluctance would be construed as fear, and that the signs of fear might condemn him to death. And while he ate Nejoumi questioned him in the silkiest voice about the fortifications of Cairo and the strength of the garrison at Assouan, and the rumours of dissension between the Khedive and the Sirdar.

But to each question Feversham replied –

'How should a Greek know of these matters?'

Nejoumi rose from his angareb and roughly gave an order. The soldiers seized upon Feversham and dragged him out again into the sunlight. They poured water upon the palm-rope which bound his wrists, so that the thongs swelled and bit into his flesh.

'Speak, Kaffir. You carry promises to Kordofan.'

Feversham was silent. He clung doggedly to the plan over which he had so long and so carefully pondered. He could not improve upon it, he was sure, by any alteration suggested by fear at a moment when he could not think clearly. A rope was flung about his neck and he was pushed and driven beneath the gallows.

'Speak, Kaffir,' said Nejoumi, 'so shall you escape death.'

Feversham smiled and grimaced, and shook his head loosely from side to side. It was astonishing to him that he could do it, that he did not fall down upon his knees and beg for mercy. It was still more astonishing to him that he felt no temptation so to demean himself. He wondered whether the oft-repeated story was true, that criminals in English prisons went quietly and with dignity to the scaffold because they had been drugged. For without drugs he seemed to be behaving with no less dignity himself. His heart was beating very fast, but it was with a sort of excitement. He did not even think of Ethne at that moment; and certainly the great dread that his strong hope would never be fulfilled did not trouble him at all. He had his allotted part to play, and he just played it; and that was all.

Nejoumi looked at him sourly for a moment. He turned to the men who stood ready to draw away from Feversham the angareb on which he was placed.

'To-morrow,' said he, 'the Kaffir shall go to Omdurman.'

Feversham began to feel then that the rope of palm-fibre tortured his wrists.

Chapter Twenty-one

ETHNE MAKES ANOTHER SLIP

Mrs Adair speculated with some uneasiness upon the consequences of the disclosures which she had made to Durrance. She was in doubt as to the course which he would take. It seemed possible that he might frankly tell Ethne of the mistake which he had made. He might admit that he had discovered the unreality of her affection for him, and the reality of her love for Feversham, and if he made that admission, however carefully he tried to conceal her share in his discovery, he would hardly succeed. She would have to face Ethne, and she dreaded the moment when her companion's frank eyes would rest quietly upon hers, and her lips demand an explanation. It was consequently a relief to her at first that no outward change was visible in the relations of Ethne and Durrance. They met and spoke as though that day on which Willoughby had landed at the garden, and the evening when Ethne had played the Melusine overture upon the violin, had been blotted from their experience. Mrs Adair was relieved at first, but when the sense of personal danger passed from her, and she saw that her interference had been apparently without effect, she began to be puzzled. A little while, and she was both angry and disappointed.

Durrance, indeed, quickly made up his mind. Ethne wished him not to know, it was some consolation to her in her distress to believe that she had brought happiness to this one man whose friend she genuinely was. And of that consolation Durrance was aware. He saw no reason to destroy it – for the present. He must know certainly whether a misunderstanding or an irreparable breach separated Ethne from Feversham before he took the steps he had in mind. He must have sure knowledge too of Harry Feversham's fate. Therefore he pretended to know nothing; he abandoned even his habit of attention and scrutiny, since for these there was no longer any need; he forced himself to a display of contentment; he made light of his misfortune, and professed to find in Ethne's company more than its compensation.

'You see,' he said to her, 'one can get used to blindness and take it as the natural thing. But one does not get used to you, Ethne. Each time one meets you, one discovers something new and fresh to delight one. Besides there is always the possibility of a cure.'

He had his reward, for Ethne understood that he had laid aside his suspicions, and she was able to set off his indefatigable cheerfulness against her own misery. And her misery was great. If for one day she had recaptured the lightness of heart which had been hers before the three white feathers came to Ramelton, she had now recaptured simething of the grief which followed upon their coming. A difference there was, of course. Her pride was restored, and she had a faint hope born of Durrance's words that Harry after all might perhaps be rescued. But she knew again the long and sleepless nights and the dull hot misery of the head as she waited for the grey of the morning. For she could no longer pretend to herself that she looked upon Harry Feversham as a friend who was dead. He was living, and in what straits she dreaded to think, and yet thirsted to know. At rare times, indeed, her impatience got the better of her will.

'I suppose that escape is possible from Omdurman,' she said one day, constraining her voice to an accent of indifference.

'Possible? Yes, I think so,' Durrance answered cheerfully. 'Of course it is difficult and would in any case take time.

Attempts, for instance, have been made to get Trench out and others, but the attempts have not yet succeeded. The difficulty is the go-between.'

Ethne looked quickly at Durrance.

'The go-between?' she asked, and then she said: 'I think I begin to understand,' and pulled herself up abruptly. 'You mean the Arab who can come and go between Omdurman and the Egyptian frontier?'

'Yes. He is usually some Dervish pedlar or merchant trading with the tribes of the Soudan who slips into Wadi Halfa or Assouan or Suakin and undertakes the work. Of course his risk is great. He would have short shift in Omdurman if his business were detected. So it is not to be wondered that he shirks the danger at the last moment. As often as not, too, he is a rogue. You make your arrangements with him in Egypt, and hand him over the necessary money. In six months or a year he comes back alone, with a story of excuses. It was summer and the season unfavourable for an escape. Or the prisoners were more strictly guarded. Or he himself was suspected. And he needs more money. His tale may be true, and you give him more money and he comes back again, and again he comes back alone.'

Ethne nodded her head.

'Exactly.'

Durrance had unconsciously explained to her a point which till now she had not understood. She was quite sure that Harry Feversham aimed in some way at bringing help to Colonel Trench, but in what way his own capture was to serve that aim she could not determine. Now she understood; he was to be his own go-between, and her hopes drew strength from this piece of new knowledge. For it was likely that he had laid his plans with care. He would be very anxious that the second feather should come back to her. And if he could fetch Trench safely out of Omdurman, he would not himself remain behind.

Ethne was silent for a little while. They were sitting on the terrace, and the sunset was red upon the water of the creek.

'Life would not be easy, I suppose, in the prison of Omdurman,' she said, and again she forced herself to indifference.

'Easy!' exclaimed Durrance; 'no, it would not be easy. A

175

hovel crowded with Arabs, without light or air, and the roof perhaps two feet above your head, into which you were locked up from sundown to morning; very likely the prisoners would have to stand all night in that foul den, so closely packed would they be. Imagine it even here in England on an evening like this! Think what it would be on an August night in the Soudan! Especially if you had memories, say, of a place like this, to make the torture worse.'

Ethne looked out across that cool garden. At this very moment Harry Feversham might be struggling for breath in that dark and noisesome hovel, dry of throat and fevered with the heat, with a vision before his eyes of the grass slopes of Ramelton and with the music of the Lennon River liquid in his ears.

'One would pray for death,' said Ethne slowly, 'unless — ' She was on the point of adding 'unless one went there deliberately with a fixed thing to do,' but she cut the sentence short. Durrance carried it on –

'Unless there was a chance of escape,' he said. 'And there is a chance – if Feversham is in Omdurman.'

He was afraid that he had allowed himself to say too much about the horrors of the prison in Omdurman, and he added: 'Of course, what I have described to you is mere hearsay, and not to be trusted. We have no knowledge. Prisoners may not have such bad times as we think,' and thereupon he let the subject drop. Nor did Ethne mention it again. It occurred to her at times to wonder in what way Durrance had understood her abrupt disappearance from the drawing-room on the night when he had told her of his meeting with Harry Feversham. But he never referred to it himself, and she thought it wise to imitate his example. The noticeable change in his manner, the absence of that caution which had so distressed her, allayed her fears. It seemed that he found for himself some perfectly simple and natural explanation. At times too, she asked herself why Durrance had told her of that meeting in Wadi Halfa, and of Feversham's subsequent departure to the south. But for that she found an explanation – a strange explanation, perhaps, but it was simple enough and satisfactory to her. She believed that the news was a message of which Durrance was only the instrument. It was meant for her ears, and for her comprehension alone, and Durrance was bound to convey it to her by the will of a power above him. His real reason she had not stayed to hear.

During the month of September, then, they kept up the pretence. Every morning when Durrance was in Devonshire he would come across the fields to Ethne at The Pool, and Mrs Adair, watching them as they talked and laughed without a shadow of embarrassment or estrangement, grew more angry, and found it more difficult to hold her peace and let the pretence go on. It was a month of strain and tension to all three, and not one of them but experienced a great relief when Durrance visited his oculist in London. And those visits increased in number, and lengthened in duration. Even Ethne was grateful for them. She could throw off the mask for a little while; she had an opportunity to be tired; she had solitude wherein to gain strength to resume her high spirits upon Durrance's return. There came hours when despair seized hold of her. 'Shall I be able to keep up the pretence when we are married, when we are always together?' she asked herself. But she thrust the question back unanswered; she dared not look forward lest even now her strength should fail her.

After the third visit Durrance said to her –

'Do you remember that I once mentioned a famous oculist at Wiesbaden? It seems advisable that I should go to him.'

'You are recommended to go?'

'Yes, and to go alone.'

Ethne looked up at him with a shrewd, quick glance.

'You think that I should be dull at Wiesbaden,' she said. 'There is no fear of that. I can rout out some relative to go with me.'

'No. It is on my own account,' answered Durrance. 'I shall perhaps have to go into a home. It is better to be quite quiet, and to see no one for a time.'

'You are sure?' Ethne asked. 'It would hurt me if I thought you proposed this plan because you felt I would be happier at Glenalla.'

'No, that is not the reason,' Durrance answered, and he answered quite truthfully. He felt it necessary for both of them that they should separate. He, no less than Ethne, suffered under the tyranny of perpetual simulation. It was only because he knew how much store she set upon carrying out her resolve that two lives should not be spoilt because of her, that he was able to hinder himself from crying out that he knew the truth.

'I am returning to London next week,' he added, 'and when I come back I shall be in a position to tell you whether I am to go to Wiesbaden or not.'

Durrance had reason to be glad that he had mentioned his plan before the arrival of Calder's telegram from Wadi Halfa. Ethne was unable to connect his departure from her with the receipt of any news about Feversham. The telegram came one afternoon, and Durrance took it across to The Pool in the evening and showed it to Ethne. There were only four words to the telegram –

'Feversham imprisoned at Omdurman.'

Durrance, with one of the new instincts of delicacy, which had been born in him lately by reason of his sufferings and the habit of thought, had moved away from Ethne's side as soon as he had given it to her, and had joined Mrs Adair, who was reading a book in the drawing-room. He had folded up the telegram, besides, so that by the time Ethne had unfolded it and saw the words, she was alone upon the terrace. She remembered what Durrance had said to her about the prison, and her imagination enlarged upon his words. The quiet of a September evening was upon the fields, a light mist rose from the creek and crept over the garden bank across the lawn. Already the prison doors were shut in that hot country at the junction of the Niles. 'He is to pay for his fault ten times over, then,' she said in revolt against the disproportion. 'And the fault was his father's, and mine too, more than his own. For neither of us understood.'

She blamed herself for the gift of that fourth feather. She leaned upon the stone balustrade with her eyes shut, wondering whether Harry would outlive this night, whether he was still alive to outlive it. The very coolness of the stones on which her hands pressed became the bitterest of reproaches.

'Something can now be done.'

Durrance was coming from the window of the drawing-room and spoke as he came to warn her of his approach. 'He was and is my friend, I cannot leave him there. I shall write to-night to Calder. Money will not be spared. He is my friend, Ethne. You will see. From Suakin or from Assouan something will be done.'

He put all the help to be offered to the credit of his own friendship. Ethne was not to believe that he imagined she had any further interest in Harry Feversham.

She turned to him suddenly, almost interrupted him.

'Major Castleton is dead?' she said.

'Castleton?' he exclaimed. 'There was a Castleton in Feversham's regiment. Is that the man?'

'Yes. He is dead.'

'He was killed at Tamai.'

'You are sure – quite sure?'

'He was within the square of the Second Brigade on the edge of the great gully when Osman Digna's men sprang out of the earth and broke through. I was in that square too. I saw Castleton killed.'

'I am glad,' said Ethne.

She spoke quite simply and distinctly. The first feather had been brought back by Captain Willoughby. It was just possible that Colonel Trench might bring back the second. Harry Feversham had succeeded once under great difficulties in the face of great peril. The peril was greater now, the difficulties more arduous to overcome; that she clearly understood. But she took the one success as an augury that another might follow it. Feversham would have laid his plans with care; he had money wherewith to carry them out; and besides she was a woman of strong faith. But she was relieved to know that the sender of the third feather could never be approached. Moreover she hated him, and there was an end of the matter.

Durrance was startled. He was a soldier of a type not so rare as the makers of war stories wish their readers to believe. Hector of Troy was his ancestor; he was neither hysterical in his language nor vindictive in his acts, he was not an elderly schoolboy with a taste for loud talk, but a quiet man who did his work without noise; who could be stern when occasion needed and of an unflinching severity; but whose nature was gentle and compassionate. And this barbaric utterance of Ethne Eustace he did not understand.

'You disliked Major Castleton so much?' he exclaimed.

'I never knew him.'

'Yet you are glad that he is dead?'

'I am quite glad,' said Ethne stubbornly.

She made another slip when she spoke thus of Major Castleton, and Durrance did not pass it by unnoticed. He remembered it and thought it over in his gun-room at Guessens. It added something to the explanation which he was building up of Harry Feversham's disgrace and disappearance. The story was gradually becoming clear to his sharpened wits. Captain Willoughby's visit and the token he had brought had given him the clue. A white feather could mean nothing but an accusation of cowardice. Durrance could not remember that he had ever detected any signs of cowardice in Harry Feversham, and the charge startled him perpetually into incredulity.

But the fact remained. Something had happened on the night of the ball at Lennon House, and from that date Harry had been an outcast. Suppose that a white feather had been forwarded to Lennon House, and had been opened in Ethne's presence? Or more than one white feather? Ethne had come back from her long talk with Willoughby holding that white feather as though there was nothing so precious in all the world.

So much Mrs Adair had told him.

It followed then that the cowardice was atoned, or in one particular atoned. Ethne's recapture of her youth pointed inevitably to that conclusion. She treasured the feather because it was no longer a symbol of cowardice but a symbol of cowardice atoned.

But Harry Feversham had not returned, he still slunk in the world's by-ways. Willoughby, then, was not the only man who had brought the accusation, there were others – two others. One of the two Durrance had long since identified. When Durrance had suggested that Harry might be taken to Omdurman, Ethne had at once replied: 'Colonel Trench is in Omdurman.' She needed no explanation of Harry's disappearance from Wadi Halfa into the southern Soudan. It was deliberate, he had gone out to be captured, to be taken to Omdurman. Moreover,

Ethne had spoken of the untrustworthiness of the go-between, and there again had helped Durrance in his conjectures. There was some obligation upon Feversham to come to Trench's help. Suppose that Feversham had laid his plans of rescue and had ventured out into the desert that he might be his own go-between. It followed that a second feather had been sent to Ramelton, and that Trench had sent it.

To-night Durrance was able to join Major Castleton to Trench and Willoughby. Ethne's satisfaction at the death of a man whom she did not know could mean but the one thing. There would be the same obligation resting upon Feversham with regard to Major Castleton if he lived. It seemed likely that a third feather had come to Lennon House, and that Major Castleton had sent it.

Durrance pondered over the solution of the problem, and more and more he found it plausible. There was one man who could have told him the truth and who had refused to tell it, who would no doubt still refuse to tell it. But that one man's help Durrance intended to enlist, and to this end he must come with the story pat upon his lips and no request for information.

'Yes,' he said, 'I think that after my next visit to London I can pay a visit to Lieutenant Sutch.'

Chapter Twenty-two

DURRANCE LETS HIS CIGAR GO OUT

Captain Willoughby was known at his club for a bore. He was a determined raconteur of pointless stories about people with whom not one of his audience was acquainted. And there was no deterring him, for he did not listen, he only talked. He took the most savage snub with a vacant and amicable face; and, wrapped in his own dull thoughts, he continued his copious monologue. In the smoking-room or at the supper-table he crushed conversation flat as a steam-roller crushes a road. He was quite irresistible. Trite anecdotes were sandwiched between aphorisms of the copybook, and whether anecdote or aphorism, all was delivered with the air of a man surprised by his own profundity. If you waited long enough you had no longer the will power to run away, you sat caught in a web of sheer dullness. Only those, however, who did not know him waited long enough, the rest of his fellow-members at his appearance straightway rose and fled.

It happened, therefore, that within half an hour of his entrance to his club he usually had one large corner of the room entirely to himself, and that particular corner up to the moment of his entrance had been the most frequented. For he made it a rule to choose the largest group as his audience. He was sitting in this solitary state one afternoon early in October when the waiter approached him and handed to him a card.

Captain Willoughby took it with alacrity, for he desired company, and his acquaintances had all left the club to fulfil the most pressing and imperative engagements. But as he read the card his countenance fell. 'Colonel Durrance!' he said, and scratched his head thoughtfully. Durrance had never in his life paid him a friendly visit before, and why should he go out of his way to do so now? It looked as if Durrance had somehow got wind of his journey to Kingsbridge.

'Does Colonel Durrance know that I am in the club?' he asked.

'Yes, sir,' replied the waiter.

'Very well. Show him in.'

Durrance had, no doubt, come to ask questions, and diplomacy would be needed to elude them. Captain Willoughby had no mind to meddle any further in the affairs of Miss Ethne Eustace. Feversham and Durrance must fight their battle without his intervention. He did not distrust his powers of diplomacy, but he was not anxious to exert them in this particular case, and he looked suspiciously at Durrance as he entered the room. Durrance, however, had apparently no questions to ask. Willoughby rose from his chair, and crossing the room guided his visitor over to his deserted corner.

'Will you smoke?' he said, and checked himself. 'I beg your pardon.'

'Oh, I'll smoke,' Durrance answered. 'It's not quite true that a man can't enjoy his tobacco without seeing the smoke of it. If I let my cigar out I should know at once. But you will see, I shall not let it out.' He lighted his cigar with deliberation, and leaned back in his chair.

'I am lucky to find you, Willoughby,' he continued, 'for I am only in town for to-day. I come up every now and then from Devonshire to see my oculist, and I was very anxious to meet you if I could. On my last visit Mather told me that you were away in the country. You remember Mather, I suppose? He was with us in Suakin.'

'Of course, I remember him quite well,' said Willoughby heartily. He was more than willing to talk about Mather; he had a hope that in talking about Mather Durrance might forget that other matter which caused him anxiety.

'We are both of us curious,' Durrance continued, 'and you can clear up the point we are curious about. Did you ever come across an Arab called Abou Fatma?'

'Abou Fatma,' said Willoughby slowly, 'one of the Hadendoas?'

'No, a man of the Kabbabish tribe.'

'Abou Fatma?' Willoughby repeated, as though for the first time he had heard the name. 'No, I never came across him;' and then he stopped. It occurred to Durrance that it was not a natural place at which to stop; Willoughby might have been expected to add, 'Why do you ask me?' or some question of the kind. But he kept silent. As a matter of fact he was wondering how in the world Durrance had ever come to hear of Abou Fatma, whose name he himself had heard for the first and last time a year ago upon the verandah of the Palace at Suakin. For he had spoken the truth. He never had come across Abou Fatma, although Feversham had spoken of him.

'That makes me still more curious,' Durrance continued. 'Mather and I were together on the last reconnaissance in '84, and we found Abou Fatma hiding in the bushes by the Sinkat fort. He told us about the Gordon letters which he had hidden in Berber. Ah! you remember his name now.'

'I was merely getting my pipe out of my pocket,' said Willoughby. 'But I do remember the name now that you mention the letters.'

'They were brought to you in Suakin fifteen months or so back. Mather showed me the paragraph in the *Evening Standard*. And I am curious as to whether Abou Fatma returned to Berber and recovered them. But since you have never come across him, it follows that he was not the man.'

Captain Willoughby began to feel sorry that he had been in such haste to deny all acquaintance with Abou Fatma of the Kabbabish tribe.

'No; it was not Abou Fatma,' he said, with an awkward sort of hesitation. He dreaded the next question which Durrance would put to him. He filled his pipe, pondering what answer he should make to it. But Durrance put no question at all for the moment.

'I wondered,' he said slowly. 'I thought that Abou Fatma would hardly return to Berber. For, indeed, whoever undertook the job undertook it at the risk of his life, and, since Gordon was dead, for no very obvious reason.'

'Quite so,' said Willoughby in a voice of relief. It seemed that Durrance's curiosity was satisfied with the knowledge that Abou Fatma had not recovered the letters. 'Quite so. Since Gordon was dead, for no reason.'

'For no obvious reason, I think I said,' Durrance remarked imperturbably. Willoughby turned and glanced suspiciously at his companion, wondering whether after all Durrance knew of his visit to Kingsbridge and its motive. Durrance, however, smoked his cigar, leaning back in his chair, with his face tilted up towards the ceiling. He seemed, now that his curiosity was satisfied, to have lost interest in the history of the Gordon letters. At all events he put no more questions upon that subject to embarrass Captain Willoughby, and indeed there was no need that he should. Thinking over the possible way by which Harry Feversham might have redeemed himself in Willoughby's eyes from the charge of cowardice, Durrance could only hit upon this recovery of the letters from the ruined wall in Berber. There had been no personal danger to the inhabitants of Suakin since the days of that last reconnaissance. The great troopships had steamed between the coral reefs towards Suez, and no cry for help had ever summoned them back. Willoughby risked only his health in that white palace on the Red Sea. There could not have been a moment when Feversham was in a position to say: 'Your life was forfeit but for me, whom you call coward.' And Durrance, turning over in his mind all the news and gossip which had come to him at Wadi Halfa or during his furloughs, had been brought to conjecture whether that fugitive from Khartum, who had told him his story in the glacis of the silent ruined fort of Sinkat during one drowsy afternoon of May, had not told it again at Suakin within Feversham's hearing. He was convinced now that his conjecture was correct.

Willoughby's reticence was in itself a sufficient confirmation. Willoughby without doubt had been instructed by Ethne to keep his tongue in a leash. Colonel Durrance was prepared for reticence, he looked to reticence as the answer to his conjecture. His trained ear besides had warned him that Willoughby was uneasy at his visit and careful in his speech. There had been pauses, during which Durrance was as sure as though he had eyes wherewith to see that his companion was staring at him suspiciously and wondering how much he knew, or how little. There had been an accent of wariness and caution in his voice which was hatefully familiar to Durrance's ears, for just with that accent Ethne had been wont to speak. Moreover, Durrance had set traps – that remark of his 'for no obvious reason I think I said,' had been one – and a little start here or a quick turn there showed him that Willoughby had tumbled into them.

He had no wish, however, that Willoughby should write off to Ethne and warn her that Durrance was making inquiries. That was a possibility, he recognised, and he set himself to guard against it.

'I want to tell you why I was anxious to meet you,' he said. 'It was because of Harry Feversham,' and Captain Willoughby, who was congratulating himself that he was well out of an awkward position, fairly jumped in his seat. It was not Durrance's policy, however, to notice his companion's agitation, and he went on quickly: 'Something happened to Feversham. It's more than five years ago now. He did something, I suppose, or left something undone – the secret, at all events, has been closely kept – and he dropped out and his place knew him no more. Now you are going back to the Soudan, Willoughby?'

'Yes,' Willoughby answered, 'in a week's time.'

'Well, Harry Feversham is in the Soudan,' said Durrance, leaning towards his companion.

'You know that?' exclaimed Willoughby.

'Yes, for I came across him this spring at Wadi Halfa,' Durrance continued. 'He had fallen rather low,' and he told Willoughby of their meeting outside of the café at Tewfikieh. 'It's strange, isn't it? A man whom one knew very well going under like that in a second; disappearing before your eyes, as it were; dropping plumb out of sight as though down an oubliette in an old French castle. I want you to look out for him, Willoughby, and do what you can to set him on his legs again. Let me know if you chance on him. Harry Feversham was a friend of mine – one of my few real friends.'

'All right,' said Willoughby cheerfully. Durrance knew at once from the tone of his voice that suspicion was quieted in him. 'I will look out for Feversham. I remember he was a great friend of yours.'

He stretched out his hand towards the matches upon the table beside him. Durrance heard the scrape of the phosphorus and the flare of the match. Willoughby was lighting his pipe. It was a well-seasoned piece of briar, and needed a cleaning; it bubbled as he held the match to the tobacco and sucked at the mouthpiece.

'Yes, a great friend,' said Durrance. 'You and I dined with him in his flat high up above St James's Park just before we left England.'

And at that chance utterance Willoughby's briar pipe ceased suddenly to bubble. A moment's silence followed, then Willoughby swore violently, and a second later he stamped upon the carpet. Durrance's imagination was kindled by this simple sequence of events, and he straightway made up a little picture in his mind. In one chair himself smoking a cigar, a round table holding a matchstand on his left hand, and on the other side of the table Captain Willoughby in another chair. But Captain Willoughby lighting his pipe and suddenly arrested in the act by a sentence spoken without significance. Captain Willoughby staring suspiciously in his slow-witted way at the blind man's face, until the lighted match, which he had forgotten, burnt down to his fingers, and he swore and dropped it and stamped it out upon the floor. Durrance had never given a thought to that dinner till this moment. It was possible it might deserve much thought.

'There were you and I and Feversham present,' he went on. 'Feversham had asked us there to tell us of his engagement to Miss Eustace. He had just come back from Dublin. That was almost the last we saw of him.' He took a pull at his cigar, and added, 'By the way, there was a third man present.'

'Was there?' asked Willoughby. 'It's so long ago.'

'Yes – Trench.'

'To be sure, Trench was present. It will be a long time, I am afraid, before we dine at the same table with poor old Trench again.'

The carelessness of his voice was well assumed; he leaned forward and struck another match and lighted his pipe. As he did so, Durrance laid down his cigar upon the table edge.

'And we shall never dine with Castleton again,' he said slowly.

'Castleton wasn't there,' Willoughby exclaimed, and quickly enough to betray that, however long the interval since that little dinner in Feversham's rooms, it was at all events still distinct in his recollections.

'No, but he was expected,' said Durrance.

'No, not even expected,' corrected Willoughby. 'He was dining elsewhere. He sent the telegram, you remember.'

'Ah, yes! a telegram came,' said Durrance.

That dinner-party certainly deserved consideration. Willoughby, Trench, Castleton – these three men were the cause of Harry Feversham's disgrace and disappearance. Durrance tried to recollect all the details of the evening; but he had been occupied himself on that occasion. He remembered leaning against the window above St James's Park; he remembered hearing the tattoo from the parade-ground of Wellington Barracks – and a telegram had come.

Durrance made up another picture in his mind. Harry Feversham at the table reading and re-reading his telegram, Trench and Willoughby waiting silently, perhaps expectantly, and himself paying no heed, but staring out from the bright room into the quiet and cool of the park.

'Castleton was dining with a big man from the War Office that night,' Durrance said, and a little movement at his side warned him that he was getting hot in his search. He sat for a while longer talking about the prospects of the Soudan, and then rose up from his chair.

'Well, I can rely on you, Willoughby, to help Feversham, if ever you find him. Draw on me for money.'

'I will do my best,' said Willoughby. 'You are going? I could have won a bet off you this afternoon.'

'How?'

'You said that you did not let your cigars go out. This one's stone cold.'

'I forgot about it; I was thinking of Feversham. Good-bye.'

He took a cab and drove away from the club door. Willoughby was glad to see the last of him, but he was fairly satisfied with his own exhibition of diplomacy. It would have been strange, after all, he thought if he had not been able to hoodwink poor old Durrance; and he returned to the smoking-room and refreshed himself with a whisky and potass.

Durrance, however, had not been hoodwinked. The last perplexing question had been answered for him that afternoon. He remembered now that no mention had been made at the dinner which could identify the sender of the telegram. Feversham had read it without a word, and without a word had crumpled it up and tossed it into the fire. But to-day Willoughby had told him that it had come from Castleton, and Castleton had been dining with a high official of the War Office. The particular act of cowardice which had brought the three white feathers to Ramelton was easy to discern. Almost the next day Feversham had told Durrance in the Row that he had resigned his commission, and Durrance knew that he had not resigned it when the telegram came. That telegram could have brought only one piece of news, that Feversham's regiment was ordered on active service. The more Durrance reflected, the more certain he felt that he had at last hit upon the truth. Nothing could be more natural than that Castleton should telegraph his good news in confidence to his friends. Durrance had the story now complete, or rather the sequence of facts complete. For why Feversham should have been seized with panic, why he should have played the coward the moment after he was engaged to Ethne Eustace – at a time, in a word, when every manly quality he possessed should have been at its strongest and truest, remained for Durrance, and, indeed, was always to remain, an inexplicable problem. But he put that question aside, classing it among the considerations which he had learnt to estimate as small and unimportant. The simple and true thing – the thing of real importance – emerged definite and clear. Harry Feversham was atoning for his one act of cowardice with a full and an overflowing measure of atonement.

'I shall astonish old Sutch,' he thought, with a chuckle. He took the night mail into Devonshire the same evening, and reached his home before mid-day.

Chapter Twenty-three

MRS ADAIR MAKES HER APOLOGY

Within the drawing-room at The Pool Durrance said good-bye to Ethne. He had so arranged it that there should be little time for that leave-taking, and already the carriage stood at the steps of Guessens with his luggage strapped upon the roof, and his servant waiting at the door.

Ethne came out with him on to the terrace, where Mrs Adair stood at the top of the flight of steps. Durrance held out his hand to her, but she turned to Ethne and said : –

'I want to speak to Colonel Durrance before he goes.'

'Very well,' said Ethne. 'Then we will say good-bye here,' she added to Durrance. 'You will write from Wiesbaden? Soon, please!'

'The moment I arrive,' answered Durrance. He descended the

steps with Mrs Adair, and left Ethne standing upon the terrace. The last scene of pretence had been acted out, the months of tension and surveillance had come to an end, and both were thankful for their release. Durrance showed that he was glad even in the briskness of his walk as he crossed the lawn at Mrs Adair's side. She, however, lagged, and when she spoke it was in a despondent voice.

'So you are going,' she said. 'In two days' time you will be at Wiesbaden and Ethne at Glenalla. We shall all be scattered. It will be lonely here.'

She had had her way; she had separated Ethne and Durrance for a time, at all events; she was no longer to be tortured by the sight of them and the sound of their voices; but somehow her interference had brought her little satisfaction.

'The house will seem very empty after you are all gone,' she said; and she turned at Durrance's side, and walked down with him into the garden.

'We shall come back, no doubt,' said Durrance reassuringly.

Mrs Adair looked about her garden. The flowers were gone and the sunlight; clouds stretched across the sky overhead, the green of the grass underfoot was dull, the stream ran grey in the gap between the trees, and the leaves from the branches were blown russet and yellow about the lawns.

'How long shall you stay at Wiesbaden?' she asked.

'I can hardly tell. But as long as it's advisable,' he answered.

'That tells me nothing at all. I suppose it was meant not to tell me anything.'

Durrance did not answer her, and she resented his silence. She knew nothing whatever of his plans; she was unaware whether he meant to break his engagement with Ethne or to hold her to it, and curiosity consumed her. It might be a very long time before she saw him again, and all that long time she must remain tortured with doubts.

'You distrust me?' she said defiantly, and with a note of anger in her voice.

Durrance answered her quite gently –

'Have I no reason to distrust you? Why did you tell me of Captain Willoughby's coming? Why did you interfere?'

'I thought you ought to know.'

'But Ethne wished the secret kept. I am glad to know, very glad. But, after all, you told me, and you were Ethne's friend.'

'Yours, too, I hope,' Mrs Adair answered, and she exclaimed, 'How could I go on keeping silence? Don't you understand?'

'No.'

Durrance might have understood, but he had never given much thought to Mrs Adair, and she knew it. The knowledge rankled within her, and his simple 'no' stung her beyond bearing.

'I spoke brutally, didn't I?' she said. 'I told you the truth as brutally as I could. Doesn't that help you to understand?'

Again Durrance said 'No,' and the monosyllable exasperated her out of all prudence, and all at once she found herself speaking incoherently the things which she had thought. And once she had begun, she could not stop. She stood as it were outside of herself, and saw that her speech was madness; yet she went on with it.

'I told you the truth brutally on purpose. I was so stung because you would not see what was so visible had you only the mind to see. I wanted to hurt you. I am a bad, bad woman, I suppose. There were you and she in the room talking together in the darkness; there was I alone upon the terrace. It was the same again to-day. You and Ethne in the room, I alone upon the terrace. I wonder whether it will always be so. But you will not say – you will not say.' She struck her hands together with a gesture of despair, but Durrance had no words for her. He walked silently along the garden path towards the stile, and he quickened his pace a little, so that Mrs Adair had to walk fast to keep up with him. That quickening of the pace was a sort of answer, but Mrs Adair was not deterred by it. Her madness had taken hold of her.

'I do not think I would have minded so much,' she continued, 'if Ethne had really cared for you. But she never cared more than as a friend cares, just a mere friend. And what's friendship worth?' she asked scornfully.

'Something surely,' said Durrance.

'It does not prevent Ethne from shrinking from her friend,' cried Mrs Adair. 'She shrinks from you. Shall I tell you why. Because you are blind. She is afraid. While I – I will tell you

191

the truth – I am glad. When the news first came from Wadi
Halfa that you were blind I was glad, when I saw you in Hill
Street I was glad, ever since I have been glad – quite glad. Because I saw that she shrank. From the beginning she shrank,
thinking how her life would be hampered and fettered,' and
the scorn of Mrs Adair's voice increased, though her voice itself
was sunk to a whisper. 'I am not afraid,' she said, and she
repeated the words passionately again and again. 'I am not
afraid. I am not afraid.'

To Durrance it seemed that in all his experience nothing so
horrible had ever occurred as this outburst by the woman who
was Ethne's friend, nothing so unforeseen.

'Ethne wrote to you at Wadi Halfa out of pity,' she went on,
'that was all. She wrote out of pity; and, having written, she
was afraid of what she had done; and being afraid, she had not
courage to tell you she was afraid. You would not have blamed
her if she had frankly admitted it; you would have remained
her friend. But she had not the courage.'

Durrance knew that there was another explanation of
Ethne's hesitations and timidities. He knew, too, that the other
explanation was the true one. But to-morrow he himself would
be gone from the Salcombe estuary and Ethne would be on her
way to the Irish Channel and Donegal. It was not worth while
to argue against Mrs Adair's slanders. Besides, he was close
upon the stile which separated the garden of The Pool from the
fields. Once across that stile he would be free of Mrs Adair. He
contented himself with saying quietly –

'You are not just to Ethne.'

At that simple utterance the madness of Mrs Adair went
from her. She recognised the futility of all that she had said,
of her boastings of courage, of her detractions of Ethne. Her
words might be true or not, they could achieve nothing. Durrance was always in the room with Ethne, never upon the
terrace with Mrs Adair. She became conscious of her degrada-
tion, and she fell to excuses.

'I am a bad woman, I suppose. But after all I have not had
the happiest of lives. Perhaps there is something to be said for
me.' It sounded pitiful and weak even in her ears; but they had
reached the stile and Durrance had turned towards her. She

saw that his face lost something of its sternness. He was standing quietly, prepared now to listen to what she might wish to say. He remembered that in the old days when he could see he had always associated her with a dignity of carriage and a reticence of speech. It seemed hardly possible that it was the same woman who spoke to him now, and the violence of the contrast made him ready to believe that there must be something to be said on her behalf.

'Will you tell me?' he said gently.

'I was married almost straight from school. I was the merest girl. I knew nothing, and I was married to a man of whom I knew nothing. It was my mother's doing, and no doubt she thought that she was acting for the very best. She was securing for me a position of a kind, and comfort and release from any danger of poverty. I accepted what she said blindly ignorantly. I could hardly have refused, indeed, for my mother was an imperious woman, and I was accustomed to obedience. I did as she told me and married dutifully the man whom she chose. The case is common enough, no doubt, but its frequency does not make it easier of endurance.'

'But Mr Adair!' said Durrance. 'After all, I knew him. He was older, no doubt, than you, but he was kind. I think, too, he cared for you.'

'Yes. He was kindness itself, and he cared for me. Both things are true. The knowledge that he did care for me was the one link, if you understand. At the beginning I was contented, I suppose. I had a house in town and another here. But it was dull,' and she stretched out her arms. 'Oh, how dull it was! Do you know the little back streets in a manufacturing town? Rows of small houses, side by side, with nothing to relieve them of their ugly regularity, each with the self-same windows, the self-same door, the self-same doorstep. Overhead a drift of smoke, and every little green thing, down to the plants in the window, dirty and black. The sort of street whence any crazy religious charlatan who can promise a little colour to their grey lives can get as many votaries as he wants. Well, when I thought over my life, one of those little streets always came into my mind. There are women, heaps of them, no doubt, to whom the management of a big house, the season in

193

London, the ordinary round of visits are sufficient. I, worse luck, was not one of them. Dull! You, with your hundred thousand things to do, cannot conceive how oppressively dull my life was. And that was not all!' She hesitated, but she could not stop midway, and it was far too late for her to recover her ground. She went on to the end.

'I married, as I say, knowing nothing of the important things. I believed at the first that mine was just the allotted life of all women. But I began soon to have my doubts. I got to know that there was something more to be won out of existence than mere dullness; at least, that there was something more for others, though not for me. One could not help learning that. One passed a man and a woman riding together, and one chanced to look into the woman's face as one passed; or one saw, perhaps, the woman alone and talked with her for a little while, and from the happiness of her looks and voice one knew with absolute certainty that there was ever so much more. Only the chance of that ever so much more my mother had denied to me.'

All the sternness had now gone from Durrance's face, and Mrs Adair was speaking with great simplicity. Of the violence which she had used before there was no longer any trace. She did not appeal for pity, she was not even excusing herself; she was just telling her story quietly and gently.

'And then you came,' she continued. 'I met you and met you again. You went away upon your duties, and you returned; and I learnt now, not that there was ever so much more, but just what that ever so much more was. But it was still of course denied to me. However, in spite of that, I felt happier. I thought that I should be quite content to have you for a friend, to watch your progress, and to feel pride in it. But you see – Ethne came, too, and you turned to her. At once – oh, at once! If you had only been a little less quick to turn to her! In a very short while I was sad and sorry that you had ever come into my life.'

'I knew nothing of this,' said Durrance. 'I never suspected. I am sorry.'

'I took care you should not suspect,' said Mrs Adair. 'But I tried to keep you, with all my wits I tried. No matchmaker in the world ever worked so hard to bring two people together as I did to bring together Ethne and Mr Feversham, and I succeeded.'

The statement came upon Durrance with a shock. He leaned back against the stile and could have laughed. Here was the origin of the whole sad business. From what small beginnings it had grown! It is a trite reflection, but the personal application of it is apt to take away the breath. It was so with Durrance as he thought himself backwards into those days when he had walked on his own path, heedless of the people with whom he came in touch, never dreaming that they were at that moment influencing his life right up to his dying day. Feversham's disgrace and ruin, Ethne's years of unhappiness, the wearying pretences of the last few months, all had their origin years ago when Mrs Adair, to keep Durrance to herself, threw Feversham and Ethne into each other's company.

'I succeeded,' continued Mrs Adair. 'You told me that I had succeeded one morning in the Row. How glad I was! You did not notice it, I am sure. The next moment you took all my gladness from me by telling me you were starting for the Soudan. You were away three years. They were not happy years for me. You came back. My husband was dead, but Ethne was free. Ethne refused you, but you went blind and she claimed you. You can see what ups and downs have fallen to me. But these months here have been the worse.'

'I am very sorry,' said Durrance. Mrs Adair was quite right, he thought. There was indeed something to be said on her behalf. The world had gone rather hardly with her. He was able to realise what she had suffered since he was suffering in much the same way himself. It was quite intelligible to him why she had betrayed Ethne's secret that night upon the terrace, and he could not but be gentle with her.

'I am very sorry, Mrs Adair,' he repeated lamely. There was nothing more which he could find to say, and he held out his hand to her.

'Good-bye,' she said, and Durrance climbed over the stile and crossed the fields to his house.

Mrs Adair stood by that stile for a long while after he had

gone. She had shot her bolt and hit no one but herself and the man for whom she cared.

She realised that distinctly. She looked forward a little too, and she understood that if Durrance did not, after all, keep Ethne to her promise, and marry her and go with her to her country, he would come back to Guessens. That reflection showed Mrs Adair yet more clearly the folly of her outcry. If she had only kept silence she would have had a very true and constant friend for her neighbour, and that would have been something. It would have been a good deal. But, since she had spoken, they could never meet without embarrassment, and, practise cordiality as they might, there would always remain in their minds the recollection of what she had said and he had listened to on the afternoon when he left for Wiesbaden.

Chapter Twenty-four

ON THE NILE

It was a callous country inhabited by a callous race, thought Calder as he travelled down the Nile from Wadi Halfa to Assouan on his three months' furlough. He leaned over the rail of the upper deck of the steamer and looked down upon the barge lashed alongside. On the lower deck of the barge among the native passengers stood an angareb,* whereon was stretched the motionless figure of a human being shrouded in a black veil. The angareb and its burden had been carried on board early that morning at Korosko by two Arabs, who now sat laughing and chattering in the stern of the barge. It might have been a dead man or a dead woman who lay still and stretched out upon the bedstead, so little heed did they give to it. Calder lifted his eyes and looked to his right and his left across glaring sand and barren rocks shaped roughly into the hard forms of pyramids. The narrow meagre strip of green close by the water's edge upon each bank was the only response

* The native bedstead of matting woven across a four-legged frame.

which the Soudan made to spring and summer and the bene-
fiçent rain. A callous country inhabited by a callous people.

Calder looked downwards again to the angareb upon the
barge's deck and the figure lying upon it. Whether it was man
or woman he could not tell. The black veil lay close about
the face outlining the nose, the hollows of the eyes and the
mouth, but whether the lips wore a moustache and the chin a
beard it did not reveal.

The slanting sunlight crept nearer and nearer to the angareb.
The natives seated close to it moved into the shadow of the
upper deck, but no one moved the angareb, and the two men
laughing in the stern gave no thought to their charge. Calder
watched the blaze of yellow light creep over the black re-
cumbent figure from the feet upwards. It burnt at last bright
and pitiless upon the face. Yet the living creature beneath the
veil never stirred. The veil never fluttered above the lips, the
legs remained stretched out straight, the arms lay close against
the side.

Calder shouted to the two men in the stern –

'Move the angareb into the shadow,' he cried, 'and be quick!'

The Arabs rose reluctantly and obeyed him.

'Is it a man or a woman?' asked Calder.

'A man. We are taking him to the hospital at Assouan, but
we do not think that he will live. He fell from a palm-tree three
weeks ago.'

'You give him nothing to eat or drink.'

'He is too ill.'

It was a common story, and the logical outcome of the belief
that life and death are written and will inevitably befall after
the manner of the writing. That man lying so quiet beneath
the black covering had probably at the beginning suffered
nothing more serious than a bruise, which a few simple remedies would have cured within a week. But he had been allowed
to lie, even as he lay upon the angareb, at the mercy of the sun
and the flies, unwashed, unfed, and with his thirst unslaked.
The bruise had become a sore, the sore had gangrened, and,
when all remedies were too late, the Egyptian Mudir of
Korosko had discovered the accident and sent the man on the
steamer down to Assouan. But, familiar though the story was,

Calder could not dismiss it from his thoughts. The immobility of the sick man upon the native bedstead in a way fascinated him, and when towards sunset a strong wind sprang up and blew against the stream, he felt an actual comfort in the knowledge that the sick man would gain some relief from it. And when his neighbour that evening at the dinner-table spoke to him with a German accent, he suddenly asked upon an impulse –

'You are not a doctor by any chance?'

'Not a doctor,' said the German, 'but a student of medicine at Bonn. I came from Cairo to see the Second Cataract, but was not allowed to go further than Wadi Halfa.'

Calder interrupted him at once. 'Then I will trespass upon your holiday and claim your professional assistance.'

'For yourself? With pleasure, though I should never have guessed you were ill,' said the student, smiling good-naturedly behind his eyeglasses.

'Nor am I. It is an Arab for whom I ask your help.'

'The man on the bedstead?'

'Yes, if you will be so good. I will warn you – he was hurt three weeks ago, and I know these people. No one will have touched him since he was hurt. The sight will not be pretty. This is not a nice country for unattended wounds.'

The German student shrugged his shoulders. 'All experience is good,' said he, and the two men rose from the table and went out on to the upper deck.

The wind had freshened during the dinner, and, blowing up stream, had raised waves so that the steamer and its barge tossed and the water broke on board.

'He was below there,' said the student as he leaned over the rail and peered downwards to the lower deck of the barge alongside. It was night, and the night was dark. Above that lower deck only one lamp, swung from the centre of the upper deck, glimmered and threw uncertain lights and uncertain shadows over a small circle. Beyond the circle all was black darkness, except at the bows, where the water breaking on board flung a white sheet of spray. It could be seen like a sprinkle of snow driven by the wind, it could be heard striking the deck like a lash of a whip.

'He has been moved,' said the German. 'No doubt he has been moved. There is no one in the bows.'

Calder bent his head downwards and stared into the darkness for a little while without speaking.

'I believe the angareb is there,' he said at length. 'I believe it is.'

Followed by the German, he hurried down the stairway to the lower deck of the steamer and went to the side. He could make certain now. The angareb stood in a wash of water on the very spot to which at Calder's order it had been moved that morning. And on the angareb the figure beneath the black covering lay as motionless as ever, as inexpressive of life and feeling, though the cold spray broke continually upon its face.

'I thought it would be so,' said Calder. He got a lantern, and with the German student climbed across the bulwarks on to the barge. He summoned the two Arabs.

'Move the angareb from the bows,' he said; and when they had obeyed, 'Now take that covering off. I wish my friend, who is a doctor, to see the wound.'

The two men hesitated, and then one of them, with an air of insolence, objected. 'There are doctors in Assouan, whither we are taking him.'

Calder raised the lantern, and himself drew the veil away from off the wounded man. 'Now, if you please,' he said to his companion. The German student made his examination of the wounded thigh, while Calder held the lantern above his head. As Calder had predicted, it was not a pleasant business; for the wound crawled. The German student was glad to cover it up again.

'I can do nothing,' he said. 'Perhaps in a hospital, with baths and dressings — ! Relief will be given at all events; but more? I do not know. Here I could not even begin to do anything at all. Do these two men understand English?'

'No,' answered Calder.

'Then I can tell you something. He did not get the hurt by falling out of any palm-tree. That is a lie. The injury was done by the blade of a spear or some weapon of the kind.'

'Are you sure?'

'Yes.'

Calder bent down suddenly towards the Arab on the angareb. Although he never moved, the man was conscious. Calder had been looking steadily at him, and saw that his eyes followed the spoken words.

'You understand English?' said Calder.

The Arab could not answer with his lips, but a look of comprehension came into his face.

'Where do you come from?' asked Calder.

The lips tried to move, but not so much as a whisper escaped from them. Yet his eyes spoke, but spoke vainly; for the most which they could tell was a great eagerness to answer. Calder dropped upon his knee close by the man's head, and, holding the lantern close, enunciated the towns.

'From Dongola?'

No gleam in the Arab's eyes responded to that name.

'From Metemneh? From Berber? From Omdurman? Ah!'

The Arab answered to that word. He closed his eyelids. Calder went on still more eagerly.

'You were wounded there? No. Where then? At Berber? Yes. You were in prison at Omdurman and escaped? No. Yet you were wounded.'

Calder sank back upon his knee and reflected. His reflections roused in him some excitement. He bent down to the Arab's ear and spoke in a lower key.

'You were helping someone to escape? Yes. Who? El Kaimakam Trench? No.' He mentioned the names of other white captives in Omdurman, and to each name the Arab's eyes answered 'No'. 'It was Effendi Feversham, then?' he said, and the eyes assented as clearly as though the lips had spoken.

But this was all the information which Calder could secure. 'I too am pledged to help Effendi Feversham,' he said, but in vain. The Arab could not speak, he could not so much as tell his name, and his companions would not. Whatever those two men knew or suspected, they had no mind to meddle in the matter themselves, and they clung consistently to a story which absolved them from responsibility. Kinsmen of theirs in Korosko, hearing that they were travelling to Assouan, had asked them to take charge of the wounded man, who was a stranger to them, and they had consented. Calder could get nothing more explicit from them than this statement, however closely he questioned them. He had under his hand the information which he desired, the news of Harry Feversham for which Durrance asked by every mail, but it was hidden from him in a locked book. He stood beside the helpless man upon the angareb. There he was, eager enough to speak, but the extremity of weakness to which he had sunk laid a finger upon his lips. All that Calder could do was to see him safely bestowed within the hospital at Assouan. 'Will he recover?' Calder asked, and the doctors shook their heads in doubt. There was a chance perhaps, a very slight chance, but at the best recovery would be slow.

Calder continued upon his journey to Cairo and Europe. An opportunity of helping Harry Feversham had slipped away; for the Arab who could not even speak his name was Abou Fatma, of the Kabbabish tribe, and his presence wounded and helpless upon the Nile steamer between Korosko and Assouan meant that Harry Feversham's carefully laid plan for the rescue of Colonel Trench had failed.

Chapter Twenty-five

LIEUTENANT SUTCH COMES OFF THE HALF-PAY LIST

At the time when Calder, disappointed at his failure to obtain news of Feversham from the one man who possessed it, stepped into a carriage of the train at Assouan, Lieutenant Sutch was driving along a high white road of Hampshire across a common of heather and gorse; and he too was troubled on Harry Feversham's account. Like many a man who lives much alone, Lieutenant Sutch had fallen into the habit of speaking his thoughts aloud. And as he drove slowly and reluctantly forward, more than once he said to himself, 'I foresaw there would be trouble. From the beginning I foresaw there would be trouble.'

The ridge of hill along which he drove dipped suddenly to a hollow. Sutch saw the road run steeply down in front of him between forests of pines to a little railway station. The sight of the rails gleaming bright in the afternoon sunlight, and the telegraph poles running away in a straight line until they seemed to huddle together in the distance, increased Sutch's discomposure. He reined his pony in and sat staring with a frown at the red-tiled roof of the station building.

'I promised Harry to say nothing,' he said; and drawing some makeshift of comfort from the words, repeated them, 'I promised faithfully in the Criterion grill-room.'

The whistle of an engine a long way off sounded clear and shrill. It roused Lieutenant Sutch from his gloomy meditations. He saw the white smoke of an approaching train stretch out like a riband in the distance.

'I wonder what brings him,' he said doubtfully; and then with an effort at courage, 'Well, it's no use shirking.' He flicked the pony with his whip and drove briskly down the hill. He reached the station as the train drew up at the platform. Only two passengers descended from the train. They were Durrance and his servant, and they came out at once on to the road. Lieutenant Sutch hailed Durrance, who walked to the side of the trap.

'You received my telegram in time, then!' said Durrance.

'Luckily it found me at home.'

'I have brought a bag. May I trespass upon you for a night's lodging?'

'By all means,' said Sutch, but the tone of his voice quite clearly to Durrance's ears belied the heartiness of the words. Durrance, however, was prepared for a reluctant welcome, and he had purposely sent his telegram at the last moment. Had he given an address, he suspected that he might have received a refusal of his visit. And his suspicion was accurate enough. The telegram, it is true, had merely announced Durrance's visit, it had stated nothing of his object; but its despatch was sufficient to warn Sutch that something grave had happened, something untoward in the relations of Ethne Eustace and Durrance. Durrance had come, no doubt, to renew his inquiries about Harry Feversham, those inquiries which Sutch was on no account to answer, which he must parry all this afternoon and night. But he saw Durrance, feeling about with his raised foot for the step of the trap, and the fact of his visitor's blindness was brought home to him. He reached out a hand, and catching Durrance by the arm, helped him up. After all, he thought, it would not be difficult to hoodwink a blind man. Ethne herself had had the same thought, and felt much the same relief as Sutch felt now. The Lieutenant, indeed, was so relieved that he found room for an impulse of pity.

'I was very sorry, Durrance, to hear of your bad luck,' he said as he drove off up the hill. 'I know what it is myself to be suddenly stopped and put aside just when one is making way and the world is smoothing itself out, though my wound in the leg is nothing in comparison to your blindness. I don't talk to you about compensations and patience. That's the gabble of people who are comfortable and haven't suffered. *We* know that for a man who is young and active, and who is doing well in a career where activity is a necessity, there are no compensations if his career's suddenly cut short through no fault of his.'

'Through no fault of his,' repeated Durrance. 'I agree with you. It is only the man whose career is cut short through his own fault who gets compensations.'

Sutch glanced sharply at his companion. Durrance had spoken slowly and very thoughtfully. Did he mean to refer to Harry Feversham, Sutch wondered. Did he know enough to be able so to refer to him. Or was it merely by chance that his words were so strikingly apposite?

'Compensations of what kind?' Sutch asked uneasily.

'The chance of knowing himself for one thing, for the chief thing. He is brought up short, stopped in his career, perhaps disgraced.' Sutch started a little at the word. 'Yes, perhaps – disgraced,' Durrance repeated. 'Well, the shock of the disgrace is, after all, his opportunity. Don't you see that? It's his opportunity to know himself at last. Up to the moment of disgrace his life has all been sham and illusion; the man he believed himself to be, he never was, and now at the last he knows it. Once he knows it, he can set about to retrieve his disgrace. Oh, there are compensations for such a man. You and I know a case in point.'

Sutch no longer doubted that Durrance was deliberately referring to Harry Feversham. He had some knowledge, though how he had gained it Sutch could not guess. But the knowledge was not to Sutch's idea quite accurate, and the inaccuracy did Harry Feversham some injustice. It was on that account chiefly that Sutch did not affect any ignorance as to Durrance's allusion. The passage of the years had not diminished his great regard for Harry, he cared for him indeed with a woman's concentration of love, and he could not endure that his memory should be slighted.

'The case you and I know of is not quite in point,' he argued. 'You are speaking of Harry Feversham.'

'Who believed himself a coward, and was not one. He commits the fault which stops his career, he finds out his mistake, he sets himself to the work of retrieving his disgrace. Surely it's a case quite in point.'

'Yes, I see,' Sutch agreed. 'There is another view, a wrong view as I know, but I thought for the moment it was your view – that Harry fancied himself to be a brave man, and was suddenly brought up short by discovering that he was a coward. But how did you find out? No one knew the whole truth except myself.'

'I am engaged to Miss Eustace,' said Durrance.

'She did not know everything. She knew of the disgrace, but she did not know of the determination to retrieve it.'

'She knows now,' said Durrance; and he added sharply, 'You are glad of that – very glad.'

Sutch was not aware that by any movement or exclamation he had betrayed his pleasure. His face, no doubt, showed it clearly enough, but Durrance could not see his face. Lieutenant Sutch was puzzled, but he did not deny the imputation.

'It is true,' he said stoutly. 'I am very glad that she knows. I can quite see that from your point of view it would be better if she did not know. But I cannot help it. I am very glad.'

Durrance laughed, and not at all unpleasantly: 'I like you the better for being glad,' he said.

'But how does Miss Eustace know?' asked Sutch. 'Who told her? I did not, and there is no one else who could tell her.'

'You are wrong. There is Captain Willoughby. He came to

Devonshire six weeks ago. He brought wih him a white feather which he gave to Miss Eustace, as a proof that he withdrew his charge of cowardice against Harry Feversham.'

Sutch stopped the pony in the middle of the road. He no longer troubled to conceal the joy which this good news caused him. Indeed, he forgot altogether Durrance's presence at his side. He sat quite silent and still, with a glow of happiness upon him such as he had never known in all his life. He was an old man now, well on in his sixties; he had reached an age when the blood runs slow, and the pleasures are of a grey, sober kind, and joy has lost its fevers. But there welled up in his heart a gladness of such buoyancy as only falls to the lot of youth. Five years ago on the pier of Dover he had watched a mail packet steam away into darkness and rain, and had prayed that he might live until this great moment should come. And he had lived and it had come. His heart was lifted up in gratitude. It seemed to him that there was a great burst of sunlight across the world, and that the world itself had suddenly grown many-coloured and a place of joys. Ever since the night when he had stood outside the War Office in Pall Mall, and Harry Feversham had touched him on the arm and had spoken out his despair, Lieutenant Sutch had been oppressed with a sense of guilt. Harry was Muriel Feversham's boy, and Sutch just for that reason should have watched him and mothered him in his boyhood since his mother was dead, and fathered him in his youth since his father did not understand. But he had failed. He had failed in a sacred trust, and he had imagined Muriel Feversham's eyes looking at him with reproach from the barrier of the skies. He had heard her voice in his dreams saying to him gently, ever so gently, 'Since I was dead, since I was taken away to where I could only see and not help, surely you might have helped. Just for my sake you might have helped, you whose work in the world was at an end.' And the long tale of his inactive years had stood up to accuse him. Now, however, the guilt was lifted from his shoulders, and by Harry Feversham's own act. The news was not altogether unexpected, but the lightness of spirit which he felt showed him how much he had counted upon its coming.

'I knew,' he exclaimed, 'I knew he wouldn't fail. Oh, I am

205

glad you came to-day, Colonel Durrance. It was partly my fault, you see, that Harry Feversham ever incurred that charge of cowardice. I could have spoken – there was an opportunity on one of the Crimean nights at Broad Place, and a word might have been of value – and I held my tongue. I have never ceased to blame myself. I am grateful for your news. You have the particulars? Captain Willoughby was in peril, and Harry came to his aid?'

'No, it was not that exactly.'

'Tell me! Tell me!'

He feared to miss a word. Durrance related the story of the Gordon letters, and their recovery by Feversham. It was all too short for Lieutenant Sutch.

'Oh, but I am glad you came,' he cried.

'You understand at all events,' said Durrance, 'that I have not come to repeat to you the questions I asked in the court-yard of my club. I am able, on the contrary, to give you information.'

Sutch spoke to the pony and drove on. He had said nothing which could reveal to Durrance his fear that to renew those questions was the object of his visit; and he was a little perplexed at the accuracy of Durrance's conjecture. But the great news to which he had listened hindered him from giving thought to that perplexity.

'So Miss Eustace told you the story,' he said, 'and showed you the feather.'

'No, indeed,' replied Durrance. 'She said not a word about it, she never showed me the feather, she even forbade Willoughby to hint of it, she sent him away from Devonshire before I knew that he had come. You are disappointed at that,' he added quickly.

Lieutenant Sutch was startled. It was true he was disappointed, he was jealous of Durrance, he wished Harry Feversham to stand first in the girl's thoughts. It was for her sake that Harry had set about his difficult and perilous work. Sutch wished her to remember him as he remembered her. Therefore he was disappointed that she did not at once come with her news to Durrance and break off their engagement. It would be hard for Durrance, no doubt, but that could not be helped.

'Then how did you learn the story?' asked Sutch.

'Someone else told me. I was told that Willoughby had come, and that he had brought a white feather, and that Ethne had taken it from him. Never mind by whom. That gave me a clue. I lay in wait for Willoughby in London. He is not very clever; he tried to obey Ethne's command of silence, but I managed to extract the information I wanted. The rest of the story I was able to put together by myself. Ethne now and then was off her guard. You are surprised that I was clever enough to find out the truth by the exercise of my own wits?' said Durrance with a laugh.

Lieutenant Sutch jumped in his seat. It was mere chance, of course, that Durrance continually guessed with so singular an accuracy; still it was uncomfortable.

'I have said nothing which could in any way suggest that I was surprised,' he said testily.

'That is quite true, but you are none the less surprised,' continued Durrance. 'I don't blame you. You could not know that it is only since I have been blind that I have begun to see. Shall I give you an instance? This is the first time that I have ever come into this neighbourhood or got out at your station. Well, I can tell you that you have driven me up a hill between forests of pines, and are now driving me across open country of heather.'

Sutch turned quickly towards Durrance.

'The hill, of course, you would notice. But the pines?'

'The air was close. I knew there were trees. I guessed they were pines.'

'And the open country?'

'The wind blows clear across it. There's a dry stiff rustle besides. I have never heard quite that sound except when the wind blows across heather.'

He turned the conversation back to Harry Feversham and his disappearance, and the cause of his disappearance. He made no mention, Sutch remarked, of the fourth white feather which Ethne herself had added to the three. But the history of the three which had come by the post to Ramelton he knew to its last letter.

'I was acquainted with the men who sent them,' he said.

'Trench, Castleton, Willoughby. I met them daily in Suakin, just ordinary officers, one rather shrewd, the second quite commonplace, the third distinctly stupid. I saw them going quietly about the routine of their work. It seems quite strange to me now. There should have been some mark set upon them, setting them apart as the particular messengers of fate. But there was nothing of the kind. They were just ordinary prosaic regimental officers. Doesn't it seem strange to you too? Here were men who could deal out misery and estrangement and years of suffering, without so much as a single word spoken, and they went about their business, and you never knew them from other men until a long while afterwards some consequence of what they did, and very likely have forgotten, rises up and strikes you down.'

'Yes,' said Sutch. 'That thought has occurred to me.' He fell to wondering again what object had brought Durrance into Hampshire, since he did not come for information; but Durrance did not immediately enlighten him. They reached the Lieutenant's house. It stood alone by the roadside looking across a wide country of downs. Sutch took Durrance over his stable and showed him his horses, he explained to him the arrangement of his garden and the grouping of his flowers. Still Durrance said nothing about the reason of his visit; he ceased to talk of Harry Feversham, and assumed a great interest in the Lieutenant's garden. But indeed the interest was not all pretence. These two men had something in common, as Sutch had pointed out at the moment of their meeting – the abrupt termination of a promising career. One of the two was old, the other comparatively young, and the younger man was most curious to discover how his elder had managed to live through the dragging profitless years alone. The same sort of lonely life lay stretched out before Durrance, and he was anxious to learn what alleviations could be practised, what small interests could be discovered, how best it could be got through.

'You don't live within sight of the sea,' he said at last, as they stood together, after making the round of the garden, at the door.

'No, I dare not,' said Sutch, and Durrance nodded his head in complete sympathy and comprehension.

'I understand. You care for it too much. You would have the full knowledge of your loss presented to your eyes each moment.'

They went into the house. Still Durrance did not refer to the object of his visit. They dined together and sat over their wine alone. Still Durrance did not speak. It fell to Lieutenant Sutch to recur to the subject of Harry Feversham. A thought had been gaining strength in his mind all that afternoon, and since Durrance would not lead up to its utterance, he spoke it out himself.

'Harry Feversham must come back to England. He has done enough to redeem his honour.'

Harry Feversham's return might be a little awkward for Durrance, and Lieutenant Sutch with that notion in his mind blurted out his sentences awkwardly, but to his surprise Durrance answered him at once.

'I was waiting for you to say that. I wanted you to realise without any suggestion of mine that Harry must return. It was with that object that I came.'

Lieutenant Sutch's relief was great. He had been prepared for an objection, at the best he only expected a reluctant acquiescence, and in the greatness of his relief he spoke again:

'His return will not really trouble you or your wife, since Miss Eustace has forgotten him.'

Durrance shook his head.

'She has not forgotten him.'

'But she kept silence even after Willoughby had brought the feather back. You told me so this afternoon. She said not a word to you. She forbade Willoughby to tell you.'

'She is very true, very loyal,' returned Durrance. 'She has pledged herself to me, and nothing in the world, no promise of happiness, no thought of Harry would induce her to break her pledge. I know her. But I know too that she only plighted herself to me out of pity, because I was blind. I know that she has not forgotten Harry.'

Lieutenant Sutch leaned back in his chair and smiled. He could have laughed outright. He asked for no details, he did not doubt Durrance's words. He was overwhelmed with pride in that Harry Feversham, in spite of his disgrace and his long

209

absence – Harry Feversham his favourite, had retained this girl's love. No doubt she was very true, very loyal. Sutch endowed her on the instant with all the good qualities possible to a human being. The nobler she was, the greater was his pride that Harry Feversham still retained her heart. Lieutenant Sutch fairly revelled in this new knowledge. It was not to be wondered at after all, he thought, there was nothing astonishing in the girl's fidelity, to anyone who was fairly acquainted with Harry Feversham, it was only an occasion of great gladness. Durrance would have to get out of the way of course, but then he should never have crossed Harry Feversham's path. Sutch was cruel with the perfect cruelty of which love alone is capable.

'You are very glad of that,' said Durrance quietly. 'Very glad that Ethne has not forgotten him. It is a little hard on me, perhaps, who have not much left. It would have been less hard if two years ago you had told me the whole truth when I asked it of you that summer evening in the courtyard of the club.'

Compunction seized upon Lieutenant Sutch. The gentleness with which Durrance had spoken, and the quiet accent of weariness in his voice, brought home to him something of the cruelty of his great joy and pride. After all, what Durrance said was true. If he had broken his word that night at the club, if he had related Feversham's story, Durrance would have been spared a great deal.

'I couldn't!' he exclaimed. 'I promised Harry in the most solemn way that I would tell no one until he came back himself. I was sorely tempted to tell you, but I had given my word. Even if Harry never came back, if I obtained sure knowledge that he was dead, even then I was only to tell his father, and even his father not all that could be told on his behalf.'

He pushed back his chair and went to the window. 'It is hot in here,' he said. 'Do you mind?' and without waiting for an answer he loosed the catch and raised the sash. For some little while he stood by the open window, silent, undecided. Durrance plainly did not know of the fourth feather broken off from Ethne's fan, he had not heard the conversation between himself and Feversham in the grill-room of the Criterion Restaurant. There were certain words spoken by Harry upon that occasion which it seemed fair Durrance should now hear. Compunction and pity bade Sutch repeat them, his love of Harry Feversham enjoined him to hold his tongue. He could plead again that Harry had forbidden him speech, but the plea would be an excuse and nothing more. He knew very well that, were Harry present, Harry would repeat them, and Lieutenant Sutch knew what harm silence had already done. He mastered his love in the end and came back to the table.

'There is something which it is fair you should know,' he said. 'When Harry went away to redeem his honour if the opportunity should come, he had no hope, indeed he had no wish, that Miss Eustace should wait for him. She was the spur to urge him, but she did not know even that. He did not wish her to know. He had no claim upon her. There was not even a hope in his mind that she might at some time be his friend – in this life at all events. When he went away from Ramelton, he parted from her, according to his thought, for all his mortal life. It is fair that you should know that. Miss Eustace, you tell me, is not the woman to withdraw from her pledged word. Well, what I said to you that evening at the club I now repeat. There will be no disloyalty to friendship if you marry Miss Eustace.'

It was a difficult speech for Lieutenant Sutch to utter, and he was very glad when he had uttered it. Whatever answer he received, it was right that the words should be spoken, and he knew that had he refrained from speech, he would always have suffered remorse for his silence. None the less, however, he waited in suspense for the answer.

'It is kind of you to tell me that,' said Durrance, and he smiled at the Lieutenant with a great friendliness. 'For I can guess what the words cost you. But you have done Harry Feversham no harm by speaking them. For, as I told you, Ethne has not forgotten him; and I have my point of view. Marriage between a man blind like myself and any woman, let alone Ethne, could not be fair or right unless upon both sides there was more than friendship. Harry must return to England. He must return to Ethne too. You must go to Egypt, and do what you can to bring him back.'

Sutch was relieved of his suspense. He had obeyed his conscience, and yet done Harry Feversham no disservice.

'I will start to-morrow,' he said. 'Harry is still in the Soudan?'

'Of course.'

'Why of course?' asked Sutch. 'Willoughby withdrew his accusation; Castleton is dead – he was killed at Tamai; and Trench – I know, for I have followed all these three men's careers – Trench is a prisoner in Omdurman.'

'So is Harry Feversham.'

Sutch stared at his visitor. For a moment he did not understand, the shock had been too sudden and abrupt. Then, after comprehension dawned upon him, he refused to believe. The folly of that refusal in its turn became apparent. He sat down in his chair opposite to Durrance, awed into silence. And the silence lasted for a long while.

'What am I to do?' he said at length.

'I have thought it out,' returned Durrance. 'You must go to Suakin. I will give you a letter to Willoughby, who is Deputy Governor, and another to a Greek merchant there whom I know, and on whom you can draw for as much money as you require.'

'That's good of you, Durrance, upon my word,' Sutch interrupted; and, forgetting that he was talking to a blind man, he held out his hand across the table. 'I would not take a penny if I could help it. But I am a poor man. Upon my soul, it's good of you.'

'Just listen to me, please,' said Durrance. He could not see the outstretched hand, but his voice showed that he would hardly have taken it if he had. He was striking the final blow at his chance of happiness. But he did not wish to be thanked for it. 'At Suakin you must take the Greek merchant's advice and organise a rescue as best you can. It will be a long business, and you will have many disappointments before you succeed; but you must stick to it until you do.'

Upon that the two men fell to a discussion of the details of the length of time which it would take for a message from Suakin to be carried into Omdurman, of the untrustworthiness of some Arab spies, and of the risks which the trustworthy ran. Sutch's house was searched for maps; the various routes by which the prisoners might escape were described by Durrance – the great forty days' road from Kordofan on the west, the straight track from Omdurman to Berber and from Berber to Suakin, and the desert journey across the Belly of Stones by the wells of Murat to Korosko. It was late before Durrance had told all that he thought necessary and Sutch had exhausted his questions.

'You will stay at Suakin as your base of operations,' said Durrance as he closed up the maps.

'Yes,' answered Sutch; and he rose from his chair. 'I will start as soon as you give me the letters.'

'I have them already written.'

'Then I will start to-morrow. You may be sure I will let both you and Miss Eustace know how the attempt progresses.'

'Let me know,' said Durrance, 'but not a whisper of it to Ethne. She knows nothing of my plan, and she must know nothing until Feversham comes back himself. She has her point of view, as I have mine. Two lives shall not be spoilt because of her. That's her resolve. She believes that to some degree she was herself the cause of Harry Feversham's disgrace – that but for her he would not have resigned his commission.'

'Yes.'

'You agree to that? At all events, she believes it. So there's one life spoilt because of her. Suppose now I go to her and say, "I know that you pretend out of your charity and kindness to care for me, but in your heart you are no more than my friend," why, I hurt her, and cruelly. For there's all that's left of the second life spoilt too. But bring back Feversham! Then I can speak – then I can say freely, "Since you are just my friend, I would rather be your friend and nothing more. So neither life will be spoilt at all." '

'I understand,' said Sutch. 'It's the way a man should speak. So till Feversham comes back the pretence remains. She pretends to care for you, you pretend you do not know she thinks of Harry. While I go eastwards to bring him home, you go back to her.'

'No,' said Durrance, 'I can't go back. The strain of keeping up the pretence was telling too much on both of us. I go to

Wiesbaden. An oculist lives there who serves me for an excuse. I shall wait at Wiesbaden until you bring Harry home.'

Sutch opened the door, and the two men went out into the hall. The servants had long since gone to bed. A couple of candlesticks stood upon a table beside a lamp. More than once Lieutenant Sutch had forgotten that his visitor was blind, and he forgot the fact again. He lighted both candles, and held out one to his companion. Durrance knew from the noise of Sutch's movements what he was doing.

'I have no need of a candle,' he said with a smile. The light fell upon his face, and Sutch suddenly remarked how tired it looked and old. There were deep lines from the nostrils to the corners of the mouth, and furrows in the cheeks. His hair was grey as an old man's hair. Durrance had himself made so little of his misfortune this evening that Sutch had rather come to rate it as a small thing in the sum of human calamities; but he read his mistake now in Durrance's face. Just above the flame of the candle, framed in the darkness of the hall, it showed white and drawn and haggard – the face of an old worn man set upon the stalwart shoulders of a man in the prime of his years.

'I have said very little to you in the way of sympathy,' said Sutch. 'I did not know that you would welcome it. But I am sorry. I am very sorry.'

'Thanks,' said Durrance simply. He stood for a moment or two silently in front of his host. 'When I was in the Soudan, travelling through the deserts, I used to pass the white skeletons of camels lying by the side of the track. Do you know the camel's way? He is an unfriendly, graceless beast, but he marches to within an hour of his death. He drops and dies with the load upon his back. It seemed to me even in those days the right and enviable way to finish. You can imagine how I must envy them that advantage of theirs now. Good night.'

He felt for the banister, and walked up the stairs to his room.

Chapter Twenty-six

GENERAL FEVERSHAM'S PORTRAITS ARE APPEASED

Lieutenant Sutch, though he went late to bed, was early astir in the morning. He roused the household, packed and repacked his clothes, and made such a bustle and confusion that everything to be done took twice its ordinary time in the doing. There never had been so much noise and flurry in the house during all the thirty years of Lieutenant Sutch's residence. His servants could not satisfy him, however quickly they scuttled about the passages in search of this or that forgotten article of his old travelling outfit. Sutch, indeed, was in a boyish fever of excitement. It was not to be wondered at, perhaps. For thirty years he had lived inactive – on the world's half-pay list, to quote his own phrase; and at the end of all that long time miraculously something had fallen to him to do – something important, something which needed energy and tact and decision. Lieutenant Sutch, in a word, was to be employed again. He was feverish to begin his employment. He dreaded the short interval before he could begin, lest some hindrance should unexpectedly occur and relegate him again to inactivity.

'I shall be ready this afternoon,' he said briskly to Durrance as they breakfasted. 'I shall catch the night mail to the Continent. We might go up to London together; for London is on your way to Wiesbaden.'

'No,' said Durrance. 'I have just one more visit to pay in England. I did not think of it until I was in bed last night. You put it into my head.'

'Oh,' observed Sutch; 'and whom do you propose to visit?'

'General Feversham,' replied Durrance.

Sutch laid down his knife and fork, and looked with surprise at his companion.

'Why in the world do you wish to see him?' he asked.

215

'I want to tell him how Harry has redeemed his honour – how he is still redeeming it. You said last night that you were bound by a promise not to tell him anything of his son's intention, or even of his son's success, until the son returned himself. But I am bound by no promise. I think such a promise bears hardly on the General. There is nothing in the world which could pain him so much as the proof that his son was a coward. Harry might have robbed and murdered. The old man would have preferred him to have committed both these crimes. I shall cross into Surrey this morning and tell him that Harry never was a coward.'

Sutch shook his head.

'He will not be able to understand. He will be very grateful to you, of course. He will be very glad that Harry has atoned his disgrace, but he will never understand why he incurred it. And after all he will only be glad because the family honour is restored.'

'I don't agree,' said Durrance. 'I believe the old man is rather fond of his son, though, to be sure, he would never admit it. I rather like General Feversham.'

Lieutenant Sutch had seen very little of General Feversham during the last five years. He could not forgive him for his share in the responsibility of Harry Feversham's ruin. Had the General been capable of sympathy with and comprehension of the boy's nature, the white feathers would never have been sent to Ramelton. Sutch pictured the old man sitting sternly on his terrace at Broad Place, quite unaware that he was himself at all to blame, and, on the contrary, rather inclined to pose as a martyr in that his son had turned out a shame and disgrace to all the dead Fevershams whose portraits hung darkly on the high walls of the hall. Sutch felt that he could never endure to talk patiently with General Feversham; and he was sure that no argument would turn that stubborn man from his convictions. He had not troubled at all to consider whether the news which Durrance had brought should be handed on to Broad Place.

'You are very thoughtful for others,' he said to Durrance.

'It's not to my credit. I practise thoughtfulness for others out of an instinct of self-preservation, that's all,' said Durrance.

'Selfishness is the natural and encroaching fault of the blind. I know that, so I am careful to guard against it.'

He travelled accordingly that morning by branch lines from Hampshire into Surrey, and came to Broad Place in the glow of the afternoon. General Feversham was now within a few months of his eightieth year, and though his back was as stiff and his figure as erect as on that night, now so many years ago, when he first presented Harry to his Crimean friends, he was shrunken in stature, and his face seemed to have grown small. Durrance had walked with the General upon his terrace only two years ago, and, blind though he was, he noticed a change within this interval of time. Old Feversham walked with a heavier step, and there had come a note of puerility into his voice.

'You have joined the veterans before your time, Durrance,' he said. 'I read of it in a newspaper. I would have written had I known where to write.'

If he had any suspicion of Durrance's visit, he gave no sign of it. He rang the bell, and tea was brought into the great hall, where the portraits hung. He asked after this and that officer in the Soudan with whom he was acquainted; he discussed the iniquities of the War Office, and feared that the country was going to the deuce.

'Everything, through ill-luck or bad management, is going to the devil, sir,' he exclaimed irritably. 'Even you, Durrance, you are not the same man who walked with me on my terrace two years ago.'

The General had never been remarkable for tact, and the solitary life he led had certainly brought no improvement. Durrance could have countered with a *tu quoque*, but he refrained.

'But I come upon the same business,' he said.

Feversham sat up stiffly in his chair.

'And I give you the same answer. I have nothing to say about Harry Feversham. I will not discuss him.'

He spoke in his usual hard and emotionless voice. He might have been speaking of a stranger. Even the name was uttered without the slightest hint of sorrow. Durrance began to wonder whether the fountains of affection had not been altogether dried up in General Feversham's heart.

'It would not please you, then, to know where Harry Feversham has been and how he has lived during the last five years?'

There was a pause – not a long pause, but still a pause – before General Feversham answered –

'Not in the least, Colonel Durrance.'

The answer was uncompromising, but Durrance relied upon the pause which preceded it.

'Nor on what business he has been engaged?' he continued.

'I am not interested in the smallest degree. I do not wish him to starve, and my solicitor tells me that he draws his allowance. I am content with that knowledge, Colonel Durrance.'

'I will risk your anger, General,' said Durrance. 'There are times when it is wise to disobey one's superior officer. This is one of the times. Of course, you can turn me out of the house. Otherwise I shall relate to you the history of your son and my friend since he disappeared from England.'

General Feversham laughed.

'Of course, I can't turn you out of the house,' he said; and he added severely, 'but I warn you that you are taking an improper advantage of your position as my guest.'

'Yes, there is no doubt of that,' Durrance answered calmly; and he told his story – the recovery of the Gordon letters from Berber, his own meeting with Harry Feversham at Wadi Halfa, and Harry's imprisonment at Omdurman. He brought it down to that very day, for he ended with the news of Lieutenant Sutch's departure for Suakin. General Feversham heard the whole account without an interruption, without even stirring in his chair. Durrance could not tell in what spirit he listened, but he drew some comfort from the fact that he did listen, and without argument.

For some while after Durrance had finished, the General sat silent. He raised his hand to his forehead and shaded his eyes, as though the man who had spoken could see; and thus he remained. Even when he did speak, he did not take his hand away. Pride forbade him to show to those portraits on the walls that he was capable even of so natural a weakness as joy at the reconquest of honour by his son.

'What I don't understand,' he said slowly, 'is why Harry ever resigned his commission. I could not understand it before; I understand it even less now since you have told me of his great bravery. It is one of the queer inexplicable things. They happen, and there's all that can be said. But I am very glad that you compelled me to listen to you, Durrance.'

'I did it with a definite object. It is for you to say, of course, but for my part I do not see why Harry should not come home and enter in again to all that he lost.'

'He cannot regain everything,' said Feversham. 'It is not right that he should. He committed the sin, and he must pay. He cannot regain his career, for one thing.'

'No; that is true. But he can find another. He is not yet so old but that he can find another. And that is all that he will have lost.'

General Feversham now took his hand away and moved in his chair. He looked quickly at Durrance; he opened his mouth to ask a question, but changed his mind.

'Well,' he said briskly, and as though the matter were of no particular importance, 'if Sutch can manage Harry's escape from Omdurman, I see no reason either why he should not come home.'

Durrance rose from his chair. 'Thank you, General. If you can have me driven to the station I can catch a train to town. There's one at six.'

'But you will stay the night, surely,' cried General Feversham.

'It is impossible. I start for Wiesbaden early to-morrow.'

Feversham rang the bell and gave the order for a carriage. 'I should have been very glad if you could have stayed,' he said, turning to Durrance. 'I see very few people nowadays. To tell the truth, I have no great desire to see many. One grows old and a creature of customs.'

'But you have your Crimea nights,' said Durrance cheerfully.

Feversham shook his head. 'There have been none since Harry went away. I had no heart for them,' he said slowly. For a second the mask was lifted and his stern features softened. He had suffered much during these five lonely years of his old age, though not one of his acquaintances up to this moment had ever detected a look upon his face or heard a sentence from his lips which could lead them so to think. He had shown a stubborn front to the world. He had made it a matter of pride that no one should be able to point a finger at him and say, 'There's a man struck down.' But on this one occasion and in these few words he revealed to Durrance the depth of his grief. Durrance understood how unendurable the chatter of his friends about the old days of war in the snowy trenches would have been. An anecdote recalling some particular act of courage would hurt as keenly as a story of cowardice. The whole history of his lonely life at Broad Place was laid bare in that simple statement that there had been no Crimean nights, for he had no heart for them.

The wheels of the carriage rattled on the gravel.

'Good-bye,' said Durrance; and he held out his hand.

'By the way,' said Feversham, 'to organise this escape from Omdurman will cost a great deal of money. Sutch is a poor man. Who is paying?'

'I am.'

Feversham shook Durrance's hand in a firm clasp. 'It is my right, of course,' he said.

'Certainly. I will let you know what it costs.'

'Thank you.'

General Feversham accompanied his visitor to the door. There was a question which he had it in his mind to ask, but the question was delicate. He stood uneasily on the steps of the house.

'Didn't I hear, Durrance,' he said, with an air of carelessness, 'that you were engaged to Miss Eustace?'

'I think I said that Harry would regain all that he had lost except his career,' said Durrance.

He stepped into the carriage and drove off to the station. His work was ended. There was nothing more for him now to do, except to wait at Wiesbaden and pray that Sutch might succeed. He had devised the plan; it remained for those who had eyes wherewith to see to execute it.

General Feversham stood upon the steps looking after the carriage until it disappeared among the pines. Then he walked slowly back into the hall. 'There is no reason why he should not come back,' he said. He looked up at the pictures. The dead Fevershams in their uniforms would not be disgraced. 'No reason in the world,' he said. 'And please God he will come back soon.' The dangers of an escape from the Dervish city remote among the sands began to loom very large on his mind. He owned to himself that he felt very tired and old, and many times that night he repeated his prayer, 'Please God, Harry will come back soon,' as he sat erect upon the bench which had once been his wife's favourite seat, and gazed out across the moonlit country to the Sussex downs.

Chapter Twenty-seven

THE HOUSE OF STONE

These were the days before the great mud wall was built about the House of Stone in Omdurman. Only a thorn zareeba as yet enclosed that noisome prison and the space about it. It stood upon the eastern border of the town, surely the most squalid capital of any Empire since the world began. Not a flower bloomed in a single corner. There was no grass nor the green shade of any tree. A brown and stony plain burnt by the sun, and, built upon it, a straggling narrow city of hovels crawling with vermin and poisoned with disease.

Between the prison and the Nile no houses stood, and at this time the prisoners were allowed, so long as daylight lasted, to stumble in their chains down the half-mile of broken sloping earth to the Nile bank, so that they might draw water for their use and perform their ablutions. For the native or the negro then escape was not so difficult. For along that bank the dhows were moored, and they were numerous; the river traffic, such as there was of it, had its harbour there, and the wide foreshore made a convenient market place. Thus the open space between the river and the House of Stone was thronged and clamorous all day, captives rubbed elbows with their friends, concerted plans of escapes, or then and there slipped into the

221

thickest of the crowd and made their way to the first black-smith, with whom the price of iron outweighed any risk he took. But even on their way to the blacksmith's shop their fetters called for no notice in Omdurman. Slaves wore them as a daily habit, and hardly a street in all that long brown treeless squalid city was ever free from the clink of a man who walked in chains.

But for the European escape was another matter. There were not so many white prisoners but that each was a marked man. Besides, relays of camels stationed through the desert, much money, long preparations, and, above all, devoted natives who would risk their lives were the first necessities for their evasion. The camels might be procured and stationed, but it did not follow that their drivers would remain at the stations; the long preparations might be made, and the whip of the gaoler overset them at the end by flogging the captive within an inch of his life on a suspicion that he had money; the devoted servant might shrink at the last moment. Colonel Trench began to lose all hope. His friends were working for him, he knew. For at times the boy who brought his food into the prison would bid him be ready; at times, too, when at some parade of the Khalifa's troops he was shown in triumph as an emblem of the destiny of all the Turks, a man perhaps would jostle against his camel and whisper encouragements. But nothing ever came of the encouragements. He saw the sun rise daily beyond the bend of the river behind the tall palm trees of Khartum and burn across the sky, and the months dragged one after the other.

On an evening towards the end of August, in that year when Durrance came home blind from the Soudan, he sat in a corner of the enclosure watching the sun drop westwards towards the plain with an agony of anticipation. For however intolerable the heat and burden of the day, it was as nothing compared with the horrors which each night renewed. The moment of twilight came, and with it Idris-es-Saier, the great negro of the Gawaamah tribe, and his fellow gaolers.

'Into the House of Stone!' he cried.

Praying and cursing with the sound of the pitiless whips falling perpetually upon the backs of the hindmost, the prisoners

jostled and struggled at the narrow entrance to the prison house.
Already it was occupied by some thirty captives, lying upon
the swamped mud floor or supported against the wall in the
last extremities of weakness and disease. Two hundred more
were driven in that night and penned there till morning. The
room was perhaps thirty feet square, of which four feet were
occupied by a solid pillar supporting the roof. There was no
window in the building; a few small apertures near the roof
made a pretence of giving air, and into this foul and pestilent
hovel the prisoners were packed, screaming and fighting. The
door was closed upon them, utter darkness replaced the twilight, so that a man could not distinguish even the outlines of
the heads of the neighbours who wedged him in.

Colonel Trench fought like the rest. There was a corner near
the door which he coveted at that moment with a greater
fierceness of desire than he had ever felt in the days when he
had been free. Once in that corner he would have some shelter
from the blows, the stamping feet, the bruises of his neighbour's shackles; he would have, too, a support against which to
lean his back during the ten interminable hours of suffocation.

'If I were to fall! If I were to fall!'

That fear was always with him when he was driven in at
night. It worked in him like a drug producing madness. For if
a man once went down amid that yelling, struggling throng
he never got up again – he was trampled out of shape. Trench
had seen such victims dragged from the prison each morning;
and he was a small man. Therefore he fought for his corner in
a frenzy like a wild beast, kicking with his fetters, thrusting
with his elbows, diving under this big man's arm, burrowing
between two others, tearing at their clothes, using his nails, his
fists, and even striking at heads with the chain which dangled
from the iron ring about his neck. He reached the corner in the
end, streaming with the heat and gasping for breath; the rest
of the night he would spend in holding it against all comers.

'If I were to fall!' he gasped. 'O God, if I were to fall!' and
he shouted aloud to his neighbour – for in that clamour nothing
less than a shout was audible – 'Is it you, Ibrahim?' and a
like shout answered him, 'Yes, Effendi.'

Trench felt some relief. Between Ibrahim, a great tall Arab

223

of the Hadendoas, and Trench a friendship born of their common necessities had sprung up. There were no prison rations at Omdurman; each captive was dependent upon his own money or the charity of his friends outside. To Trench from time to time there came money from his friends brought secretly into the prison by a native who had come up from Assouan or Suakin; but there were long periods during which no help came to him, and he lived upon the charity of the Greeks who had sworn conversion to the Mahdist faith, or starved with such patience as he could. There were times, too, when Ibrahim had no friend to send him his meal into the prison. And thus each man helped the other in his need. They stood side by side against the wall at night.

'Yes, Effendi, I am here,' and groping with his hand in the black darkness he steadied Trench against the wall.

A fight of even more than common violence was raging in an extreme corner of the prison, and so closely packed were the prisoners that with each advance of one combatant and retreat of the other the whole jostled crowd swayed in a sort of rhythm, from end to end, from side to side. But they swayed fighting to keep their feet, fighting even with their teeth, and above the din and noise of their hard breathing, the clank of their chains and their imprecations, there rose now and then a wild sobbing cry for mercy, or an inhuman shriek stifled as soon as uttered, which showed that a man had gone down beneath the stamping feet. Missiles, too, were flung across the prison, even to the foul earth gathered from the floor, and, since none knew from what quarter they were flung, heads were battered against heads in the effort to avoid them. And all these things happened in the blackest darkness.

For two hours Trench stood in that black prison ringing wiith noise, rank with heat, and there were eight hours to follow before the door would be opened and he could stumble into the clean air and fall asleep in the zareeba. He stood upon tiptoe that he might lift his head above his fellows, but even so he could barely breathe, and the air he breathed was moist and sour. His throat was parched, his tongue was swollen in his mouth and stringy like a dried fig. It seemed to him that the imagination of God could devise no worse hell than the House of Stone on an August night in Omdurman. It could add fire, he thought, but only fire.

'If I were to fall!' he cried, and as he spoke his hell was made perfect, for the door was opened, and Idris-es-Saier appeared in the opening.

'Make room,' he cried, 'make room,' and he threw fire among the prisoners to drive them from the door. Lighted tufts of dried grass blazed in the darkness and fell upon the bodies of the prisoners. The captives were so crowded they could not avoid the missiles, in places even they could not lift their hands to dislodge them from their shoulders or their heads.

'Make room,' cried Idris. The whips of his fellow-gaolers enforced his command, the lashes fell upon all within reach, and a little space was cleared within the door. Into that space a man was flung and the door closed again.

Trench was standing close to the door; in the dim twilight which came through the doorway he had caught a glimpse of the new prisoner, a man heavily ironed, slight of figure, and bent with suffering.

'He will fall,' he said, 'he will fall to-night. God if I were to fall!' and suddenly the crowd swayed against him, and the curses rose louder and shriller than before.

The new prisoner was the cause. He clung to the door with his face against the panels, through the chinks of which actual air might come. Those behind plucked him from his vantage, jostled him, pressed him backwards that they might take his place. He was driven, as a wedge is driven by a hammer, between this prisoner and that, until at last he was flung against Colonel Trench.

The ordinary instincts of kindness could not live in the nightmare of that prison-house. In the daytime, outside, the prisoners were often drawn together by their bond of a common misery, the faithful as often as not helped the infidel. But to fight for life during the hours of darkness without pity or cessation was the one creed and practice of the House of Stone. Colonel Trench was like the rest. The need to live, if only long enough to drink one drop of water in the morning and draw one clean mouthful of fresh air, was more than uppermost in his mind. It was the only thought he had.

225

'Back,' he cried violently, 'back, or I strike,' and as he wrestled to lift his arm above his head that he might strike the better, he heard the man who had been flung against him incoherently babbling English.

'Don't fall,' cried Trench, and he caught his fellow captive by the arm. 'Ibrahim, help! God, if he were to fall!' and while the crowd swayed again, and the shrill cries and curses rose again, deafening the eares, piercing the brain, Trench supported his companion, and, bending down his head, caught again after so many months the accent of his own tongue. And the sound of it civilised him like the friendship of a woman.

He could not hear what was said; the din was too loud. But he caught, as it were, shadows of words which had once been familiar to him, which had been spoken to him, which he had spoken to others – as a matter of course. In the House of Stone they sounded most wonderful. They had a magic, too. Meadows of grass, cool skies, and limpid rivers rose in grey, quiet pictures before his mind. For a moment he was insensible to his parched throat, to the stench of that prison-house, to the oppressive blackness. But he felt the man whom he supported totter and slip, and again he cried to Ibrahim –

'If he were to fall!'

Ibrahim helped as only he could. Together they fought and wrestled until those about them yielded, crying –

'Shaitan! They are mad!'

They cleared a space in that corner, and, setting the Englishman down upon the ground, they stood in front of him lest he should be trampled. And behind him upon the ground Trench heard every now and then in the lull of the noise the babble of English.

'He will die before morning,' he cried to Ibrahim; 'he is in a fever!'

'Sit beside him,' said the Hadendoa. 'I can keep them back.'

Trench stooped and squatted in the corner, Ibrahim set his legs well apart, and guarded Trench and his new friend.

Bending his head, Trench could now hear the words. They were the words of a man in delirium, spoken in a voice of great pleading. He was telling some tale of the sea, it seemed.

'I saw the riding lights of the yachts – and the reflections shortening and lengthening as the water rippled – there was a band, too, as we passed the pier-head. What was it playing? Not the overture – and I don't think that I remember any other tune . . .' And he laughed with a crazy chuckle. 'I was always pretty bad at appreciating music, wasn't I? Except when you played,' and again he came back to the sea. 'There was the line of hills upon the right as the boat steamed out of the bay – you remember there were woods on the hillside – perhaps you have forgotten. Then came Bray, a little fairyland of lights close down by the water at the point of the ridge . . . you remember Bray, we lunched there once or twice, just you and I before everything was settled . . . it seemed strange to be steaming out of Dublin Bay and leaving you a long way off to the north among the hills . . . strange, and somehow not quite right . . . for that was the word you used when the morning came behind the blinds – it is not right that one should suffer so much pain . . . the engines didn't stop though, they just kept throbbing and revolving and clanking as though nothing had happened whatever . . . one felt a little angry about that . . . the fairyland was already only a sort of golden blot behind . . . and then nothing but sea and the salt wind . . . and the things to be done.'

The man in his delirium suddenly lifted himself upon an elbow and with the other hand fumbled in his breast as though he searched for something. 'Yes, the things to be done,' he repeated in a mumbling voice, and he sank to unintelligible whisperings with his head fallen upon his breast.

Trench put an arm about him and raised him up. But he could do nothing more, and even to him, crouched as he was close to the ground, the noisome heat was almost beyond endurance. In front the din of shrill voices, the screams for pity, the swaying and struggling went on in that appalling darkness. In one corner there were men singing in a mad frenzy, in another a few danced in their fetters, or rather tried to dance; in front of Trench Ibrahim maintained his guard; and beside Trench there lay in the House of Stone, in the town beyond the world, a man who one night had sailed out of Dublin Bay past the riding lanterns of the yachts, and had seen Bray, that fairyland of lights, dwindle to a golden blot. The thought of the sea and the salt wind, the sparkle of light as the water split at the ship's bows, the illuminated deck, perhaps the sound of a bell telling the hour, and the cool, dim night about and above, so wrought upon Trench that, practical unimaginative creature as he was, for very yearning he could have wept. But the stranger at his side began to speak again.

'It is funny that those three faces were always the same . . . the man in the tent with the lancet in his hand, and the man in the back room off Piccadilly . . . and mine. Funny, and not quite right. No, I don't think that was quite right either. They get quite big, too, just when you are going to sleep in the dark – quite big, and they come very close to you, and won't go away . . . they rather frighten one . . .' And he suddenly clung to Trench with a close, nervous grip, like a boy in an extremity of fear. And it was in the tone of reassurance that a man might use to a boy that Trench replied, 'It's all right, old man, it's all right.'

But Trench's companion was already relieved of his fear. He had come out of his boyhood, and was rehearsing some interview which was to take place in the future.

'Will you take it back?' he asked, with a great deal of hesitation and timidity. 'Really? The others have, all except the man who died at Tamai. And you will, too!' He spoke as though he could hardly believe some piece of great good fortune which had befallen him. Then his voice changed to that of a man belittling his misfortunes. 'Oh, it hasn't been the best of times, of course. But then one didn't expect the best of times. And at the worst one had always the afterwards to look forward to . . . supposing one didn't run . . . I'm no sure that when the whole thing's balanced it won't come out that you have really had the worst time. I know you . . . it would hurt you through and through, pride and heart and everything, and for a long time just as much as it hurt that morning when the daylight came through the blinds. And you couldn't do anything! And you hadn't the afterwards to look forward to . . . it was all over and done with for you . . .' and he lapsed again into mutterings.

Colonel Trench's delight in the sound of his native tongue had now given place to a great curiosity as to the man who spoke and what he said. Trench had described himself a long while ago, as he stood opposite the capstand in the south-west corner of St James's Square: 'I am an inquisitive, methodical person,' he had said, and he had not described himself amiss. Here was a life history, it seemed, being unfolded to his ears, and not the happiest of histories, perhaps indeed with something of tragedy at the heart of it. Trench began to speculate upon the meaning of that word 'afterwards', which came and went among the words like the *motif* in a piece of music, and very likely was the life *motif* of the man who spoke them.

In the prison the heat became stifling, the darkness more oppressive, but the cries and shouts were dying down; their volume was less great, their intonation less shrill; stupor and fatigue and exhaustion were having their effect. Trench bent his head again to his companion, and now heard more clearly.

'I saw your light that morning . . . you put it out suddenly . . . did you hear my step on the gravel? . . . I thought you did, it hurt rather,' and then he broke out into an emphatic protest. 'No, no, I had no idea that you would wait. I had no wish that you should. Afterwards perhaps, I thought, but nothing more, upon my word. Sutch was quite wrong . . . Of course there was always the chance that one might come to grief one's self – get killed, you know, or fall ill and die – before one asked you to take your feather back; and then there wouldn't even have been a chance of the afterwards. But that is the risk one had to take.'

The allusion was not direct enough for Colonel Trench's comprehension. He heard the word 'feather', but he could not connect it as yet with any action of his own. He was more curious than ever after that 'afterwards;' he began to have a glimmering of its meaning, and he was struck with wonderment at the thought of how many men there were going about the world with a calm and commonplace demeanour, beneath which were hidden quaint fancies and poetic beliefs, never to be so much as suspected, until illness deprived the brain of its control.

'No, one of the reasons I never said anything that night to you about what I intended was, I think, that I did not wish you to wait or to have any suspicion of what I was going to attempt.' And then expostulation ceased and he began to speak in a tone of interest. 'Do you know? It has only occurred to me since I came to the Soudan, but I believe that Durrance cared.'

The name came with something of a shock upon Trench's ears. This man knew Durrance! He was not merely a stranger of Trench's blood, but he know Durrance even as Trench knew him. There was a link between them, they had a friend in common. He knew Durrance, had fought in the same square with him perhaps, at Tokar or Tamai or Tamanib, just as Trench had done! And so Trench's curiosity as to the life history in its turn gave place to a curiosity as to the identity of the man. He tried to see, knowing that in that black and noisesome hovel sight was impossible. He might hear, though, enough to be assured. For if the stranger knew Durrance, it might be that he knew Trench as well. Trench listened; the sound of the voice, high-pitched and rambling, told him nothing. He waited for the words and the words came.

'Durrance stood at the window, after I had told them about you, Ethne.' And Trench repeated the name to himself. It was a woman, then, that his new-found compatriot, this friend of Durrance, in his delirium imagined himself to be speaking – a woman named Ethne. Trench could recall no such name; but the voice in the dark went on.

'All the time when I was proposing to send in my papers, after the telegram had come, he stood at the window of my rooms with his back to me, looking out across the park. I fancied he blamed me. But I think now he was making up his mind to lose you . . . I wonder.'

Trench uttered so startled an exclamation that Ibrahim turned round.

'Is he dead?'

'No, he lives, he lives.'

It was impossible, Trench argued. He remembered quite clearly Durrance standing by a window with his back to the room. He remembered a telegram coming which took a long while in the reading – which diffused among all except Durrance an inexplicable suspense. He remembered, too, a man who spoke of his betrothal and of sending in his papers. But surely this could not be the man. Was the woman's name Ethne? A woman of Donegal – yes; and this man had spoken of sailing out of Dublin Bay. He had spoken, too, of a feather.

'Good God!' whispered Trench. 'Was the name Ethne? Was it? Was it?'

But for a while he received no answer. He heard only talk of a mud-walled city and an intolerable sun burning upon a wide round of desert, and a man who lay there all the day with his linen robe drawn over his head, and slowly drew one face towards him across three thousand miles, until at sunset it was near, and he took courage and went down into the gate. And after that four words stabbed Trench.

'Three little white feathers' were the words. Trench leaned back against the wall. It was he who had devised that message. 'Three little white feathers,' the voice repeated. 'This afternoon we were under the elms down by the Lennon River – do you remember, Harry? – just you and I. And then came three little white feathers; and the world's at an end.'

Trench had no longer any doubts. The man was quoting words, and words, no doubt, spoken by this girl Ethne on the night when the three feathers came. 'Harry,' she had said. 'Do you remember, Harry?' Trench was certain.

'Feversham!' he cried, 'Feversham!' And he shook the man whom he held in his arms, and called to him again. 'Under the elms by the Lennon River.' Visions of green shade touched with gold and of the sunlight flickering between the leaves caught at Trench and drew him like a mirage in that desert of which Feversham had spoken. Feversham had been under the elms of the Lennon River on that afternoon before the feathers came, and he was in the House of Stone at Omdurman. But why? Trench asked himself the question, and was not spared the answer.

'Willoughby took his feather back'–and upon that Feversham broke off. His voice rambled. He seemed to be running somewhere amid sandhills, which continually shifted and danced about him as he ran, so that he could not tell which way he went. He was in the last stage of fatigue too, so that his voice in his delirium became querulous and weak. 'Abou Fatma!' he cried; and the cry was the cry of a man whose throat is parched and whose limbs fail beneath him. 'Abou Fatma! Abou Fatma!' He stumbled as he ran, picked himself up, ran and stumbled again; and about him the deep, soft sand piled itself into pyramids, built itself into long slopes and ridges, and levelled itself flat with an extraordinary and a malicious rapidity. 'Abou Fatma!' cried Feversham; and he began to argue in a weak, obstinate voice. 'I know the wells are here – close by – within half a mile. I know they are – I know they are.'

The clue to that speech Trench had not got. He knew nothing of Feversham's adventure at Berber; he could not tell that the wells were the wells of Obak, or that Feversham, tired with the hurry of his travelling and after a long day's march without water, had lost his way among the shifting sandhills. But he did know that Willoughby had taken back his feather; and he made a guess as to the motive which had brought Feversham now to the House of Stone. Even on that point, however, he was not to remain in doubt; for in a while he heard his own name upon Feversham's lips.

Remorse seized upon Colonel Trench. The sending of the feathers had been his invention, and his alone. He could not thrust the responsibility of his invention upon either Willoughby or Castleton; it was just his doing. He had thought it rather a shrewd and clever stroke, he remembered, at the time – a vengeance eminently just. Eminently just no doubt it was, but he had not thought of the woman. He had not imagined that she might be present when the feathers came. He had, indeed, almost forgotten the episode. He had never speculated upon the consequences, and now they rose up and smote the smiter.

And his remorse was to grow. For the night was not nearly at its end. All through the dark, slow hours he supported Feversham and heard him talk. Now Feversham was lurking in the bazaar at Suakin, and during the siege.

'During the siege,' thought Trench. 'While we were there, then, he was herding with the camel-drivers in the bazaar, learning their tongues, watching for his chance. Three years of it!'

At another moment Feversham was slinking up the Nile to Wadi Halfa with a zither in the company of some itinerant musicians, hiding from any who might remember him and accuse him with his name. Trench heard of a man slipping out from Wadi Halfa, crossing the Nile, and wandering, with the assumed manner of a lunatic, southwards, starving and waterless, until one day he was snapped up by a Mahdist caravan and dragged to Dongola as a spy. And at Dongola things had happened of which the mere mention made Trench shake. He heard of leather cords which had been bound about the prisoner's wrists, and upon which water had been poured until the cords swelled and the wrists burst; but this was among the minor brutalities. Trench waited for the morning as he listened, wondering whether indeed it would ever come.

He heard the bolts dragged back at the last; he saw the door open, and the good daylight. He stood up, and, with Ibrahim's help, protected his new comrade until the eager rush was past. Then he supported him out into the zareeba. Worn, wasted in body and face, with a rough beard straggled upon his chin, and his eyes all sunk and very bright, it was still Harry Feversham. Trench laid him down in a corner of the zareeba where there would be shade, and in a few hours shade would be needed. Then with the rest he scrambled to the Nile for water, and brought it back. As he poured it down Feversham's throat Feversham seemed for a moment to recognise him. But it was only for a moment; and the incoherent tale of his adventures began again. Thus, after five years, and for the first time since Trench had dined as Feversham's guest in the high rooms overlooking St James's Park, the two met in the House of Stone.

Chapter Thirty-three

PLANS OF ESCAPE

For three days Feversham rambled and wandered in his talk, and for three days Trench fetched him water from the Nile, shared his food with him, and ministered to his wants; for three nights, too, he stood with Ibrahim and fought in front of Feversham in the House of Stone. But on the fourth morning Feversham waked to his senses, and, looking up with his own eyes, saw bending over him the face of Trench. At first the face

233

seemed a part of his delirium – one of those nightmare faces which used to grow big and had come so horribly close to him in the dark nights of his boyhood as he lay in bed. He put out a weak arm and thrust it aside. But he gazed about him. He was lying in the shadow of the prison-house, and the hard blue sky above him, the brown bare trampled soil on which he lay, and the figures of his fellow-prisoners dragging their chains or lying prone upon the ground in some extremity of sickness, gradually conveyed their meaning to him. He turned to Trench, caught at him as if he feared the next moment would snatch him out of reach, and then smiled.

'I am in the prison of Omdurman,' he said. 'Actually in the prison! This is Umm Hagar, the House of Stone. It seems too good to be true.'

He leaned back against the wall with an air of extreme relief. To Trench the words, the tone of satisfaction in which they were uttered, sounded like some sardonic piece of irony. A man who plumed himself upon indifference to pain or pleasure – who posed as a being of so much experience that joy and trouble could no longer stir a pulse or cause a frown, and who carried his pose to perfection – such a man, thought Trench, might have uttered Feversham's words in Feversham's voice. But Feversham was not that man, his delirium had proved it. The satisfaction, then, was genuine, the words were sincere. The peril of Dongola was past, he had found Trench, he was in Omdurman. The prison-house was his longed-for goal, and he had reached it. He might have been dangling on a gibbet hundreds of miles away down the stream of the Nile, with the vultures perched upon his shoulders, the purpose for which he lived quite unfulfilled. But he was in the enclosure of the House of Stone in Omdurman.

'You have been here a long while,' he said.

'Three years.'

Feversham looked round the zareeba. 'Three years of it,' he murmured. 'I was afraid that I might not find you alive.'

Trench nodded.

'The nights are the worst, the nights in there. It's a wonder any man lives through a week of them. Yet I have lived through a thousand nights.' And even to him who had endured them his endurance seemed incredible. 'A thousand nights of the House of Stone!' he exclaimed.

'But we may go down to the Nile by daytime,' said Feversham, and he started up with alarm as he gazed at the thorn zareeba. 'Surely we are allowed so much liberty. I was told so. An Arab at Wadi Halfa told me.'

'And it's true,' returned Trench. 'Look!' He pointed to the earthen bowl of water at his side. 'I filled that at the Nile this morning.'

'I must go,' said Feversham, and he lifted himself up from the ground. 'I must go this morning,' and since he spoke with a raised voice and a manner of excitement, Trench whispered to him –

'Hush! There are many prisoners here, and among them many tale bearers.'

Feversham sank back on to the ground as much from weakness as in obedience to Trench's warning.

'But they cannot understand what we say,' he objected in a voice from which the excitement had suddenly gone.

'They can see that we talk together and earnestly. Idris would know of it within the hour, the Khalifa before sunset. There would be heavier fetters and the courbatch if we spoke together at all. Lie still. You are weak, and I, too, am very tired. We will sleep, and later in the day we will go together down to the Nile.'

Trench lay down beside Feversham and in a moment was asleep. Feversham watched him, and saw, now that his features were relaxed, the mark of those three years very plainly in his face. It was towards noon before he awoke.

'There is no one to bring you food?' he asked, and Feversham answered –

'Yes. A boy should come. He should bring news as well.'

They waited until the gate of the zareeba was opened and the friends or wives of the prisoners entered. At once that enclosure became a cage of wild beasts. The gaolers took their dole at the outset. Little more of the 'aseeda' – that moist and pounded cake of dhurra which was the staple diet of the town – than was sufficient to support life was allowed to reach the

235

prisoners, and even for that the strong fought with the weak and the group of four did battle with the group of three. From every corner men gaunt and thin as skeletons hopped and leaped as quickly as the weight of their chains would allow them towards the entrance. Here one weak with starvation tripped and fell, and, once fallen, lay prone in a stolid despair, knowing that for him there would be no meal that day. Others seized upon the messengers who brought the food, and tore it from their hands, though the whips of the gaolers laid their backs open. There were thirty gaolers to guard that enclosure, each armed with his rhinoceros-hide courbatch, but this was the one moment in each day when the courbatch was neither feared, nor, as it seemed, felt.

Among the food-bearers a boy sheltered himself behind the rest, and gazed irresolutely about the zareeba. It was not long, however, before he was detected; he was knocked down, and his food snatched from his hands; but the boy had his lungs, and his screams brought Idris-es-Saier himself upon the three men who had attacked him.

'For whom do you come?' asked Idris, as he thrust the prisoners aside.

'For Joseppi, the Greek,' answered the boy, and Idris pointed to the corner where Feversham lay. The boy advanced, holding out his empty hands as though explaining how it was that he brought no food. But he came quite close, and, squatting at Feversham's side, continued to explain with words. And as he spoke he loosed a gazelle skin which was fastened about his waist beneath his jibbeh, and he let it fall by Feversham's side. The gazelle skin contained a chicken, and upon that Feversham and Trench breakfasted and dined and supped. An hour later they were allowed to pass out of the zareeba and make their way to the Nile. They walked slowly and with many halts, and during one of these Trench said –

'We can talk here.'

Below them at the water's edge some of the prisoners were unloading dhows, others were paddling knee-deep in the muddy water. The shore was crowded with men, screaming and shouting and excited for no reason whatever. The gaolers were within view, but not within earshot.

'Yes, we can talk here. Why have you come?'

'I was captured in the desert, on the Arbaîn road,' said Feversham slowly.

'Yes, masquerading as a lunatic musician who had wandered out of Wadi Halfa with a zither. I know. But you were captured by your own deliberate wish. You came to join me in Omdurman. I know.'

'How do you know?'

'You told me. During the last three days you have told me much;' and Feversham looked about him suddenly in alarm. 'Very much,' continued Trench. 'You came to join me because five years ago I sent you a white feather.'

'And was that all I told you?' asked Feversham anxiously.

'No,' Trench replied, and he dragged out the word. He sat up while Feversham lay on his side, and he looked towards the Nile in front of him, holding his head between his hands, so that he could not see or be seen by Feversham. 'No, that was not all – you spoke of a girl, the same girl of whom you spoke when Willoughby and Durrance and I dined with you in London a long while ago. I know her name now – her Christian name. She was with you when the feathers came. I had not thought of that possibility. She gave you a fourth feather to add to our three. I am sorry.'

There was a silence of some length, and then Feversham replied slowly –

'For my part I am not sorry. I mean I am not sorry that she was present when the feathers came. I think on the whole that I am rather glad. She gave me the fourth feather, it is true, but I am glad of that as well. For without her presence, without that fourth feather snapped from her fan, I might have given up there and then. Who knows? I doubt if I could have stood up to the three long years in Suakin. I used to see you and Durrance and Willoughby and many men who had once been my friends, and you were all going about the work which I was used to. You can't think how the mere routine of a regiment to which one had become accustomed, and which one cursed heartily enough when one had to put up with it, appealed as something very desirable. I could so easily have run away. I could so easily have slipped on to a boat and gone back to Suez.

And the chance for which I waited never came – for three years.'

'You saw us?' said Trench. 'And you gave no sign?'

'How would you have taken it if I had?' And Trench was silent. 'No, I saw you, but I was careful that you should not see me. I doubt if I could have endured it without the recollection of that night at Ramelton, without the feel of the fourth feather to keep the recollection actual and recent in my thoughts. I should never have gone down from Obak into Berber. I should certainly never have joined you in Omdurman.'

Trench turned quickly towards his companion.

'She would be glad to hear you say that,' he said. 'I have no doubt she is sorry about her fourth feather, sorry as I am about the other three.'

'There is no reason that she should be, or that you either should be sorry. I don't blame you or her,' and in his turn Feversham was silent and looked towards the river.

The air was shrill with cries, the shore was thronged with a motley of Arabs and negroes, dressed in their long robes of blue and yellow and dirty brown, the work of unloading the dhows went busily on; across the river and beyond its fork the palm trees of Khartum stood up against the cloudless sky, and the sun behind them was moving down to the west. In a few hours would come the horrors of the House of Stone. But they were both thinking of the elms by the Lennon River and a hall of which the door stood open to the cool night and which echoed softly to the music of a waltz, while a girl and a man stood with three white feathers fallen upon the floor between them; the one man recollected, the other imagined the picture, and to both of them it was equally vivid.

Feversham smiled at last.

'Perhaps she has now seen Willoughby, perhaps she has now taken his feather.'

Trench held out his hand to his companion.

'I will take mine back now.'

Feversham shook his head.

'No, not yet;' and Trench's face suddenly lighted up. A hope, which had struggled up in his hopeless breast during the three days and nights of his watch, a hope which he had striven to repress for very fear lest it might prove false, sprang to life.

'Not yet – then you *have* a plan for our escape;' and the anxiety returned to Feversham's face.

'I said nothing of it,' he pleaded, 'tell me that! When I was delirious in the prison there, I said nothing of it, I breathed no word of it? I told you of the four feathers, I told you of Ethne, but of the plan for your escape I said nothing.'

'Not a single word. So that I myself was in doubt, and did not dare to believe;' and Feversham's anxiety died away. He had spoken with his hand trembling upon Trench's arm, and his voice itself had trembled with alarm.

'You see if I spoke of that in the House of Stone,' he exclaimed, 'I might have spoken of it in Dongola. For in Dongola as well as Omdurman I was delirious. But I didn't, you say – not here at all events. So perhaps not there either. I was afraid that I should – how I was afraid! There was a woman in Dongola who spoke some English – very little, but enough. She had been in the "Kauneesa" of Khartum when Gordon ruled there. She was sent to question me. I had unhappy times in Dongola.'

Trench interrupted him in a low voice. 'I know. You told me things which made me shiver,' and he caught hold of Feversham's arm and thrust the loose sleeve back. Feversham's scarred wrists confirmed the tale.

'Well, I felt myself getting light-headed there,' he went on. 'I made up my mind to think of something else with all my might when I was going off my head.' And he laughed a little to himself. 'That was why you heard me talk of Ethne,' he explained.

Trench sat nursing his knees and looking straight in front of him. He had paid no heed to Feversham's last words. He had dared now to give his hopes their way.

'So it's true,' he said in a quiet wondering voice. 'There will be a morning when we shall not drag ourselves out of the House of Stone. There will be nights when we shall sleep in beds – actually in beds. There will be —' He stopped with a sort of shy air like a man upon the brink of a confession. 'There will be – something more,' he said lamely, and then he got up on to his feet.

239

'We have sat here too long. Let us go forward.'

They moved a hundred yards nearer to the river and sat down again.

'You have more than a hope. You have a plan of escape?' Trench asked eagerly.

'More than a plan,' returned Feversham. 'The preparations are made. There are camels waiting in the desert ten miles west of Omdurman.'

'Now?' exclaimed Trench – 'now?'

'Yes, man, now. There are rifles and ammunition buried near the camels, provisions and water kept in readiness. We travel by Metemneh, where fresh camels wait, from Metemneh to Berber. There we cross the Nile; camels are waiting for us five miles from Berber. From Berber we ride in over the Kokreb Pass to Suakin.'

'When?' exclaimed Trench. 'Oh! when, when?'

'When I have strength enough to sit a horse for ten miles and a camel for a week,' answered Feversham. 'How soon will that be? Not long, Trench, I promise you not long,' and he rose up from the ground.

'As you get up,' he continued, 'glance round. You will see a man in a blue linen dress, loitering between us and the gaol. As we came past him he made me a sign. I did not return it. I shall return it on the day we escape.'

'He will wait?'

'For a month. We must manage on one night during that month to escape from the House of Stone. We can signal him to bring help. A passage might be made in one night through that wall, the stones are loosely built.'

They walked a little further and came to the water's edge. There amid the crowd they spoke again of their escape, but with the air of men amused at what went on about them.

'There is a better way than breaking through the wall,' said Trench, and he uttered a laugh as he spoke, and pointed to a prisoner with a great load upon his back who had fallen upon his face in the water, and, encumbered by his fetters, pressed down by his load, was vainly struggling to lift himself again. 'There is a better way. You have money?'

'Ai, ai!' shouted Feversham, roaring with laughter as the

240

prisoner half rose and soused again. I have some concealed on me. Idris took what I did not conceal.'

'Good!' said Trench. 'Idris will come to you to-day or to-morrow. He will talk to you of the goodness of Allah, who has brought you out of the wickedness of the world to the holy city of Omdurman. He will tell you at great length of the peril of your soul and of the only means of averting it, and he will wind up with a few significant sentences about his starving family. If you come to the aid of his starving family and bid him take fifteen dollars of your store, you may get permission to sleep in the zareeba outside the prison. Be content with that for a night or two. Then he will come to you again, and again you will assist his starving family, and this time you will ask for permission for me to sleep in the open too. Come! There's Idris shepherding us home.'

It fell out as Trench had predicted. Idris read Feversham an abnormally long lecture that afternoon. Feversham learned that now God loved him, and how Hicks Pasha's army had been destroyed. The holy angels had done that; not a single shot was fired, not a single spear thrown by the Mahdi's soldiers. The spears flew from their hands by the angels' guidance and pierced the unbelievers. Feversham heard for the first time of a most convenient spirit, Nebbi Khiddr, who was the Khalifa's eyes and ears, and reported to him all that went on in the gaol. It was pointed out to Feversham that if Nebbi Khiddr reported against him he would have heavier shackles riveted upon his feet, and many unpleasant things would happen. At last came the exordium about the starving children, and Feversham begged Idris to take fifteen dollars.

Trench's plan succeeded. That night Feversham slept in the open, and two nights later Trench lay down beside him. Overhead was a clear sky and the blazing stars.

'Only three more days,' said Feversham, and he heard his companion draw in a long breath. For a while they lay side by side in silence, breathing the cool night air, and then Trench said –

'Are you awake?'

'Yes.'

'Well,' and with some hesitation he made that confidence

241

which he had repressed on the day when they sat upon the foreshore of the Nile. 'Each man has his particular weak spot of sentiment, I suppose. I have mine. I am not a marrying man, so it's not sentiment of that kind. Perhaps you will laugh at it. It isn't merely that I loathe this squalid, shadeless, vile town of Omdurman, or the horrors of its prison. It isn't merely that I hate the emptiness of those desert wastes. It isn't merely that I am sick of the palm trees of Khartum, or these chains, or the whips of the gaolers. But there's something more. I want to die at home, and I have been desperately afraid so often that I should die here. I want to die at home – not merely in my own country, but in my own village, and be buried there under the trees I know, in the sight of the church and the houses I know, and the trout stream where I fished when I was a boy. You'll laugh, no doubt.'

Feversham was not laughing. The words had a queer ring of familiarity to him, and he knew why. They never had actually been spoken to him, but they might have been, and by Ethne Eustace.

'No, I am not laughing,' he answered. 'I understand.' And he spoke with a warmth of tone which rather surprised Trench. And indeed an actual friendship sprang up between the two men, and it dated from that night.

It was a fit moment for confidences. Lying side by side in that enclosure, they made them one to the other in low voices. The shouts and yells came muffled from within the House of Stone and gave to them both a feeling that they were well off. They could breathe, they could see, no low roof oppressed them. They were in the cool of the night air. That night air would be very cold before morning and wake them to shiver in their rags and huddle together in their corner. But at present they lay comfortably upon their backs with their hands clasped behind their heads, and watched the great stars and planets burn in the blue dome of sky.

'It will be strange to find them dim and small again,' said Trench.

'There will be compensations,' answered Feversham with a laugh, and they fell to making plans of what they would do when they had crossed the desert and the Mediterranean and the Continent of Europe, and had come to their own country of dim small stars. Fascinated and enthralled by the pictures which the simplest sentence, the most commonplace phrase, through the magic of its associations was able to evoke in their minds, they let the hours slip by unnoticed. They were no longer prisoners in that barbarous town which lay a murky stain upon the solitary wide spaces of sand; they were in their own land, following their old pursuits. They were standing outside clumps of trees, guns in their hands, while the sharp cry 'Mark! mark!' came to their ears. Trench heard again the unmistakable rattle of the reel of his fishing-rod as he wound in his line upon the bank of his trout-stream. They talked of theatres in London and the last plays which they had seen, the last books which they had read six years ago.

'There goes the Great Bear,' said Trench suddenly. 'It is late.' The tail of the constellation was dipping behind the thorn hedge of the zareeba. They turned over on their sides.

'Three more days,' said Trench.

'Only three more days,' Feversham replied. And in a minute they were neither in England nor the Soudan. The stars marched to the morning unnoticed above their heads. They were lost in the pleasant countries of sleep.

Chapter Twenty-nine

COLONEL TRENCH ASSUMES A KNOWLEDGE OF CHEMISTRY

'Three more days.' Both men fell asleep with these words upon their lips. But the next morning Trench waked up and complained of a fever; and the fever rapidly gained upon him, so that before the afternoon had come he was light-headed, and those services which he had performed for Feversham, Feversham had now to perform for him. The thousand nights of the House of Stone had done their work. But it was no mere coincidence that Trench should suddenly be struck down by them at

243

the very moment when the door of his prison was opening. The great revulsion of joy which had come to him so unexpectedly had been too much for his exhausted body. The actual prospect of escape had been the crowning trial which he could not endure.

'In a few days he will be well,' said Feversham. 'It is nothing.'

'It is *Umm Sabbah*,' answered Ibrahim, shaking his head, the terrible typhus fever which had struck down so many in that infected gaol and carried them off upon the seventh day.

Feversham refused to believe. 'It is nothing,' he repeated in a sort of passionate obstinacy, but in his mind there ran another question: 'Will the men with the camels wait?' Each day as he went to the Nile he saw Abou Fatma in the blue robe at his post; each day the man made his sign, and each day Feversham gave no answer. Meanwhile with Ibrahim's help he nursed Trench. The boy came daily to the prison with food; he was sent out to buy tamarinds, dates, and roots, out of which Ibrahim brewed cooling draughts. Together they carried Trench from shade to shade as the sun moved across the zareeba. Some further assistance was provided for the starving family of Idris, and the forty-pound chains which Trench wore were subsequently removed. He was given vegetable marrow soaked in salt water, his mouth was packed with butter, his body anointed and wrapped close in camel-clothes. The fever took its course, and on the seventh day Ibrahim said –

'This is the last. To-night he will die.'

'No,' replied Feversham; 'that is impossible. 'In his own parish,' he said, 'beneath the trees he knew. Not here, no.' And he spoke again with a passionate obstinacy. He was no longer thinking of the man in the blue robe outside the prison walls, or of the chances of escape. The fear that the third feather would never be brought back to Ethne, that she would never have the opportunity to take back the fourth of her own free will, no longer troubled him. Even that great hope of 'the afterwards' was for the moment banished from his mind. He thought only of Trench and the few awkward words he had spoken in the corner of the zareeba on the first night when they lay side by side under the sky. 'No,' he repeated, 'he must not die here.' And through all that day and night he watched by

Trench's side the long hard battle between life and death. At one moment it seemed that the three years of the House of Stone must win the victory, at another that Trench's strong constitution and wiry frame would get the better of the three years.

For that night, at all events, they did, and the struggle was prolonged. The dangerous seventh day was passed. Even Ibrahim began to gain hope; and on the thirteenth day Trench slept and did not ramble during his sleep, and when he waked it was with a clear head. He found himself alone, and so swathed in camel-cloths that he could not stir; but the heat of the day was past, and the shadow of the House of Stone lay black upon the sand of the zareeba. He had not any wish to stir, and he lay wondering idly how long he had been ill. While he wondered he heard the shouts of the gaolers, the cries of the prisoners outside the zareeba and in the direction of the river. The gate was opened, and the prisoners flocked in. Feversham was among them, and he walked straight to Trench's corner.

'Thank God!' he cried. 'I would not have left you, but I was compelled. We have been unloading boats all day.' And he dropped in fatigue by Trench's side.

'How long have I lain ill?' asked Trench.

'Thirteen days.'

'It will be a month before I can travel. You must go, Feversham. You must leave me here and go while you still can. Perhaps when you come to Assouan you can do something for me. I could not move at present. You will go to-morrow?'

'No, I should not go without you in any case,' answered Feversham. 'As it is, it is too late.'

'Too late?' Trench repeated. He took in the meaning of the words but slowly; he was almost reluctant to be disturbed by their mere sound; he wished just to lie idle for a long time in the cool of the sunset. But gradually the import of what Feversham had said forced itself into his mind.

'Too late? Then the man in the blue gown has gone?'

'Yes. He spoke to me yesterday by the river. The camel men would wait no longer. They were afraid of detection, and meant to return whether we went with them or not.'

'You should have gone with them,' said Trench. For himself

he did not at that moment care whether he was to live in the prison all his life, so long as he was allowed quietly to lie where he was for a long time: and it was without any expression of despair that he added, 'So our one chance is lost.'

'No; deferred,' replied Feversham. 'The man who watched by the river in the blue gown brought me paper, a pen, and some wood-soot mixed with water. He was able to drop them by my side as I lay upon the ground. I hid them beneath my jibbeh, and last night – there was a moon last night – I wrote to a Greek merchant who keeps a café at Wadi Halfa. I gave him the letter this afternoon, and he has gone. He will deliver it and receive money. In six months, in a year at the latest, he will be back in Omdurman.'

'Very likely,' said Trench. 'He will ask for another letter, so that he may receive more money, and again he will say that in six months or a year he will be back in Omdurman. I know these people.'

'You do not know Abou Fatma. He was Gordon's servant over there, before Khartum fell; he has been mine since. He came with me to Obak, and waited there while I went down to Berber. He risked his life in coming to Omdurman at all. Within six months he will be back, you may be very sure.'

Trench did not continue the argument. He let his eyes wander about the enclosure, and they settled at last upon a pile of newly turned earth which lay in one corner.

'What are they digging?' he asked.

'A well,' answered Feversham.

'A well?' said Trench fretfully, 'and so close to the Nile! Why? What's the object?'

'I don't know,' said Feversham. Indeed he did not know, but he suspected. With a great fear at his heart he suspected the reason why the well was being dug in the enclosure of the prison. He would not, however, reveal his suspicion until his companion was strong enough to bear the disappointment which belief in it would entail. But within a few days his suspicion was proved true. It was openly announced that a high wall was to be built about the House of Stone. Too many prisoners had escaped in their fetters along the Nile bank. Henceforward they were to be kept from year's beginning to year's end within the wall. The prisoners built it themselves of mud-bricks dried in the sun. Feversham took his share in the work, and Trench, as soon as he could stand, was joined with him.

'Here's our last hope gone,' he said; and though Feversham did not openly agree, in spite of himself his heart began to consent.

They piled the bricks one upon the other and mortised them. Each day the wall rose a root. With their own hands they closed themselves in. Twelve feet high the wall stood when they had finished it – twelve feet high, and smooth and strong. There was never a projection from its surface on which a foot could rest; it could not be broken through in a night. Trench and Feversham contemplated it in despair. The very palm trees of Khartum were now hidden from their eyes. A square of bright blue by day, a square of dark blue by night, jewelled with points of silver and flashing gold, limited their world. Trench covered his face with his hands.

'I daren't look at it,' he said in a broken voice. 'We have been building our own coffin, Feversham, that's the truth of it.' And then he cast up his arms and cried aloud, 'Will they never come up the Nile, the gunboats and the soldiers? Have they forgotten us in England! Good God! have they forgotten us?'

'Hush!' replied Feversham. 'We shall find a way of escape, never fear. We must wait six months. Well, we have both of us waited years. Six months: what are they?'

But, though he spoke stoutly for his comrade's sake, his own heart sank within him.

The details of their life during the six months are not to be dwelt upon. In that pestilent enclosure only the myriad vermin lived lives of comfort. No news filtered in from the world outside. They fed upon their own thoughts, so that the sight of a lizard upon the wall became an occasion for excitement. They were stung by scorpions at night; they were at times flogged by their gaolers by day. They lived at the mercy of the whims of Idris-es-Saier and that peculiar spirit Nebbi Khiddr, who always reported against them to the Khalifa just at the moment when Idris was most in need of money for his starving family. Religious men were sent by the Khalifa to convert them to the only true religion; and indeed the long theological disputations in the enclosure became events to which both men looked forward with eagerness. At one time they would be freed from the heavier shackles and allowed to sleep in the open; at another, without reason, those privileges would be withdrawn, and they struggled for their lives within the House of Stone.

The six months came to an end. The seventh began; a fortnight of it passed, and the boy who brought Feversham food could never cheer their hearts with word that Abou Fatma had come back.

'He will never come,' said Trench in despair.

'Surely he will – if he is alive,' said Feversham. 'But is he alive?'

The seventh month passed, and one morning at the beginning of the eighth there came two of the Khalifa's bodyguard to the prison, who talked with Idris. Idris advanced to the two prisoners.

'Verily God is good to you, you men from the bad world,' he said. 'You are to look upon the countenance of the Khalifa. How happy you should be!'

Trench and Feversham rose up from the ground in no very happy frame of mind. 'What does he want with us? Is this the end?' The questions started up clear in both their minds. They followed the two guards out through the door and up the street towards the Khalifa's house.

'Does it mean death?' said Feversham.

Trench shrugged his shoulders and laughed sourly. 'It is on the cards the Nebbi Khiddr has suggested something of the kind,' he said.

They were led into the great parade-ground before the mosque, and thence into the Khalifa's house, where another white man sat in attendance upon the threshold. Within the Khalifa was seated upon an angareb, and a grey-bearded Greek stood beside him. The Khalifa remarked to them that they were both to be employed upon the manufacture of gunpowder, with which the armies of the Turks were shortly to be overwhelmed.

Feversham was on the point of disclaiming any knowledge of the process, but before he could open his lips he heard Trench declaring in fluent Arabic that there was nothing connected with gunpowder which he did not know about; and upon his words they were both told they were to be employed at the powder factory under the supervision of the Greek.

For that Greek both prisoners will entertain a regard to their dying day. There was in the world a true Samaritan. It was out of sheer pity, knowing the two men to be herded in the House of Stone, that he suggested to the Khalifa their employment, and the same pity taught him to cover the deficiencies of their knowledge.

'I know nothing whatever about the making of gunpowder except that crystals are used,' said Trench. 'But we shall leave the prison each day, and that is something, though we return each night. Who knows when a chance of escape may come!'

The powder factory lay in the northward part of the town and on the bank of the Nile just beyond the limits of the great mud wall, and at the back of the slave market. Every morning the two prisoners were let out from the prison door, they tramped along the river bank on the outside of the town wall, and came into the powder factory past the storehouses of the Khalifa's bodyguard. Every evening they went back by the same road to the House of Stone. No guard was sent with them, since flight seemed impossible, and each journey that they made they looked anxiously for the man in the blue robe. But the months passed, and May brought with it the summer.

'Something has happened to Abou Fatma,' said Feversham. 'He has been caught at Berber perhaps. In some way he has been delayed.'

'He will not come,' said Trench.

Feversham could no longer pretend to hope that he would. He did not know of a sword-thrust received by Abou Fatma, as he fled through Berber on his return from Omdurman. He had been recognised by one of his old gaolers in that town, and had got cheaply off with the one thrust in his thigh. From that wound he had through the greater part of this year been slowly recovering in the hospital at Assouan. But though Feversham heard nothing of Abou Fatma, towards the end of May he received news that others were working for his escape. As Trench and he passed in the dusk of one evening between the storehouses and the town wall, a man in the shadows of one of the narrow alleys which opened from the storehouses whispered

249

to them to stop. Trench knelt down upon the ground and examined his foot as though a stone had cut it, and as he kneeled the man walked past them and dropped a slip of paper at their feet. He was a Suakin merchant, who had a booth in the grain market of Omdurman. Trench picked up the paper, hid it in his hand, and limped on, with Feversham at his side. There was no address or name upon the outside, and as soon as they had left the houses behind, and had only the wall upon their right and the Nile upon their left, Trench sat down again. There was a crowd upon the water's edge, men passed up and down between the crowd and them. Trench took his foot into his lap and examined the sole. But at the same time he unfolded the paper in the hollow of his hand and read the contents aloud. He could hardly read them, his voice so trembled. Feversham could hardly hear them, the blood so sang in his ears.

'A man will bring to you a box of matches. When he comes trust him. – SUTCH.' And he asked, 'Who is Sutch?'

'A great friend of mine,' said Feversham. 'He is in Egypt, then! Does he say where?'

'No; but since Mohamed Ali, the grain merchant, dropped the paper, we may be sure he is at Suakin. A man with a box of matches! Think, we may meet him to-night!'

But it was a month later when, in the evening, an Arab pushed past them on the river bank and said, 'I am the man with the matches. To-morrow by the storehouse at this hour.' And as he walked past them he dropped a box of coloured matches on the ground. Feversham stooped instantly.

'Don't touch them,' said Trench, and he pressed the box into the ground with his foot and walked on.

'Sutch!' exclaimed Feversham. 'So he comes to our help! How did he know that I was here?'

Trench fairly shook with excitement as he walked. He did not speak of the great new hope which so suddenly came to them, for he dared not. He tried even to pretend to himself that no message at all had come. He was afraid to let his mind dwell upon the subject. Both men slept brokenly that night, and every time they waked it was with a dim consciousness that something great and wonderful had happened. Feversham, as he lay upon his back and gazed upwards at the stars, had a fancy that he had fallen asleep in the garden of Broad Place, on the Surrey Hills, and that he had but to raise his head to see the dark pines upon his right hand and his left, and but to look behind to see the gables of the house against the sky. He fell asleep towards dawn, and within an hour was waked up by a violent shaking. He saw Trench bending over him with great fear on his face.

'Suppose they keep us in prison to-day,' he whispered in a shaking voice, plucking at Feversham. 'It has just occurred to to me. Suppose they did that!'

'Why should they?' answered Feversham, but the same fear caught hold of him, and they sat dreading the appearance of Idris lest he should have some such new order to deliver. But Idris crossed the yard and unbolted the prison door without a look at them. Fighting, screaming, jammed together in the entrance, pulled back, thrust forward, the captives struggled out into the air, and among them was one who ran, foaming at the mouth, and dashed his head against the wall.

'He is mad!' said Trench, as the gaolers secured him, and since Trench was unmanned that morning he began to speak rapidly and almost with incoherence. 'That's what I have feared, Feversham, that I should go mad. To die, even here, one could put up with that without overmuch regret; but to go mad!' and he shivered. 'If this man with the matches proves false to us, Feversham, I shall be near to it – very near to it. A man one day, a raving, foaming idiot the next – a thing to be put away out of sight, out of hearing. God, but that's horrible!' and he dropped his head between his hands, and dared not look up until Idris crossed to them and bade them go about their work. What work they did in the factory that day neither knew. They were only aware that the hours passed with an extraordinary slowness, but the evening came at last.

'Among the storehouses,' said Trench. They dived into the first alley which they passed, and turning a corner saw the man who had brought the matches.

'I am Abdul Kader,' he began at once. 'I have come to arrange for your escape. But at present flight is impossible;' and Trench swayed upon his feet as he heard the word.

'Impossible?' asked Feversham.

'Yes. I brought three camels to Omdurman, of which two have died. The Effendi at Suakin gave me money, but not enough. I could not arrange for relays, but if you will give me a letter to the Effendi telling him to give me two hundred pounds, then I will have everything ready and come again within three months.'

Trench turned his back so that his companion might not see his face. All his spirit had gone from him at this last stroke of fortune. The truth was clear to him, appallingly clear. Abdul Kader was not going to risk his life; he would be the shuttle going backwards and forwards between Omdurman and Suakin as long as Feversham cared to write letters and Sutch to pay money. But the shuttle would do no weaving.

'I have nothing with which to write,' said Feversham, and Abdul Kader produced them.

'Be quick,' he said. 'Write quickly, lest we be discovered.' And Feversham wrote; but though he wrote as Abdul suggested, the futility of his writing was as clear to him as to Trench.

'There is the letter,' he said, and he handed it to Abdul, and, taking Trench by the arm, walked without another word away.

They passed out of the alley and came again to the great mud wall. It was sunset. To their left the river gleamed with changing lights – here it ran the colour of an olive, there rose pink, and here again a brilliant green; above their heads the stars were coming out, in the east it was already dusk; and behind them in the town drums were beginning to beat with their barbaric monotone. Both men walked with their chins sunk upon their breasts, their eyes upon the ground. They had come to the end of hope, they were possessed with a lethargy of despair. Feversham thought not at all of the pine trees on the Surrey Hills, nor did Trench have any dread that something in his head would snap and that which made him man be reft from him. They walked slowly, as though their fetters had grown ten times their weight, and without a word. So stricken, indeed, were they that an Arab turned and kept pace beside them, and neither noticed his presence. In a few moments the Arab spoke –

'The camels are ready in the desert, ten miles to the west.'

But he spoke in so low a voice, and those whom he spoke were so absorbed in misery, that the words passed unheard. He repeated them, and Feversham looked up. Quite slowly their meaning broke in on Feversham's mind; quite slowly he recognised the man who uttered them.

'Abou Fatma!' he said.

'Hoosh!' returned Abou Fatma, 'the camels are ready.'

'Now?'

'Now.'

Trench leaned against the wall with his eyes closed, and the face of a sick man. It seemed that he would swoon, and Feversham took him by the arm.

'Is it true?' Trench asked faintly; and before Feversham could answer Abou Fatma went on –

'Walk forward very slowly. Before you reach the end of the wall it will be dusk. Draw your cloaks over your heads, wrap these rags about your chains, so that they do not rattle. Then turn and come back, go close to the water beyond the storehouses. I will be there with a man to remove your chains. But keep your faces well covered, and do not stop. He will think you slaves.'

With that he passed some rags to them, holding his hands behind his back, while they stood close to him. Then he turned and hurried back. Very slowly Feversham and Trench walked forward in the direction of the prison, the dusk crept across the river, mounted the long slope of sand, enveloped them. They sat down and quickly wrapped the rags about their chains and secured them there. From the west the colours of the sunset had altogether faded, the darkness gathered quickly about them. They turned and walked back along the road they had come. The drums were more numerous now, and above the wall there rose a glare of light. By the time they had reached the water's edge opposite the storehouses it was dark. Abou Fatma was already waiting with his blacksmith. The chains were knocked off without a word spoken.

'Come,' said Abou. 'There will be no moon to-night. How long before they discover you are gone?'

'Who knows? Perhaps already Idris has missed us. Perhaps he will not till morning. There are many prisoners.'

They ran up the slope of sand, between the quarters of the tribes, across the narrow width of the city, through the cemetery. On the far side of the cemetery stood a disused house; a man rose up in the doorway as they approached, and went in.

'Wait here,' said Abou Fatma, and he too went into the house. In a moment both men came back, and each one led a camel, and made it kneel.

'Mount,' said Abou Fatma. 'Bring its head round and hold it as you mount.'

'I know the trick,' said Trench.

Feversham climbed up behind him, the two Arabs mounted the second camel.

'Ten miles to the west,' said Abou Fatma, and he struck the camel on the flanks.

Behind them the glare of the lights dwindled, the tapping of the drums diminished.

Chapter Thirty

THE LAST OF THE
SOUTHERN CROSS

The wind blew keen and cold from the north. The camels, freshened by it, trotted out at their fastest pace.

'Quicker,' said Trench, between his teeth. 'Already Idris may have missed us.'

'Even if he has,' replied Feversham, 'it will take time to get men together for a pursuit, and those men must fetch their camels, and already it is dark.'

But although he spoke hopefully he turned his head again and again towards the glare of light above Omdurman. He could no longer hear the tapping of the drums, that was some consolation. But he was in a country of silence, where men could journey swiftly and yet make no noise. There would be no sound of galloping horses to warn him that pursuit was at his heels. Even at that moment the Ansar soldiers might be riding within thirty paces of them, and Feversham strained his eyes backwards into the darkness and expected the glimmer of a white turban. Trench, however, never turned his head. He rode with his teeth set, looking forward. Yet fear was no less strong in him than in Feversham. Indeed, it was stronger, for he did not look back towards Omdurman because he did not dare; and though his eyes were fixed directly in front of him, the things which he really saw were the long, narrow streets of the town behind him, the dotted fires at the corners of the streets, and men running hither and thither among the houses, making their quick search for the two prisoners escaped from the House of Stone.

Once his attention was diverted by a word from Feversham, and he answered without turning his head –

'What is it?'

'I no longer see the fires of Omdurman.'

'The golden blot, eh, very low down?' Trench answered in an abstracted voice. Feversham did not ask him to explain what his allusion meant, nor could Trench have disclosed why he had spoken it; the words had come back to him suddenly with a feeling that it was somehow appropriate that the vision which was the last thing to meet Feversham's eyes as he set out upon his mission he should see again now that that mission was accomplished. They spoke no more until two figures rose out of the darkness in front of them, at the very feet of their camels, and Abou Fatma cried in a low voice –

'Instanna!'

They halted their camels and made them kneel.

'The new camels are here?' asked Abou Fatma, and two of the men disappeared for a few minutes and brought four camels up. Meanwhile the saddles were unfastened and removed from the camels Trench and his companion had ridden out of Omdurman.

'They are good camels?' asked Feversham, as he helped to fix the saddles upon the fresh ones.

'Of the Anafi breed,' answered Abou Fatma. 'Quick! Quick!' and he looked anxiously to the East and listened.

'The arms?' said Trench. 'You have them? Where are they?' and he bent his body and searched the ground for them.

'In a moment,' said Abou Fatma, but it seemed that Trench could hardly wait for that moment to arrive. He showed even more anxiety to handle the weapons than he had shown fear that he would be overtaken.

'There is ammunition?' he asked feverishly.

'Yes, yes,' replied Abou Fatma, 'ammunition and rifles and revolvers.' He led the way to a spot about twenty yards from the camels where some long desert grass rustled about their legs. He stooped and dug into the soft sand with his hands.

'Here,' he said.

Trench flung himself upon the ground beside him and scooped with both hands, making all the while an inhuman whimpering sound with his mouth, like the noise a foxhound makes at a cover. There was something rather horrible to Feversham in his attitude as he scraped at the ground on his knees, in the action of his hands, quick like the movements of a dog's paws, and in the whine of his voice. He was sunk for the time into an animal. In a moment or two Trench's fingers touched the lock and trigger of a rifle, and he became man again. He stood up quietly with the rifle in his hands. The other arms were unearthed, the ammunition shared.

'Now,' said Trench, and he laughed with a great thrill of joy in the laugh. 'Now I don't mind. Let them follow from Omdurman! One thing is certain now. I shall never go back there; no, not even if they overtake us,' and he fondled the rifle which he held and spoke to it as though it lived.

Two of the Arabs mounted the old camels and rode slowly away to Omdurman. Abou Fatma and the other remained with the fugitives. They mounted and trotted north-eastwards. No more than a quarter of an hour had elapsed since they had first halted at Abou Fatma's word.

All that night they rode through halfa grass and mimosa trees and went but slowly, but they came about sunrise on to flat, bare ground broken with small hillocks.

'Are the Effendi tired?' asked Abou Fatma. 'Will they stop and eat? There is food upon the saddle of each camel.'

'No; we can eat as we go.'

Dates and bread and a draught of water from a zamsheyeh

256

made up their meal, and they ate it as they sat their camels. These, indeed, now that they were free of the long desert grass, trotted at their quickest pace. And at sunset that evening they stopped and rested for an hour. All through that night they rode and the next day, straining their own endurance and that of the beasts they were mounted on, now ascending on to high and rocky ground, now traversing a valley, and now trotting fast across plains of honey-coloured sand. Yet to each man the pace seemed always as slow as a funeral. A mountain would lift itself above the rim of the horizon at sunrise, and for the whole lifelong day it stood before their eyes, and was never a foot higher or an inch nearer. At times some men tilling a scanty patch of sorghum would send the fugitives' hearts leaping in their throats, and they must make a wide detour; or again a caravan would be sighted in the far distance by the keen eyes of Abou Fatma, and they made their camels kneel and lay crouched behind a rock, with their loaded rifles in their hands. Ten miles from Abu Klea a relay of fresh camels awaited them, and upon these they travelled, keeping a day's march westward of the Nile. Thence they passed through the desert country of the Ababdeh, and came in sight of a broad grey tract stretching across their path.

'The road from Berber to Merowi,' said Abou Fatma. 'North of it we turn east to the river. We cross that road to-night, and if God wills to-morrow evening we shall have crossed the Nile.'

'If God wills,' said Trench. 'If only He wills,' and he glanced about him in a fear which only increased the nearer they drew towards safety. They were in a country traversed by the caravans; it was no longer safe to travel by day. They dismounted, and all that day they lay hidden behind a belt of shrubs upon some high ground and watched the road and the people like specks moving along it. They came down and crossed it in the darkness, and for the rest of that night travelled hard towards the river. As the day broke Abou Fatma again bade them halt. They were in a desolate open country, whereon the smallest projection was magnified by the surrounding flatness. Feversham and Trench gazed eagerly to their right. Somewhere in that direction and within the range of their eyesight flowed the Nile, but they could not see it.

'We must build a circle of stones,' said Abou Fatma, 'and you must lie close to the ground within it. I will go forward to the river, and see that the boat is ready and that our friends are prepared for us. I shall come back after dark.'

They gathered the stones quickly and made a low wall about a foot high; within this wall Feversham and Trench laid themselves down upon the ground with a water-skin and their rifles at their sides.

'You have dates, too,' said Abou Fatma.

'Yes.'

'Then do not stir from the hiding-place till I come back. I will take your camels, and bring you back fresh ones in the evening.' And in company with his fellow Arab he rode off towards the river.

Trench and Feversham dug out the sand within the stones and lay down, watching the horizon between the interstices. For both of them this perhaps was the longest day of their lives. They were so near to safety and yet not safe. To Trench's thinking it was longer than a night in the House of Stone, and to Feversham longer than even one of those days six years back, when he had sat in his rooms above St James's Park and waited for the night to fall before he dared venture out into the streets. They were so near to Berber, and the pursuit must needs be close behind. Feversham lay wondering how he had ever found the courage to venture himself in Berber. They had no shade to protect them; all day the sun burnt pitilessly upon their backs, and within the narrow circle of stones they had no room wherein to move. They spoke hardly at all. The sunset, however, came at the last, the friendly darkness gathered about them, and a cool wind rustled through the darkness across the desert.

'Listen!' said Trench, and both men as they strained their ears heard the soft padding of camels very near at hand. A moment later a low whistle brought them out of their shelter.

'We are here,' said Feversham quietly.

'God be thanked,' said Abou Fatma. 'I have good news for you and bad news too. The boat is ready, our friends are waiting for us, camels are prepared for you on the caravan track by the river bank to Abu Hamed. But your escape is known, and the roads and the ferries are closely watched. Before sunrise we must have struck inland from the eastern bank of the Nile.'

They crossed the river cautiously about one o'clock of the morning, and sank the boat upon the far side of the stream. The camels were waiting for them, and they travelled inland and more slowly than suited the anxiety of the fugitives. For the ground was thickly covered with boulders, and the camels could seldom proceed at any pace faster than a walk. And all through the next day they lay hidden again within a ring of stones while the camels were removed to some high ground where they could graze. During the next night, however, they made good progress, and, coming to the groves of Abu Hamed in two days, rested for twelve hours there and mounted upon a fresh relay. From Abu Hamed their road lay across the great Nubian Desert.

Nowadays the traveller may journey through the two hundred and forty miles of the waterless plain of coal-black rocks and yellow sand, and sleep in his berth upon the way. The morning will show to him, perhaps, a tent, a great pile of coal, a water tank, and a number painted on a white sign-board, and the stoppage of the train will inform him that he had come to a station. Let him put his head from the window, he will see the long line of telegraph poles reaching from the sky's rim behind him to the sky's rim in front, and huddling together, as it seems, with less and less space between them the farther they are away. Twelve hours will enclose the beginning and the end of his journey, unless the engine break down or the rail be blocked. But in the days when Feversham and Trench escaped from Omdurman progression was not so easy a matter. They kept eastward of the present railways and along the line of wells among the hills. And on the second night of this stage of their journey Trench shook Feversham by the shoulder and waked him up.

'Look,' he said, and he pointed to the south. 'To-night there's no Southern Cross.' His voice broke with emotion. 'For six years, for every night of six years, until this night, I have seen the Southern Cross. How often have I lain awake watching it, wondering whether the night would ever come when I should not see those four slanting stars! I tell you, Feversham, this is

259

the first moment when I have really dared to think that we should escape.'

Both men sat up and watched the southern sky with prayers of thankfulness in their hearts; and when they fell asleep it was only to wake up again and again with a fear that they would after all still see that constellation blazing low down towards the earth, and to fall asleep again confident of the issue of their desert ride. At the end of seven days they came to Shof-el-Ain, a tiny well set in a barrel valley between featureless ridges, and by the side of that well they camped. They were in the country of the Amrab Arabs, and had come to an end of their peril.

'We are safe,' cried Abou Fatma. 'God is good. Northwards to Assouan, westwards to Wadi Halfa, we are safe!' And spreading a cloth upon the ground in front of the kneeling camels, he heaped dhurra before them. He even went so far in his gratitude as to pat one of the animals upon the neck, and it immediately turned upon him and snarled.

Trench reached out his hand to Feversham.

'Thank you,' he said simply.

'No needs of thanks,' answered Feversham, and he did not take the hand. 'I served myself from first to last.'

'You have learned the churlishness of a camel,' cried Trench. 'A camel will carry you where you want to go, will carry you till it drops dead, and yet if you show your gratitude it resents and bites. Hang it all, Feversham, there's my hand.'

Feversham untied a knot in the breast of his jibbeh and took out three feathers, two small, the feathers of a heron, the other large, an ostrich feather broken from a fan.

'Will you take yours back?'

'Yes.'

'You know what to do with it.'

'Yes. There shall be no delay.'

Feversham wrapped the remaining feathers carefully away in a corner of his ragged jibbeh and tied them safe.

'We shake hands, then,' said he, and as their hands met he added, 'To-morrow morning we part company.'

'Part company, you and I – after the year in Omdurman, the

weeks of flight?' exclaimed Trench. 'Why? There's no more to be done. Castleton's dead. You keep the feather which he sent, but he is dead. You can do nothing with it. You must come home.'

'Yes,' answered Feversham, 'but after you, certainly not with you. You go to Assouan and Cairo. At each place you will find friends to welcome you. I shall not go with you.'

Trench was silent for a while. He understood Feversham's reluctance, he saw that it would be easier for Feversham if he were to tell his story first to Ethne Eustace, and without Feversham's presence.

'I ought to tell you no one knows why you resigned your commission, or of the feathers we sent. We never spoke of it. We agreed never to speak, for the honour of the regiment. I can't tell you how glad I am that we all agreed and kept to the agreement,' he said.

'Perhaps you will see Durrance,' said Feversham; 'if you do, give him a message from me. Tell him that the next time he asks me to come and see him, whether it is in England or Wadi Halfa, I will accept the invitation.'

'Which way will you go?'

'To Wadi Halfa,' said Feversham, pointing westwards over his shoulder. 'I shall take Abou Fatma with me and travel slowly and quietly down the Nile. The other Arab will guide you into Assouan.'

They slept that night in security beside the well, and the next morning they parted company. Trench was the first to ride off, and as his camel rose to its feet, ready for the start, he bent down towards Feversham, who passed him the nose rein.

'Ramelton, that was the name? I shall not forget.'

'Yes, Ramelton,' said Feversham; 'there's a ferry across Lough Swilly to Rathmullen. You must drive the twelve miles to Ramelton. But you may not find her there.'

'If not there, I shall find her somewhere else. Make no mistake, Feversham, I shall find her.'

And Trench rode forward, alone with his Arab guide. More than once he turned his head and saw Feversham still standing by the well; more than once he was strongly drawn to stop and ride back to that solitary figure, but he contented himself with waving his hand, and even that salute was not returned.

Feversham, indeed, had neither thought nor eyes for the companion of his flight. His six years of hard probation had come this morning to an end, and yet he was more sensible of a certain loss and vacancy than of any joy. For six years, through many trials, through many falterings, his mission had strengthened and sustained him. It seemed to him now that there was nothing more wherewith to occupy his life. Ethne? No doubt she was long since married . . . and there came upon him all at once a great bitterness of despair for that futile, unnecessary mistake made by him six years ago. He saw again the room in London overlooking the quiet trees and lawns of St James's Park, he heard the knock upon the door, he took the telegram from his servant's hand.

He roused himself finally with the recollection that, after all, the work was not quite done. There was his father, who just at this moment was very likely reading his *Times* after breakfast upon the terrace of Broad Place among the pine trees upon the Surrey hills. He must visit his father, he must take the fourth feather back to Ramelton. There was a telegram, too, which must be sent to Lieutenant Sutch at Suakin.

He mounted his camel and rode slowly with Abou Fatma westwards towards Wadi Halfa. But the sense of loss did not pass from him that day, nor his anger at the act of folly which had brought about his downfall. The wooded slopes of Ramelton were very visible to him across the shimmer of the desert air. In the greatness of his depression, Harry Feversham upon this day, for the first time, doubted his faith in the 'afterwards'.

Chapter Thirty-one

FEVERSHAM RETURNS TO RAMELTON

On an August morning of the same year, Harry Feversham rode across the Lennon bridge into Ramelton. The fierce sun of the Soudan had tanned his face, the years of his probation had left their marks; he rode up the narrow streets of the town unrecognised. At the top of the hill he turned into the broad highway which, descending valleys and climbing hills, runs in one straight line to Letterkenny. He rode rather quickly in a company of ghosts.

The intervening years had gradually been dropping from his thoughts all through his journey across Egypt and the Continent. They were no more than visionary now. Nor was he occupied with any dream of the things which might have been but for his great fault. The things which had been, here, in this small town of Ireland, were too definite. Here he had been most happy, here he had known the uttermost of his misery; here his presence had brought pleasure, here too he had done his worst harm. Once he stopped when he was opposite to the church, set high above the road upon his right hand, and wondered whether Ethne was still at Ramelton – whether old Dermod was alive, and what kind of welcome he would receive. But he waked in a moment to the knowledge that he was sitting upon his horse in the empty road and in the quiet of an August morning. There were larks singing in the pale blue above his head; a landrail sent up its harsh cry from the meadow on the left; the crow of a cock rose clear from the valley. He looked about him, and rode briskly on down the incline in front of him and up the ascent beyond. He rode again with his company of ghosts – phantoms of people with whom upon this road he had walked and ridden and laughed, ghosts of old thoughts and recollected words. He came to a thick grove of trees, a broken

263

fence, a gateway with no gate. Inattentive to these evidences of desertion, he turned in at the gate and rode along a weedy and neglected drive. At the end of it he came to an open space before a ruined house. The aspect of the tumbling walls and unroofed rooms roused him at last completely from his absorption. He dismounted, and, tying his horse to the branch of a tree, ran quickly into the house and called aloud. No voice answered him. He ran from deserted room to deserted room. He descended into the garden, but no one came to meet him; and he understood now from the uncut grass upon the lawn, the tangled disorder of the flowerbeds, that no one would come. He mounted his horse again, and rode back at a sharp trot. In Ramelton he stopped at the inn, gave his horse to the ostler, and ordered lunch for himself. He said to the landlady who waited upon him –

'So Lennon House has been burned down? When was that?'

'Five years ago,' the landlady returned, 'just five years ago this summer.' And she proceeded, without further invitation, to give a voluminous account of the conflagration and the cause of it, the ruin of the Eustace family, the inebriety of Bastable, and the death of Dermod Eustace at Glenalla. 'But we hope to see the house rebuilt. It's likely to be, we hear, when Miss Eustace is married,' she said, in a voice which suggested that she was full of interesting information upon the subject of Miss Eustace's marriage. Her guest, however, did not respond to the invitation.

'And where does Miss Eustace live now?'

'At Glenalla,' she replied. 'Half-way on the road to Rathmullen there's a track leads up to your left. It's a poor mountain village is Glenalla, and no place for Miss Eustace at all, at all. Perhaps you will be wanting to see her?'

'Yes. I shall be glad if you will order my horse to be brought round to the door,' said the man; and he rose from the table to put an end to the interview.

The landlady, however, was not so easily dismissed. She stood at the door and remarked –

'Well, that's curious – that's most curious. For only a fortnight ago a gentleman burnt just as black as yourself stayed a night here on the same errand. He asked for Miss Eustace's address, and drove up to Glenalla. Perhaps you have business with her?'

'Yes, I have business with Miss Eustace,' the stranger returned. 'Will you be good enough to give orders about my horse?'

While he was waiting for his horse he looked through the leaves of the hotel-book, and saw under a date towards the end of July the name of Colonel Trench.

'You will come back, sir, to-night?' said the landlady as he mounted.

'No,' he answered, 'I do not think I shall come again to Ramelton.' And he rode down the hill, and once more that day crossed the Lennon bridge. Four miles on he came to the track opposite a little bay of the Lough, and, turning into it, he rode past a few white cottages up to the purple hollow of the hills. It was about five o'clock when he came to the long, straggling village. It seemed very quiet and deserted, and built without any plan. A few cottages stood together, then came a gap of fields, beyond that a small plantation of larches and a house which stood by itself. Beyond the house was another gap, through which he could see straight down to the water of the Lough, shining in the afternoon sun, and the white gulls poising and swooping above it. And after passing that gap he came to a small grey church, standing bare to the winds upon its tiny plateau. A pathway of white shell-dust led from the door of the church to the little wooden gate. As he came level with the gate a collie dog barked at him from behind it.

The rider looked at the dog, which was very grey about the muzzle. He noticed its marking, and stopped his horse altogether. He glanced towards the church, and saw that the door stood open. At once he dismounted; he fastened his horse to the fence, and entered the churchyard. The collie thrust its muzzle into the back of his knee, sniffed once or twice doubtfully, and suddenly broke into an exuberant welcome. The collie dog had a better memory than the landlady of the inn. He barked, wagged his tail, crouched and sprang at the stranger's shoulders, whirled round and round in front of him, burst into sharp, excited screams of pleasure, ran up to the church door and barked furiously there, then ran back and

265

jumped again upon his friend. The man caught the dog as it stood up with its forepaws upon his chest, patted it, and laughed. Suddenly he ceased laughing, and stood stock-still with his eyes towards the open door of the church. In the doorway Ethne Eustace was standing. He put the dog down, and slowly walked up the path towards her. She waited on the threshold without moving, without speaking. She waited, watching him, until he came close to her. Then she said simply –

'Harry.'

She was silent after that; nor did he speak. All the ghosts and phantoms of old thoughts in whose company he had travelled the whole of that day vanished away from his mind at her simple utterance of his name. Six years had passed since his feet crushed the gravel on the dawn of a June morning beneath her window. And they looked at one another, remarking the changes which those six years had brought. And the changes, unnoticed and almost imperceptible to those who had lived daily in their company, sprang very distinct to the eyes of these two. Feversham was thin, his face was wasted. The strain of life in the House of Stone had left its signs about his sunken eyes and in the look of age beyond his years. But these were not the only changes, as Ethne noticed; they were not, indeed, the most important ones. Her heart, although she stood so still and silent, went out to him in grief for the great troubles which he had endured; but she saw, too, that he came back without a thought of anger towards her for that fourth feather snapped from her fan. But she was clear-eyed even at this moment. She saw much more. She understood that the man who stood quietly before her now was not the same man whom she had last seen in the hall of Ramelton. There had been a timidity in his manner in those days, a peculiar diffidence, a continual expectation of other men's contempt, which had gone from him. He was now quietly self-possessed; not arrogant; on the other hand, not diffident. He had put himself to a long, hard test; and he knew that he had not failed. All that she saw; and her face lightened as she said –

'It is not all harm which has come of these years. They were not wasted.'

But Feversham thought of her lonely years in this village of

Glenalla – and thought with a man's thought, unaware that no-
where else would she have chosen to live. He looked into her
face, and saw the marks of the years upon it. It was not that
she had aged so much. Her big grey eyes shone as clearly as
before, the colour was still as bright upon her cheeks. But there
was more of character; she had suffered; she had eaten of the
tree of knowledge.

'I am sorry,' he said. 'I did you a great wrong six years ago,
and I need not.'

She held out her hand to him.

'Will you give it to me, please?'

And for a moment he did not understand.

'That fourth feather,' she said.

He drew his letter-case from his coat, and shook two feathers
out into the palm of his hand. The larger one, the ostrich
feather, he held out to her. But she said –

'Both.'

There was no reason why he should keep Castleton's feather
any longer. He handed them both to her, since she asked for
them, and she clasped them, and with a smile treasured them
against her breast.

'I have the feathers now,' she said.

'Yes,' answered Feversham; 'all four. What will you do with
them?'

Ethne's smile became a laugh.

'Do with them!' she cried in scorn. 'I shall do nothing with
them. I shall keep them. I am very proud to have them to keep.'

She kept them, as she had once kept Harry Feversham's
portrait. There was something perhaps in Durrance's conten-
tion that women so much more than men gather up their
experiences and live upon them, looking backwards. Feversham, at all events, would now have dropped the feathers then
and there and crushed them into the dust of the path with his
heel; they had done their work. They could no longer reproach,
they were no longer needed to encourage, they were dead things.
Ethne, however, held them tight in her hand; to her they were
not dead.

'Colonel Trench was here a fortnight ago,' she said. 'He told
me you were bringing it back to me.'

'But he did not know of the fourth feather,' said Feversham. 'I never told any man that I had it.'

'Yes. You told Colonel Trench on your first night in the House of Stone at Omdurman. He told me. I no longer hate him,' she added, but without a smile and quite seriously, as though it was an important statement which needed careful recognition.

'I am glad of that,' said Feversham. 'He is a great friend of mine.'

Ethne was silent for a moment or two. Then she said –

'I wonder whether you have forgotten our drive from Ramelton to our house when I came to fetch you from the quay? We were alone in the dog-cart, and we spoke — '

'Of the friends whom one knows for friends the first moment, and whom one seems to recognise even though one has never seen them before,' interrupted Feversham. 'Indeed I remember.'

'And whom one never loses whether absent or dead,' continued Ethne. 'I said that one could always be sure of such friends, and you answered — '

'I answered that one could make mistakes,' again Feversham interrupted.

'Yes, and I disagreed. I said that one might seem to make mistakes, and perhaps think so for a long while, but that in the end one would be proved not to have made them. I have often thought of those words. I remembered them very clearly when Captain Willoughby brought me the first feather, and with a great deal of remorse. I remember them again very clearly to-day, although I have no room in my thoughts for remorse. I was right, you see, and I should have clung firmly to my faith. But I did not.' Her voice shook a little, and pleaded as she went on: 'I was young. I knew very little. I was unaware how little. I judged hastily, but to-day I understand.'

She opened her hand and gazed for a while at the white feathers. Then she turned and went inside the church. Feversham followed her.

Chapter Thirty-two

IN THE CHURCH AT GLENALLA

Ethne sat down in the corner of a pew next to the aisle, and Feversham took his stand beside her. It was very quiet and peaceful within that tiny church. The afternoon sun shone through the upper windows and made a golden haze about the roof. The natural murmurs of the summer floated pleasantly through the open door.

'I am glad that you remembered our drive and what we said,' she continued. 'It is rather important to me that you should remember. Because, although I have got you back, I am going to send you away from me again. You will be one of the absent friends whom I shall not lose because you are absent.'

She spoke slowly, looking straight in front of her without faltering. It was a difficult speech for her to deliver, but she had thought over it night and day during this last fortnight, and the words were ready to her lips. At the first sight of Harry Feversham, recovered to her after so many years, so much suspense, so much suffering, it had seemed to her that she never would be able to speak them, however necessary it was that they should be spoken. But as they stood over against one another she had forced herself to remember that necessity until she actually recognised and felt it. Then she had gone back into the church and taken a seat, and gathered up her strength.

It would be easier for both of them, she thought, if she should give no sign of what so quick a separation cost her. He would know surely enough, and she wished him to know; she wished him to understand that not one moment of his six years, so far as she was concerned, had been spent in vain. But that could be understood without the signs of emotion. So she spoke her speech, looking steadily straight forward and speaking in an even voice.

'I know that you will mind very much just as I do. But there

269

is no help for it,' she resumed. 'At all events you are at home again, with the right to be at home. It is a great comfort to me to know that. But there are other, much greater reasons from which we can both take comfort. Colonel Trench told me enough of your captivity to convince me that we both see with the same eyes. We both understand that this second parting, hard as it is, is still a very slight small thing compared with the other, our first parting over at the house six years ago. I felt very lonely after that, as I shall not feel lonely now. There was a great barrier between us then separating us for ever. We should never have met again here or afterwards. I am quite sure of that. But you have broken the barrier down by all your pain and bravery during these last years. I am no less sure of that. I am absolutely confident about it, and I believe you are too. So that although we shall not see one another here and as long as we live, the afterwards is quite sure for us both. And we can wait for that. You can. You have waited with so much strength all these years since we parted. And I can too, for I get strength from your victory.'

She stopped, and for a while there was silence in that church. To Feversham her words were gracious as rain upon dry land. To hear her speak them uplifted him so that those six years of trial, of slinking into corners out of sight of his fellows, of lonely endurance, of many heart-sinkings and much bodily pain, dwindled away into insignificance. They had indeed borne their fruit to him. For Ethne had spoken in a gentle voice just what his ears had so often longed to hear as he lay awake at night in the bazaar at Suakin, in the Nile villages, in the dim wide spaces of the desert, and what he had hardly dared to hope she ever would speak. He stood quite silently by her side, still hearing her voice though the voice had ceased. Long ago there were certain bitter words which she had spoken, and he had told Sutch, so closely had they clung and stung, that he believed in his dying moments he would hear them again, and so go to his grave with her reproaches ringing in his ears. He remembered that prediction of his now and knew that it was false. The words he would hear would be those which she had just uttered.

For Ethne's proposal that they should separate he was not unprepared. He had heard already that she was engaged, and he did not argue against her wish. But he understood that she had more to say to him. And she had. But she was slow to speak it. This was the last time she was to see Harry Feversham; she meant resolutely to send him away. When once he had passed through that church door, through which the sunlight and the summer murmurs came, and his shadow gone from the threshold, she would never talk with him or set her eyes on him until her life was ended. So she deferred the moment of his going by silences and slow speech. It might be so very long before that end came. She had, she thought, the right to protract this one interview. She rather hoped that he would speak of his travels, his dangers; she was prepared to discuss at length with him even the politics of the Soudan. But he waited for her.

'I am going to be married,' she said at length, 'and immediately. I am to marry a friend of yours, Colonel Durrance.'

There was hardly a pause before Feversham answered –

'He has cared for you a long while. I was not aware of it until I went away, but, thinking over everything, I thought it likely, and in a very little time I became sure.'

'He is blind.'

'Blind!' exclaimed Feversham. 'He, of all men, blind!'

'Exactly,' said Ethne. 'He – of all men. His blindness explains everything – why I marry him, why I send you away. It was after he went blind that I became engaged to him. It was before Captain Willoughby came to me with the first feather. It was between those two events. You see, after you went away one thought over things rather carefully. I used to lie awake and think, and I resolved that two men's lives should not be spoilt because of me.'

'Mine was not,' Feversham interrupted. 'Please believe that.'

'Partly it was,' she returned, 'I know very well. You would not own it for my sake, but it was. I was determined that a second should not be. And so when Colonel Durrance went blind – you know the man he was, you can understand what blindness meant to him, the loss of everything he cared for —'

'Except you.'

'Yes,' Ethne answered quietly, 'except me. So I became engaged to him. But he has grown very quick – you cannot guess how quick. And he sees so very clearly. A hint tells him the whole hidden truth. At present he knows nothing of the four feathers.'

'Are you sure?' suddenly exclaimed Feversham.

'Yes. Why?' asked Ethne, turning her face towards him for the first time since she had sat down.

'Lieutenant Sutch was at Suakin while I was at Omdurman. He knew that I was a prisoner there. He sent messages to me; he tried to organise my escape.'

Ethne was startled.

'Oh,' she said. 'Colonel Durrance certainly knew that you were in Omdurman. He saw you in Wadi Halfa, and he heard that you had gone south into the desert. He was distressed about it; he asked a friend to get news of you, and the friend got news that you were in Omdurman. He told me so himself, and – yes, he told me that he would try to arrange for your escape. No doubt he has done that through Lieutenant Sutch. He has been at Wiesbaden with an oculist; he only returned a week ago. Otherwise he would have told me about it. Very likely he was the reason why Lieutenant Sutch was at Suakin, but he knows nothing of the four feathers. He only knows that our engagement was abruptly broken off; he believes that I have no longer any thought of you at all. But if you came back, if you and I saw anything of each other, however calmly we met, however indifferently we spoke, he would guess. He is so quick, he would be sure to guess.' She paused for a moment, and added in a whisper, 'And he would guess right.'

Feversham saw the blood flush her forehead and deepen the colour of her cheeks. He did not move from his position, he did not bend towards her, or even in voice give any sign that would make this leavetaking yet more difficult to carry through.

'Yes, I see,' he said. 'And he must not guess.'

'No, he must not,' returned Ethne. 'I am so glad you see that too, Harry. The straight and simple thing is the only thing for us to do. He must never guess, for, as you said, he has nothing left but me.'

'Is Durrance here?' asked Feversham.

'He is staying at the vicarage.'

'Very well,' he said. 'It is only fair that I should tell you I had no thought that you would wait. I had no wish that you should; I had no right to such a wish. When you gave me that fourth feather in the little room at Ramelton, with the music coming faintly through the door, I understood your meaning. There was to be a complete, an irrevocable end. We were not to be the merest acquaintances. So I said nothing to you of the plan which came clear and definite into my mind at the very time when you gave me the feathers. You see, I might never have succeeded. I might have died trying to succeed. I might even perhaps have shirked the attempt. It would be time enough for me to speak if I came back. So I never formed any wish that you should wait.'

'That was what Colonel Trench told me.'

'I told him that too?'

'On your first night in the House of Stone.'

'Well, it's just the truth. The most I hoped for – and I did hope for that every hour of every day – was that, if I did come home, you would take back your feather, and that we might – not renew our friendship here, but see something of one another afterwards.'

'Yes,' said Ethne. 'Then there will be no parting.'

Ethne spoke very simply, without even a sigh, but she looked at Harry Feversham as she spoke and smiled. The look and the smile told him what the cost of the separation would be to her. And, understanding what it meant now, he understood, with an infinitely greater completeness than he had ever reached in his lonely communings, what it must have meant six years ago when she was left with her pride stricken as sorely as her heart.

'What trouble you must have gone through!' he cried, and she turned and looked him over.

'Not I alone,' she said gently. 'I passed no nights in the House of Stone.'

'But it was my fault. Do you remember what you said when the morning came through the blinds? "It's not right that one should suffer so much pain." It was not right.'

'I had forgotten the words – oh, a long time since – until Colonel Trench reminded me. I should never have spoken them. When I did I was not thinking they would live so in your thoughts. I am sorry that I spoke them.'

'Oh, they were just enough. I never blamed you for them,'

said Feversham with a laugh. 'I used to think that they would be the last words I should hear when I turned my face to the wall. But you have given me others to-day wherewith to replace them.'

'Thank you,' she said quietly.

There was nothing more to be said, and Feversham wondered why Ethne did not rise from her seat in the pew. It did not occur to him to talk of his travels or adventures. The occasion seemed too serious, too vital. They were together to decide the most solemn issue in their lives. Once the decision was made, as now it had been made, he felt that they could hardly talk on other topics. Ethne, however, still kept him at her side. Though she sat so calmly and still, though her face was quiet in its look of gravity, her heart ached with longing. Just for a little longer, she pleaded to herself. The sunlight was withdrawing from the walls of the church. She measured out a space upon the walls where it still glowed bright. When all that space was cold grey stone she would send Harry Feversham away.

'I am glad that you escaped from Omdurman without the help of Lieutenant Sutch or Colonel Durrance. I wanted so much that everything should be done by you alone without anybody's help or interference,' she said, and after she had spoken there followed a silence. Once or twice she looked towards the wall, and each time she saw the space of golden light narrowed, and knew that her minutes were running out. 'You suffered horribly at Dongola,' she said in a low voice. 'Colonel Trench told me.'

'What does it matter now?' Feversham answered. 'That time seems rather far away to me.'

'Have you anything of mine with you?'

'I had your white feather.'

'But anything else? Any little thing which I had given you in the other days?'

'Nothing.'

'I had your photograph,' she said. 'I kept it.'

Feversham suddenly leaned down towards her.

'You did!'

Ethne nodded her head.

'Yes. The moment I went upstairs that night I packed up your presents and addressed them to your rooms.'

'Yes, I got them in London.'

'But I put your photograph aside first of all to keep. I burnt all your letters after I had addressed the parcel and taken it down to the hall to be sent away. I had just finished burning your letters when I heard your step upon the gravel in the early morning underneath my windows. But I had already put your photograph aside. I have it now. I shall keep it and the feathers together.' She added after a moment –

'I rather wish that you had had something of mine with you all the time.'

'I had no right to anything,' said Feversham.

There was still a narrow slip of gold upon the grey space of stone.

'What will you do now?' she asked.

'I shall go home first and see my father. It will depend upon the way we meet.'

'You will let Colonel Durrance know. I would like to hear about it.'

'Yes, I will write to Durrance.'

The slip of gold was gone, the clear light of a summer evening filled the church, a light without radiance or any colour.

'I shall not see you for a long while,' said Ethne, and for the first time her voice broke in a sob. 'I shall not have a letter from you again.'

She leaned a little forward, and bent her head, for the tears had gathered in her eyes. But she rose up bravely from her seat, and together they went out of the church side by side. She leaned towards him as they walked so that they touched.

Feversham untied his horse and mounted it. As his foot touched the stirrup Ethne caught her dog close to her.

'Good-bye,' she said. She did not now even try to smile, she held out her hand to him. He took it and bent down from his saddle close to her. She kept her eyes steadily upon him though the tears brimmed in them.

'Good-bye,' he said. He held her hand just for a little while, and then releasing it, rode down the hill. He rode for a hundred yards, stopped and looked back. Ethne had stopped too, and

275

with this space between them and their faces towards one another they remained. Ethne made no sign of recognition or farewell. She just stood and looked. Then she turned away and went up the village street towards her house, alone and very slowly. Feversham watched her till she went in at the gate, but she became dim and blurred to his vision before even she had reached there. He was able to see, however, that she did not look back again.

He rode down the hill. The bad thing which he had done so long ago was not even by his six years of labour to be destroyed. It was still to live, its consequence was to be sorrow till the end of life for another than himself. That she took the sorrow bravely and without complaint, doing the straight and simple thing as her loyal nature bade her, did not diminish Harry Feversham's remorse. On the contrary, it taught him yet more clearly that she least of all deserved unhappiness. The harm was irreparable. Other women might have forgotten, but not she. For Ethne was of those who neither lightly feel nor lightly forget, and if they love cannot love with half a heart. She would be alone now, he knew, in spite of her marriage, alone up to the very end and at the actual moment of death.

Chapter Thirty-three

ETHNE AGAIN PLAYS THE MELUSINE OVERTURE

The incredible words were spoken that evening. Ethne went into her farmhouse and sat down in the parlour. She felt cold that summer evening and had the fire lighted. She sat gazing into the bright coals with that stillness of attitude which was a sure sign with her of tense emotion. The moment so eagerly looked for had come and it was over. She was alone now in her remote little village, out of the world in the hills, and more alone than she had been since Willoughby sailed on that August morning down the Salcombe estuary. From the time of Willoughby's coming she had looked forward night and day to the one half-hour during which Harry Feversham would be with her. The half-hour had come and passed. She knew now how she had counted upon its coming, how she had lived for it. She felt lonely in a rather empty world. But it was part of her nature that she had foreseen this sense of loneliness; she had known that there would be a bad hour for her after she had sent Harry Feversham away, that all her heart and soul would clamour to her to call him back. And she forced herself as she sat shivering by the fire to remember that she had always foreseen and had always looked beyond it. To-morrow she would know again that they had not parted for ever, to-morrow she would compare the parting of to-day with the parting on the night of the ball at Lennon House, and recognise what a small thing this was to that. She fell to wondering what Harry Feversham would do now that he had returned, and while she was building up for him a future of great distinction she felt Dermod's old collie dog muzzling at her hand with his sure instinct that his mistress was in distress. Ethne rose from her chair and took the dog's head between her hands and kissed it. He was very old, she thought; he would die soon and leave her, and then there would be years and years, perhaps, before she lay down in her bed and knew the great moment was at hand.

There came a knock upon the door, and a servant told her that Colonel Durrance was waiting.

'Yes,' she said, and as he entered the room she went forward to meet him. She did not shirk the part which she had allotted to herself. She stepped out from the secret chamber of her grief as soon as she was summoned.

She talked with her visitor as though no unusual thing had happened an hour before, she even talked of their marriage and the rebuilding of Lennon House. It was difficult, but she had grown used to difficulties. Only that night Durrance made her path a little harder to tread. He asked her, after the maid had brought in the tea, to play to him the Melusine Overture upon her violin.

'Not to-night,' said Ethne. 'I am rather tired.' And she had hardly spoken before she changed her mind. Ethne was determined that in the small things as well as in the great she must not shirk. The small things with their daily happenings were just those about which she must be most careful. 'Still, I think that I can play the overture,' she said, with a smile, and she took down her violin. She played the overture through from the beginning to the end. Durrance stood at the window with his back towards her until she had ended. Then he walked to her side.

'I was rather a brute,' he said quietly, 'to ask you to play that overture to-night.'

'I wasn't anxious to play,' she answered as she laid the violin aside.

'I know. But I was anxious to find out something, and I knew no other way of finding it out.'

Ethne turned up to him a startled face.

'What do you mean?' she asked in a voice of suspense.

'You are so seldom off your guard. Only indeed at rare time when you play. Once before when you played that over- times when you play. Once before when you played that over- to play it again to-night – the overture which was once strummed out in a dingy café at Wadi Halfa – to-night again I should find you off your guard.'

His words took her breath away and the colour from her cheeks. She got up slowly from her chair and stared at him wide-eyed. He could not know. It was impossible. He did not know.

But Durrance went quietly on.

'Well? Did you take back your feather? The fourth one?'

These to Ethne were the incredible words. Durrance spoke them with a smile upon his face. It took her a long time to understand that he had actually spoken them. She was not sure at the first that her overstrained senses were not playing her tricks, but he repeated his question, and she could no longer disbelieve or misunderstand.

'Who told you of any fourth feather?' she asked.

'Trench,' he answered. 'I met him at Dover. But he only told me of the fourth feather,' said Durrance. 'I knew of the three before. Trench would never have told me of the fourth had I not known of the three. For I should not have met him as he landed from the steamer at Dover. I should not have asked him: "Where is Harry Feversham?" And for me to know of the three was enough.'

'How do you know?' she cried in a kind of despair, and coming close to her he took gently hold of her arm.

'But since I know!' he protested, 'what does it matter how I know? I have known a long while, ever since Captain Willoughby came to The Pool with the first feather. I waited to tell you that I knew until Harry Feversham came back, and he came to-day.'

Ethne sat down in her chair again. She was stunned by Durrance's unexpected disclosure. She had so carefully guarded her secret, that to realise that for a year it had been no secret came as a shock to her. But, even in the midst of her confusion, she understood that she must have time to gather up her faculties again under command. So she spoke of the unimportant thing to gain the time.

'You were in the church then? Or you heard us upon the steps? Or you met – him as he rode away?'

'Not one of the conjectures is right,' said Durrance with a smile. Ethne had hit upon the right subject to delay the statement of the decision to which she knew very well that he had come. Durrance had his vanities like others; and in particular one vanity which had sprung up within him since he had become blind. He prided himself upon the quickness of his perception. It was a delight to him to make discoveries which no one expected a man who had lost his sight to make, and to announce them unexpectedly. It was an additional pleasure to relate to his puzzled audience the steps by which he had reached his discovery. 'Not one of your conjectures is right, Ethne,' he said, and he practically asked her to question him.

'Then how did you find out?' she asked.

'I knew from Trench that Harry Feversham would come some day, and soon. I passed the church this afternoon. Your collie dog barked at me. So I knew you were inside. But a saddled horse was tied up beside the gate. So someone else was with you, and not anyone from the village. Then I got you to play, and that told me who it was who rode the horse.'

'Yes,' said Ethne vaguely. She had barely listened to his

words. 'Yes, I see.' Then in a definite voice, which showed that she had regained all her self-control, she said –

'You went away to Wiesbaden for a year. You went away just after Captain Willoughby came. Was that the reason why you went away?'

'I went because neither you nor I could have kept up the game of pretences we were playing. You were pretending that you had no thought for Harry Feversham, that you hardly cared whether he was alive or dead. I was pretending not to have found out that beyond everything in the world you cared for him. Some day or other we should have failed, each one in turn. I dared not fail, nor dared you. I could not let you, who had said, "Two lives must not be spoilt because of me," live through a year thinking that two lives had been spoilt. You on your side dared not let me, who had said, "Marriage between a blind man and a woman is only possible when there is more than friendship on both sides," know that upon one side there was only friendship, and we were so near to failing. So I went away.'

'You did not fail,' said Ethne quietly; 'it was only I who failed.'

She blamed herself most bitterly. She had set herself, as the one thing worth doing, and incumbent on her to do, to guard this man from knowledge which would set the crown on his calamities, and she had failed. He had set himself to protect her from the comprehension that she had failed, and he had succeeded. It was not any mere sense of humiliation, due to the fact that the man whom she had thought to hoodwink had hoodwinked her, which troubled her. But she felt that she ought to have succeeded, since by failure she had robbed him of his last chance of happiness. There lay the sting for her.

'But it was not your fault,' he said. 'Once or twice, as I said, you were off your guard, but the convincing facts were not revealed to me in that way. When you played the Melusine Overture before, on the night of the day when Willoughby brought you such good news, I took to myself that happiness of yours which inspired your playing. You must not blame yourself. On the contrary, you should be glad that I have found out.'

'Glad!' she exclaimed.

'Yes, for my sake, glad.' And as she looked at him in wonderment he went on: 'Two lives should not be spoilt because of you. Had you had your way, had I not found out, not two but three lives would have been spoilt because of you – because of your loyalty.'

'Three?'

'Yours. Yes – yes, yours, Feversham's, and mine. It was hard enough to keep the pretence during the few weeks we were in Devonshire. Own to it, Ethne! When I went to London to see my oculist it was a relief, it gave you a pause, a rest wherein to drop pretence and be yourself. It could not have lasted long even in Devonshire. But what when we came to live under the same roof, and there were no visits to the oculist, when we saw each other every hour of every day. Sooner or later the truth must have come to me. It might have come gradually, a suspicion added to a suspicion, and another to that until no doubt was left. Or it might have flashed out in one terrible moment. But it would have been made clear. And then, Ethne? What then? You aimed at a compensation; you wanted to make up to me for the loss of what I love – my career, the army, the special service in the strange quarters of the world. A fine compensation to sit in front of you knowing you had married a cripple out of pity, and in so doing had crippled yourself and forgone the happiness which is yours by right. Whereas now —'

'Whereas now?' she repeated.

'I remain your friend, which I would rather be, than your unloved husband,' he said very gently.

Ethne made no rejoinder. The decision had been taken out of her hands.

'You sent Harry away this afternoon,' said Durrance. 'You said good-bye to him twice.'

At the 'twice' Ethne raised her head, but before she could speak Durrance explained –

'Once in the church, again upon your violin,' and he took up the instrument from the chair on which she had laid it. 'It has been a very good friend, your violin,' he said. 'A good friend to me, to us all. You will understand that, Ethne, very soon. I stood at the window while you played it. I had never heard anything in my life half so sad as your farewell to Harry Feversham, and yet it was nobly sad. It was true music, it did not complain.' He laid the violin down upon the chair again.

'I am going to send a messenger to Rathmullen. Harry cannot cross Lough Swilly to-night. The messenger will bring him back to-morrow.'

It had been a day of many emotions and surprises for Ethne. As Durrance bent down towards her, he became aware that she was crying silently. For once tears had their way with her. He took his cap and walked noiselessly to the door of the room. As he opened it, Ethne got up.

'Don't go for a moment,' she said, and she left the fireplace and came to the centre of the room.

'The oculist at Wiesbaden?' she asked. 'He gave you a hope?'

Durrance stood meditating whether he should lie or speak the truth.

'No,' he said at length. 'There is no hope. But I am not so helpless as at one time I was afraid that I should be. I can get about, can't I? Perhaps one of these days I shall go on a journey, one of the long journeys amongst the strange people in the East.'

He went from the house upon his errand. He had learned his lesson a long time since, and the violin had taught it him. It had spoken again that afternoon, and, though with a different voice, had offered to him the same message. The true music cannot complain.

Chapter Thirty-four

THE END

In the early summer of next year two old men sat reading their newspapers after breakfast upon the terrace of Broad Place. The elder of the two turned over a sheet.

'I see Osman Digna's back at Suakin,' said he. 'There's likely to be some fighting.'

'Oh,' said the other. 'He will not do much harm.' And he laid down his paper. The quiet English countryside vanished from before his eyes. He saw only the white city by the Red Sea shimmering in the heat, the brown plains about it with their tangle of halfa grass, and in the distance the hills towards Khor Gwob.

'A stuffy place Suakin, eh, Sutch?' said General Feversham.

'Appallingly stuffy. I heard of an officer who went down on parade at six o'clock of the morning there, sun-struck in the temples right through a regulation helmet. Yes, a town of dank heat! But I was glad to be there – very glad,' he said with some feeling.

'Yes,' said Feversham briskly; 'ibex, eh?'

'No,' replied Sutch. 'All the ibex had been shot off by the English garrison for miles round.'

'No? Something to do, then. That's it?'

'Yes, that's it, Feversham. Something to do.'

And both men busied themselves again over their papers. But in a little while a footman brought to each a small pile of letters. General Feversham ran his envelopes with a quick eye, selected one letter, and gave a grunt of satisfaction. He took a pair of spectacles from a case and placed them upon his nose.

'From Ramelton?' asked Sutch, dropping his newspaper on to the terrace.

'From Ramelton,' answered Feversham. 'I'll light a cigar first.'

He laid the letter down on the garden table which stood between his companion and himself, drew a cigar-case from his pocket and in spite of the impatience of Lieutenant Sutch, proceeded to cut and light it with the utmost deliberation. The old man had become an epicure in this respect. A letter from Ramelton was a luxury to be enjoyed with all the accessories of comfort which could be obtained. He made himself comfortable in his chair, stretched out his legs, and smoked enough of his cigar to assure himself that it was drawing well. Then he took up his letter again and opened it.

'From him?' asked Sutch.

'No; from her.'

'Ah!'

General Feversham read the letter through slowly, while Lieutenant Sutch tried not to peep at it across the table. When the General had finished he turned back to the first page, and began it again.

'Any news?' said Sutch with a casual air.

'They are very pleased with the house now that it's rebuilt.'

'Anything more?'

'Yes. Harry's finished the sixth chapter of his history of the war.'

'Good!' said Sutch. 'You'll see, he'll do that well. He has imagination, he knows the ground, he was present while the war went on. Moreover, he was in the bazaars, he saw the under side of it.'

'Yes. But you and I won't read it, Sutch,' said Feversham. 'No; I am wrong. You may, for you can give me a good many years.'

He turned back to his letter, and again Sutch asked –

'Anything more?'

'Yes. They are coming here in a fortnight.'

'Good,' said Sutch. 'I shall stay.'

He took a turn along the terrace and came back. He saw Feversham sitting with the letter upon his knees and a frown of great perplexity upon his face.

'You know, Sutch, I never understood,' he said. 'Did you?'

'Yes, I think I did.'

Sutch did not try to explain. It was as well, he thought, that Feversham never would understand. For he could not understand without much self-reproach.

'Do you ever see Durrance?' asked the General suddenly.

'Yes, I see a good deal of Durrance. He is abroad just now.'

Feversham turned towards his friend.

'He came to Broad Place when you went to Suakin, and talked to me for half an hour. He was Harry's best man. Well, that too I never understood. Did you?'

'Yes, I understood that as well.'

'Oh!' said General Feversham. He asked for no explana-

tions, but, as he had always done, he took the questions which
he did not understand and put them aside out of his thoughts.
But he did not turn to his other letters. He sat smoking his
cigar, and looked out across the summer country and listened
to the sounds rising distantly from the fields. Sutch had read
through all of his correspondence before Feversham spoke
again.

'I have been thinking,' he said. 'Have you noticed the date
of the month, Sutch?' and Sutch looked up quickly.

'Yes,' said he, 'this day next week will be the anniversary of
our attack upon the Redan, and Harry's birthday.'

'Exactly,' replied Feversham. 'Why shouldn't we start the
Crimean nights again?'

Sutch jumped up from his chair.

'Splendid!' he said. 'Can we muster a table full, do you
think?'

'Let's see,' said Feversham, and ringing a hand-bell upon the
table, sent the servant for the Army List. Bending over that
Army List the two veterans may be left.

But of one other figure in this story a final word must be said.
That night, when the invitations had been sent out from Broad
Place, and no longer a light gleamed from any window of the
house, a man leaned over the rail of a steamer anchored at
Port Said and listened to the song of the Arab coolies as they
tramped up and down the planks with their coal baskets between the barges and the ship's side. The clamour of the streets
of the town came across the water to his ears. He pictured to
himself the flare of braziers upon the quays, the lighted port-
holes, and dark funnels ahead and behind in the procession of
the anchored ships. Attended by a servant, he had come back to
the East again. Early the next morning the steamer moved
through the canal, and towards the time of sunset passed out
into the chills of the Gulf of Suez. Kassasin, Tel-el-Kebir,
Tamai, Tamanieb, the attack upon McNeil's zareeba – Durrance lived again through the good years of his activity, the
years of plenty. Within that country on the west the long preparations were going steadily forward which would one day
roll up the Dervish Empire and crush it into dust. Upon the
glacis of the ruined fort of Sinkat Durrance had promised him-

self to take a hand in that great work, but the desert which he loved had smitten and cast him out. But at all events the boat steamed southwards into the Red Sea. Three nights more and, though he would not see it, the Southern Cross would lift slantwise into the sky.

Famous War Novels in Fontana

Trapp's War   Brian Callison

The Dawn Attack   Brian Callison

A Flock of Ships   Brian Callison

U-Boat   Lothar Günther Buchheim

The Sea Chase   Andrew Geer

The Enemy Below   D. A. Rayner

Send Down a Dove   Charles MacHardy

The Tunnel   Eric Williams

The Wooden Horse   Eric Williams

The Bridge on the River Kwai   Pierre Boulle

Night   Elie Wiesel

 *Fontana Books*

Fontana Books

Fontana is a leading paperback publisher of fiction and non-fiction, with authors ranging from Alistair MacLean, Agatha Christie and Desmond Bagley to Solzhenitsyn and Pasternak, from Gerald Durrell and Joy Adamson to the famous Modern Masters series.

In addition to a wide-ranging collection of internationally popular writers of fiction, Fontana also has an outstanding reputation for history, natural history, military history, psychology, psychiatry, politics, economics, religion and the social sciences.

All Fontana books are available at your bookshop or newsagent; or can be ordered direct. Just fill in the form and list the titles you want.

FONTANA BOOKS, Cash Sales Department, G.P.O. Box 29, Douglas, Isle of Man, British Isles. Please send purchase price, plus 8p per book. Customers outside the U.K. send purchase price, plus 10p per book. Cheque, postal or money order. No currency.

NAME (Block letters)

ADDRESS

While every effort is made to keep prices low, it is sometimes necessary to increase prices on short notice. Fontana Books reserve the right to show new retail prices on covers which may differ from those previously advertised in the text or elsewhere.